M

WIT

MASTER'S CHOICE

VOLUME II

MASTER'S CHOICE

VOLUME II

*Mystery Stories by Today's Top Writers
and the Masters Who Inspired Them*

EDITED BY

LAWRENCE BLOCK

BERKLEY PRIME CRIME, NEW YORK

This is a work of fiction. Names, characters, places, and incidents are either the product of the author's imagination or are used fictitiously, and any resemblance to actual persons, living or dead, business establishments, events, or locales is entirely coincidental.

MASTER'S CHOICE, VOLUME II

A Berkley Prime Crime Book
Published by The Berkley Publishing Group,
a division of Penguin Putnam Inc.,
375 Hudson Street
New York, New York 10014

The Penguin Putnam Inc. World Wide Web site address is
http://www.penguinputnam.com

First edition: November 2000

Library of Congress Cataloging-in-Publication Data

Master's choice: mystery stories by today's top writers and the
masters who inspired them / edited by Lawrence Block.
    p. cm.
  ISBN 0-425-17676-2
  1. Detective and mystery stories, American. I. Block, Lawrence.
PS648.D4M37 1999
813'.087208—dc21   99-30270
                                                    CIP

PRINTED IN THE UNITED STATES OF AMERICA

10 9 8 7 6 5 4 3 2 1

ACKNOWLEDGMENTS

All story introductions are copyright © 2000 by the respective authors.

"Puppyland" by Doug Allyn. Copyright © 1996 by Doug Allyn. Reprinted by permission of the author and his agent, James Allen.

"Child of Another Time" by William Bankier. Copyright © 1983 by William Bankier. Reprinted by permission of the author and his agents, Curtis Brown, Ltd.

"The Man Next Door" by Mary Higgins Clark. Copyright © 1998 by Mary Higgins Clark. Reprinted by permission of the author and her agent, McIntosh & Otis, Inc.

"The Criminal" by Joe Gores. Copyright © 1970 by the Knight Publishing Corp. Reprinted by permission of the author.

"The Knife" by John Russell. Copyright © 1925 by John Russell.

"True Thomas" by Reginald Hill. Copyright © 1993 by Reginald Hill. Reprinted by permission of the author.

"The Detective's Wife" by Edward D. Hoch. Copyright © 1990 by Edward D. Hoch. Reprinted by permission of the author.

"You Can't Be a Little Girl All Your Life" by Stanley Ellin. Copyright © 1958 by Stanley Ellin. Reprinted by permission of the agent for the author's Estate, Curtis Brown, Ltd.

CONTENTS

MASTER'S CHOICE

VOLUME II

INTRODUCTION

IF THERE'S ANYTHING easier than presenting the following twenty-six stories to you, I don't know what it is. Let me just list the names of the writers who have so generously participated: Doug Allyn, Mary Higgins Clark, Joe Gores, Reginald Hill, Edward D. Hoch, Clark Howard, Evan Hunter, Stuart Kaminsky, Sharyn McCrumb, Joyce Carol Oates, Ian Rankin, and Carolyn Wheat. Impressive, no? And here are the authors *they* selected: William Bankier, Mat Coward, Stanley Ellin, Susan Glaspell, Edgar Allan Poe, Jack Ritchie, John Russell, Saki, Robert Louis Stevenson, Robert Turner, and that perennial favorite, Anonymous. (And, I blush to admit, I'm here myself, presenting a story by the incomparable Fredric Brown.)

This is the second volume of *Master's Choice*—the numeral in the title may have tipped you off—and the premise remains unchanged. A group of writers, masters of the short story, were invited to select two stories—one they're particularly proud to have written, and one they're particularly pleased to have read. In this volume, as in the first, the result has not merely been a collection of outstanding short stories but a fascinating glimpse of who likes what, and why.

Looking over the selections, I thought of the profound impact a really good short story has on the reader, and how it lingers in the mind. Sometimes, alas, the story hangs on after one has forgotten its title and author.

And that brings me to my own real reason for writing this introduction for a book which clearly needs none. I'm hoping that someone out there can point me to a pair of stories I've been unable to track down.

The first of the two is one I never read, so I can't really be expected to remember it. Decades ago, Donald E. Westlake and I were sitting around, as was our wont, and talking, as was also our wont, and Don spoke at length about a story he said had considerable impact. I could believe it; the story made a powerful impression on me, and all I had of it was his summary.

As I recall, it went like this: A perfectly ordinary guy gets up one morning, puts on a suit and tie, has breakfast, reads the paper, kisses his wife goodbye, and leaves the house. On his way to work he stops at a house, chosen apparently at random, enters it, and massacres an entire family, butchers the lot of them. Then he cleans up, straightens his tie, and continues on his way to the office.

"Wow," I said. Or words to that effect.

Well, a few years ago I tried to track down the story. First thing I did, logically enough, was ask Don. He said the story sounded terrific, all right, but that he'd never read it or anything like it. The conversation I recalled so vividly was one he remembered not at all. Maybe I'd had the conversation with someone else, he suggested. If so, and if I managed to pin down the story, would I please let him know? Because he'd love to read it.

It seemed to me he'd originally attributed the story to Anthony Boucher. I thought I'd read everything of Boucher's at one time or another, but you never know with short stories. If they don't wind up in a collection, they can slip through the cracks. So I asked some people who would know, and nobody recognized the story, and several people volunteered the opinion that it sure didn't sound like something Tony Boucher would have written.

Here's the second story: A woman is in some isolated rural location, and she hears an announcement on the radio that a homicidal maniac has escaped from the nearby hospital for the murderously insane. The escapee is described as monomaniacal on the subject of Germany. The woman's in a panic. Her car won't start, or something like that. She can't get away, and she's convinced the maniac's going to show up any minute.

And then a man does show up, a man who'll be able to save her, and she's overjoyed and tells him about the news item, and how the maniac's obsessed on the subject of Germany. "You know," he says, "I went to Germany just two years ago. What a beautiful country! I cycled from Munich to Baden-Baden, and then—"

And she knows he's the maniac!

Well, she manages to save herself. There's someone at the door, the guy's distracted, and she sticks a knife in him or does something else, but one way or another the guy's dead and she's alive, and there's this priest at the door, or maybe he's a cop, he could even be a fireman, I don't know what he is, but he's there, and she throws herself into his arms and babbles about how she was almost done in by this maniac, this bastard who *seemed* perfectly normal, until, wouldn't you know it, he started talking about *Germany*.

"Germany," her deliverer muses. "Germany. Do you know, the physical territory of Germany is XYZ square miles, and the gross national product of Germany for the year 1927 was XYZ deutschmarks, and . . ."

And she realizes that she killed an innocent man, and she's about to be killed by this wacko, and there's not a thing she can do about it.

Let me tell you, it was a hell of a story—or at least I thought so at the time. It's been at least forty-five years since I read it, and it might be closer to fifty, and I was young enough to pay scant attention to titles and authors. I remember it was in a collection of stories housed on the second shelf from the bottom of our living room bookcase, to the right of the fireplace. And a fat lot of good it does me to know that.

Well, Dear Reader? Does either story ring a bell? If so, I trust you'll get in touch (LawBloc@aol.com, or a fax to 212.675.4341). If I can locate them, I'll include them in future Master's Choice volumes. And if I can't, if absolutely nobody remembers either story, I'll decide these are phantom memories and that my own unconscious created both stories. In which case I'll steal them and see if I can make them come out as good as I remember them.

There is, I submit, a point to this beyond my yearning to find those two stories, and that's the extraordinary impression a really fine short story can make. I think you'll find, in the following pages, quite a few stories that will stay with you long after you've finished the book. I know I did.

LAWRENCE BLOCK
Greenwich Village

DOUG ALLYN

Some stories come easy. The writing witch parks on your shoulder, jabbering ideas faster than you can type, then hones your prose to a razor edge while you're pouring a second cup of coffee. The tale flows like the scribbling we all did in Writing for Fun 101.

"Puppyland" came tougher. It felt so personal I wasn't sure it would make sense to anyone else. When readers of Ellery Queen voted this story one of the best of the year, I was very surprised. It meant a lot. Because . . .

I wrote this story for my friend Nadine, whose spirit burned like a flare in a hurricane, brightening the world for anyone lucky enough to wander into her circle of light.

She never saw it. Uncertain of her reaction, I put off showing it to her. Time has made that problem academic.

Perhaps she'll see it now.

• • •

Pick a story that matters to me out of the eight billion or so that I've read? No problem. A dozen summers ago when I was just beginning to write, a friend suggested that I read a few mysteries. I bought an Alfred Hitchcock's Mystery Magazine and an Ellery Queen. Whoa! A revelation.

I'd thought mysteries were Col. Mustard conking Miss Plum with a candlestick in a veddy, veddy English library. Not so.

While many stories in the magazines were excellent, "Child of Another Time" really lit it up for me. William Bankier is that rare writer who can tell a tantalizing tale wrapped around a real-life problem. Sometimes things end unsatisfactorily. Life's like that.

"Child of Another Time" is one of the first mystery stories I ever read. Eight billion stories later (okay, maybe seven billion), including umpteen of my own, it's still one of the best. Bankier is a wizard. If you've not read him before, you're in for a treat.

PUPPYLAND

Doug Allyn

THE BITCH HAD golden eyes, liquid and deep. Her coat was sleek, a lustrous liver color with white ticking on her shoulders and rump. She was a four-year-old German shorthaired pointer, weight, about seventy-five pounds. She looked exhausted. She was lying on her side on a red velvet pillow in an elaborate wicker dog basket. Her name was engraved on an ornate brass plate on the front. Hilda Von Holzweg. Five squirming furballs were sucking at her swollen breasts.

A sixth wasn't squirming anymore. She'd pushed it to the edge of the basket away from the others. David picked up the dead pup. It was already cooling. Hilda raised her head a moment and glowered at him, but didn't growl. Probably didn't have the energy.

"How long was she in labor?" David asked.

"I'm not sure," Ted Crane said. "She had them in the night. I checked her at eleven just before I went to bed. Then this morning, about seven, there they were."

"And this pup was alive then?" David said, turning the small body over, examining it for injuries or obvious flaws.

"I believe so. I can't honestly say I took special notice of it, I mean, they all look pretty much alike, except for the solid white one. Is it an albino?" Crane was a bit of an albino himself, a handsome one, tall and fair, with sandy hair and nearly invisible eyebrows. He was dressed for the office in a mocha-brown three-piece power suit. His Sulka tie probably cost more than the loden-green corduroy sport coat David was wearing.

"I doubt he's a true albino," David said. "His nose is dark. Can't be certain until his eyes are open, though. Solid-white shorthair pups are quite valuable, I understand. Did the dead pup try to suckle at all?"

"I think so. I didn't really pay any special attention to it until I noticed it was just stumbling around, kind of wheezing. And then it died. The other one was wheezing too, but it was all right afterward."

"The other one?"

"Another pup was behaving oddly. My wife has it in her room, feeding it with a bottle."

"And it's taking the bottle?" David frowned.

"Seems to be. But only when she holds it. It stops trying when she puts it down."

"I see. Is she cradling it? Like a baby, I mean?" David demonstrated what he meant by cradling the dead pup in the crook of his arm, with its head upright.

"Something like that," Ted acknowledged, wincing at the casual way David handled the tiny corpse. "But she can't hold it for long. She's . . . quite ill herself. Look, I can't hang around here all day, I have to get back to the office. I have a luncheon meeting at one."

"I'll just be a few more minutes," David said, examining the dead pup's face more carefully. There were bubbles of dried milk in its nostrils. He tried to force its mouth open with a fingertip but it was locked shut. Rigor mortis had already set in. "I don't think this is anything serious, Mr. Crane. The mother and the rest of the pups look healthy as horses. I'd guess this fella's problem was a birth defect rather than an illness. I'd better examine the other sickly pup, though, if you don't mind."

"My wife's room is at the head of the stairs," Crane said impatiently. "I really have to go. Will you take care of the dead one?"

"You mean dispose of it?" David said.

"I'd appreciate it," Crane said. "I don't like having to mess with . . . dead things."

"I thought you worked at the hospital," David said.

"I'm Director of Public Relations," Crane said, trying not to sound smug, and failing. "I deal with fund-raising, not patients. Frankly, I try to have as little to do with corpses as possible."

"I'll see to this one," David said. "Do you have a plastic bag?"

"In the kitchen. Thanks for coming by, Dr. Westbrook. I really have to go." Ted Crane hurried off. Grateful for an excuse to be away from the messy business of life and death, David thought.

David left Hilda and her pups in their basket and wandered into the living room. The Crane home was a mansion, really, filled with antiques. The Persian rugs were rich, but showed signs of wear. Tudor furniture was covered in white damask, and an honest-to-God *Gone with the Wind* staircase swept up to the floors above. The stairway had been modified to accommodate a wheelchair lift. David followed the lift rails up to the second floor. The first door was ajar and he rapped lightly.

"Mrs. Crane?" No answer.

"Hello?" He peered cautiously around the door. A woman was propped up in bed, surrounded by pillows, cradling a puppy in her arms. "Hi," David said, "I'm Dr. Westbrook, the veterinarian. Your husband said you were having a spot of trouble with some of the pups. May I come in?"

She nodded, closing her eyes a moment. Her hair was auburn and very fine, like a wispy halo of fire. She was wearing a jade-green embroidered silk bed jacket. It matched her eyes, which were a deep, deep emerald. And very sunken. She was probably in her mid thirties, but illness was ageing her. There was a rack of medical equipment beside her bed, a humidifier, a heart monitor, and a respirator the size of a small microwave. A length of flexible tubing connected the respirator to a breathing mask on the pillow beside her.

"I'm sorry," she whispered, "I have some difficulty talking. How's Hilda?"

"She's fine," David said. "So are her pups. How's this little guy doing?"

"Not well. He'll only eat if I hold him."

"May I?" David took the pup from her arms. He stepped over to the window for better light, then worked his finger into the hinge of the pup's jaw, pried it open, and peered in. Damn. There was a narrow schism in the roof of its mouth. Double damn.

"What is it?"

David hesitated.

"Just say it, Doctor. I'm used to hearing bad news."

"He has a birth defect, Mrs. Crane, a cleft palate. I expect the one that died had the same problem. I'm sorry."

"Call me Inga, please. How bad is it?"

"It's usually fatal, I'm afraid. They can't suck very well, you see, so they either starve, or milk gets into their airways. The pup downstairs probably suffocated."

"But this one seems to be feeding all right."

"That's because you were holding him upright. He doesn't have to suckle. The milk's trickling down the back of his throat."

"Well, what's wrong with that?"

"Nothing, for now. But he won't be able to eat solid food that way, or even drink water normally. He could choke, or get fluid into his lungs and die of pneumonia."

"Isn't there anything you can do?"

"Well, on an adult dog, I could repair the palate by inserting a plate, perhaps, but the procedure's not practical and the surgery would be both risky and expensive in any case."

"But it would be possible? On an adult dog?"

"Mrs. Crane, Inga, forgive me for being blunt, but pups with this problem rarely reach adulthood."

"Really? Take a look at all the machinery beside my bed, Doctor. Do you know what it's for?"

David glanced at the rack of equipment on the left side of the bed against the wall. "A heart monitor," he said. "And . . . some kind of a respirator?"

"That's right. I have ALS, Lou Gehrig's disease. I had an auto accident nearly three years ago, shattered my right shoulder and hip. And while I was in the hospital, in traction, they diagnosed the ALS. They gave me eighteen months to live, or less. That was three years ago. I need a wheel-chair to get around now, and the respirator breathes for me much of the time, but I'm still here. Maybe that's why life seems very precious to me these days. If I care for this pup properly, will he have a chance to live?"

"That depends. He won't be a pup for long, you know. He'll only drink milk for a few weeks, then he'll need solid food and it'll have to bypass his mouth. Are you up to feeding him through a tube? Several times a day?"

"If that's what it takes to save his life, then I'll either do it myself or see that it's done. I'm not alone here, my mother can help, and my niece. And you? Are you willing to help?"

"I don't know," David said. "What you're suggesting would be difficult for anyone, let alone someone in your condition. No offense, ma'am, but you seem to have troubles enough of your own."

"Trust me, a few puppy-sized troubles will make a pleasant change from the rest," she said, smiling. It was a wan, but fine, smile.

"Then I guess we'll all have to do the best that we can," David said, handing her the pup.

"Good," Inga Crane said. She cradled the pup to her breast. "Can you sit a minute? I don't have much company. You're the newcomer Yvonne LeClair married, aren't you?"

"Not such a newcomer," David said, easing into the chair beside her bed. "I've been practicing in Algoma for about four years."

"In northern Michigan, unless you're born here you're a flatlander forever. Ted, my husband, moved here . . . My God. Is it five years now? It seems like so much longer. We hadn't been married long when . . . this happened." She indicated her wasted form with a wave of her free hand. "He tries, but he's such an active man, he has a little trouble dealing with illness, I think."

"On the other hand, you seem to be handling it well enough," David said.

"But I have no choice, have I?" she countered. "Oh! Is something wrong? The puppy's twitching."

David peered at it intently, then relaxed. "No, nothing to worry about," he said. "He's just dreaming, that's all."

"Dreaming? About what?"

"What do you mean?"

"Well, he was just born last night. He hasn't been anyplace or done anything yet. His eyes aren't even open," Inga said. "So what can he possibly be dreaming about?"

"I don't know. I guess I never thought of it that way."

"Maybe he's dreaming about Puppyland," she said.

"About what?"

"Puppyland. My family has always had dogs, so my mother never told us the stork story. She said that baby dogs came from Puppyland, kind of a hound heaven, where they can run and play all day. When I was a girl, this house was my Puppyland. My grandparents built it and I grew up here. Ted thinks we should sell it now. I know it's expensive to maintain, but I doubt my mother'd be happy anywhere else, and I love it too. God, I used to run like a deer in the hills out back when I was a kid. I still dream about it sometimes. I'm running flat-out with the wind in my face, and I can breathe easily again. I almost hate to wake up. I hope this little guy won't be too disappointed when his eyes open and he finds out he's not in Puppyland anymore. He's stuck in our world now." She smothered a cough with her hand. She was clearly tiring.

"At least he'll have a friend," David said, rising to leave. "What are you going to call him?"

"I don't think I'll name him yet," she said, thoughtfully tracing his silken ears with her fingertip. "It will be harder to lose him if he has a name. I'll wait a few weeks. See how he does. Thanks for coming by, Dr. Westbrook."

"Call me David," he said. "Would you mind if I stopped by now and again? No charge."

"I'd like that," she said. "Maybe you can help me choose a name. If he . . . needs one."

"He's going to need one," David said.

• • •

SHE named the pup Hector, after the old phrase "since Hector was a pup." Neither of them could remember who the original Hector the pup was, but it didn't matter. Inga's Hector soon developed a quirky personality of his own. Despite his defect, he cheerfully adapted to his circumstances, learning to feed and drink in Inga's arms, first liquids, then solid food through a tube. Over the next several months, as spring warmed into summer, David stopped by once or twice each week to check on the pup and to chat with Inga Crane. The visits often stretched into an hour or more, talking about dogs, or mutual friends, or just life in general. David rarely saw Ted on these visits, but he did meet Inga's mother, Clare, a charming, drifty old soul who seemed to wander through the house like a ghost. She'd obviously been a beauty once, but her mind was as cloudy now as Inga's was clear.

Most of the scutwork and heavy lifting involved in caring for an invalid fell to Inga's niece, Cindy, a stolid, pudgy girl of twenty or so. She wore her dun-colored hair in an MTV-style shambles and her ears were pierced with three studs each. She never complained, but David sensed that she resented his visits a little, so he generally took her arrival as his signal to leave.

The truth was, his visits had become more personal than professional anyway. Hector was healthy and growing like the national debt, and David really couldn't afford the time away from his practice, but there are some things you have to do for yourself. For your soul.

In any case, he knew that the visits wouldn't continue for long. He was a vet, not an M.D., but it was clear that even as Hector was flourishing under Inga's devoted care, Inga herself was wasting away, as though the fire of her spirit was consuming her shrunken body. It should have been depressing, but he found her struggle an inspiration instead. He'd read Dylan Thomas in college, but he'd never truly understood the line "Rage, rage against the dying of the light," until he met Inga. Her thirsts to savor every last drop of her life, however bitter, personified the indomitability of the human spirit more than anyone he'd ever known. And in the end, she did not "go gentle into that good night . . ." Not gentle at all.

• • •

THE phone dragged David up from the depths of a dark dream. He glanced at the nightstand as he fumbled for the receiver. Four-thirty. What the hell?

"Hello."

"Dr. Westbrook? This is Sheriff Wolinski. I'm sorry to bother you this time of the morning, Doc, but I've got a special problem. Are you awake?"

"I am now. What is it, Stan?"

"I'm at the Crane place on Stillmeadow Road. Do you know it?"

Damn. "Yes, I know it," David said. "Is it Inga?"

"Yeah, she's gone all right. Thing is, it looks like her dog may have killed her."

"What?"

"Look, Doc, I can show you a helluva lot faster than I can explain it over the phone. Can you get out here, please? Now?"

"Right," David said, fully awake now. "I'm on my way."

• • •

THE emergency flashers of the Algoma County Sheriff's patrol car and the EMT van were already being washed out by the first light of dawn when David pulled into the red brick drive of the Crane estate. Sheriff Stan Wolinski was waiting for him on the porch, pacing impatiently. Stan's concrete-block build and gray uniform were both in perfect order and his eyes were clear. A grayish stubble of beard was his only concession to the early hour. David wondered if he ever actually slept, or just caught catnaps at his desk at the county jail.

"Morning, Doc," Stan said, leading the way into the house toward the winding staircase. "Sorry to drag you out like this, but I've got a bit of a situation here."

"What's happened?"

"Mrs. Crane's mother called nine-one-one about three A.M., said her daughter'd passed away, then started mumbling. When the EMT techs got here they found the mother sitting by the bed. The dog was on the bed, guarding the body. The old lady seemed to be pretty much in a fog."

"She's on quite a bit of medication," David said.

"Anyway, Mrs. Crane was dead, probably had been for an hour or so. The bedclothing was disarranged a little, as though she'd thrashed around some at the end. And as the technician was checking over the body, he noticed the respirator was unplugged."

"The respirator?"

"Right. Apparently she could only breathe without it for short periods. I guess she was in pretty bad shape. Thing is, the machine's quite close to the wall, and there's other equipment near it. The mother said she hadn't touched it, and the tech thought it was unlikely it could have been unplugged by accident. It looked odd to him, so he called me."

"And you called me? What the hell for?"

"I'm coming to that. By the time I got here, the husband had showed up—"

"What do you mean, showed up?"

"Came upstairs. He said he was asleep, but the EMT guys had been there half an hour at that point, and hadn't been particularly quiet."

"Maybe Crane's a heavy sleeper."

"Maybe. He said he'd had a few scotches before he turned in and I believe him. He smelled like a brewery. On the other hand, he was wearing street clothes. I ask you, if you had a sick wife and heard noises in the night, would you bother to get dressed? Anyway, when the tech tells Crane the respirator was unplugged, he goes ballistic. He says the dog must have pulled it out, that he'd been prowling around back there before. And there are some marks on the plug that coulda been made by a dog. So I called you."

"To look at a plug?"

"Dave, what I got here is a dead woman who probably would have passed away naturally in a month or two anyway. Maybe a few things don't quite add up about it, but that's not unusual. Death is a messy business sometimes. I've got no real reason to doubt the husband's story, I just want to be sure. If the marks on the plug look like tooth marks to you, we can all go home."

"What the hell is he doing here?" Ted Crane bellowed. He was blocking the head of the stairway in his stocking feet. His shirttail was half out of his dark dress slacks. He was weaving and his face was flushed. "This is his fault!"

"Mr. Crane—" Stan began.

"He knew that damned dog had a birth defect! If he'd done the right thing and put it down before my wife got so attached to it—" Crane lunged at David, swinging wildly at his head. Stan grabbed his arm but the force of Crane's rush carried all three men down in a heap, struggling dangerously at the top of the stairs.

"Damn it, Crane, get hold of yourself!" Stan roared, twisting Ted's arm behind his back and hauling him to his feet.

"Let go of me, you bastard! This is my house!"

"This is a crime scene until I say otherwise!" Stan said, forcing Crane against the wall. "Now you settle down or I'll cuff you and lock you in the back of my patrol car. Are you all right, Doc?"

"I'll live," David said, getting to his feet, more shaken than he cared to admit. He touched his cheek with his fingertips. They came away bloody. Terrific.

"You've got a nick on your cheek."

"It's nothing," David said. "Crane's cufflink grazed me, that's all. Mr. Crane, I'm terribly sorry about your wife, and I know this must be an awful time for you. So why don't you let me take care of my business and I'll get out of here."

"You'd better take that dog with you," Crane snarled over his shoulder. "You get it out of here or I'll kill it! I swear I will!"

Stan marched Crane over to a chair and parked him in it, none too gently. David left them in the hall and stepped into Inga's room. A burly, uniformed medical tech was standing just inside the door, his arms folded. Inga's mother was sitting beside the bed in her robe and slippers. One of her hands was beneath the sheet that covered Inga's body and David guessed she was still holding her daughter's hand. He touched the elderly woman's shoulder. She glanced up at him without a hint of recognition, then looked away.

David eased cautiously around the bed, knelt beside the respirator, and picked up the plug. Tooth marks. He'd seen them a thousand times on everything from fine furniture to briar pipes. Puppies test their strength against the world by grabbing and tugging on things. Or they just chew things up for the sheer joyful hell of it. There were several other cords plugged into the multiple socket, for the other medical equipment and her bedside lamp. They'd been chewed as well. He examined the respirator plug closely to be sure, but there was little doubt. Damn it. Sometimes it seemed like the Almighty had an almighty warped sense of humor . . .

He rose slowly, dusting off his hands.

"What do you think?" the medic asked. The tech was a heavyset man with a beer-barrel build and a dark stubble of beard. He looked tired, probably nearing the end of his shift.

"I'd say her husband is right. There are tooth marks on that plug," David said, gazing down at the shrouded body. "How did she . . . die?"

"Heart failure, I think, triggered by anoxia. Actually, in her condition that mask was barely adequate to keep her going anyway. Her doctor wanted to hospitalize her weeks ago to have a ventilator tube inserted. She refused."

"Can't say I blame her for that," David said. "It can be a pretty uncomfortable situation."

"True blue," the medic agreed, "and it's not like it would have cured her. It would only have prolonged her dyin' a bit. Maybe it's best this way. If she woke up at all, she was probably too groggy to realize what had happened."

"I hope so," David said. "She was quite a lady."

"Well?" Stan Wolinski said from the doorway.

"They . . . certainly look like tooth marks to me," David said. "Proper depth, proper spacing. Maybe a lab could tell you more."

"Do you think a lab's necessary?"

"No," David said. "They're tooth marks all right."

"Anything wrong, Doc? You look a little bummed."

"Just upset," David said. "The lady was a friend of mine."

"In that case, considering Crane just decked you, I'll assume your opinion's as close to objective as I'm likely to get. Thanks for coming down."

"I'll send you a bill," David said. "Where's Hector?"

"Hec—oh, the dog, you mean?"

"We shut it up in the next bedroom," the medical tech volunteered. "He wouldn't let us near her."

"You gonna take him with you, Doc?" Stan asked.

"I think I'd better, under the circumstances, don't you?" David said. "There's been enough trouble here for one night." He collected Hector from the adjoining bedroom. Ted Crane was still in the hallway chair where Stan had left him, sitting with his head in his hands. He didn't look up as David passed.

David put Hector in the back of his Jeep. He clipped a lead to the pup's collar, but it wasn't really necessary. Hector made no move to escape. He seemed dazed and disoriented, barely aware of his surroundings. And David knew exactly how he felt.

• • •

DURING the course of the day, David tried to feed Hector several times. He'd seen Inga do it, cradling the pup lovingly in her arms, slipping the feeding tube into the corner of his mouth to bypass the schism in his palate. Hector had seemed to enjoy every moment of it. Why not? It was the only way he'd ever been fed by the only mother he'd ever known. When David tried it, though, the pup snapped out of his apathy long enough to snarl at him and spit the tube out. An hour later David's second attempt failed as well. He decided to have his assistant, Bettina, try the next one. Perhaps a woman's touch . . .

"Doctor?" Bettina stuck her head around his office doorjamb. "There's a Cindy Meyers to see you. She says it's urgent."

"Meyers? Oh, that would be Inga Crane's niece. I'd better see her now, if no one's bleeding to death on the waiting-room floor."

"Nope, everything out front routine. I'll send her back."

David met Cindy at the door. She was wearing a Def Leppard sweatshirt and jeans. Her eyes were red, but she seemed more nervous than sad. She scanned the office warily, as if she were scheduled for some uncomfortable procedure.

"I'm very sorry about your aunt," David said, taking her hand and leading her to the chair beside his desk. "If there's anything I can do . . ."

"Actually, maybe there is," Cindy said, glancing uneasily around the office. "I need to talk to you privately. Would you mind closing the door?"

David hesitated, then complied. "What is it?" he asked.

"Ted called me around ten this morning," she said. "I was visiting a girl-friend over at Central Michigan. He . . . he sounded pretty loaded, you know, drunk?"

"I suppose that's understandable, wouldn't you say?"

"I guess it is," she said, taking a deep breath. "Anyway, I drove straight back, but the more I thought about it, the more I thought I'd better talk to you before I went home."

"I don't understand."

"The thing is, Ted said that Hector killed Aunt Inga. That he'd been chewing on the respirator plug and pulled it out somehow. He said the sheriff even called you out to look at it."

"That's right. There were tooth marks on the plug—"

"How many marks were there?" Cindy interrupted. "I mean, was it all chewed up? Or were there just a few?"

"Well, I didn't actually count the marks but the cord wasn't badly chewed. They were definitely tooth marks, though."

"I know they were," she said. "I've seen them."

"What do you mean you've seen them?"

"Hector's been chewing up things for the past few weeks," Cindy said carefully, her voice tautly controlled. "Slippers, shoes, table legs, anything he can reach, really. And Inga caught him chewing on the cord a couple of days ago. She had me paddle his bottom good."

"He's just a pup," David said. "Sometimes one lesson isn't enough."

"You don't understand. Inga and Ted had a big fight about it. He wanted her to get rid of the dog, said if it happened again, he'd get rid of it whether she agreed or not. So she was real careful to watch Hector when he was with her, and she's been shutting him out of her room at night."

"What are you saying?" David asked.

"I'm not saying anything," Cindy said. "I'm just trying to . . . understand how Inga died. Ted said it must have happened during the night, right?"

"I believe the EMT people got there about three-thirty," David said.

"And Inga seldom went to sleep before midnight," Cindy said. "So, let's say Clare forgot and left the door open or something and Hector got in. The first thing he would have done was jump on her bed to say hello. He always did."

David started to speak but she waved him off.

"I know," she said. "He's only a pup. So maybe he didn't say hello. Maybe he went straight to that cord and chewed on it until he pulled it out. But he couldn't have done that without drooling on it, could he?"

"No," David said, "I suppose not."

"So? Was the plug damp?"

"No," David said slowly, remembering. "It was dry. A little dusty, in fact. I . . . brushed my hands off after I handled it." Neither of them spoke for a moment, each of them considering what the other had said.

"You don't think the pup unplugged that cord, do you?" David asked at last.

"I don't know what to think," Cindy said. "You've got to understand, I'm in kind of a shaky situation here. Inga took me in when my parents died, but everything will belong to Ted now and he can put me out in a heartbeat if he wants to. I wouldn't mind so much for myself, but who'll take care of Clare? She can't fend for herself and she loves that house. So I don't want to make waves, but I think I'd better take a look at that cord. After all the fuss about it earlier, I'm pretty sure I'll be able to tell if Hector chewed on it again. The thing is, I think I should have a witness, but if I ask the sheriff to go with me and nothing's wrong, Ted might . . . Look, these past weeks you've been the closest friend Inga had. Would you come with me? Please."

"I—of course," David said abruptly. "Let's go."

· · ·

CINDY entered the house without knocking. "With any luck, we'll be in and outa here before anybody knows it," she said quietly. "I'm probably just making a fuss over nothing anyway."

David followed her quietly up the main staircase. He felt a bit like a burglar, but he hoped to avoid trouble with Ted Crane if possible. Clare was still in Inga's room, sitting beside the empty bed where David last saw her, hours before. She might have been there the whole time, except that she'd exchanged her bathrobe for a prim gray housedress and sensible shoes.

"Hello, Dr. Westbrook," she said vaguely. "Inga's not here now."

"It's all right, Gran," Cindy said, swallowing. "Everything will be all right. We'll just be a moment." She moved around the bed, knelt beside the respirator, and examined the plug. Her mouth narrowed to a thin line. She rose slowly.

"I can't be absolutely positive, of course," she said grimly, "but I'd swear the plug doesn't look any different than it did before. Gran, when you . . . found Inga last night, was Hector in the room with her?"

"Hector?" the old woman echoed.

"Just tell us what happened," Cindy said impatiently. "One step at a time. You came into the room, right?"

"Yes, something woke me . . . The phone? Or the doorbell? I can't remember. I thought at first it was morning. The pills I take . . . usually I sleep very soundly. But when I woke up I had a bad feeling about Inga. And so I went to her room. But . . . she wasn't there anymore. She was gone." Clare looked away.

"The room," Cindy prompted. "Tell us about the room."

"It was . . . a little messy," Clare said. "And you know how fussy Inga was about things being neat. So I straightened up a bit. I didn't want . . . strangers to see it like that."

"And Hector?" Cindy asked. "Was he in the room?"

"Hector? No," Clare said. "He was on his blanket in the hall. He came in with me and jumped on the bed but . . . he didn't get all excited the way he usually does. He just . . . licked at Inga's face a little, and then he curled up at the foot of her bed. He didn't move after that until the ambulance men came. He got excited then, tried to keep them away from her, so they put him in the next room."

"So he was out in the hall until you let him in," Cindy said. Her eyes met David's for a moment.

"Yes." Clare nodded. "Hector was outside."

Cindy took a deep breath. "You said you straightened up the room? Why, Gran? Was it messed up?"

"The . . . bedclothes were disarranged," Clare said vaguely. "As though . . . she must have had trouble . . . at the last."

"And is that all you did? Fix the bedclothes?"

"No, I . . . her book was on the bed," Clare said. "It was open and I knew she wouldn't want people to read it, so I put it away."

"Her book?" David echoed.

"Her diary," Cindy said, moving to the bookcase and picking out a slim volume.

"You shouldn't touch that," Clare said. "Inga will be angry. . . ." Her voice trailed off as she realized what she'd said.

Cindy leafed through the diary, then froze. She passed the book to David. The paragraph at the top of the page was dated and neatly written in a careful hand. But below it was a wobbly scrawl that covered half the page. *Ted unplu . . .* The line sagged away at the end. Unfinished.

There was a rustle from the hallway, and suddenly Ted Crane was standing unsteadily in the doorway, his face flushed, his hair disheveled. "What's going on here?" he mumbled blearily. "What the hell are you doing here, Westbrook?"

David carefully closed the journal. "What I'm doing, Mr. Crane," he said, picking up the bedside phone, "is calling the police."

• • •

CRANE made it easy. When Stan Wolinski tried to question him about the diary Ted was so outraged he took a swing at the sheriff. A big mistake. Stan took him into custody for attempted assault and hauled him off in the back of his patrol car.

David left Cindy and her grandmother on the porch, arm in arm. The elderly woman didn't seem to comprehend what had happened, and David recalled Cindy's earlier question, "Who'll take care of Clare?" Perhaps the answer was beside her now. He hoped so.

David hadn't liked Ted Crane all that much initially and his recent behavior hadn't helped matters. Still, the thought that Ted might have killed Inga or contributed to her death was hard to stomach. People killed each other in Detroit or New York or L.A., not in Algoma. Folks moved to the north country to live happily ever after. Maybe that had been Ted's problem. Knowing that he and Inga would never have a happily ever after.

David didn't know what to do about Hector. The pup was still rejecting the feeding tube. If he didn't start eating in the next few days, force-feeding him while he was sedated would be the only option left. It was a tough choice. Hector wouldn't be mature enough for a surgical repair of his palate for another twelve to fourteen months, minimum. David doubted the pup could survive more than a few weeks of force-feeding, to say nothing of a year. Besides, he'd seen this behavioral syndrome before.

Dogs that are strongly attached to their masters or their mates will sometimes mourn their deaths so keenly that they lose their own will to live. They don't whine or howl or carry on, they simply sink into a numbed apathy and refuse to eat. Exactly as Hector was doing.

David was in a black mood for the rest of the afternoon, curt with his clients and Bettina. His temper didn't improve when his last client at the end of the day turned out to be Stan Wolinski.

"Doc," the sheriff said, following David back to his office, "I think I need another favor, or rather, Ted Crane does."

"I don't owe Crane any favors," David said grimly, waving Stan toward the chair beside his desk. "I don't owe you any either, for that matter. What's happened?"

"Well, for openers, I've caught Mr. Crane in a half-dozen lies," Stan said. "At first he said he was home, asleep, but when I showed him Inga's diary he changed his story. Swore he was with a lady friend whom he preferred not to name. I told him chivalry was a helluva nice idea but it wouldn't do him much good in the state pen. Them hardcase cons ain't big on Mother may I, you know? At which point he caved in and named . . . a prominent local lady. Who happens to be more'n slightly married to a prominent local gentleman."

"Who?" David asked, his curiosity piqued.

"I'm coming to that," Stan said. "I called the lady in question. She told me she barely knew Crane, couldn't even remember his first name."

"So what's your problem? It sounds open and shut to me."

"That's the problem," Stan said. "It is open and shut. Now maybe Ted Crane's not one of my favorite human beings at the moment, but he's an educated man. He's not stupid. So why would he give me an alibi that was so easy to disprove? For that matter, why would he bother to murder his wife? She was dying anyway. All he had to do was wait, and probably not for very long, either."

"Maybe he got tired of waiting."

"Maybe so. But that still leaves me with his alibi. He claims he can prove he and the lady were more than acquaintances. He says he gave her a puppy as a gift. Says it was a pure white one, worth a lot of money. Do you know anything about it?"

"There was a pure white pup in the litter," David acknowledged. "And he's right about it being worth a lot of money. White German shorthairs are rare. I'd guess it would be worth at least a thousand dollars, probably more."

"So if the lady in question actually has this dog, then she and Crane are probably better friends than she wants to admit."

"I suppose they could be," David said. "Where are you going with this?"

"It's not where I'm going, Doc, it's where you're going. Would you recognize this dog if you saw it?"

"A white shorthair? Probably. But so could you. Why not just go check?"

"Because I've already asked the lady and she said she doesn't know Crane. So if I show up on her doorstep asking to inventory her dogs, she may just infer that I doubt her word."

"So? Since when did you get sensitive about offending a suspect?"

"But the lady isn't a suspect, she's only a witness. And she also happens to be Senator Holcomb's wife."

"Diane Holcomb?" David whistled. "She's Crane's alibi?"

"So he claims. And since I have to run for election in this county, the senator and his wife aren't people I'd care to tick off unless it's absolutely necessary."

"So you want me to tick them off instead?"

"I'm hoping to avoid offending anyone, period. The Holcombs have a kennel attached to their guesthouse. If you drive past you can probably spot the dog from the road. If it's there, then I'll make an official call on Mrs. Holcomb."

"And if it's not?"

"If you don't see it, then it comes down to her word against Crane's, and he's already lied to me. The funny part is, you're the reason I tend to believe him. That nick on your face you got in the scuffle this morning? He grazed you with his cufflink. Most guys don't wear cufflinks except on special occasions."

"Like a hot date with someone else's wife, for instance?" David said, touching the cut gingerly with his fingertips. "All right, I'll take a drive past the Holcombs' kennel, but that's all I'm doing. Don't expect me to stick my neck out for Ted Crane."

"All I'm asking for is a look, okay?"

"Right," David said grimly. "A look."

• • •

EASIER said than done. The Holcombs lived in a rambling brown brick ranch house that sprawled along a ridge west of Algoma. There was a four-car garage behind it with guest or servants' quarters above and a kennel attached to its rear wall. The impeccably landscaped grounds were enclosed by a decorative split-rail fence. It was an expensive home, but most of the homes nearby were equally posh, built on ten-acre lots with three-car garages standard and rolling lawns large enough for polo. Which meant it wasn't a neighborhood where a strange car could linger for any length of time without being noticed.

Fortunately, the next home was a Windsor manor set well back from the road. Its long driveway ran parallel to the rear of the Holcombs' guesthouse, which gave it a clear view of the kennels.

David swung the Jeep into the driveway, slowing as he approached the kennels. Beagles. The first three runs held pairs of beagles. The dogs raised their heads to watch him pass, but otherwise ignored him. The last two kennels were a problem. They were larger than the beagles' pens, but one stood open and empty. No way to be sure what lived there, except that it was probably larger than a beagle. The last pen held a white dog. It was the right size to be Crane's pup, but it was sleeping in the afternoon sun with its back to him and David couldn't be sure one way or the other.

He stopped the Jeep abruptly and climbed out. He vaulted the low fence and trotted to the kennels. The beagles came to life, raising the alarm, yawping and yapping as he approached.

The white pup in the last kennel stirred and rose to check him out, but it didn't deign to join in the clamor. Barking was for beagles, and this pup was no hound. He was a German shorthaired pointer, a solid-white male. And he was almost certainly Hector's one-time littermate.

David knelt for a closer look, to be absolutely sure. The pup approached him curiously and sniffed his hand.

"What are you doing here?"

A woman had appeared at the corner of the building. She was strikingly attractive, with fine, aquiline features and honey-blond hair tied back in a lustrous ponytail. Her eyes were hidden behind dark glasses. She was dressed for country life, riding breeches, boots, and a flannel shirt, but there was nothing working class about her. She oozed the confidence that comes with old money and social position. Or perhaps her confidence came from the fiery-eyed Doberman that was straining at the short leash she held in her gloved hand. The dog wasn't growling or even baring its fangs, but its gaze was locked on David's throat. All business. Probably a trained attack dog.

David rose slowly. "I guess I could say I was just passing, Mrs. Holcomb, but I'm not much at fibbing, even in a good cause. My name is Dr. David Westbrook. I'm a veterinarian. Sheriff Wolinski asked me to stop by in order to verify some information, an alibi actually."

"This has to do with that . . . Crane person, doesn't it? I've already told the sheriff that I scarcely know him. My husband and I may have met him at some function, we're quite active socially—"

"Mrs. Holcomb, you don't have to convince me of anything," David interrupted. "I'm not a policeman. On the other hand, this is a very unusual pup you have here. Pedigreed and AKC registered, I imagine."

"What business is that of yours?"

"None at all, ma'am. But if you wouldn't mind an observation by your friendly neighborhood veterinarian, this dog will be awfully easy to trace, which means you're likely going to be involved in a murder investigation whether you like it or not. Ted Crane named you as his alibi. He also said he gave you this dog and here it is. Rather an expensive gift from a man you scarcely know, wouldn't you say?"

She started to reply, then bit it off.

"Ma'am, if you really want to get clear of this thing, the smart thing to do is to just tell Stan Wolinski the truth. He may seem like a rube to you, but you can trust his discretion. He doesn't want to cause any problems for you, and he certainly doesn't want trouble with your husband. That's why he asked me to stop by instead of coming himself."

"And what's your part in this?" she asked coldly.

"I don't have one. I'm only here because I can identify the dog."

"But I'm supposed to rely on your discretion too?"

"I can only give you my word for that, but I live in Algoma now, and practice here. I'm not looking to make enemies either."

"No," she said, releasing a long, ragged breath, "I suppose not. All right then, Ted was here last night. My husband is in Lansing for the week. He spends much of his time there, and I . . . Anyway, Ted arrived about midnight, I believe, and left a few hours later. I'm not really sure of the time, we . . . were drinking quite heavily." She took a deep breath and squared her shoulders. Her eyes were coldly unreadable behind her smoked glasses. "That's really all I have to say on the matter," she said firmly. "I'd appreciate if you'd pass it along to Sheriff Wolinski for me. I'm leaving for Lansing within the hour to join my husband. We're dining with the governor tonight."

She tugged the Doberman's leash and turned away, but then hesitated. "Please tell Sheriff Wolinski that I am relying on his discretion. And yours. And by God, I'd better be able to. Do you understand?"

"Yes, ma'am," David said, eyeing the Doberman. "Definitely."

• • •

"I don't like it," Stan Wolinski said. "I should have questioned her myself." They were in Tubby's Restaurant in downtown Algoma, seated at Wolinski's favorite table. The room was paneled in knotty pine, the furniture was dark oak, and the only decorations were trophy mounts of white-tailed bucks. The chandeliers were made of elk antlers. North-country chic.

"You can still question her if you like," David said, sipping his coffee. "Lansing's only an hour and a half away. If you leave now you can probably roust her in the middle of the governor's after-dinner speech."

"Very funny."

"Sorry. The truth is, I'm a little disappointed too. I was hoping Crane was lying."

"Maybe Mrs. Holcomb's lying. Maybe she's covering for him."

"I doubt it," David said. "She didn't strike me as the sacrificial-lamb type. I got the impression that she only bothered to tell me the truth because it was expedient. If it had been more convenient to let Ted hang, she would have."

"Poor Crane. He doesn't seem to have much luck in love, does he?"

"That depends on how you define luck," David said. "I'd say Inga Crane, as ill as she was, was ten times the woman Diane Holcomb is. And a lot better than Ted deserved."

"But as you say, Inga was in rough shape and that can be a terrible drag, emotionally and financially," Stan said. "Personally, I don't think Crane has the backbone to carry the weight. Alibi or not, I still like him for the killing. And he's the one Inga named."

"Yeah, so she did. I've been chewing on that all the way back to town. Why did she name him?"

"Maybe because he did it," Stan snorted. "Or at the very least, she thought he did."

"You mean she woke up in the night, suffocating, realized her respirator was shut down, and just assumed Ted unplugged it? I doubt that. She couldn't function without the machine for long and she couldn't get out of bed without help. So with her dying breath she managed to scrawl his name? Very dramatic."

"Sometimes death is dramatic."

"But she didn't want to die. At least, not yet. So why did she bother to scrawl his name? Why didn't she just pick up the phone and dial nine-one-one? Her bedside phone worked, I used it to call you today."

Stan stared at him a moment. "Are you sure about that?"

"Absolutely."

"Then maybe whoever unplugged the machine did the same to the phone, or at least moved it."

"Or perhaps Inga simply never woke up. The machine stopped breathing and a few moments later, so did she. But either way, she couldn't have written the note blaming Ted."

"Why not?"

"Because her mother said the book was open on the bed. She put it away to protect Inga's privacy. If Ted killed her, he must have either unplugged the phone or moved it out of her reach and then replaced it afterward. But if he did that, he would have seen the diary."

"But the only other person in the house was Inga's mother. Surely you don't think she could have done this thing?"

"If she had, she'd hardly have put the diary away, would she? No, I think the person that killed Inga knew Ted would be visiting his ladylove and knew Clare would be too zonked on medication to hear the machine's alarm or any sounds Inga might make. Inga once told me that Ted was worried about how much her care was costing, that he wanted her to sell the house. With Ted out of the picture and the old lady clearly incompetent, I wonder who will inherit the estate?"

"You mean the niece? But she was out of town, staying with a girlfriend."

"Was she? Did you actually check her story out, Stan?"

"No, I didn't," the sheriff said slowly. "I had no reason to. Until now."

• • •

DAVID was in his kitchen making a cup of midnight cocoa when he heard the crunch of tires on the driveway. He poured a second cup as Stan Wolinski eased quietly in the back door.

"Thanks, Doc," Stan said, gratefully accepting the steaming cup. "Thought you might be waiting up for news. I've arrested Cindy Meyers. She claims it was a mercy killing. Says poor Inga was suffering and she only wanted to put an end to it."

"Maybe that's how it was," David said, waving Stan to a seat at the kitchen table.

"She'll have a tough time making that fly," Stan said. "She arranged an alibi for herself and forged that death note to frame her uncle. I doubt a judge will buy the idea that she did Inga in out of the goodness of her heart. The friend Cindy claimed she stayed with in Alma folded like an accordion when she learned it was a murder case. She admitted Cindy'd told her she was seeing someone secretly and borrowed her car to drive back here."

"A secret lover? Maybe she got that idea from Ted."

"Possibly, although she's certainly sly enough to have thought of it on her own. She stuck to her story about being out of town until I hit her with the phone record."

"Phone record?"

"Sure. The thing is, Cindy knew about Ted's little midnight visits and she wanted to be sure the EMT guys would find Inga's respirator unplugged and Ted gone. So I figured she must have made a call to wake Clare on the way back to her friend's place. I checked the records, and there was a call from a gas station pay phone just outside of Algoma to the Crane home. Cindy even used her credit card."

"Not very clever of her."

"She didn't have any change," Stan said wryly. "And she didn't want to ask the attendant for any. She was afraid he might remember her. And now I've got a question for you, Doc. Something's been bothering me all day. You don't have to answer if you don't want to."

"Maybe I won't," David said. "What is it?"

"This morning at the Crane place when I asked you about the tooth marks on that plug? I got the feeling you had some doubts."

"No, they were tooth marks all right."

"I'm not saying you lied about anything, only that you might have had some doubts."

"It did seem awfully . . . convenient," David conceded. "There were several cords back there and Hector'd chewed on all of them. It seemed odd that the only one he unplugged was the one that really mattered."

"But you didn't say anything."

"No. It was early in the morning and I hadn't had time to think. It occurred to me that Crane might have pulled the plug, but if so, I wasn't sure I should point the finger at him."

"Why not?"

"Because Inga was my friend and she was in a lot of pain," David said evenly. "It cost her every time she drew a breath. To be honest, I'd thought about pulling that plug myself more than once."

"I see. But later, when Cindy asked for your help in implicating Ted, you went along."

"I'd thought things through by then," David said with a shrug. "And I realized that if Inga wanted to end things, she could have done so anytime just by leaving her mask off. But she didn't. I think she intended to live long enough to see Hector healthy and strong and able to stand on his own. Maybe it was a foolish idea, but no one had the right to take it from her, not her friends, nor her family. Only Inga."

"That's straight enough," Stan said, rising. "But next time, if you have any doubts, you tell me about 'em, okay?"

"I hope to God there won't be a next time," David said. "At least not like this one."

"It came down pretty hard, I'll admit," Stan said, pausing in the doorway. "But at least one good thing came out of it. Your friend was in a lot of pain, and now it's over."

David nodded without answering. But he knew it wasn't true. It wasn't over. Not yet.

• • •

FOUR days after Inga's funeral, Hector died. At the end, David eased his passing with an injection. The pup wouldn't accept food from anyone but Inga and he was wasting away. David decided against trying to anesthetize Hector in order to force-feed him. It would only have prolonged the inevitable, and he couldn't find it in his heart to compel Hector to abide in this world when he so clearly wanted to be gone.

Later that afternoon, David placed the pup's small body in the Crawford furnace behind his office and cremated it. His ashes barely filled an envelope.

Dusk was falling and a hint of rain was in the air as David drove his Jeep through the gates of Holy Cross Cemetery. He parked near the entrance, then followed the tiled walkway to Inga's grave. Her resting place seemed more final somehow than it had the day of her funeral. The flowers were gone now and fresh strips of green sod had been neatly laid down over the mound of raw earth.

He knelt in the grass beside her grave for a moment. He didn't pray. He'd never been a religious man and it would have seemed hypocritical. After a few moments, he glanced around to be sure he wasn't being observed. No one was near. The cemetery stretched away to the foothills beyond. The only other mourner in view was an elderly woman in a dark raincoat and she was far off and lost in her own thoughts.

David carefully raised the corner of a sod strip and slid the small envelope of ashes into the soil beneath, then gently patted the grass back into place. He wasn't sure if what he was doing made any sense, even to himself. But he hoped that it might mean something to Inga.

He lingered as the shadows lengthened, waiting in silence for . . . something. Anything, really. A sign, perhaps. Some indication that he'd done the right thing. But nothing happened, nothing changed. He'd thought that burying Hector's ashes here might give him a sense of closure. It didn't. It felt like an empty, futile gesture. Maybe the cynics are right. Maybe the grave is truly the end of things after all. Eventually he tired of waiting, and rose on stiffened knees. But he hesitated. Something in the distance caught his eye. A movement. Probably just the wind in the trees. The Algoma hills rolled away into the dusky distance like shadowy waves, bathed in the blaze of the lowering sun. And in the dying light, the hills seemed to glow from within, as though they were being magically transmuted into gold, like the hills of Oz or . . .

Puppyland. That's what Inga'd said those hills meant to her when she was a child. And perhaps that was why he felt no sense of her presence at the grave. She wasn't here anymore. If she was anywhere, she would be there, in those shining hills, running free. Breathing free. But not alone. Hector had been so eager to follow her, surely he must be with her now. Perhaps he'd gone to show her the way back to the place he'd come from. Puppyland. Where the air is sweet, and the hills are so lush and lovely that puppies are born dreaming of them.

CHILD OF ANOTHER TIME

William Bankier

THEIR EYES MET and Blake Metcalfe felt as if he had been kicked in the stomach. She couldn't be older than seventeen, young enough to be his daughter. But she held out her glass, and as he filled it with red wine she said; "Hi, my name's Tina Flanagan. I'm the new girl in town."

He introduced himself and heard that she was just down from Toronto. Her father had used influence to get her a job in a Montreal ad agency. It had been her wish to get away from home.

They stood side by side at the drinks table, watching couples dancing in the area occupied by desks and drawing boards during the working day. "I've been watching you," she said. "Do you work here?"

Metcalfe nodded. "I'm one of the old originals. The oldest," he added, providing emphasis that was hardly necessary. At forty-eight, he was going heavy, trousers rolling at the waist, cheekbones covered by a mask of fat. Life was good these days, life was easy. Apex Art Studio was charging clients a premium for his illustrations and he was collecting part of that money. He ate big lunches, drank out of habit, went home and made love with Laura as often as most men might with a wife of twenty-five years' standing. Having his ailing mother-in-law in the house was a problem, but then.

Metcalfe found himself looking down at Tina's hair. It was chestnut, thick and wavy, and the way it grew and glistened reminded him of somebody—

yes, his daughter Maggie. Good thing Maggie had not made it to the party or she would have been casting sarcastic glances his way, seeing him chatting up the young talent like this. Still only twenty-three, Maggie Metcalfe was fast becoming one of the better illustrators in the advertising department at Rambeau's.

"I have to say it." Tina looked up at him. "I go for older men. I hope you don't mind."

"I'd be lying if I said I mind." There was something so attractive about this plump, pretty kid. Metcalfe couldn't express it other than to admit he felt inclined to pick her up and hold her in his arms. And although there was an element of lust, the attraction was not totally sexual. No, he felt an overpowering affection for her, a disturbing urge to nuzzle her big, smooth face, to tuck his nose into the dimple in her cheek, to inhale whatever soapy fragrance he might find clinging to her.

"It's because I never had a father," she confessed. "I was adopted. My parents leveled with me when I was twelve. I think that's a good idea, don't you? They told me I was chosen because they love me so much." She sipped some wine. "My father is Horace Flanagan, the real-estate man. You must have heard of him."

"Who hasn't. He's the cover story this month in *Locus* magazine."

"See how clever I am." She gave Metcalfe a smile that interrupted his heartbeat. "If you're going to be adopted, choose somebody like Horace Flanagan."

Some of the party left to go to the baseball game, where they would be guests in the Apex box at the Olympic Stadium. The reduced crowd seemed to be settling in for heavy drinking and close dancing. Metcalfe looked at his watch. He had told Laura to expect him around nine. He never stayed till the end at company parties.

"If you're getting ready to go, I'd appreciate a lift," Tina said.

They walked from the building along Notre Dame Street through a cool summer night. The girl fell into step, matching his stride naturally. Not many people did this—most of them asked him where the fire was.

In the car, he asked her where she lived. She told him she had an apartment on Durocher Street. "But I don't want to go home yet. Can we go somewhere for coffee?"

Metcalfe avoided the restaurants where he was known, drove to a place down east where he took late nourishment after his occasional solo debaucheries in the strip clubs on The Main. Tina seemed fascinated, listening to the foreign hum of the place, flashing a friendly smile at their French-Canadian waitress.

"This is so nice of you to take me out."

"My pleasure." Had she really forgotten it was her suggestion? He felt like nothing more than coffee and pie but Tina ordered barbecue chicken, fries, roll, and a vanilla milkshake. As she tucked in, she said:

"I love Montreal. For some reason it feels like home to me. Maybe I was born here—my parents have never said where I came from when they adopted me. Is it possible I feel something in my soul, like a salmon that goes back to where it was spawned?"

"It's possible."

"Talk to me while I eat. Tell me about yourself."

Metcalfe seldom opened up to anybody but now he found himself telling this child everything, eager to describe his life to her. He spoke of his early dreams of becoming a fine artist, of having a studio in Paris—a city he had never even visited. He explained his acceptance of the security in the illustrator's life, where he was usually bored, never stretched, by the assignments.

He glowed when he spoke of Maggie and her burgeoning career at the department store. "She's better than I am already." He produced a snapshot from his wallet.

"Looks like somebody I know," Tina said, frowning, dipping a french-fry into a pot of spicy sauce.

Metcalfe went on to talk about his wife, who had resumed her career teaching languages until her mother's illness became so far advanced that the old lady had to be taken into the house where Laura could devote full time to looking after her.

"What is Parkinson's disease?" Tina asked. "I've never come across it."

"I hope you never do. The victim shakes constantly, can't do much of anything for herself, wastes away but very slowly. It can go on for years and years."

"No cure?"

"Sometimes a very tricky brain operation can help if they get to it soon enough. Laura's mum is too late for that." Thinking of the old lady with her hideous life sentence and Laura trapped at home as nurse, Metcalfe felt impotent rage.

When they were finished, Tina went to the ladies room. As Metcalfe gave money to the waitress, she said: "Your daughter is a chip off the old block. I can see the family resemblance. She looks like you."

Metcalfe felt weak in the legs. Seventeen years fell away and he was back in the waiting room of the maternity hospital facing a troubled Dr. Fox, trying to understand what the man was saying. "Something is the matter with the baby. She's having trouble breathing. We'll do everything we can, but I think you should prepare yourself. No, we won't say anything yet to Mrs. Metcalfe."

So the baby they had planned to call Angela came and went in one shocking weekend in October. Metcalfe called the department store and managed to get rid of the new crib before Laura came home from the hospital. Somehow they recovered, concentrated on six-year-old Maggie, but the wound never healed completely. To this day, when he remembered the death of Angela, Metcalfe wept.

"Are you all right?" Tina searched his face as she joined him at the restaurant entrance.

"Come on, I'll drive you home."

The suspicion was no more than a whisper in Metcalfe's mind. It was the most incredible nonsense but he listened to it. She was the right age. There was this instant rapport between them, which was much more than an ordinary physical attraction. And now the waitress had said they were father and daughter, she emphasized the resemblance.

Saying goodnight outside Tina's apartment building, he was deluged by clues. That laugh—it was like Maggie's. When she turned her eyes down, they were Laura's eyes. The broad forehead was his own—and the overlapping teeth in the bottom row, why hadn't he noticed them before? That was the Metcalfe bite, his dentist would recognize it.

He drove home at twenty-five miles an hour. The suspicion was right or it was wrong. If wrong, Tina's appearance here, her very existence, was an incredible coincidence. If the suspicion was right, the explanation was even more overwhelming. It would suggest a crime that hardly bore thinking about. Had Dr. Stanley Fox deliberately lied about the baby's condition? Did he, somehow, fake Angela's death, present to Metcalfe through the undertaker a small white coffin—empty—then provide a healthy baby to the millionaire Toronto realtor, Horace Flanagan? It *could* be done. Anything could be done with money and Flanagan had plenty of money. But why?

"Why my baby?" Metcalfe said aloud, sitting parked in front of his house.

"Are you staying out there all night?" Laura called in a stage whisper from the open front door.

He went in and pretended he was sick to his stomach to cover his shell-shocked condition. He drank a bromo, then took a cup of black coffee. There was no way he could breathe a word of his theory to Laura. Seventeen years ago, losing the baby had almost wiped her out. To this day, the subject could hardly be discussed.

"How's your mum?"

"She had one of her bad spells this afternoon."

"You should have called me."

"I knew you had the party. I called the doctor, I explained she was getting violent—it's the depression. She brought my silver hand-mirror down, cracked the glass top on the dresser."

"And you were here alone." He had stopped suggesting they institutionalize the old lady. Laura wouldn't consider the provincial hospital—it was a nightmare, the wards and corridors populated with pitiful human wreckage out of an engraving from the Middle Ages. The acceptable alternative was a private nursing-home, but this would cost the world.

"The doctor told me to increase her medication. I don't think she'll act up again." Laura's face was showing new creases, her mouth set in the familiar determined line. She lowered her eyes and Metcalfe saw for a fraction of a second the expression that had crossed Tina Flanagan's face. "Will you go in and speak to her before we go to bed? She looks forward to seeing you."

Metcalfe pulled a chair close to the bed and turned the lamp so his cheery face was illuminated. "Evening, Mum," he said. "I've come from a drunken party. Don't worry, I drank your share, too."

The pale, drugged eyes looked up at him. Her lips parted as she tried to smile and the palsied hand crept towards him across the blanket. Leaning forward to give her a kiss on the cheek, Metcalfe kept smiling but he closed his eyes and held his breath.

• • •

FOR two days, Metcalfe carried the fantastic theory around. It did not evaporate, made ludicrous by the passage of time. It hardened into reality, like an excavated relic of some ancient war. He was going to have to dig in order to verify his suspicion or to dispel the delusion. But he would need help and there was only one place where he could find it, one man who would go along without trying to talk him out of it.

Metcalfe took Tuesday afternoon off and drove to the apartment building on Decelles Avenue. The building looked sadly familiar—red brick, three tiers of iron balconies, an entrance decorated with curved concrete like something out of an Alexander Korda film. This was the doorway through which he and Laura had carried baby Maggie on the proud return from the hospital twenty-three years ago. Six years later they had crept in alone, empty-handed, guilty, nothing to show.

On the first occasion, Alphonse Ferrier had been coming up from his basement apartment. Al was the building superintendent, a former policeman expelled for drinking and insubordination. When he saw Maggie, his Indian features produced a proud smile—she might have been his baby.

After the loss of Angela, while Laura was still in the hospital, Metcalfe had wandered into the Texas Tavern around the corner for a few beers to help him sleep. Alphonse Ferrier was alone at a table near the door. He must have heard the news. When Metcalfe sat down, Ferrier pushed one of three glasses of beer toward him and said, "Not very good, is it." There was something stoical, an acceptance of bad luck, in the understatement that reinforced Metcalfe more than all the effusions of sympathy poured over him in the past two days. He relaxed, relieved of the hideous embarrassment.

"Thanks, Al," he said. "Cheers." He drank the glass of beer at one draft and ordered four more. He and the super closed the tavern that night. After that, they drank together once a week until Laura suggested a year later that they get out of the apartment with its melancholy nursery and move closer into the city. Since then, he only managed drinks with Ferrier at Christmas.

Metcalfe parked the car. Ferrier was washing the glass in the front doors. He looked a few pounds heavier. The glossy black hair fell in a thick curtain as he bent to his work.

"Time for a beer, Al."

He stood up with a chamois in one hand, the dark Iroquois eyes finding out everything there was to know about his former tenant who had come back so unexpectedly. "What's the matter?"

"I've got big trouble."

"What can I do?"

"Come and listen to me. Tell me if you think I'm crazy."

"I can tell you that right now. But I could use a beer."

The tavern wasn't crowded. They took a table by the door, said nothing till the beer came and they had tasted the first one. "You're getting fat, Al."

"I had to stop running." Ferrier used to walk every day to the steps leading up to Beaver Lake. He used to go there, fair weather or foul, and run for miles over pathways covering the mountain. "I did something to a bone in my foot. It's getting better—I'll get back to it."

Metcalfe finished the first glass, drew the next one to him. "Remember when Angela died the day after she was born? Well. You aren't going to believe this. I don't think she died. I think I've seen her."

Ferrier did not look surprised. He never looked surprised. "She'd be a big girl by now. Seventeen years?"

"That's right. I've met a girl that age. From Toronto. She told me she was adopted. A waitress saw us together in a restaurant and said my daughter looks just like me. But, Al, it's more than that. I had a feeling about her right from the start. Before I knew any of this."

Ferrier looked through the doorway, far away down the street. "How could it be?"

"I don't know. The doctor would have had to take my baby out of the hospital somehow. Convince people she died. I don't know why he'd do that."

"Are you going to ask him?"

"Not yet. He'd say I'm crazy, he'd simply deny it. For all I know, he'd be telling the truth. No, Al, I have to do something—"

During their drinking sessions, Ferrier had always been able to read Metcalfe's mind. Now he drew lines with a fingertip in the condensation from the beer glasses, traced the shape of a cross on the table top. "Will you be able to do that?" he asked. "Look in your own baby's grave?"

• • •

THE weather was good, the risks would never be less. Ferrier took Metcalfe back to the apartment building and fitted them both out with gardener's overalls. He found two pairs of grass clippers, a rake, a spade, and a large canvas bag. With the tools in the bag, they went back to Metcalfe's car and drove to the base of the steps at the side of the mountain.

"If we go in through the cemetery gate," Ferrier said, "they'll ask us what we want. But there's another way in."

They climbed the steps, Ferrier carrying the bag, walked past Beaver Lake and the chalet, then continued up a grassy slope until they came to a bluff overlooking the cemetery.

"This is the hard part. Follow me." Ferrier began to scramble down the steep face, clutching at shrubs and rocks, sending a cascade of gravel ahead of them. Halfway down, the slope began to level out and the passage became easier. Soon they were on grass, moving through a stand of young birch trees, then they were on a path between marble gravestones.

"You know the way from here?" Ferrier asked.

"I visited once or twice years ago. There's an area set aside for the children."

It was a quiet time of afternoon, the cemetery almost deserted. Metcalfe led the way past rows of monuments, the larger ones casting shadows over the path. They moved into an area where the stones were smaller and beyond to where the graves were marked only by rectangular plaques. "This is it." He was occupying his mind with extraneous details, the length of the grass, the number of lace-holes in Ferrier's boot. If he thought about what they were about to do, he knew he would not be able to proceed.

"People over there," Ferrier said, handing his companion a pair of clippers. They bent to the edge of the path and began trimming grass.

Ferrier stood up a while later and made a few passes with the rake. "Okay," he said. "Let's make it fast." He took the spade and went to work, Metcalfe more than willing to leave him to it. The spade was sharp; it cut the turf into neat squares Ferrier dragged to one side. Now he was into dark earth.

Metcalfe had not come with the undertaker to the cemetery. The ceremony in the funeral parlor was enough; he had listened to the prayers and watched them take the small white casket away, then he had gone up to the hospital to sit with Laura.

Ferrier's spade struck something solid. He scraped away the earth to reveal crumbling wood. "Want to leave it to me?"

"Yes, go ahead." Metcalfe turned away, bent to examine a patch of clover, tugged at tendrils of weed twisted through the roots of grass. Ferrier's call brought him around.

"You were right, my friend."

"What?"

"This is an empty casket." He stirred some fragments of wood as Metcalfe peered over his shoulder. "There was never anything in this box but the lining."

• • •

THE building had once been somebody's home. Now it was a suite of offices. The automatic switchboard, the telex terminal, the massive electric typewriter all looked expensive. The girl at the reception desk appeared a bit pricey as well. She had been talking on the telephone when Metcalfe came in. Now she set down the phone, picked up a glitter earring, and fastened it to a shell-like lobe.

"Can I help you?"

"I'd like to speak to Mr. Fox. I rang earlier."

"Mr. Metcalfe? Yes, go on through. I'll buzz and tell him you're on the way."

The former Dr. Fox had put on weight. Metcalfe remembered him as a nervous young man with the build of a hungry schoolboy. Now that frame was concealed inside a suitful of flesh. When he stood to greet his visitor, the fat on Fox's chest kept his arms from touching his sides.

"What can I do for you?"

Metcalfe sat down. He could see in Fox's eyes that the man had decided not to remember him. The gun he had borrowed from Alphonse Ferrier felt heavy in his jacket pocket. "When did you stop being a doctor?"

"Quite some time ago. I decided real estate was better for me. After all those years of study, too." Fox made a coarse sound between a cough and a laugh. "Ain't it a bitch!"

Metcalfe decided to get on with it. "Seventeen years ago, you delivered my daughter Angela. You told me she had hyaline membrane, couldn't breathe properly, you said she died the next day. Recently I met a seventeen-year-old girl from Toronto who could be my daughter. I've been told we have a strong resemblance. She's adopted. What do you say, Dr. Fox?"

The heavy face was like damp clay. Mottled patches suggested worms below the surface. "I remember the case, of course. Very tragic. But this girl—you mustn't let something like that play on your imagination."

"I agree. That's why I went to the cemetery and opened the grave. I've just come from there." Metcalfe held onto the gun butt as if he would fall without it. "It's an empty coffin. As you well know."

"Oh, God." Fox buried his face in two bunches of fleshy fingers. A couple of gaudy rings stared at Metcalfe. "What are you going to do?"

It was time to show the gun. Metcalfe took it out and let the barrel rest on the edge of the desk to keep it from waving like a baton. "I haven't made up my mind. I may shoot you in the gut. But first I want to know what happened. I want to know who. And why."

"It was Horace Flanagan. He offered me money—so much money I couldn't let it go. Can you imagine somebody putting a quarter of a million dollars in front of you—tax free? He wanted a baby. He and his wife couldn't conceive. They couldn't adopt, either—not in Quebec because they were different religions."

"I don't see the problem. These things happen underground all the time. Girls are in trouble, they have babies and they farm them out."

"Flanagan is a crackpot. He believes the infant from an unwed mother carries bad blood. It wasn't good enough for him. He came to me and told me what he wanted, a child of good parents, cultivated people, talented people. He was ready to buy that baby. I told him no way, but then he named this incredible sum of money. I wanted out—medical practice was killing me, I owed people from my years in college. Flanagan had found this out."

Hearing his suspicion confirmed was almost beyond Metcalfe's belief. "How did you get away with it?"

Fox explained. The maternity hospital was a small place with only a few patients. He had arranged to have Laura Metcalfe induced so the baby would arrive on a Sunday night when a young, inexperienced nurse was on duty. He convinced the nurse the infant needed emergency treatment, said he would drive it to Montreal General himself. He took the newborn child to the Flanagan residence, where a private nurse took over the post-natal care. It was a healthy girl, there were no complications.

"But the undertaker? He staged a funeral service."

"Staged is right. I gave him twenty thousand dollars. Only one man knew about it. I said I performed an autopsy so the coffin was sealed, nobody would want to look inside." Fox took his hands away from his face. "I did a terrible thing."

Metcalfe got up and went to the door. "I'm not sure what I'm going to do with you. I may bring in the police. I may kill you myself." He put the gun in his pocket. "First I want to go and see Flanagan."

Incredibly, Fox tried to mitigate his crime. "Babies do die. It happens all the time. It's a terrible thing for the parents but they get over it. Life goes on."

"There's only one thing wrong with that," Metcalfe said. "My baby *didn't* die."

• • •

IN the days that followed, Metcalfe tried to decide what to do. He was bricked up, he realized, like a frog in a cornerstone. He couldn't tell Laura about his discovery—she would go out of her mind. Nor could he go to Tina Flanagan and explain that he was her real father. The revelation might turn the girl upside down. He had observed during their time together that she had a crush on him. Sexual fantasies had probably taken place in her mind. To learn he was her father—

On the other hand, if he went to Toronto, looked up Horace Flanagan, and faced him with his outrage, the tycoon would surely have him killed. How could the holder of such a threatening secret be allowed to live?

What if Metcalfe were to kill Flanagan? If he did it precipitately and was caught, then the secret would be revealed with Laura and Maggie and Tina left to live with it. And he himself would spend the rest of his life in prison.

What if he took care, murdered Flanagan, and managed to go undetected? It would be a shocking loss for Tina, who obviously loved her adoptive father. How could he do that to her?

There was no direction in which Metcalfe could turn, and yet the urge for revenge was so overpowering he could taste it like a mouthful of copper coins.

A further chilling thought was the realization that Dr. Fox must have telephoned Flanagan the same day and told him about Metcalfe's discovery. The millionaire, a great believer in insurance, could well have set the wheels in motion by this time to have the threat eliminated. So whether Metcalfe took action or not, fate, having shown him the truth about a devastating aspect of his past, might now be about to sort out his future.

• • •

"I'D like to have you guys down to the loft for supper in a couple of weeks," Maggie said. She had come for a meal and a visit and was now playing stud poker with her father at the dining-room table, using matches for chips. Laura was in a deep chair marking French papers, a job she did freelance for one of her former colleagues at the school. Her face lit up.

"Sounds lovely," she said. The evenings at Maggie's place were always entertaining. Odd friends dropped in, there was wine and much spontaneous laughter. The loft was part of a converted clothing factory—spacious, mattress on the floor, painted bricks hung with bright, original work. "Let's make it soon."

"I may have to go to Toronto," Metcalfe said in a tone that cancelled all other plans.

"What does it take to raise a smile around here?" Maggie complained. She shuffled the cards. "New game. Seven-card stud. Deuces, treys, one-eyed Jacks, and low-in-the-hole wild. Everybody prospers."

• • •

Two days later, Metcalfe was at the drawing board in his private room at the art studio. The telephone rang. "Metcalfe?" said a resonant voice. "This is Horace Flanagan. Can you come out and talk to me? I'm outside the building."

Metcalfe tried to visualize the tycoon in a telephone booth. "Why not come in here?"

"Better we not be seen together. For both of us. And for Tina."

That was direct enough. Metcalfe felt reassured, as if now the matter was on the table and this man, whose career was built on problem-solving, would do something to make Metcalfe's agony go away. "I'll be right out."

Flanagan had not been calling from a booth. The telephone was in a grey limousine stationed outside the building like a slab of polished glacial rock. The back door opened and Metcalfe climbed into an upholstered interior that resembled a corner of the lobby in an expensive hotel. Horace Flanagan blended into the grey-plush fabric. Only his face emerged—pink-and-white skin, sea-green eyes, sparse white hair, a long upper lip curved in a mild smile, a dimple in a plump, square jaw. This is the man Tina accepts as her father, Metcalfe thought, understanding how it could be so. She loves him. She looks forward to seeing him.

"Thanks for coming out." The car began to roll. "It's after eleven. Have a drink?"

"Rye and water." Metcalfe watched Flanagan open a cherrywood panel and measure whisky into crystal glasses. Here is the man who did this unspeakable thing to me, he thought. Why aren't I at his throat?

"Cheers." Was it actually the best booze he had ever tasted or was it the influence of the experience—drifting silently with a gentle surging movement through surroundings tinted green by glass that was probably bulletproof? If the gods went about the world, this was how they did it.

"To the point," Flanagan said. "A terrible coincidence has taken place. I should never have allowed Tina to move to Montreal. But the chance that she would encounter her father, or that you would recognize her, seemed infinitely remote."

"She encountered me," Metcalfe intoned with a hint of mockery. "I recognized her."

"And you went further, Dr. Fox tells me. You opened the grave and established the case. Well, I give you credit, Mr. Metcalfe, for not running amok. I can't say I would have been as controlled. In your position, I reckon I'd have grabbed a gun. There would have been bodies, Tina would have lost two fathers. She would be the ultimate loser."

"And her mother. My wife."

"Of course." The millionaire put his hand on a black despatch case beside him. "But you didn't do that. You have kept the secret, which means there is still a chance for a happy ending."

"I doubt it." Metcalfe's sense of outrage was rising as Flanagan talked on about civilized behavior.

"We can't turn back the clock. I can't give you back your baby. She doesn't exist. She's a young woman and she accepts me and my wife as her parents. We have a sound relationship—we love each other."

"You'd better let me out of the car."

"No, listen. We have only two courses of action open to us. This case contains a lot of money. Half a million dollars. It may sound crass, Metcalfe, but what else can I offer you as compensation? Believe me, money *does* buy happiness. A lot of people achieve it in no other way."

Metcalfe was thinking of Ferrier's gun. It was in his desk at the office, in a bottom drawer buried under a couple of art pads. "You said two courses of action."

Flanagan looked genuinely troubled. "If you refuse to cooperate, I'll have

to take steps to protect my own position and the contentment of my family."
He glanced through the glass panel at the back of the chauffeur's neck.
The driver was not a large man. Narrow shoulders, tendons in the neck,
and signs of a scaly scalp suggested an impatient individual, one who took
pleasure in carrying out antisocial assignments under the protection of a
wealthy patron.

When Metcalfe said nothing, Flanagan snapped the catches on the despatch case, opened the lid, and placed it on his passenger's knees. The
money was real, it was half a million dollars. The sick old lady could be
installed in a proper home where she would receive the best of care. Freed
from her slavery, Laura could pursue her teaching career, could return to
McGill to obtain a better degree. Or why not the Sorbonne—while Metcalfe
took that studio within sight of the Seine and gave himself one real chance
to develop the talent that had come down to him through the generations?
It wasn't too late.

"What's to stop me taking the money," he heard himself saying, "and
then going to the police with the story about you and Dr. Fox?"

"Your common sense. Imagine what such an action would do to Tina. I
know you love her, she's your daughter. But the man she accepts as her
father—and she loves me, believe it—would be involved in a nasty court
case. Think of the publicity and how it would affect her."

"At least you'd be in prison where you belong."

"Never. I could buy the Canadian prison system and turn it into a chain
of holiday camps. No, I'd suffer from the exposure, but I'd keep my freedom. You, on the other hand, would lose your life in some sort of accident.
So your wife would be a widow, your daughter would be fatherless, Tina's
life would be a shambles, and you'd be dead. While against that—" Flanagan
passed his hand over the case of money.

They were back outside the studio building. By closing the case himself,
Metcalfe took possession of the payoff. Clasping the door handle, he said,
"Just so you don't think you hold all the cards, I wasn't alone when I opened
the grave. A friend was with me. An influential friend. If anything should
happen to me, he could tell the whole story."

Flanagan looked respectful. "Who is this influential friend?"

"If you think I'd tell you his name," Metcalfe said as he opened the door,
"you must believe I'm suicidal. And homicidal."

• • •

METCALFE spent the afternoon working, then carried the despatch case
home with him. He was afraid to let it out of his sight. "It's part of a job
I'm working on," he told Laura.

"Al Ferrier telephoned you."

"When?"

"This morning, just after you left for work."

"I'd better see what he wants." He dialed the number on the kitchen phone. "Al, it's me."

"I thought you'd like to know I'm helping you." The former policeman sounded pleased with himself. "Early this morning I went around to the house of that Dr. Fox. I put a little fear into him, showed him my old department identification. How was he to know it's no longer valid? Anyway, I told him he better cooperate with you."

"Thanks, Al. But I'm not sure that was such a wise thing to do."

"Why not? He looked shook up."

"I can't talk about it. I'm coming to see you, are you home?"

At the door, Laura said, "What's the mysterious business with Al Ferrier?"

"He's getting involved in a betting thing and I'm trying to talk him out of it. I won't be long."

Metcalfe drove to the apartment building on Decelles Avenue. He went inside and hurried down the marble steps to the superintendent's apartment on the basement level. Reaching for the bell, he noticed the crack of the open door. A cold wind seemed to flow from the place, though when he stepped inside he discovered the apartment was stuffy and there was an unfamiliar musky smell in the air.

He stumbled over Ferrier's body in the kitchen. His throat had been cut and a lake of blood had collected at the low end of the uneven floor. Metcalfe stood over his friend for a full minute. Then he went upstairs and out of the building and drove to the nearest public telephone from which he placed an anonymous call to the police.

Throughout the whole procedure, Metcalfe now realized, he had been carrying the despatch case. He opened it on the car seat beside him and stared at the money. It seemed to be the only thing of value in his life, including the life itself. Because of him, Alphonse Ferrier was dead. Had he not involved him in his morbid investigation, Al would be alive.

But it was *not* morbid. His own Angela had made her way back into his life. There were many clues to her identity. Naturally, he had followed it up.

There seemed to be a message here for bereaved parents: don't go searching for your dead children—they may prove to be alive.

He switched on and drove to Maggie's address on Crescent Street. She was up in the loft, propped on her mattress with a bottle of chianti and a slab of cheese, watching a movie she'd seen four times. "It's a good thing I love you more than Robert Redford," she snarled, turning off the set and pouring her father some wine.

"Maggie, you have to do something for me. Hold onto your hat." He opened the case.

"New bills for the Sunday-afternoon Monopoly game," she said in a subdued tone.

"It's real. There's half a million there."

"When do the cops start firing through the windows?"

"I promise you, this is legal money. It's ours. You can smile if you want. You're the oldest unmarried daughter of a wealthy father."

"Where did you get it?"

"I can't tell you at the moment. It's a thing I've become involved in."

"You're in trouble."

"Not yet. But if it turns out that way, you'll have to take over. I want you to hire a safety-deposit box tomorrow and stow the money in it. Tonight, I want you to go and see your mother."

Maggie sensed what was coming. "Why can't you see her? Daddy, what's happening?" Her hands gripped his hard enough so he would have to struggle to free himself.

"I have to go away for a while. You know your mum—if I start to tell her this, there'll be a big scene. Believe me, Maggie, I'm doing the only thing I can."

• • •

METCALFE stopped off at the office and collected Ferrier's gun. Then he drove to the building on Durocher where Tina Flanagan lived. He hadn't seen her since the night he dropped her off after the party. He felt he had to have a word with her though he had no idea what he would say.

Her name was hand-lettered on a card over the doorbell. Metcalfe's heart turned over as he studied the printing—it could have been done by Maggie or himself. He rang four times and was turning to go when a woman came out of a ground-floor apartment and smiled at him.

"The Flanagan girl? She's gone for a while. But she's keeping the place. She paid two months in advance."

Metcalfe drove up Decarie Boulevard, put the car on Highway 401, and aimed it at Toronto. He was halfway there when his mind began to emerge from the shock of discovering Al's body. It was almost midnight. At this rate, he would arrive in Flanagan's city in the small hours of the morning. He might better try to get some sleep.

Finding a motel with a vacancy sign, he checked in and lay between chilly sheets in a room that smelled of damp plaster and emulsion paint. What alternative did he have now that the mistakes had been made?

The first and worst one was to have let his imagination loose on the identity of Tina. Another drink and home early to bed that night could have saved all this. But he had taken her to eat, had watched her, listened to her, accepted the idle comment of a waitress who was simply being flattering. Crazy little accidents like that could make the world come to an end.

The other serious mistake was involving Al Ferrier, and then telling Flanagan he had an accomplice.

Al had, of course, contributed to his own fate by running to Dr. Fox and identifying himself.

Metcalfe turned over on sagging springs. If he did nothing, if he went home and pretended he had spent a night out drinking, would all end well? Never. Having killed Ferrier, Flanagan was committed now to doing away with the only man who could connect him with the crime.

No, he was doing the best thing, the only thing he could do. In his childhood, Metcalfe had listened to Foster Hewitt broadcasting NHL hockey from Toronto on the radio. One of the commentator's favorite clichés was, "The best defense is a good offense." This was what Metcalfe was doing— defending himself. By four o'clock, he was up and shaved and back on the road.

The current issue of *Locus* magazine supplied a photograph of the Flanagan mansion as well as an indication of its location. Metcalfe knew the city well enough to find the district. Then he cruised the early-morning streets until he came across the house, a colonial front set back behind an iron fence, trees, and a curving gravel road. The sleek grey limousine was parked opposite the entrance.

Driving half a block ahead, Metcalfe parked in a position where he could watch the front of the house. There was no point in going up and ringing the bell. A man in Flanagan's position would have layers of people between himself and the public. The time to make the move would be when he came out to get into the car. But it would have to be done quickly.

At eight o'clock, the chauffeur appeared from the side of the house and opened the limousine door by the driver's seat. He took a chamois and began polishing a fender. This was the warning Metcalfe needed. He left his car quietly and hurried to a position where he was hidden by a clump of shrubbery.

Footsteps on gravel. The chauffeur was approaching. Metcalfe's hand tightened on the gun in his pocket. A squeal of iron hinges as the man swung open the gates. Then retreating footsteps. Metcalfe's luck was holding. The rich man worked to a schedule and he was about to leave for the office.

Metcalfe peered between branches at the door of the house. The chauffeur was yawning, looking at his watch. The chamois was at the ready—like an old soldier, he wanted to be occupied when the colonel appeared.

The door opened, the chauffeur turned to his polishing, and Metcalfe darted from his place through the gateway and over thirty yards of cropped lawn. Horace Flanagan, splendid in a white suit and straw hat, saw the running man and saw the gun but only as Metcalfe raised it and aimed from a range of five yards.

"Just a minute," the millionaire said.

"It's all I can do!" Metcalfe called. The chauffeur was reaching inside his jacket but Metcalfe wasn't worried. He would have time for them both.

Then Tina Flanagan came through the open doorway. She saw Metcalfe and the gun. "What is it?" she said. "What are you doing here?"

Her eyes and Metcalfe's eyes came together. She was smiling, as if at a performance. Then she sensed something and her brow lowered, her mouth formed a silent question. In far less than a second, information flowed between them, not all the questions, not all the answers, but a flood of near-understanding, enough for her to work on for the rest of her life.

Metcalfe's gun wavered as the chauffeur's gun appeared. Flanagan observed the indecision on his assailant's face and called out to his bodyguard, but he was too late. The chauffeur fired twice and Metcalfe fell.

"Daddy, what's going on?" Tina cried, "I know him! He works in Montreal!"

"Don't go there, Tina. Come with me. Come inside."

"Why was he going to shoot you?"

"People do crazy things. Leave it, come inside."

Metcalfe had only seconds left for considering what had happened. He was not in pain. He was slipping into a condition that was not unpleasant. It was a good ending. Laura and Maggie would be well off. Laura's mother would be cared for properly. His own life was finished but it had to be, it was the only way. This was far better than if he had killed Flanagan and been left to cope with the aftermath.

The chauffeur was kneeling over him, observing him with neutral eyes. "The truth doesn't set you free," Metcalfe said, puzzling the man who had shot him. "You have to set yourself free."

MARY HIGGINS CLARK

When I'm asked, I've always maintained that I have no favorites among my novels. It's like asking me to name my favorite child.

The short stories are a bit different. In my own mind a few feel the most satisfying to me. The one I'd call a favorite is "The Man Next Door." I choose it because I think it does follow faithfully a premise I find terribly frightening. In this story, Bree is in her town house with the security on and feels totally safe. The mild-mannered serial killer gains entrance by removing cinderblocks from their common basement wall. I believe that, in our own minds, we feel that our home is our sanctuary. When it is invaded, even after we take all the normal precautions, the situation takes on a special degree of horror.

• • •

In the same vein, a story I read when I was in my early teens jumps out at me as a favorite long remembered. It was "The Tell-Tale Heart," by Edgar Allan Poe.

The elements that I enjoy most in a story are present there: an unbalanced mind, an innocent victim, invasion of the sanctuary.

In that story I can feel with the old man the sheer terror of knowing that someone whom he cannot see is present in the dark with him. I am emotionally satisfied by the irony intrinsic in the fact that while the victim's eye was the cause of his death, his heart was the reason his killer was brought to justice.

The last line, "It is the beating of his hideous heart!" still chills me.

THE MAN NEXT DOOR

Mary Higgins Clark

HE HAD KNOWN for weeks that it was time to invite another guest to the secret place, the space he had fashioned out of the utility room in the basement. It had been six months since Tiffany, the last one. She had lasted twenty days, longer than most of the others.

It didn't make sense to invite Bree Matthews—he knew that. Every day as he followed his routine—washing the windows, vacuuming the carpets, polishing the furniture, sweeping the walk—he reminded himself that it was dangerous to choose a next-door neighbor. Much too dangerous. But ever since the day she had rung his bell and he had invited her in, she had not been out of his mind. She had stood in his foyer, arms folded, and insisted that the leaks in her adjoining town house were originating from *his* roof.

"My contractor could have redone Buckingham Palace for what I paid him to renovate," she said, "but whenever it rains hard, you'd think I lived under Niagara Falls! Anyway, he *insists* that whoever did your work caused the problem."

Her anger thrilled him. She was beautiful in a bold, Celtic way, with midnight-blue eyes, fair skin and blue-black hair. He guessed her to be in her late twenties, older than the women he usually favored, but very appealing. He wanted to reach out and touch her, to push the door closed, to lock her in.

He had blushed and stammered as he explained that there was no possibility that the leaks were coming from his roof, or else he'd have leaks himself. He suggested she call another contractor for an opinion. He had almost explained that he had worked for a builder for fifteen years and knew that the man she'd hired was doing a shoddy job, but he managed to stop himself. He didn't want to admit that he had any interest in her or her home, didn't want her to know that he had even noticed. . . .

A few days later, as he was outside planting impatiens along the driveway, she came over to apologize. She had followed his advice and called in another contractor, who confirmed that the first one had done a sloppy job. "He's going to hear from me in court," she vowed. "I've had a summons issued for him."

Then, emboldened by her friendliness, he did something foolish. As he stood with her, facing their semi-detached town houses, he once again noticed the lopsided blind on her front window. It drove him crazy. The blinds on his front windows and those on hers lined up perfectly, which made the sight of the lopsided one bother him as much as hearing a fingernail screech across a blackboard. So he offered to fix it for her.

She looked at the offending blind as if she had never seen it before. "Thanks, but why bother?" she said. "The decorator has draperies ready to put up as soon as the damage from the leaks is repaired. It'll get fixed then."

"Then," of course, could be months from now, but still he was glad she had said no. When she disappeared, the police would ask questions. "Mr. Mensch, did you see Ms. Matthews leave with anyone?" they would ask. "Did you notice anyone visiting her lately? How friendly were you with her?"

He could answer truthfully: "We spoke casually on the street if we ran into each other. She has a young man she seems to be dating. I've exchanged a few words with him from time to time—tall, brown hair, about thirty or so. Believe he said his name is Carter. Kevin Carter."

The police would probably already know about Carter. When Bree Matthews disappeared they would talk to her close friends first.

He had never even been questioned about Tiffany. There had been no reason for anyone to ask. Occasionally they had run into each other in museums—he had found several of his young women in museums. The third or fourth time they met, he made it a point to ask Tiffany her impression of a painting she was looking at.

He had liked her instantly. Beautiful Tiffany, so appealing, so intelligent. She believed that because he claimed to share her enthusiasm for Gustav Klimt, he was a kindred spirit, a man who could be trusted. She had been grateful for his offer of a ride back to Georgetown. He had picked her up as she was walking to the Metro station.

Tiffany had scarcely felt the prick of the needle that knocked her out. She slumped on the floor of the car. As he pulled into his driveway, Bree Matthews was just leaving her house; he nodded to her as he clicked the garage-door opener. At that time, of course, he had no idea that she would be next.

· · ·

EVERY morning for the next three weeks, he had spent all his free time with Tiffany. He'd loved having her there. The secret place was bright and cheerful. The floor was covered by a thick yellow pad, like a comfortable mattress, and he had filled the room with books and games.

He had even painted the windowless bathroom adjacent to it a cherry red and yellow and installed a portable shower. He would lock her in the bathroom, and while she was showering he would vacuum and scrub the secret place. He kept it immaculate; he couldn't abide untidiness. He washed and ironed the clothes she had arrived in, and laid them out clean for her every day, just as he had with the others. He had even had her jacket cleaned; that spot on the sleeve drove him crazy.

He knew he was fortunate. He was able to spend all his time with the women he chose because he didn't have to work. He didn't need the money. After high school, when he had begun working for the builder, his father demanded he turn his paycheck over to him. "I'm saving for you, August," his father had said. "It's wasteful to spend money on women. They're all like your mother—taking everything you have and leaving you for another man. She said she was too young when we got married, that nineteen was too young to have a baby. Not too young for my mother, I told her."

Ten years ago his father had died, and August had been astonished to find that during all those years of penny-pinching, his father had invested in stocks. At thirty-four, he, August Mensch, was worth over a million dollars. Suddenly he could afford to travel and to live the way he wanted to, the way he had dreamed about during all those years of sitting at home at night, listening to his father tell him how his mother had neglected him when he was a baby. "She left you in the playpen for hours. When you cried, she'd toss a bottle or some crackers to you. You were her prisoner, not her baby. She wouldn't even read to you. I'd come home from work and find you sitting in spilled milk and crumbs, neglected."

August had moved to Washington last year, rented this furnished, run-down town house cheaply and made the necessary repairs himself. He had painted it and scrubbed the kitchen and bathrooms until they shone. But his lease would run out on May 1, only twenty days from now, and he had already told the owner he was planning to leave. By then he would have had Bree Matthews, and it would be time to move on. The only thing he would have to take care of was to paint over all the improvements he had made to the secret place, so no one would ever guess what had happened there.

How many cities had he lived in during the last ten years? He had lost track. Seven? Eight? More? He liked Washington, would stay here longer. But he knew that after Bree it wouldn't be a good idea.

What kind of guest will she be? he wondered. Tiffany had been both frightened and angry. She had ridiculed the books he had bought for her, refusing to read to him. She'd told him her family had no money, as if that was what he wanted. When she'd told him she wanted to paint, he'd even bought an easel and art supplies for her.

She actually started one painting while she was visiting—a copy of Klimt's *The Kiss*. He tore it off the easel and told her to copy one of the nice illustrations in the children's books he had given her. That was when she had picked up an open jar of paint and thrown it at him.

Mensch didn't quite remember the next few minutes—just that when he looked down and saw the sticky mess on his jacket and trousers, he'd lunged at her.

When her body was pulled out of a Washington canal the next day, the police had questioned her ex-boyfriends. The local papers and TV newscasts had been full of the case, full of speculation as to where she had been during the three weeks she was missing.

Mensch sighed. He didn't want to think of Tiffany now. He wanted to clean the room again to make it ready for Bree. Then he had to finish chiseling mortar from the cinder blocks in the wall that separated his basement from hers. He would remove enough blocks to gain entry into her basement, bring her in through the opening, then replace them.

It was Sunday night. He had watched her house all day; she hadn't gone out at all. Lately she had stayed in on Sundays, since Carter had stopped coming around. Mensch had last seen him there a couple of weeks ago.

Tomorrow at this time she would be here with him. He had bought a stack of Dr. Seuss books for her to read to him. He had thrown out all the other books. Some had been splattered with red paint. All of them reminded him of how Tiffany had refused to read to him.

Over the years, he had always tried to make his guests comfortable. It wasn't his fault that they were ungrateful. He remembered how the one in Kansas City told him she wanted a steak. He had bought a thick one, the very best he could find. When he came back, he could see that she had used the time he was out to try to escape, and he'd lost his temper. He couldn't remember exactly what happened after that.

He hoped Bree would be nicer.

• • •

"WHAT is that?" Bree muttered to herself the next morning as she stood at the head of the stairs leading to her basement. She could hear a faint scraping sound coming from the basement of the adjoining town house. She shook her head. *Only six o'clock on a Monday morning, and Mr. Mensch was already on some do-it-yourself project!*

She sighed. There was no point in getting up so early, but she wasn't sleepy. She had a lousy cold and had felt so miserable yesterday that she'd stayed in bed all day, dozing. She hadn't even bothered to answer the phone, just listened to messages. Her folks were away. Gran hadn't called, and a certain Mr. Kevin Carter hadn't either.

Now, cold or no cold, she was due in court at 9 A.M. to try to force that contractor to pay for the repairs she'd had to make to the roof he was supposed to have fixed. To say nothing of getting him to pay for the interior damage caused by the leaks. She closed the door to the basement decisively and went into the kitchen, squeezed some grapefruit juice, made coffee, toasted an English muffin and settled at the breakfast bar. *I've never testified in court,* she thought. *That's the reason I'm so nervous.*

Bree—short for Bridget—Matthews was admittedly jumpy by nature. Buying this town house last year had been an expensive mistake. She had begun to refer to it as the dwelling from hell. Still, once all the damage was repaired, she had to admit it would be lovely.

She reviewed everything she would tell the judge: "The wallpaper's stained and peeling. My grandmother's Persian carpet is rolled and wrapped in plastic to make sure no new leaks damage it further, and the polish on the parquet floors is dull and stained. Now I'm waiting for the painter and the floor guy to come back to charge a fortune to redo what they did perfectly well four months ago.

"I asked the contractor to take care of the leaks. Then, when he told me the water was coming from my neighbor's roof, I believed him and accused poor Mr. Mensch of causing all the problems. You see, Your Honor, we share a common wall. . . ."

Bree thought of her next-door neighbor, the balding guy with the graying ponytail, who looked embarrassed just to say hello if they ran into each other on the street. The day she had gone storming over, he had invited her in. At first he had listened to her rant with calm, unblinking eyes. Then he had blushed and almost whispered that it couldn't be his roof, because surely he would have a leak too. She should call in another contractor, he said.

"I scared the poor guy out of his wits," she'd told Kevin that night. "I should have known the minute I saw the way he keeps his place that he'd never tolerate a leaking roof. I bet when he was a kid he got a medal for being the neatest boy in camp."

Kevin. Try as she might, she couldn't keep him from coming to mind. She would be seeing him this morning, the first time in quite a while. He had insisted on meeting her in court even though they were no longer dating. *Going to court is definitely not my idea of a good time,* she told herself, *and I absolutely do not want to see Kevin!*

Their fight had started out small but soon took on epic proportions. Kevin had said she was foolish not to accept the settlement the contractor offered—that she probably wouldn't get much more by going to court—but that she was stubborn and loved a fight and always shot from the hip. She was becoming irrational about this, he'd said, and she'd had no business going after that shy little guy next door.

Bree reminded him that she'd apologized profusely, and Mr. Mensch was so sweet about it that he'd even offered to fix that broken blind in her living room window. But then, instead of letting it go, she'd told Kevin that *he* seemed to be the one who loved a fight, and why did he have to always take everybody else's side? That was when he said maybe they should step back and examine their relationship. And Bree had said angrily: "If it has to be examined, then it doesn't exist!"

She sighed. It had been a very long two weeks.

Again the scraping sound came from the basement. *Knock it off,* she almost said aloud. Then the noise abruptly stopped, followed by a hollow silence. Was that a footstep on the basement stairs? She whirled around to see her next-door neighbor standing there, a hypodermic needle in hand.

As she dropped her coffee cup, he plunged the needle into her arm.

• • •

KEVIN Carter felt the level of his irritability hit the danger zone. *This is just another example of Bree's total inability to listen to reason,* he thought. *She's downright pigheaded. So where in hell is she?*

The contractor, Richie Ombert, had shown up on time. A surly-looking man, he kept looking at his watch and mumbling about being due on a job. He raised his voice as he reiterated his position to his lawyer: "I offered to fix the leak, but by then she'd had it done—for about six times what I coulda done it for. Anyhow, I offered to pay what it woulda cost me."

Furious that Bree had not shown up, Kevin went to his job at the State Department. He did not call her at the public-relations firm where she worked; nor did he attempt to call her at home. The next call was going to come from her. He tried to forget that he'd planned to tell her, after she'd had her day in court, that he'd missed her like hell.

• • •

MENSCH slid Bree's limp body down the basement stairs, step by step, until he reached the bottom; then he bent down and picked her up. He had made the opening in the wall in the boiler room, where it would be least noticed. He had pulled the cinder blocks into his basement, so now all he had to do was to secure her in the secret place, go back to get her some extra clothing, then replace and remortar the blocks.

She was still knocked out, so there was no resistance as he carried her to the secret place. He attached restraints to her wrists and ankles and, as a precaution, tied a scarf loosely around her mouth. He could tell from her breathing that she had a cold. He certainly did not want her to suffocate. He straightened her robe and tucked it around her.

Now that she was here, he felt strong, calm. But he had to move quickly: to get her clothes and her purse, to wipe up that spilled coffee. It had to look as if she had disappeared *after* she left her house.

He looked at the answering machine in her kitchen, the blinking light indicating that there had been calls. That was odd, he thought. He knew she hadn't gone out all day yesterday. Was it possible she hadn't bothered to answer the phone?

He played the messages back. All calls from friends. "How are you?" . . . "Let's get together soon." . . . "Good luck in court." . . . "Hope you make that contractor pay."

Mensch erased the messages and took a moment to sit down at the breakfast bar. It was very important that he think all this through. She had not gone out at all yesterday and apparently hadn't answered her phone. Suppose instead of just taking her clothes to make it look as if she'd left for work this morning, he tidied up the house so people would think she hadn't reached home at all on Saturday night? After all, he had seen her go out, and then come in alone at around eleven, a newspaper under her arm. Who was there to say she had arrived safely?

He got up, put on his latex gloves and started looking about. The garbage bin under the kitchen sink was empty. He took a fresh disposable bag from the drawer and put in the grapefruit rind, the coffee grounds and the pieces of the cup Bree had dropped. Working methodically, he cleaned the kitchen, even taking time to scour the pot she had left on the stove.

Upstairs in her bedroom, he made the bed and picked up the Sunday edition of the *Washington Post* that was on the floor next to it. He put the paper in the garbage bag. She had left a suit lying on the bed. He hung it in the closet.

Next he cleaned the bathroom. Her clothes washer and dryer were in the bathroom, concealed by louvered doors. On top of the washer he found the jeans and sweater he had seen her wearing on Saturday. It hadn't been raining at the time, but she had also had on a yellow raincoat. He collected the clothes. Then from her dresser he selected undergarments. From her closets he took a few more sweaters and pairs of slacks.

He found her raincoat and shoulder bag in the foyer by the front door. He looked at his watch. It was seven-thirty—time to go. He had to take care of those cinder blocks.

He looked around to be sure he had missed nothing. His eye fell on the lopsided blind in the front window. It made him almost physically ill. He put the clothing, purse and garbage bag on the floor, and in quick, determined steps went to the window. The cord on the blind was broken, but there was enough slack to tie it and still level it.

He sighed in relief when he finished the task. The blind now stopped at exactly the same level as the other two and, like his, just grazed the sill. He quickly gathered up Bree's coat, shoulder bag, clothing and the garbage bag. Two minutes later he was back in his own basement, replacing the cinder blocks.

• • •

AT first Bree thought she was having a nightmare—a Disney World nightmare. She opened her eyes to see cinder-block walls painted with evenly shaped brown slats to resemble a railing. The space was small, not much more than six by nine feet, and she was lying on a bright yellow plastic mattress. Above the "railing," decals lined the walls: Mickey Mouse, Cinderella, Kermit, Miss Piggy, Sleeping Beauty, Pocahontas.

She realized there was a gag over her mouth. She tried to push it away but could move her arm only a few inches. Her arms and legs were held in some kind of restraints.

The grogginess was lifting now. Where was she? What had happened? Panic overwhelmed her as she remembered turning around to see Mensch, her neighbor, standing in her kitchen. She looked around slowly, her eyes widening. This room, wherever it was, resembled an oversize playpen. In one corner was a stack of children's books. She could read the lettering on one of them: *Grimm's Fairy Tales.*

How had she gotten here? She remembered she had been about to get dressed to go to court. She had tossed the suit she'd planned to wear across the bed. It was new. She wanted to look good—in truth, more for Kevin than for the judge. Now she admitted that much to herself.

Kevin. Of course he would come looking for her when she didn't show up in court. He'd know something had happened to her.

Ica, her cleaning woman, would look for her too. She came in on Mondays. Ica would know something was wrong. Bree remembered dropping the coffee cup. It had shattered on the kitchen floor when Mensch grabbed her. Ica would know she wouldn't leave a broken cup for her to clean up.

As her head cleared, she remembered that just before she had turned and seen Mensch, she had heard a footstep on the basement stairs. Her mouth went dry at the thought that somehow he had come in through the basement. But how? Her basement door was double bolted, the window barred.

Then panic swept through her. Clearly this hadn't just happened; it had been carefully planned. She tried to scream but could make only a muffled gasping cry. She tried to pray, a single sentence that she repeated over and over: *Please, God, let Kevin find me.*

• • •

LATE Tuesday afternoon Kevin received a worried phone call from Bree's office. Had he heard from her? She had not shown up for work today or Monday, and she hadn't phoned. They thought she might have been stuck in court all day Monday, but now they were concerned.

Fifteen minutes later, Mensch surreptitiously watched as Kevin Carter held his finger on the doorbell of Bree's town house. Then he watched as Carter crossed the front lawn and looked in her living room window. He half expected Carter to ring his doorbell, but that didn't happen. Instead, Carter stood for a few minutes looking irresolute, then peered in the window of Bree's garage. Mensch knew her car was there. He wished he could have gotten rid of it, but that had been impossible.

He watched until Carter walked slowly back to his car and drove away. With a satisfied smile, he went down to his basement and, as always, admired his tools and paints and polishes, all in perfect order on shelves or hanging in precise rows from pegboard. Snow shovels hung over the cinder blocks he'd removed to gain entry into Bree's basement. Beneath them the mortar had dried; now nothing showed. He went through the boiler room and beyond it, to the secret place.

Bree was lying on the yellow mat, the restraints still on her arms and legs. She looked up at him, and he could see that underneath the anger, fear was beginning to take hold. He knelt and removed the gag from her mouth. "Your boyfriend was looking for you," he told her. "He's gone now."

He loosened the restraints on her left arm and leg. "What book will you read to me, Mommy?" he asked, his voice suddenly childlike, begging.

• • •

ON Thursday morning Kevin sat in the office of FBI agent Lou Ferroni. Washington was awash with cherry blossoms, but as he stared out the window he was unaware of them. Everything was a blur, especially the last two days: his frantic call to the police, the questions, the calls to Bree's family, the involvement of the FBI.

"She's been gone long enough for us to consider her a missing person," Ferroni was saying. The agent knew Carter was the boyfriend, or ex-boyfriend; he'd freely admitted that he and Bridget Matthews had quarreled. But he seemed an unlikely suspect, and his alibi checked out.

Bridget—or Bree, as she was called—had been in her house on Saturday; that much they knew. They had not been able to locate anyone who had seen or spoken to her on Sunday, however, and she had failed to show up for her court appointment on Monday.

"Let's go over it again," Ferroni suggested. "You say that Ms. Matthews's cleaning woman was surprised to find the bed made and dishes done when she came in Monday morning?" He had already spoken with the woman but wanted to see if there were any discrepancies in Carter's story.

Kevin nodded. "I called Ica as soon as I realized Bree was missing. She has a key to Bree's place, and she let me in. Ica told me that when she went in on Monday morning she couldn't understand why the bed was made and the dishes run through the dishwasher. It just wasn't normal. Bree never made her bed on Monday because that was always the day Ica changed it. So that meant the bed hadn't been slept in Sunday night, and that Bree could have disappeared any time between Saturday and Sunday night."

Ferroni's gut instinct told him that the misery he was seeing in Kevin Carter's face was genuine. So who did that leave? Richie Ombert, the contractor Matthews was suing, had had several complaints filed against him for using abusive language and threatening gestures toward disgruntled customers. He had a nasty edge, and for the moment he was a prime suspect.

There was one aspect of this case Ferroni was not prepared to reveal to Carter. The computer of VICAP, the FBI's Violent Criminal Apprehension Program, had been tracking a particular pattern of disappearing young women. The trail had begun nearly ten years ago in California, when a young acting student disappeared. Her body had shown up three weeks later; she had been strangled. The weird part was that when she was found, she was dressed in the same clothes as when she had disappeared, but they were freshly washed and pressed. There was no sign of molestation, no hint of violence beyond the obvious cause of death. But where had she been those three weeks?

Shortly afterward the VICAP computer spat out a case in Arizona with striking similarities. One followed in New Mexico, then Colorado . . . Wisconsin . . . Kansas . . . Missouri . . . Indiana . . . Ohio . . . Pennsylvania. . . . Finally, six months ago, here in DC, an art student, Tiffany Wright, had disappeared. Her body was fished out of a Washington canal three weeks later, but it had been there only a short time. Except for the effect the water had had on her clothes, they were neat. The only odd note was a faint spot of red oil paint, the kind artists use, on her blouse.

That little clue had started them working on the art-student angle, looking among her classmates. So far, however, it had led nowhere. Odds were that the disappearance of Bridget Matthews was not tied to the death of Tiffany Wright. It would be a marked departure in the serial killer's method of operation for him to strike twice in the same city. . . .

"By any chance is Ms. Matthews interested in art?" Ferroni asked. "Does she paint as a hobby, for example?"

Kevin shook his head. "She was really more into music and the theater," he said. "We went to the Kennedy Center pretty frequently."

Went? he thought. *Why am I using the past tense? God, no!*

Ferroni consulted the notes in his hand. "Mr. Carter, I want to go over this again. You were familiar with the house. There may be something you noticed when you went in with the housekeeper."

Kevin stared at him, frowning.

"What is it?" Ferroni asked quickly.

Kevin's face was haggard. "There *was* something different," he said. "I sensed it at the time. But I don't know what it was."

• • •

How long have I been here? Bree asked herself. She had lost count of the days. Three? Four? They were all blending together. Mensch had just gone upstairs with her breakfast tray. She knew he'd be back within the hour for her to begin reading to him again.

He had a strict routine. In the morning he came down carrying fresh clothing for her, a blouse or sweater and jeans or slacks. Obviously he had taken the time to go through her closet after he had knocked her out. He had been careful to bring only clothes that were washable.

Next he would unshackle her hands, connect the leg restraints to each other at the ankles, then lead her to the bathroom, drop the clean clothes on a chair and lock her in. Even before she turned on the shower, she'd hear the whir of the vacuum.

No matter how she tried to think of a way to escape, she knew she couldn't manage it. The ankle restraints forced her to shuffle, so she clearly couldn't outrun him. And there was nothing she could use to stun him long enough to get up the stairs and out the door.

She knew where she was now—the basement of his town house. The wall on the right was the one they shared. Surely by now the police were looking for her. Kevin would tell them how she'd accused Mensch of causing the leaks in her roof. They'd investigate him and realize there was something weird about him. But unless Mensch radically altered his routine, she'd have no opportunity to let anyone know she was here. She would just have to wait and hope, keep him appeased until help came. As long as she read to him, he seemed to be satisfied.

Last night she had given him a list of books by Roald Dahl that he should get. He had been pleased. "None of my guests have been as nice as you," he told her.

What had he done to those women? *Don't think about that,* Bree warned herself fiercely—*it worries him when you show you're afraid.* She realized that early on, when she had broken down, sobbing, begging him to release her.

"You're making too much noise," he'd told her and put one hand over her mouth while the other encircled her throat. For a moment she thought he was going to strangle her. But then he hesitated and said, "Promise to be quiet, and I'll let you read to me. Please, Mommy, don't cry."

Since then she had managed to hold her emotions in check.

Suddenly she heard the doorknob turning, and Mensch came in, looking troubled. "My landlord phoned," he told her. "According to the contract, he has the right to show this place two weeks before the lease is up. That's Monday, and it's Friday already. So I have to take all the decorations down from here and paint the walls and also the walls of the bathroom and give them time to dry. That will take the whole weekend. So this has to be our last day together, Bridget. I'm sorry. I guess you should try to read to me a little faster. . . ."

• • •

AT ten o'clock that morning—Friday—Kevin was once again in Lou Ferroni's office in the FBI Building. "Thanks to the publicity, we've been able to pretty much cover Ms. Matthews's activities on Saturday," Ferroni told him. "Several neighbors reported seeing her walking down the street at about two o'clock Saturday afternoon. They agree that she was wearing a yellow raincoat and jeans and carrying a shoulder bag. The raincoat and bag are missing from her home. We don't know what she did later Saturday afternoon, but we do know she had dinner alone at Antonio's in Georgetown that night and went to the nine o'clock showing of the new *Lethal Weapon* film at the Beacon."

Bree had dinner alone on Saturday night, Kevin thought. *So did I. And she genuinely likes those wild Mel Gibson films. We've laughed about that. . . .*

"No one seems to have seen her after that," Ferroni continued. "But we do have one significant piece of information. We've learned that the contractor she was suing was at the same movie that night, the same showing. He claims he drove directly home afterward, but there's no one to back up his story. He apparently separated from his wife recently." Ferroni did not add that the contractor had mouthed off to a number of people about what he'd like to do to the dame who was hauling him into court. "We're working on the theory that Ms. Matthews did not get home that night," he continued. "Did she often use the Metro instead of her car?"

"The Metro, or a cab if she was going directly from one place to another," Kevin said. "She said trying to park was too much of a nuisance." He could see that Ferroni was starting to believe the contractor was responsible for Bree's disappearance. He thought of Richie Ombert in court this past Monday—angry, then noisily elated when the judge had dismissed the complaint. *But the guy hadn't been acting,* Kevin thought. He had seemed genuinely surprised and relieved when Bree failed to show up. No, Ombert was not the answer. "There are no other leads?" he asked Ferroni.

The FBI agent thought of the briefly considered theory that Bree Matthews had been abducted by a serial killer. "No," he said firmly. Then: "How is her family? Has her father gone back to Connecticut?"

"He had to. Bree's grandmother had a mild heart attack Tuesday evening—one of those horrible coincidences. Bree's mother is with her. That's why Mr. Matthews went back. We're in touch every day, though."

Ferroni sighed. "I wish we had some good news for them." He realized that in a way it would have been better if he thought the serial killer *did* have Bree. All the women the man had abducted had lived for several weeks after disappearing. That would at least give the FBI some time.

"What about her answering machine?" Kevin asked. "Were there any messages on it?"

"Not from Sunday, or if there were, they were erased," Ferroni replied. "Of course, she could have called in and gotten them just by using the machine's code."

Kevin shook his head. He had to get out of there. He'd promised to phone Ica right after his meeting with Ferroni, but now he decided to wait and call her from Bree's house. Somehow, just being at Bree's made him feel closer to her. . . .

• • •

HER neighbor, the guy with the ponytail, was coming down the block as Kevin parked in front of the house. He was carrying a shopping bag from the bookstore. Their eyes met, but neither man spoke. Instead, the neighbor nodded, then turned to go up his walk. *Wouldn't you think he'd have the decency to at least ask about Bree?* Kevin thought. *Or maybe he's embarrassed—afraid of what he'll hear.*

Kevin took out the key Ica had given him, let himself into the house and phoned her. "Can you come over and help me?" he asked. "There's something about this place that's bugging me, and I can't figure out what it is. Maybe you can help."

While he waited for Ica to arrive, he paced restlessly around the downstairs. He stopped at the door of the living room. The contrast to the cheerful kitchen and den was striking. Here, as in the dining room, the furniture and carpet were covered with plastic and pushed to the center of the floor because of the water damage. The wallpaper, a soft ivory with a faint stripe, was stained and bubbled.

Kevin remembered how happy Bree had been three months ago when all the decorating was supposedly finished. They'd even talked around the subject of marriage, mentioning her town house and the marvelous old farmhouse in Virginia he had bought for weekends. *Too damn cautious to commit ourselves,* Kevin thought bitterly. *But not too cautious to have a fight over nothing.* It had all been so stupid!

Ica rang the doorbell then, interrupting his train of thought. The Jamaican woman's handsome face mirrored the misery he felt. "I haven't slept two hours straight this week," she said. "Looks to me like you haven't been sleeping either."

Kevin nodded. "Ica, there's something about this house that's bothering me, something I ought to be noticing."

She nodded. "It's funny you say that, 'cause I felt that way too, but blamed it on finding the bed made and the dishes done. But if Bree didn't get home Saturday night, then that would explain those things. She never left the place untidy."

Together they walked up the stairs to the bedroom. Ica looked around uncertainly. "This room felt different when I got here Monday," she said hesitantly.

"In what way?"

"It was . . . well, it was way too neat." Ica walked over to the bed. "Those throw pillows—Bree just tossed them around, like the way they are now."

"What are you telling me?" Kevin asked, grabbing her arm.

"The whole place felt just . . . too neat. I stripped the bed even though it was made because I wanted to change the sheets. I had to dig and pull the sheets and blanket loose, they were tucked in so tight. And the throw pillows on top of the quilt were all lined up against the headboard like little soldiers."

"Anything else?"

"Yes," Ica said excitedly. "Last week Bree let a pot boil over. I scoured it as best I could and left a note for her to pick up some steel wool and scouring powder; I said I'd finish it when I came back. Monday morning that pot was sitting out on the stove, scrubbed clean as could be. I know my Bree—she never would have done that."

They went downstairs and into the kitchen. From the cupboard Ica pulled out a gleaming pot and looked at Kevin. "Things just weren't right," she said. "The bed was too neat. This pot is too clean."

"And . . . and that blind in the front window has been fixed!" Kevin shouted. "It's lined up like the ones next door." He didn't know he had been about to say that, but suddenly he realized what had been bothering him about Bree's house all along.

Now that he had brought it into focus, he thought of the man next door, who was always washing his windows or trimming his lawn or sweeping his walk. What did anyone know about him? If he had rung her bell, Bree might have let him in. And he had offered to fix the blind—Bree had mentioned that. Kevin pulled Ferroni's card from his pocket and handed it to Ica. "I'm going next door. Call Ferroni and tell him to get over there fast."

• • •

"JUST one more book. That's all we'll have time for. Then you'll leave me again, Mommy, just like she did—just like all of them did."

In the two hours she had been reading to him, Bree had watched Mensch regress from adoring to angry child. *He's working up the courage to kill me,* she thought.

He was sitting cross-legged beside her on the mat. "But I want to read all of them to you," she said, her voice soothing. "I know you'll love them. Then tomorrow I could help you paint the walls. We could get it done so much faster if we worked together. Then we could go away somewhere, so I can keep reading to you."

Mensch stood up abruptly. "You're trying to trick me. You don't want to go with me. You're just like all the others." He stared at her, his eyes squinting with anger. "I saw your boyfriend go into your house a little while ago. He's too nosy. It's good that you're wearing the jeans. I have to get your raincoat and shoulder bag." He looked as if he were about to cry. "There's no time for any more books," he said and rushed out of the room.

I'm going to die, Bree thought. Frantically she tried to pull her arms and legs free of the restraints. Her right arm swung up and she realized he'd forgotten to refasten the shackle to the wall. He had said Kevin was next door. She closed her eyes and concentrated: *Kevin, help me. Kevin, I need you.*

She had to play for time. She would have only one chance at him, one moment of surprise. She would swing at his head with the dangling shackle, try to stun him. But then what? Her eyes lighted on the stack of children's books. Maybe there was a way. She grabbed the first book and began tearing out the pages, scattering the pieces, flinging them hither and yon across the bright yellow mattress. . . .

I must have known today was the day, Mensch thought as he retrieved Bree's raincoat and shoulder bag from his bedroom closet. *I laid out jeans and the red sweater she was wearing that Saturday. When they find her, it will be the same as with the others. And they'll ask that same question: Where was she for the days she was missing?*

He started down the stairs but stopped suddenly. The doorbell was ringing. He put down the bag and the coat. Should he answer? Would it seem suspicious if he didn't? No. Better to get rid of her, get her out of here. He picked up the raincoat and rushed down the basement stairs.

• • •

I know he's in there, Kevin thought, *but he's not answering. I've got to get inside.*

Ica was running across the lawn toward him. "Mr. Ferroni is on his way," she said breathlessly. "He said to absolutely wait for him. Not to ring the bell any more. He got all excited when I talked about everything being so neat. He said if it's what he thinks it is, Bree will still be alive."

Kevin ran to Mensch's front window and strained to see in. Through the slats he could see the rigidly neat living room. Craning his neck, he could see the stairway in the foyer. Then his blood froze. A woman's leather shoulder bag was on the bottom step. He recognized it—he had given it to Bree for her birthday.

Kevin ran to the front sidewalk, where a refuse can stood waiting to be emptied. He dumped the contents into the street, ran back with the can and overturned it under the window. As Ica steadied it for him, he climbed up and kicked in the window. Then he kicked away the sharp edges of shattered glass and jumped into Mensch's house. He raced up the stairs, shouting Bree's name.

Finding no one there, he clattered downstairs again, pausing only long enough to open the front door. "Tell the FBI I'm inside, Ica." He raced through the rooms on the ground floor, then headed for the basement.

• • •

FINALLY the ringing had stopped. Whoever had been at the door had gone away. Mensch knew he had to hurry. With Bree's raincoat and a plastic bag over his arm, he opened the door to the secret place. Then he froze. Bits of paper littered the yellow plastic. The woman was tearing up his books, his baby books. "Stop it!" he shrieked.

His head hurt, his throat was closing. He had a pain in his chest. The room was a shambles—he had to clean it up so he could breathe! Then he would kill her.

He ran into the bathroom, grabbed the wastebasket, ran back and began scooping up the torn paper and mangled books. He worked quickly, efficiently, until there were no scraps left. Bree was cowering against the mattress. He knelt beside her, the plastic bag clutched in his hands. Then her arm swung up, and the shackle on her wrist slammed into his face.

He cried out, and for an instant he was stunned. Then, with a snarl, he snapped his fingers around her throat.

• • •

THE basement was empty too. Where *was* she? Kevin was about to run into the garage when from somewhere behind the boiler room he heard Mensch howl in pain. And then came a scream. Bree was screaming!

As Mensch tightened his hands on Bree's neck, he suddenly felt his head yanked back, and a violent punch to the jaw caused his knees to buckle. Dazed, he shook his head and then, with a guttural cry, he sprang to his feet.

Bree reached out and grabbed his ankle, pulling him off balance as Kevin caught him in a hammerlock around the throat.

Feet pounded heavily on the basement stairs, and Ferroni and two other agents crowded into the room, their guns drawn. Moments later Bree, from the shelter of Kevin's arms, watched as Mensch was manacled at his wrists and ankles and led up the stairs.

Two days later, Bree and Kevin stood at her grandmother's bedside in Connecticut. "The doctor says you'll be fine, Gran," Bree told her.

"Of course I'm fine! But let's hear about your house. I bet you made that contractor squirm in court, didn't you?"

Bree grinned at Kevin's raised eyebrows. "Oh, Gran, I decided to accept his settlement offer after all," she said. "I've finally realized that I really hate getting into fights."

THE TELL-TALE HEART

Edgar Allan Poe

TRUE!—NERVOUS—VERY, very dreadfully nervous I had been and am; but why *will* you say that I am mad? The disease had sharpened my senses—not destroyed—not dulled them. Above all was the sense of hearing acute. I heard all things in the heaven and in the earth. I heard many things in hell. How, then, am I mad? Hearken! and observe how healthily—how calmly I can tell you the whole story.

It is impossible to say how first the idea entered my brain; but once conceived, it haunted me day and night. Object there was none. Passion there was none. I loved the old man. He had never wronged me. He had never given me insult. For his gold I had no desire. I think it was his eye! Yes, it was this! One of his eyes resembled that of a vulture—a pale blue eye, with a film over it. Whenever it fell upon me, my blood ran cold; and so by degrees—very gradually—I made up my mind to take the life of the old man, and thus rid myself of the eye for ever.

Now this is the point. You fancy me mad. Madmen know nothing. But you should have seen *me.* You should have seen how wisely I proceeded—with what caution—with what foresight— with what dissimulation I went to work! I was never kinder to the old man than during the whole week before I killed him. And every night, about midnight, I turned the latch of his door and opened it—oh, so gently! And then, when I had made an opening sufficient for my head, I put in a dark lantern, all closed, closed, so that no light shone out, and then I thrust in my head. Oh, you would have laughed to see how cunningly I thrust it in! I moved it slowly—very, very, slowly, so that I might not disturb the old man's sleep. It took me an hour to place my whole head within the opening so far that I could see him as he lay upon his bed. Ha!—would a madman have been so wise as this? And then, when my head was well in the room, I undid the lantern cautiously—oh, so cautiously—cautiously (for the hinges creaked)—I undid it just so much that a single thin ray fell upon the vulture eye. And this I did for seven long nights—every night just at midnight—but I found the eye always closed; and so it was impossible to do the work; for it was not the old man who vexed me, but his Evil Eye. And every morning, when the day broke, I went boldly into the chamber, and spoke courageously to him, calling him by name in a hearty tone, and inquiring how he had passed the night. So you see he would have been a very profound old man, indeed, to suspect that every night, just at twelve, I looked in upon him while he slept.

Upon the eighth night I was more than usually cautious in opening the door. A watch's minute hand moves more quickly than did mine. Never before that night had I *felt* the extent of my own powers—of my sagacity. I could scarcely contain my feelings of triumph. To think that there I was, opening the door, little by little, and he not even to dream of my secret deeds or thoughts. I fairly chuckled at the idea; and perhaps he heard me; for he moved on the bed suddenly, as if startled. Now you may think that I drew back—but no. His room was as black as pitch with the thick darkness (for the shutters were close fastened, through fear of robbers), and so I knew that he could not see the opening of the door, and I kept pushing it on steadily, steadily.

I had my head in, and was about to open the lantern, when my thumb slipped upon the tin fastening, and the old man sprang up in the bed, crying out—"Who's there?"

I kept quite still and said nothing. For a whole hour I did not move a muscle, and in the meantime I did not hear him lie down. He was still sitting up in the bed listening;—just as I have done, night after night, hearkening to the death watches in the wall.

Presently I heard a slight groan, and I knew it was the groan of mortal terror. It was not a groan of pain or of grief—oh, no!—it was the low stifled sound that arises from the bottom of the soul when overcharged with awe. I knew the sound well. Many a night, just at midnight, when all the world slept, it has welled up from my own bosom, deepening, with its dreadful echo, the terrors that distracted me. I say I knew it well. I knew what the old man felt, and pitied him, although I chuckled at heart. I knew that he had been lying awake ever since the first slight noise, when he had turned in the bed. His fears had been ever since growing upon him. He had been trying to fancy them causeless, but could not. He had been saying to himself—"It is nothing but the wind in the chimney—it is only a mouse crossing the floor," or "it is merely a cricket which has made a single chirp." Yes, he has been trying to comfort himself with these suppositions; but he had found all in vain. *All in vain;* because Death, in approaching him, had stalked with his black shadow before him, and enveloped the victim. And it was the mournful influence of the unperceived shadow that caused him to feel—although he neither saw nor heard—to *feel* the presence of my head within the room.

When I had waited a long time, very patiently, without hearing him lie down, I resolved to open a little—a very, very little crevice in the lantern. So I opened it—you cannot imagine how stealthily, stealthily—until, at length, a single dim ray, like the thread of the spider, shot from out the crevice and full upon the vulture eye.

It was open—wide, wide open—and I grew furious as I gazed upon it. I saw it with perfect distinctness—all a dull blue, with a hideous veil over it that chilled the very marrow in my bones; but I could see nothing else of the old man's face or person: for I had directed the ray as if by instinct, precisely upon the damned spot.

And now have I not told you that what you mistake for madness is but over-acuteness of the senses?—now, I say, there came to my ears a low, dull, quick sound, such as a watch makes when enveloped in cotton. I knew *that* sound well too. It was the beating of the old man's heart. It increased my fury, as the beating of a drum stimulates the soldier into courage.

But even yet I refrained and kept still. I scarcely breathed. I held the lantern motionless. I tried how steadily I could maintain the ray upon the eye. Meantime the hellish tattoo of the heart increased. It grew quicker and quicker, and louder and louder every instant. The old man's terror *must* have been extreme! It grew louder, I say, louder every moment!—do you mark me well? I have told you that I am nervous: so I am. And now at the dead hour of the night, amid the dreadful silence of that old house, so strange a noise as this excited me to uncontrollable terror. Yet, for some minutes longer I refrained and stood still. But the beating grew louder, louder! I thought the heart must burst. And now a new anxiety seized me— the sound would be heard by a neighbor! The old man's hour had come! With a loud yell, I threw open the lantern and leaped into the room. He shrieked once—once only. In an instant I dragged him to the floor and pulled the heavy bed over him. I then smiled gaily, to find the deed so far done. But, for many minutes, the heart beat on with a muffled sound. This, however, did not vex me; it would not be heard through the wall. At length it ceased. The old man was dead. I removed the bed and examined the corpse. Yes, he was stone, stone dead. I placed my hand upon the heart and held it there many minutes. There was no pulsation. He was stone dead. His eye would trouble me no more.

If still you think me mad, you will think so no longer when I describe the wise precautions I took for the concealment of the body. The night waned, and I worked hastily, but in silence. First of all I dismembered the corpse. I cut off the head and the arms and the legs.

I then took up three planks from the flooring of the chamber, and deposited all between the scantlings. I then replaced the boards so cleverly, so cunningly, that no human eye—not even *his*—could have detected any thing wrong. There was nothing to wash out—no stain of any kind—no blood-spot whatever. I had been too wary for that. A tub had caught all— ha! ha!

When I had made an end of these labors, it was four o'clock—still dark as midnight. As the bell sounded the hour, there came a knocking at the street door. I went down to open it with a light heart,—for what had I *now* to fear? There entered three men, who introduced themselves, with perfect suavity, as officers of the police. A shriek had been heard by a neighbor during the night; suspicion of foul play had been aroused; information had been lodged at the police office, and they (the officers) had been deputed to search the premises.

I smiled,—for *what* had I to fear? I bade the gentlemen welcome. The shriek, I said, was my own in a dream. The old man, I mentioned, was absent in the country. I took my visitors all over the house. I bade them search— search *well.* I led them, at length, to *his* chamber. I showed them his treasures, secure, undisturbed. In the enthusiasm of my confidence, I brought chairs into the room, and desired them *here* to rest from their fatigues, while I myself, in the wild audacity of my perfect triumph, placed my own seat upon the very spot beneath which reposed the corpse of the victim.

The officers were satisfied. My *manner* had convinced them. I was singularly at ease. They sat, and while I answered cheerily, they chatted familiar things. But, ere long, I felt myself getting pale and wished them gone. My head ached, and I fancied a ringing in my ears: but still they sat and still chatted. The ringing became more distinct:—it continued and became more distinct: I talked more freely to get rid of the feeling: but it continued and gained definitiveness—until, at length, I found that the noise was *not* within my ears.

No doubt I now grew *very* pale;—but I talked more fluently, and with a heightened voice. Yet the sound increased—and what could I do? It was *a low, dull, quick sound—much such a sound as a watch makes when enveloped in cotton.* I gasped for breath—and yet the officers heard it not. I talked more quickly—more vehemently; but the noise steadily increased. I arose and argued about trifles, in a high key and with violent gesticulations, but the noise steadily increased. Why *would* they not be gone? I paced the floor to and fro with heavy strides, as if excited to fury by the observation of the men—But the noise steadily increased. Oh God! what *could* I do? I foamed— I raved—I swore! I swung the chair upon which I had been sitting, and grated it upon the boards, but the noise arose over all and continually increased. It grew louder—louder—*louder!* And still the men chatted pleasantly, and smiled. Was it possible they heard not? Almighty God!—no, no! They heard!—they suspected!—they *knew!*—they were making a mockery of my horror!—this I thought, and this I think. But any thing was better than this agony! Any thing was more tolerable than this derision! I could bear those hypocritical smiles no longer! I felt that I must scream or die!—and now—again!—hark! louder! louder! louder! *louder!*—

"Villains!" I shrieked, "dissemble no more! I admit the deed!—tear up the planks!—here, here!—it is the beating of his hideous heart!"

JOE GORES

In 1957 I was living in a thatch-roof house on Tahiti. You got to Tahiti, then, by freighter, yacht, or an old PBY flying boat that landed in the lagoon twice a month from the Fijis. There was no airport. You got around the islands by copra schooner. Tahiti hosted seven hundred tourists during my year there.

During that year I was able to see the last shadowy remnants—just before they were gutted by progress—of the mystical South Seas that had captivated Paul Gauguin. I also started reading such real South Seas tale-spinners as John Russell, Louis Beck, Robert Dean Frisbie, and Eugene Burdick. Later, I wrote my master's thesis for Stanford on these writers, throwing in Conrad, London, Michener and Maugham as a sop for my bewildered thesis advisor.

After that I lived for three years in East Africa, where my life was changed by Robert Ardrey's study of the origins of man, African Genesis. Ardrey made me understand that my favorite Gauguin mural—"Where Do We Come From, What Are We, Where Are We Going?"—actually was posing the key questions of human survival.

I came to realize that Russell and Beck and the rest had been illuminating man's most basic nature by setting their stories in the South Seas, the pre–World War Two equivalent of outer space. In this world their characters could be stripped of all support: they had to succeed on their own, or die.

By 1970, when I wrote this futuristic tale, "The Criminal," the South Seas had become a mere tourist vacation stop. But meanwhile, Ardrey had suggested the horrors of a new solitude: a soulless, mechanistic future society whose only goal was control of mankind. In such a society, the individual was the enemy.

Thus the narrator of "The Criminal," who fits into his society, is not the hero. The hero is the criminal, because he is, like Russell's Jimmy

Lee in "The Knife," a man who has been thrust outside the pale, and must succeed on his own—or die.

He and Jimmy Lee would recognize each other instantly.

• • •

Until the Second World War, the vast South Seas occupied the same place in our psyche that outer space occupies today. The limitless stretches of the Pacific, with its monster-infested abyssal depths, stirred our prewar imaginations in ways that a space walk, Star Wars, or Star Trek do today. Anything could happen "out there." Anything could be out there.

A fortune in pearls might lie below the keel of your schooner in some crystal lagoon—but "black fellas" might also crouch in the bushes, ready to take your head should you venture ashore. A Polynesian girl might love you on a black coral beach one night, then murder you the next. Love, cruelty, weakness, chicanery, nobility—all of the seven virtues and the seven deadly vices were played out against a backdrop of azure seas, hurricanes, coral atolls, and lush volcanic islands.

John Russell knew the South Seas well and was a relentless storyteller besides—he once wrote all seven stories in a pulp magazine under seven different names. He lived the adventures that he wrote about, wandering the vast Pacific world when it was still the Heart of Darkness to most Americans. Indeed, the Russell Islands near Guadalcanal are named after him.

Russell's tales, despite their sudden, gripping violence in exotic sun-drenched locales, always have mystery, sometimes almost magic, at their core. And they always turn on a point of character: black against white, strong against weak, unscrupulous trader against lazy beachcomber, man against indifferent and suddenly deadly nature.

"The Knife," published in 1925, is quintessential Russell, a deceptively simple tale that has it all—shipwreck, despair, terror, hope, finally self-reliance, then ultimate vindication—against all odds. In an odd way, it inspired my own story that precedes this one.

THE CRIMINAL

Joe Gores

It BEGAN WITH the routine reporting of an individual transmitter failure. These are not common, but component fatigue does sometimes develop. When there is such a failure in the miniaturized circuitry of some citizen's subcutaneous transmitter, the monitor computer reports loss of contact and a minimal security drill is gone through. I tele'd Sergeant 1418; in a moment his image flashed on my screen.

"Contacting on transmitter failure report number 31. Do you have the suspect's personnel tape up yet?"

"I just was about to tele it to you, Controller, sir."

The statistical segment of a personnel tape flashed on the screen. The suspect was repulsively muscular, dark-haired and dark-eyed, with a square face and ugly thick neck. Weight, 85 kilos; height, 1.87 meters: name 36/204/GS/8219. A citizen of State 36, City 204, employed by Communications Center.

"What is his ComCen Station, Sergeant?"

The sergeant's face was worried. "Ah . . . Controller, sir, he . . . ah . . . Artifacts, sir."

"*Artifacts?* Did he work in Audio-Visual, 1418, or was—"

"Negative, Controller, sir. He was a . . . a Reading Material Indexer, sir."

"He had access to the book storage tapes?"

"Affirmative, Controller, sir."

"Has 8219 been warned that he has one hour to report to a medical center for replacement of his transmitter?"

"We . . . Negative, sir. 8219 did not report to his work station today, Controller, sir."

This was rapidly becoming very serious. "Has he reported ill, 1418?"

"Negative, Controller, sir. We sent a Helitrans to his dwelling unit, but their report also was negative."

My palms suddenly were wet. We *were out of contact with Citizen 8219!* A faulty individual transmitter was one thing, a misdemeanor only; but a *deliberate* break in contact was a felony because it might possibly involve Norm Deviation.

"Orders in two minutes," I barked crisply.

I blanked the screen and, drenched in sweat, pushed the computer control combination for the applicable action manual. While waiting, I estimated my anxiety level and took the psychotropic tranquilizer dosage recommended by manual for that degree of agitation. The microtapes were fed into my audioscanner; as instructions crackled in my earphones, I reactived the telecom screen and relayed them to Sergeant 1418.

"Cordon suspect's dwelling unit immediately, but delay the search of his individual premises until my arrival. Detain incommunicado all residents present, apprehend all others at work stations, and initiate Action Plan Yellow: all-points, intensive, all-ground coordinated search for Suspect 8219."

"Understood, Controller, sir."

"All individuals in his work station will be charged under section 18.9 of the Criminal Code: Failure to Report an Absence."

"Affirmative, Controller, sir."

My tranquilizers were steadying my voice. "I will report to NORMDEV Control for further instructions. Have a Helitrans ready for my use at Port Seven."

I rode the personnel transport belt down broad, restfully pale halls, my hands tremoring slightly. We had not had a case of Norm Deviation in City 204 since I had taken over as security controller five years before. What if Higher Authority found there had been security negligence in clearing the suspect for access to the book storage tapes? It was unpleasant to contemplate. I enjoyed the perquisites of my office: my tele, my supervised sexual activities, my chemical enjoyment aids; I even had been considering a sperm submission to the Genes Bank so that a satisfactory wife could be selected for me.

At NORMDEV Control, I reported name and rank to the telescreen; when a responding image appeared, my fists clenched and acrid sweat started under my arms: it was Medic One himself, head of NORMDEV Research Section and a member of Higher Authority.

"Come in, Controller." He smiled genially from the screen. "Security has been through on tele concerning your mission."

His inner office had picture windows overlooking the dazzling white towers of the city. Far away, toward the ocean and the broad plankton farms, was the green slash of Park Three. Medic One himself was a small, quick, active man, bald and wearing heavy eyeglasses. These and his slight limp would in themselves have marked him as Higher Authority: only in someone born of genetically uncontrolled parents could such physical idiosyncracies have occurred, and only one in Higher Authority could have been allowed to reach maturity with them.

He motioned me to a chair by his heavy plastic desk, fixed me with piercing eyes from behind the thick glasses, and showed yellowed teeth in a smile.

"You have shown considerable dispatch in reacting to this security breach, Controller. If Criminal 8219 is quickly apprehended, you will receive nothing more serious than a reprimand."

Relief flooded through me as he turned again from the window, so disks of reflected light flashed in his glasses.

"Several points are suggestive. Genes Bank records indicate his father was a decent, hardworking fellow in spaceship telemetry; but his mother died of a massive overdose of chemical aids after *deliberately smashing her home telescreen.*"

"I . . . can see the significance of that, sir. She—"

"Can you, Controller?" His mood suddenly had changed. "I doubt that, the overdose . . . destruction of the telescreen . . ."

"Misdemeanor first offense, felony second," I said automatically. My hands were tremoring again after his outburst. But Medic One's brief rage seemed spent.

"Quite so, since four hours' viewing a night is of course mandatory. Now, despite the mother's criminal instability, 8219 was a brilliant child: brilliant. And since he showed absolutely no Norm Deviation tendencies himself, eventually he was *cleared by Security* and given the Reading Material Index position he requested. *Requested,* Controller: a position which is hardly one for which workers clamor, eh? We should have been suspicious."

Taking advantage of his apparently lightened mood, I began, "Yes, sir, I can see that, sir. I—"

"I sincerely hope you can, Controller."

"Sir?" My stomach had begun churning again.

"*Your* department turned him loose with *books. Your* department has so miserably mishandled the investigation up to this point." His malevolent gaze drained the blood from my face. "There is nothing, for example, in your preliminary report concerning the physician who performed the illegal operation."

"Illegal operation, sir? I don't—"

"Removing 8219's transmitter!" he shrieked. A fleck of foam appeared at one corner of his mouth. But then he abruptly smiled again, and clicked his yellow teeth together. In an academic voice, he said, "There are three possibilities concerning the Criminal, Controller. Enumerate, please."

I stammered, "First, sir I...I think an overdose of a high methamphetamine-content chemical aid." His benign nod made the words flow more easily. "Second: mental or emotional derangement, sir—both common. Third . . ."

I stopped. There was no third possibility.

But Medic One's face paled visibly; his slight, malformed body seemed to swell. Behind the thick lenses his eyes grew large and round.

"Idiot!" he shrieked. Foam again flecked the corners of his mouth and his body became momentarily rigid, as if he were about to have a catatonic seizure. "A genetic sport, you fool! He may be a genetic sport! Find him! Seize him!"

I fled down echoing halls toward the heliport, his maledictions ringing in my ears. The tension made me want to throw up. What could I do? How could I cope? Somehow, en route in the Helitrans, I managed to swallow some tranquilizers and so arrived at 8219's dwelling unit in some semblance of control. Those residents present, mostly wives and children, already had been tranquilized and were chatting gaily with the security police detaining them in their individual premises. I could hear them as I was elevated in the man lift to the correct dwelling tier level.

The silence of the criminal's premises was broken only by the hum of the environmental control unit. Per regulation, the central unit's long wall was taken up by the telescreen and the other walls were bare. There were no windows, of course; they are allowed only for Higher Authority. It was pathetically easy to uncache the Norm Deviation material: it was in the criminal's sleeping room, in the tunic drawer. A notebook removed from ComCen supplies—itself a misdemeanor—was neatly filled with quotes and aphorisms illegally copied from the book tapes.

I believe there are more instances of the abridgment of the freedom of the people by gradual and silent encroachments of those in power than by violent and sudden usurpations.

The people never give up their liberties but under some delusion.

We, and all others who believe as deeply as we do, would rather die on our feet than live on our knees.

What sane man in our enlightened and totally free society would risk Deprivation of Existence merely to dwell on such maunderings? Well, I knew, I would soon find out. But it was not to be that easy. The criminal proved most difficult to apprehend.

For one thing, other cases intervened to make security's work more difficult. A berserk plankton farm laborer killed a dozen of his fellow workers, and there was a series of rapes in Map Sectors 11.4 and 11.5. Murder and rape, of course, are not serious crimes like Norm Deviation; but investigating them and recommending the proper fines tied up field agents. Also, to show Medic One where the laxity in the department had existed, I had recommended that Sergeant 1418 be castrated and reassigned to the plankton farms for his dereliction of duty in connection with Criminal 8219's escape. Training his replacement had taken time.

But on the fifteenth day after 8219's escape, Sergeant 1419's calm, efficient face appeared on my telescreen. "Controller, sir, Criminal 8219 has been surrounded. Map Sector 11.6, coordinates Ac, Bf."

My visualscanner flashed this sector on my screen. Park Three, that dense wooded area approximating our primitive ancestors' "natural environment," which I had seen from Medic One's window. No wonder we hadn't found him before now! How had he ever survived in there? Park Three does not even have power connections for setting up a portable environmental control unit!

"We will go directly, Sergeant."

Manual states that Norm Deviation Criminals must be taken unharmed to serve as subjects for NORMDEV medics' diagnostic experiments, so we had a few tense moments. At one point the criminal, a physically powerful brute with rippling, unsightly muscles, broke through the cordon, felled the Helitrans Unit Guard, and was halfway up the boarding ladder before a net rifle was fired and he was rendered helpless.

I began preliminary examination the next day under telescreen monitoring by high NORMDEV officials including, perhaps, even Medic One himself.

"Criminal 8219, once this preliminary examination has established your guilt of Norm Deviation, NORMDEV officials will examine you to determine whether you can be made fit for society again by leucotomy, or whether you will be subject to experimental dissection instead."

"*Sans* anesthesia, of course?" He did not seem disturbed by the prospect; he even grinned engagingly when he said it.

"Unfortunately, that is the scientific necessity. For the moment, forcible detranquilization will begin today—"

"I'm not on the psychotropics anyway."

I glanced at his Physical Examination Data Sheet; it confirmed the almost incredible fact that he did not use any chemical aids. How was he able to stand it? But this fact made him a much more formidable opponent. I began to bear down.

"Criminal 8219, we must have the name of your accomplice: the corrupt medic who surgically removed the individual transmitter from your back."

He gave me that oddly engaging grin again. "I did it myself, Con, with a food preparation knife and two mirrors."

I quickly checked the laboratory reports from his premises. Two small hand mirrors had been found, and a knife had borne a trace of his blood on the blade. A fragment of individual transmitter circuitry component had been found beside the base of his excrement disposal unit. But how to withstand the pain?

"How much pain is there in removing something the size of a baby's fingernail from beneath the epidermal layer, Con?"

"My name is Controller," I said coldly.

He jerked a thumb at the telescreen monitor. "Afraid you'll get in trouble with the boys from NORMDEV?" He shook his head. "They know you're incorruptible, Con. Generations of genetic control have made sure of that. Of course the inbred little band of psychopaths called Higher Authority is scared of me for just that reason: they're afraid I might have genetically uncontrolled—"

"Genetic controls were initiated for the best of reasons!" I snapped, stung by his vicious slander of Higher Authority.

"Because population levels a dozen generations ago were so high, human overcrowding so intense, that a humanity with its aggressions intact probably would have exploded into continual violence? Sure. But how much control can you exercise before people stop being people and become . . . something else?"

I terminated the interrogation abruptly; the man sickened me. And I *was* a little apprehensive, with NORMDEV medics looking in on us. But the next day he started right in again.

"You know, Con, the controls have made the vast mass of humanity a mass of intelligent but unwilled cattle, no more important to Higher Authority than individual dinoflagellates and coelenterates in those plankton farms out there. Of course no one fools around with the genetic structure of those in Higher Authority . . ."

"There are good and sufficient reasons—"

"Sure. Without his aggressions, his competitive spirit, man can't make decisions; to run things, Higher Authority has to be uncontrolled. But even more, men in Higher Authority need those aggressions for the power struggle which has to rage among them at all times."

Though he sickened me, I kept trying to draw him out. "We hear no reports on such a struggle . . ."

"Of course not," he grinned. "But I'll bet the losers are stripped of power, offspring, and the ability to make any more. So . . . that makes me unique: the only person with uncontrolled genes outside the power structure. You can see why I had to be apprehended."

"Indeed? How did you come by these 'uncontrolled genes' as you call them?"

"Mutation. Had to be. I'm a natural sport, a throwback. My parents, like everyone's parents, were themselves products of the Genes Bank, so that's the only explanation for the differences I observed between myself and everyone else."

"And as soon as you observed these differences, you traitorously removed classified material from the book tapes; you deliberately broke contact with Computor Control; you destroyed—"

He spread his arms wide and laughed. "See, Con? A classic example of Norm Deviation. As for *why* I did it: who knows?"

Who knew indeed? My interrogation was complete. I escorted him to NORMDEV Control on the personal transport belt. Since we were free from audio monitoring in the corridor, I asked him a personal question.

"You have done all of this deliberately, Criminal 8219; yet you are not a madman. Why didn't you just remain a Reading Material Indexer, even though you hid Norm Deviation impulses in your brain?"

He flashed that sudden grin and clapped me on the shoulder. "Read my final notebook entry, Con. Think about minor crimes and map sectors. And then read up on the physical properties of mutants. And then, if you figure it out: happy nightmares. Because you won't do anything to stop it."

As Apprehending Official, I had to be watching from behind the observation window at the NORMDEV Experimental Laboratory when they brought him in to strap down on the dissection table. How could any man, completely untranquilized, face so coolly the systematic surgical removal, without anesthesia, of his bodily organs one at a time?

Yet the criminal was oddly jolly, even jumping up to perch on the edge of the operating table, swinging his feet like a little child. And for that critical moment, he held the eyes, the minds, of all in that room with his defiance. It was enough.

"Bet you don't make me say 'ouch,' " he said, grinning.

And then his hand swept up a gleaming scalpel from the instrument tray and jerked it across his throat with a flashing movement. Scarlet arterial blood jumped out, splattering guards, medics, and Higher Authority impartially.

That self-murder triggered a series of tragic events. The NORMDEV agents responsible were sentenced to Deprivation of Existence in the geriatric disposal crematoria; but that was only justice. They had been lax. But a bare two days after Criminal 8219's death, a Helitrans Unit accident between the City and Medic One's country estate left him without wife and children. And before he could recover from the terrible loss—the very next day, in fact—he inadvertantly was locked in the NORMDEV radiation room and accidentally sterilized. Higher Authority, with great sorrow, announced his permanent, premature retirement.

So it was not until several days later that I could prepare to close Criminal File 36/204/GS/8219. I idly leafed through that infamous notebook to the final entry. It was nothing: one of those silly sentiments I had noted the day I'd found the notebook. *We, and all others who believe as deeply as we do, would rather die on our feet than live on our knees.*

I supposed it was indeed an explanation, of sorts, for a disturbed mind. But what else was it? Minor crimes. And map sectors. And . . . the physical properties of mutants? Yes.

Curious now, I fed the map sector grid into the visualscanner, at the same time directing the computer to run an information tape on mutants through my audioscanner.

He had been apprehended in map sector . . . what? 11.4? 11.5? No. There had been that series of rapes in those sectors. Park Three was in the adjoining 11.6. But wait a minute. Rape was a minor crime. And the map sectors were adjoining. And the rapes had occurred *during the same fifteen days* that Criminal 8219 had been hiding in Park Three. And—

Sport or Mutant, intoned my earphones. *A sudden departure from the parent type in one or more heritable characteristics, caused by a change in a gene or chromosome with an individual or new species resulting.*

Sudden terror bent me, moaning, over the desk, sent my hand scrabbling for a tranquilizer. Heritable characteristics: *mutants could reproduce their own mutations by breeding with females of the parent species!* Nightmares, had he said? Stark terror!

How many raped and impregnated women had *not* reported? Married women, perhaps, from whom even genetic control has never been able to completely eradicate the protective motherhood urge? Or teenage girls who would not mind the abortion, but who would not want to be sterilized as is automatic with reporting rape victims? Girls who could name a boyfriend as father, thus assuring that the child would be born and then reared by the State?

How many women?

My tranquilizer was letting me breathe again, letting me think, consider. If even *one* offspring resulted and lived, the very fabric of the State would be threatened. A whole strain of the old, unruly men might result. My duty was clear. Report to NORMDEV. Then, an immediate sweep through the affected sectors, aborting all pregnancies, sterilizing all women.

I tele'd NORMDEV. "Medic One, at once. Security Control."

"He is in conference, Controller. He will be alerted."

I waited. And then new terror struck. Criminal 8219 had been *my* responsibility! His suicide had made me his unwitting partner in this monstrous crime of Norm Deviation. As an accessory to Criminal 8219's crime, I would be Deprived of Existence!

"Yes, Controller?" The new Medic One glared at me from the screen, eyes slightly bulging, lank hair plastered across his cranium like strands of beached kelp.

"I . . . sir . . ." But it wasn't *fair!* "Sir, I . . . is further action contemplated on Criminal File 36/204/GS/8219?"

"Closed file," he barked. "Reprimand going into *your* personal folder, Controller, for requesting information on a closed file."

The screen was blanked, and I released my pent breath. A reprimand only, instead of death. What harm, really? Higher Authority had *decreed* that all was well: the file was closed. And Higher Authority *always* is correct. And yet . . . And yet . . .

Higher Authority, even now, did not know of the criminal's diabolic plot. That he, knowing it would mean his own death, had plotted to reproduce himself and his genetic aberrations in the sole way he could without there being genetic scrutiny of the offspring. Nor had Higher Authority foreseen, as the criminal had, that *my* genetic code with its built-in apprehensions made me *incapable* of denouncing his foul plot against the State. Higher Authority was *always* correct?

My hands shook so badly that I could hardly open my desk drawer and remove from it what I needed; I performed the only action which was possible for me.

I took a tranquilizer.

THE KNIFE

John Russell

THE THING THAT saved Jimmy Lee was his finding the knife. This is certain. If he had not found it he must have curled up and died of sheer helplessness with the sea-slugs and jelly-fish and the other stranded specimens that festered in the sun on Rose Island beach. But while he was crawling along a coral ledge beside the lagoon, whimpering feebly and searching with vague notions of salvage from the wreck, he chanced to peer down into a purple-green pool. And there he caught the familiar shimmer of a knife-blade, two fathom deep.

It is possible that much abler individuals than Jimmy Lee would have derived no consolation whatever from the discovery. Crusoe, for example. Crusoe would have scorned it. But then, that bloke Crusoe, he was blooming careful to get hisself cast away with all manner of fixings proper to a man-size shipwreck—wasn't he? Muskets and swords and bags of biscuit and kegs of rum. Crikey! Why couldn't it have happened to Jimmy Lee that way?

Jimmy knew about that bloke Crusoe. There had been some tattered pages of a book aboard the *Dundee*, pilfered from a Sailor's Mission in Auckland, on which he had feasted word by word at furtive moments of delight behind the galley stove. And as a matter of fact—talk of knowing things— he knew perfectly well why such splendid luck had not happened and never could have happened to him. . . . Not being man-size Jimmy Lee was aware of it.

Like all the failures of his oppressed and drudging life, this was just another failure—humiliating, self-convicting and thumb-handed, as usual—that now he had fallen into a real adventure, now his actual turn had come to be shipwrecked himself, he had neither food nor tool nor weapon of any kind.

Nothing—literally—except his six-penny shirt and the ragged trousers he stood in.

And even the trousers were an out-worn pair of Cookie Anderson's, flung at him by that dreaded tyrant months before—"so y' won't 'ave to pig it with the niggers in the foc'sle, quite. . . ."

"Not as y're any ways too good fer it, y' dirty wharf-rat," was Cookie's amiable method of presenting the gift. "Gawd knows y' got less spirit than the blackest woolly-head kanaka of the lot. But y're white-colored—or might be if y' ever washed!" Here he twisted Jimmy's ears until Jimmy yelled, then kicked him out through the galley door and the trousers after him. "Whoop-ee: whee-whee-whee!" It was Cookie's war-cry: something between a crow and a squeal: a hateful sound. "Skinny-legs. Pie-face. Left-over shank o' soup-meat!" he shrilled. "Get aht o' this, and don't show back till y're dressed like the bleedin' image of a man!"

Afterward he had the infernal inspiration to make an issue of those trousers. There was a pocket in them—the first pocket Jimmy had ever owned. It pleased a morbid streak in the cook's nature to point the possibilities of that pocket, on the theory—tacitly supposed if never admitted—that his victim might be meditating a desperate revenge.

"Nar then—nar then, wot y' 'iding in them britches?" he would nag, making painful inquisition with the toe of his boot or the flat of his hand. "A knife? Don't tell me y' gone and 'id a knife abaht y'!" Jimmy never risked hiding so much as a crust of bread, but Cookie would thrust forward his whittled, chinless face and lower his voice with subtly evil suggestion. "Count 'em out—d' y' 'ear? Count the knives out and let me see y' do it. Lord 'elp you if I ever catch y' sneaking one—mind that!"

For the most part of Jimmy's weary round had to do with knives. Hours and hours he spent on them, with pumice and whetstone.

There were the knives of the galley, first of all: butcher knives and carving knives and the knives for meals. They hung in gleaming ranks against the bulkhead—all kinds of knives, from the great two-foot cleaver that could unjoint an ox to the tiny, accurate blade designed for surgical operations on a potato. There were the broad and heavy oyster knives, brought into hard usage when the *Dundee* struck a strictly-preserved pearl bank and did a rare stroke of business while the shell rotted out through a hurried and smell-some week. There were the sheath-knives of the men—even the black deckhands were privileged to carry their own, belted in swagger fashion against their lean rumps as a badge of independence and of manhood.

And every one of those knives had to pass under Jimmy's anxious care, to be kept bright and shiny and razor-keen. Cookie Anderson saw to that, though the best Jimmy could do never satisfied him. It was the man's obsession.

• • •

To the other whites on the schooner, naturally, the thing became in time an accepted jest, as any such current ugliness tends to be among tough and tarry minds. They witnessed this little drama of master and slave with a detached humor. And when the big mate, Gulbranson, might poke his shaggy head in at the scuttle, Jimmy would be whetting steadily away. Cookie at his own work would be keeping a watchful, malignant eye. And Gulbranson would chuckle his warning in a hoarse aside:

"Look out for that young coot, Anderson. Look out he don't turn on y', some time. I see it in his eye—he'll get even on y' sure, some day!"

"Get aht! 'Im? I'd skin 'im like one of these 'ere spuds. Like to see 'im try it. Yes, or you either, y' big tripe. Or anyone." And the cook would flap his arms and crow excitedly only at the thought of it. "Whee-whee-whee! . . . My word, if anybody 'as a 'ankering, let 'im turn on me—that's all!"

Then Gulbranson would grin half contemptuously at the febrile creature, and half speculatively at the thin, yellow-haired, unformed youngster who sat so humbly by. Gulbranson never interfered. None of the others, from Cap'n Joe Brett down, ever interfered. They were open-air, unfanciful men, neither better nor worse than the run of island trading crews. They had served their own apprenticeships. If he survived, the lad must win his rightful rating for himself: meanwhile his net value lay in valeting the knives.

This was the age-old law of the sea that governed the case of Jimmy Lee: and this was the particular reason why Jimmy took his first effective impulse from a mere flickering reflection.

• • •

THROUGH the water, churned by a wash of ground swell over the rocks, he could not see the thing clearly. But he made out its flat, clean, metallic lustre. A knife. Being a knife it was the thing he knew: a thing of daily use and habit. Being a knife it offered an object and a means—the whole difference between life and death.

It came in good time for Jimmy.

Rose Island, to which his fate had drifted him, is one of the innumerable left-over remnants of the Pacific: a hummock of rock about the bigness of a battleship, ringed with shattered beach and the enclosing coral reef—the whole no more than a pinprick on any chart. Nobody goes to Rose Island. Messrs. Cook do not sell tickets to it. It lies on no route of trader or fisherman. . . . According to official legend it was visited once by a Naval Governor to set up an imposing notice:

ROSE ISLAND

AMERICAN SAMOA

NO TRESPASSING

Why any person should trespass, how he was to keep alive or in what manner go about removing himself if cast up as an unwilling trespasser, the Governor did not state. There stood his defiance amid the wastes of ocean: a stern reminder to marauding frigate birds and the piratical sea turtle.

By the time of the *Dundee's* venture hereabouts, however, this triumph of human prescience must have disappeared. The *Dundee* came on a fortune hunt, in hope of tracing a certain valuable lumber derelict, the *Yackarra,* last reported somewhere near the Manua group. She sighted Rose Island on the fourteenth of April. But it was no signboard that warned her off. She came close enough to observe how poor was the picking and to drop a comment in the higher criticism.

"They say Gawd made such places with the rest," remarked Cap'n Joe Brett. "Just as well for 'Im 'E didn't 'ave to put in no bill for this job. . . . What's the good of it, Gulbranson?"

To which the mate, a philosopher of sorts: "Well, you can't never tell, Cap'n. It maybe might come useful yet for some poor soul."

Three days later and some twelve miles farther south they could have used the shelter of that isle themselves—poor souls!—and thankful. This occurred on the seventeenth of April: a date to be memorable throughout that region below the Line where history is counted in devastating storms. . . .

They had found their derelict, right enough: an old three-master kept afloat by her cargo of deals and tin-bound stacks of cedar shingles. They were in the act of passing a hawser aboard when a squall swept upon them like the black wings of Azrael. The kanaka at the wheel promptly lost his head, the *Dundee's* fore-boom jibed and carried away its tackle, and the foremast snapped short.

Cookie Anderson, eager with the promise of loot, had been the first man overside. He was standing in the dinghy with Jimmy Lee to bear a hand at the moment all hell broke loose. The dinghy smashed against the channels. Cookie grabbed for a rope. Jimmy was in the way. With a shriek, Cookie snatched him back and sprang to safety on his sprawling body just as the dinghy went under.

What happened after that: how he was borne up in wreckage and flung to leeward on the *Yackarra's* rail; how he lay partly stunned and nearly drowned while the *Dundee* disappeared like a draggle-winged bird in the smother, how the derelict finally crashed on Rose Island reef and he came ashore among the shingles—serviceable life preservers with their bindings of tin strips—these events were mercifully dim.

The first dependable fact he gripped was the presence of that knife.

As he crouched there by the ledge he had reached the fever stage of thirst. He began to think (a queer process for Jimmy) and he thought that if he had the knife he might slash the sappy vines and young trees that grew so thickly 'round about. In one place, too, were things like big green melons, hanging high up. With the knife fixed to a branch he might hack them loose. They might be good to suck. Crikey! He had the feel of cool juice squashing out and trickling down his throat, and he made puppy noises and bit his fingers in desire and despair.

For Jimmy could not swim. Worse than that, his ingrained terror of the water had been most horridly confirmed. Worse than all, he was aware of dreadful dangers lurking down yonder, in the pool—he glimpsed their wavering fins and slow, snaky tentacles: mysterious and unnameable monsters.

. . . No. He dared not plunge in after the knife. Still, it was there; something to strive for. So instead of dying just yet, he stumbled along where the big fruits grew and tried to climb a tree.

He never had learned how to climb a tree. He slipped and floundered and very grievously barked his nose and his shins, and sat down and wept. But nobody being on hand to kick him and the process of thought continuing, after a while he took off his six-penny shirt and tied it between his ankles as a loose bandage. And therewith when he tried again he hiked himself up, topside of a leaning trunk, exactly as the island natives do—the trick they have used time out of mind.

He knocked off a fruit. It proved unreasonably tough, but he managed to worry the fibre apart at one end. He jabbed into the core with a stick: something spurted, and he clapped his salt-tortured mouth to the most delicious, vivifying, heart-lifting draught that ever rejoiced an amateur castaway. A miracle to Jimmy, it might pass as a very fair miracle anyhow. He had discovered the aërial fountain of half the tropical world—the common green coconut!

Such was Jimmy's immediate salvation. Actually, he had broken the spell of horror, of loneliness, of hopelessness. Actually, he had derived motive and accomplishment from the one simple cause. And he continued to derive.

• • •

THAT night he had his first rest, undisturbed by lions and bears and other noxious beasts. By day he could see that there was no such game and scant cover to hide a cat. But in the dark, roaring with voices of wind and reef: who could be sure? He felt much safer to spread his dry seaweed beside the ledge, handy to a weapon which he might perhaps reach in desperate need—if he could ever bring himself to the risk.

Next day he tried to fork it out with a length of splintered bamboo. He nearly lost it altogether, but prodding around he chanced to impale a curious arrangement like a bunch of wriggling, soft, semitranslucent ribbons. Jimmy was mortally hungry. He tore the creature apart. He bit into it—with shrinkings, at first, and then with gusto. Later he improved his spear by wedging the splinters apart and sharpening them on the coral: and about the same time he began to regard the doings of the late Mr. Crusoe with rather less awe.

Again he blundered on a lucky discovery when he twisted some threads of coconut fibre into a crude net, weighted with pebbles. The clumsy device was no good as a dredge: it would not catch the knife at all. But when he buzzed it about his head and threw it at a huddle of sea-birds on the beach it brought down one ensnared, so that he made an easy captive, and might have gone into the poultry business on a large scale if he had been able to stomach raw fowl as readily as raw rock-squid.

The matter of cookery, however, was reserved for his best performance. . . .

It came to an issue weeks afterward—after he had contrived his hut of pandanus thatch, his coco-husk sandals for wading the sharp reefs and his little coral hammer for gathering shell-fish at low tide; his throwing stones and his sling and his dagger of cane. After he had domesticated himself.

He still dwelt on the ledge above the purple-green pool. Between flaming sunrise and blazing sunset, under fierce noons that made the rocks dance in the heat haze, within the whole thunderous ring of his prison was no other refuge for a poor wharf-rat. The *Yackarra* had broken up long since, dispersed as flotsam. But there was no help in battered planks and shingle bundles. Whereas he was always conscious of the knife as a piece of man's handiwork: a comfort and a prize to be struggled for: a vision that enforced the trembling will to live.

Once, as he sat brooding and glooming over it, he pictured how he might get at it with a hook of some sort. Hooks would be useful for his fishing, too. They might be carved of clam-shell, he imagined, and he remembered how Cookie Anderson through quiet evenings had used cunningly and patiently to drill out shell bracelets with an instrument he called a "Yankee fiddle."

Now a hook after all is nothing but the segment of a bracelet, and a Yankee fiddle is nothing in the world but a stout bow and arrow, with two loops of string to twirl the shaft. Jimmy had already made rude experiments in that direction, so he took his own bow and arrow and put his weight to them as he had seen Cookie do, and set to work.

First he tried on shell, and when he noticed what surprising heat sprang up under his fingers, on slips of wood. He failed many times. But there came a moment when he started a curling blue wisp, and then a live spark from the bamboo dust. . . .

On all accounts, this marks the climax of Jimmy's adventure. It is the point for wonder, and for pride in human potential, that alone and unaided by any Crusoe fixings whatever the cook's-boy had wrested from a howling wilderness food, shelter, tools and finally—fire. No mean achievement, it may be said: the sort of achievement easily doubted by a generation too wise to believe in desert islands. But the fact stands indubitably attested—the sole cause and the direct cause of Jimmy's rescue.

> June 6—Friday. 14° 30' S. 68° 11' W. Fresh breeze out of S.E. No sign of derelict which likely drifted too far or smashed up. If not sighted tomorrow we shape for Butaritari. . . . Afternoon, smoke observed to south. Supposing it might be wreckers or ship on fire, bore up toward Rose Island.

Thus the log of the schooner *Dundee.*

The log of the *Dundee* was, and it continues to be, a strictly unfanciful, open-air chronicle: and that is why it contains no mention of a missing cook's-boy—regretful or otherwise—between the dates of his tragic disappearance and his most unexpected recovery. The *Dundee* herself had been laying up for repairs these last two months in Apia roadstead. Once more at sea, she had put in some few days' perfunctory search. Not for Jimmy, of course, but for the lost *Yackarra.* Not for Jimmy, whose existence had never occurred as a possibility until the *Dundee's* surf-boat entered the lagoon and her crew blinked toward the beach. . . . Even then they were slow enough about it.

"Now what t' Sam Hill sort of guy would you take that to be?" inquired Gulbranson.

At the edge of the rocks popped up a figure, squinting through the slanted sunlight. A stalwart figure, nearly naked, with the remnant of ragged trousers about its waist. Weathered to a ruddy bronze, with a skin fine-drawn on the coiling muscles—startled and alert as he stood at gaze—the fellow might have seemed some able young native of the isles. But no native ever wore a great shock of blond hair—yellow as corn-silk! And certainly no native would ever have given the curious, wild shout of recognition he loosed across at them.

"Whee-whee-whee!" So it sounded.

Cap'n Joe Brett was sitting in the stern sheets: Gulbranson beside him. On the next thwart sat Cookie Anderson, a volunteer under the pious plea of gathering turtles' eggs for dinner. Two white sailors were rowing—for Cap'n Joe, not knowing what he might find, had not cared to bring the blacks.

All hands stared beachward, and stared at each other. "Good Gosh!" remarked Gulbranson. "It's Jimmy Lee!"

They were close enough to be sure, for all the mad improbability of it. They could see it was Jimmy Lee. And they saw more. . . . Suddenly the little brown apparition broke into the strangest activity. It began to leap: it began to dance. It hammered its chest and flapped its arms and crowed abroad like a game-cock.

" 'E's gone crazy!" opined Cap'n Joe.

Gulbranson put up a hand.

"Listen—"

"Whoopee!" came the amazing challenge: a voice harsh with disuse, and with something else—sheer exultation. "I see you there: I'm talkin' to you, y' dirty sea-cook!" Followed the name of Cookie Anderson, three times run- • ning. "You 'ear me? Kettle-scraper. 'Ash-slinger. I'm lookin' for you. I been waitin' for you! . . . Whoopee-whee-whee!"

They listened, all of them, dumbly, while comprehension began to creep over each bewildered face. . . . But the figure on the rock still held them in its singular demonstration. It turned. It paused. It poised for an instant with an indefinable last gesture of suspense and hesitation: then with a triumphant yell it sprang forward, cleaving the water in a clean, deep dive. When it reappeared and climbed the rock again it held an object that flashed in the sun.

The four others in the boat glanced around at Cookie Anderson. They remembered. They had a perfectly clear sequence of that little galley drama aboard the *Dundee* between master and slave: the misery, the cruelty and the crowning treachery. And with the simple humor of tough and tarry minds, they understood: that is to say, they got the situation well enough— the essential justice of it as Cap'n Joe Brett summed up for them, grimly:

"Not so bloomin' crazy, after all!"

The boat had drawn very near the ledge. Cookie Anderson sat crouched like a thing of venom. His lips were lifted on the yellow teeth: his little eyes showed red. " 'E's got a knife!" he squealed.

All the evil of his twisted nature spat in the word. He bunched himself eagerly toward the gunwale, and swiftly his own dirk was out and gleaming. . . . But Gulbranson knocked it from his grip and overboard with one contemptuous sweep.

"No, he ain't. Look there!"

For Jimmy Lee had cast his own weapon aside. He was coming to meet the boat, and coming empty-handed. "Knife be damned!" said Gulbranson.

"I tol' you how it would be," he chuckled. "I tol' you he'd turn on y'! The young coot was bound to get square some day. . . . Man to man. Even-Stephen—and we'll all see fair play!"

He laughed: they all laughed. Cookie was like a snake deprived of its sting. He would have shrunk away, but they boosted him forward. At the last he would have begged and cringed, but they booted him out on the strand and stood 'round him as a ring, until for mere shame he took position. As Gulbranson stepped over to referee, his foot caught in something so that he almost tripped. It was the thing that Jimmy had plunged for: the thing he had finally thrown away—a thin band of shimmery metal—one of those tin strips in which shingle bundles are bound. . . . But it meant nothing to Gulbranson. And it meant nothing to Jimmy Lee. Smiling, confident—hard and able—he came up to settle his score and to take his rightful rating at last with nothing but his two fists, man-fashion, in the age-old way of the sea.

REGINALD HILL

I've always loved the old Border Ballad which tells how Thomas the Rhymer (which is to say, a guy who, like myself, makes a living out of invention) is snatched into Elfland, whence he returns after seven years with the parting gift from the Elfin Queen that he will thereafter always tell the truth. Now this is a very ambiguous present! Me it would simply put out of work. But what, I asked myself, would it do to a cop? The idea intrigued me because, basically, it's a problem which touches us all. So I looked for a way of presenting it which would be serious without getting too heavy, and entertaining without getting too light. "True Thomas" was the result.

• • •

Good storytellers are a surprisingly rare breed. Good storytellers who are also fine stylists are even rarer, and Stevenson must rate in the first rank of these. Oddly, these gifts can work against each other insomuch as narrative insistence can drive the reader on at too fast a pace to savour mere beauties of language, and I would recommend that "Markheim" be read at least twice to get the most out of it. But this is a redundant recommendation. Once read, it will call you back again and again in your efforts to understand the mystery at its heart.

TRUE THOMAS

Reginald Hill

It was mirk, mirk night, there was nae starlight.
They waded thro' red blude to the knee;
For a' the blude that's shed on earth
Rins through the springs o' that countrie.

"NOT GUILTY!"

Disbelief. Shock. Anger. The need for a drink.

DI Tom Tyler was heading for the court exit before the judge had pronounced the dismissal. But quick as he was, Chuck Orgill was even quicker, bounding out of the dock to ignore Miss bloody Morphet QC's congratulatory hand and crush her instead in a joyous bear-hug.

Over the lawyer's skewed wig, his gaze met Tom's. For a second his lips pursed in a derisive moue. Then, which was worse, they spread in an almost sympathetic smile and his left eyelid dropped knowingly, ironically, conspiratorially.

Scotch became essential to sanity. Tom shouldered his way to the exit till he met a body too solid to be shouldered.

"Lost it then, did you?" said Superintendent Missendon. "I got here in time to see little Miss Muffet take you to the cleaners."

"Sodding lawyers. I hate them!"

"We had one on our side too, remember?"

"That prancing ponce! If he pissed in a snowdrift, he'd miss."

He tried to resume his progress but Missendon caught his arm.

"Smithson's here from the Prosecutor's office. He's got a spare hour and would like to go over the Bryden case with us. And Tom, do me a favour. Go easy on the prancing ponce line, eh?"

It was a quarter to two before Tom made it into the murk masquerading as afternoon in wintry Lancashire. On the law court steps Missendon said, "Fancy a drink? We can make the Sailors before closing."

Tom hesitated. The need was still strong, but not for the company of colleagues he'd find in the Sailors.

He said, "I'll pass if you don't mind, sir. I ought to get down to South to check those points Smithson brought up."

"Such devotion to duty. I'm impressed," said Missendon unconvincingly. "Catch you later then."

He strode away. Tom watched him out of sight then headed over the road to the Green Tree.

The Tree had its disadvantages too. The nearest pub to the law courts, it was the traditional trough of sodding lawyers. Sodden lawyers, too. Despite the lateness of the hour, it was still crowded with the bastards, red in tooth and glass. Using his shoulder as a ram, Tom took a direct line to the bar, filling the air with protest and claret.

He was served quickly. Studying himself in the bar mirror, he understood why. A stocky, muscular thirty-year-old with a lowering, truculent expression, he looked the kind of troublemaker the police warned the public against approaching.

He raised his drink in a mock toast. "Long life," he said. "And up yours, Miss Muffet."

He drank, and as if by magic, his image vanished to be replaced by a view of the woman he was so abusively toasting.

The door linking the saloon with the small bar serving the dining-room had swung open. Miss Morphet, brandy balloon before her, was shaking hands with a man Tom recognised as Orgill's brief, Walter Lime, "Harry" to his friends. "Slime" to the constabulary. They'd probably just finished a celebratory lunch and Slime was oozing off to keep another of his crooked clients out of jail. Miss bloody Muffet on the other hand didn't need to rush her cognac. Crooks were dusted down and cleaned up before being ushered into her hygienic presence.

She was laughing now at some farewell pleasantry, probably some crack about how easy it was to stuff the police.

Tom turned from the bar with an abruptness which set the claret flying once more and headed purposefully for the dining-room.

The brief had gone. Miss Morphet looked up at him with the expression of interested puzzlement she'd worn as she insinuated that most of the police evidence was pathetic forgery.

Tom said, "I'd like a word."

She said, "I'm sorry, I know we've met, but I just can't place you . . ."

"No? You don't look at people you call liars then?"

"Ah," she said. "Inspector Tyler, isn't it? I don't believe that in fact I used that term . . ."

"Of course you didn't. A bit too plain for a lawyer. What was it you said? Oh yes. My notes had clearly been composed so long after the event that, like Shakespeare's *Richard the Third*, they might be great entertainment, but they were hardly history."

"Did I say that?" she said with amused complacency. "Oh dear.

"Though I'm sure it sounds far worse with a strong masculine delivery. Now I really ought to get back to chambers, so perhaps if there were anything else . . ."

"I just wanted to know what it feels like to put a dangerous criminal back on the streets."

She pursed her ripe cherry lips and said, "I don't know, Inspector. Perhaps you can tell me. Keeping people on or off our streets is more in your line, I believe."

"That's right," he said. "You just stand up in court, play with words, never give a damn for the consequences of what you're saying . . ."

She was gathering her bag from under her chair and her jacket from its back.

"I think it best if I didn't hear this, Inspector," she said. "And to tell the truth—"

"What the hell do you know about telling the truth?" he exploded. "Before you rush off to make your official complaint, why don't you try it, just for once in your life. Is Orgill guilty? Yes or no?"

"The jury found him Not Guilty, don't you recall?"

"Sod the jury! That's a verdict, not a fact. In truth, in honest simple truth, is Orgill guilty? Did he do it? Yes or no?"

For a brief moment he thought he saw the professional mask of that narrow, fine-boned, Siamese-cat-like face fracture.

Then she said, "Won't you sit down, Inspector?"

Tom's anger, though still strong, had lost its head of steam and he was aware that other eyes in the dining-room were watching the encounter with undisguised interest. He sat.

She said, "You clearly pride yourself on plain speaking, so why not say exactly what you've got on your mind."

He took a deep breath and said, "All right I will. I believe—I *know* there's a dangerous man roaming free because he didn't get sent down for a crime I *know* he committed. I reckon you're far too bright not to know that he did it too. But this didn't stop you asserting as true things you knew were lies, and smearing as lies things you knew were true. OK. I've heard all that garbage you people trot out about everyone being entitled under law to a defense. I just want to know how you as an individual human being can live with twisting the truth like this."

He fell silent and sipped his whisky.

She toyed with her brandy balloon then said, "My trouble is, I don't really know you, Inspector. I mean, I don't know enough about you to help me decide whether I should just tell you to go screw yourself, or whether I should simply get on the phone to the Chief."

"And how much would you need to know to make you try to answer my question honestly?" he sneered.

"Oh, very little," she said. "I'd just need to be persuaded it was the question of an honest man. Are you that rare creature, Inspector?"

"I'm on the side of truth," he growled, annoyed with himself now because it sounded pompous. "And I don't believe you can get there through lies."

"A real True Thomas," she said, smiling as though at a secret joke.

"Sorry?"

"Thomas the Rhymer in the old ballad who went to Elfland and when he came back he could never tell a lie."

"Look, I'm not saying I've never told a lie, but . . ."

"But they are not necessary for your way of life whereas they are for mine?"

"Something like that."

"So you wouldn't find it difficult to manage, say, twenty-four hours telling nothing but the truth? What's up, Inspector? You look disconcerted. You want to condemn me for allegedly doing something you couldn't avoid yourself for a mere day? Surely not?"

"Of course I could but—"

"Then that's my best offer. You go twenty-four hours without telling a lie and I'm yours to do with as you wish."

She saw his eyes widen slightly at her choice of phrase and gave a wicked smile.

"I mean, *morally*, of course, Inspector. So what do you say?"

He looked at her, trying to show his scorn for such a daft idea. She had green eyes, and those lips, which in court had lured him into so many damning uncertainties and qualifications, were full and moist. As he hesitated she picked a Cox's pippin from the bowl of fruit in front of her, polished it against her breast and offered it to him.

"What's this for?" he asked.

"In the ballad, the Queen of Elfland gives Thomas a magic apple which makes him incapable of telling a lie," she said. "I'm beginning to wonder if you don't need a bit of magic too, Inspector."

The mockery stung. She'd done the same in court, provoking him into responses he knew were unwise. But even as he recalled his resolve never to be so provoked again, he heard himself saying, "Not tell a lie for a day? No problem."

"Oh good." She nibbled a tiny wedge out of the apple, then offered it to him once more. "A bargain, then?"

He took the fruit, said, "A bargain," and sank his teeth deep into the incision she'd made, filling his mouth with the crisp juicy flesh.

"That's fine. What's the time?" As if at command, the old wall clock above the kitchen door began to chime. "Two o'clock. You've started. See you here in the Tree tomorrow. Or perhaps I should say under the Tree."

The secret mocking smile again.

"Suits me," he said trying to sound indifferent as he watched her wriggle her supple, slender arms into the sleeves of her jacket.

She caught his eyes and suddenly looked serious.

"One thing more, Tom. I may call you Tom? And you must call me Sylvie. Tell me, Tom, are you happily married?"

"Yes," he said. "I mean, most of the time, we have our ups and downs but . . ."

He stopped, not just because of the tangles his search for the precise truthful answer was leading him on to, but also because she had brought her face so close that he could feel the warmth of her five-star scented breath while under the table her long, red-nailed fingers gently caressed the inside of his thigh.

"But would you fancy sleeping with me, Tom?" she whispered.

"What?" He pushed back his chair in confusion.

She stood up, laughing.

"No need to answer, Tom. Dirty trick, you reckon? I think you may be surprised just how many dirty tricks twenty-fours can play on a man devoted to the truth. See you tomorrow. Or, if not, I'll know why."

He watched her go then he picked up the whisky glass he had set on the table. He still needed a drink but it was no longer to feed his anger.

• • •

HE spent the afternoon at his desk catching up with paperwork. Scrupulously, he applied as strict a regulation here as he knew he'd need when speaking, and the truth cost him frequent revisions and would probably cost him even more frequent rebukes when his reports were read.

But by six o'clock he felt satisfied he'd made an excellent start to his twenty-four hours. Now with a bit of luck he'd have till eight-thirty the next morning, safe from the testing pressures of the job. Not that he doubted his ability to meet Miss bloody Muffet's challenge, but he knew that his working life offered all kinds of traps to the unwary.

One of them was coming along the corridor as he came out of his room.

"Tom, just off?" said Missendon. "You got things sorted with South did you?"

"Sorry?"

"You said you were heading off to South to tidy up some loose ends on the Bryden case."

"That's right. I did."

"Did sort things out, you mean?"

"Did say I was going," said Tom.

"Ah." Missendon was looking nonplussed. "And did you go?"

"No," said Tom.

"Oh," said Missendon. "Why not?"

"Because," said Tom carefully, "I'd already got everything sorted that needed sorting."

He smiled in valediction as he spoke and started to move towards the stairs. Missendon fell into step beside him.

"So why did you say you were going?" he persisted.

Tom sighed inwardly and said, "It was an excuse."

"For what?"

"For not going to the Sailors with you, sir."

"You mean you didn't fancy a drink? Why not say so?"

"That's not what I meant, sir."

"What then?"

"I didn't fancy a drink with you, sir, at the Sailors."

Missendon was looking at him very strangely.

"Are you feeling all right, Tom?" he asked. "You've been acting a bit odd lately."

"Yes, sir. I feel fine."

"That's all right then. I'll see you in the morning. Good night."

"Good night, sir," said Tom.

He heaved a sigh of relief as he made it to his car without further encounters. This truth business wasn't quite as straightforward as he'd asserted. Of course, the kind of lie he'd told Missendon at the law court was pure white, a bit of that social mortar which holds the fabric of relationships together. But it made him aware that perhaps simply being away from his work wasn't going to give him the easy ride he'd hoped.

His fears were confirmed almost as soon as he entered his house.

Mavis appeared at the head of the stairs dressed only in her underwear, but not to offer him the soldier's welcome after a long campaign.

"Tom, there you are! Get a move on. We're due there at seven."

It came to him instantly. It was a Very Special Day, to wit, his parents-in-law's wedding anniversary, and the whole Masterman family were going out to dinner.

"What kept you so late? You didn't forget, did you?"

This was a form of reproach rather than a serious accusation. Mavis didn't believe it was humanly possible for anyone to forget so important an occasion. The correct answer was something on the lines of, "Of course not, darling. It was just that Missendon wanted to chat and with my promotion board coming up, you know I've got to keep on the right side of the old sod."

Tonight was different.

He said, "Yes. I forgot."

Fortunately she hadn't stayed for an answer but turned back into the bedroom. He watched her heavy buttocks wobble away. He didn't mind that she had started putting on weight, in fact he found the extra pounds in most places a real turn-on. But he wished that she would acknowledge the change in her choice of clothes. The fact that her skimpy silk pants now almost disappeared into her rear cleavage affected only her own personal comfort, but when he came out of the shower and saw her struggling into the kind of figure-hugging dress she'd once looked so devastating in, his heart sank.

"There," she said, pirouetting. "What do you think?"

"Oh yes," he said, nodding vigorously and smacking his lips. "I'd better get a move on. Mustn't be late."

"You mean, oh yes, you like it?" she said, unhappy as always with anything less than hyperbole.

He said. "It's a very nice dress. Super. Shall I wear my plain blue shirt?"

He knew she hated the blue shirt because it looked like official police issue, but even this provocation only provided a temporary diversion.

As he buttoned up the pearl grey pinstripe which nipped him under the arms but which Mavis thought made him look distinguished (i.e., not like a policeman) she said, "You don't like it, do you?"

He sought for further evasion, saw how close he was skirting the boundaries of truth, and said. "No, not really. The dress is all right but . . ."

"But not on me, you mean? Why? What's wrong with me?"

"It looks a bit tight, that's all. Perhaps you got the wrong size . . ."

"No, I didn't. I got the size I always get. What you mean is I'm fat, that's it, isn't it?"

She was glaring at him angrily, waiting for the reassurance, the explanation, the full frontal flattery.

He sighed and said, "Yes."

Only the fact that her parents were waiting to be picked up and must on no account be kept waiting on this Very Special Day saved him. Nothing must be allowed to interfere with the smooth running of a Masterman VSD. He'd long since given up the attempt to count exactly how many VSDs Mavis's family celebrated per year, but he was pretty certain if they were all made public holidays, it would solve the unemployment problem at a stroke.

They drove to his in-laws' house in a frost of silence beyond the reach of the car's heating system. Mummy and Daddy's presence warmed things up superficially with Mavis exuding enough heat for two, but his in-laws' attempts to bring him into the conversation created more problems.

"So how's work, Tom?" asked Father Masterman in his hearty down-to-earth, am-I-right-or-am-I-right, self-made Northerner's voice.

"Much the same."

"And your promotion board, is that looking hopeful?"

"There's always hope," said Tom.

"Well, don't forget our little agreement. The moment you feel things have stopped moving for you in the police, there's that nice comfortable seat waiting for you at Masterman's."

Father Masterman was a builder, one of the biggest in Lancashire, and for years now he and his daughter had been urging Tom to take charge of the firm's security. So long as Tom could imply that he was moving steadily onwards and upwards towards the socially acceptable level of Chief Constable, he could fend them off. But somehow a purely unilateral "agreement" had evolved whereby they understood that any hiatus in his upward progress meant he would resign and join the firm.

Tom grunted unintelligibly.

From the rear seat Mother Masterman piped up, "I dare say Tom's secretly hoping he doesn't get his promotion so's he can leave and join Father. Isn't that right, Tom?"

He didn't reply.

Mavis said sweetly, "Tom, Mummy asked you a question, didn't you hear?"

"Yes, I heard," said Tom.

"So why don't you answer? Polite people reply when they're asked civil questions."

"What was the civil question again?" asked Tom.

"Wouldn't you rather give up this awful trying police work and take a nice nine-to-five job with Father," said his mother-in-law, choosing a bad moment for one of her rare excursions into precision.

Tom considered, then said, "No. I think I'd rather pick cotton."

There was a long silence, ended when his father-in-law began to laugh.

"*Pick cotton!* That's a good 'un, Mother. Pick cotton! They're too sharp for us, these youngsters. *I'd rather pick cotton.* I'll have to remember that one."

That got them over that hurdle without much immediate pain. But as they got out of the car and he gave Mavis a ruefully apologetic smile, all he got in return was a cold stare which promised payment deferred with interest.

He sighed deeply. He hadn't been lying to Miss Muffet when he said his marriage was generally speaking a happy one. He and Mavis shared far more than they were divided by. Unhappily, Mavis's family was one of the divisors, and various guilt feelings of her own meant that no compromises were permitted here.

The rest of the family was already waiting in the restaurant. There was his brother-in-law, Trevor, weak son of a strong father who tried to compensate by eschewing charm and embracing fascism. With him was his wife, Joanna, whose alcoholism might be either a cause or an effect of her husband's growing impotence. Tom quite liked her, but he had never been able to grow fond of his sister-in-law, Trudi, who spoke as rarely as she bathed, which was not often. And to make up the party there was Trudi's husband, Fred, shambling and uncoordinated, who had finally been found a job in Accounts to keep him away from machinery and sharp edges.

The meal followed much the usual pattern.

As their orders were being taken, Joanna announced with the piercing clarity of the chronically pissed, "Spinach. My husband will have spinach. They say it helps with erections."

At the same time Fred, who despite his utter lack of physical coordination, loved sport, was describing to Mavis how he'd built a break of six in his last game of snooker. Drawing his right arm back to illustrate the shot, he drove his elbow into the crotch of the wine waiter who was uncorking the mandatory champagne. The man doubled up with a strangulated scream, the cork blew off like a bullet and hit a woman at the next table plumb between the eyes, while the jet of wine caught her dining companion on the back of his head with such force it removed his toupee.

What puzzled Tom on these occasions was the fact that no matter what outrageous observations Joanna made, no matter how much of the infrastructure Fred destroyed, their behaviour never drew more than a resigned chuckle from his father-in-law, while he, Tom Tyler, who stayed stone-cold sober and could eat his prawn cocktail without breaking the dish, was clearly regarded as the disruptive member of the family.

Tonight, however, he at last caught up with his reputation.

He kept out of trouble till well into the main course. Then: "How's crime, Tom?" asked Trevor.

"There's a lot of it about."

"You're telling me. It's the courts I blame. Too much wrist slapping. It's time the legislature got its act together. Right?"

After his experience in court that morning, Tom couldn't disagree.

"Right," he said.

"Slap their wrists with a sharp axe if they're caught thieving, that's what they need," continued Trevor, warming to his thesis. "The stuff we lose off our sites, you wouldn't believe it. It's the Irish, too many bloody Irish, why we let them in I can't fathom. And if we do catch them red-handed, what happens? Nothing! They're off robbing some other poor devil the next day. We need to make a few examples, encourage the others. Am I right, Tom?"

Tom said judiciously, "As a general principle, even-handedly applied, I think a rational man might make a rational case for that approach, Trev."

It was, he felt, in the circumstances a rather good answer. But the trouble with the Mastermans was, they didn't just want a polite nod in the general direction of the family faith, they needed you inside the temple, flat on your belly, kissing the idol's big toe.

"So why don't you join us, Tom?" said father. "Or if you're not yet ready to do that, at least give us the benefit of your expertise. Sort of consultant."

"That's right, Tom," said Trevor. "Family's got to stick together, eh? So as an expert law man, where would you start to clean up Mastermans?"

At the top, was the answer that rose in Tom's throat, but he let it stick there.

"Look," he said, "the kind of petty thieving on the job you're talking about, it sounds to me like it all comes down to how much supervision you want to pay for."

"Private security, you mean?" said Trevor. "That's a bit rich, coming from you."

"Sorry?"

"Well, haven't I heard you going on about the evils of private education? And private medicine? And private everything else? Why's it all right all of a sudden for your own family to be expected to pay for private security? What's happened to the forces of law and order, then? I mean, just because we're not the undeserving poor, aren't we entitled to the law's protection too? After all it's people like us who pay for it, isn't it? We're not on state benefits. We're paying our taxes. So shouldn't whoever pays the piper call the tune?"

"Depends."

"On what?"

"On all kinds of things. Whether the piper's getting paid full whack for instance. Fred, could you pass me the horse-radish?"

His attempt at diversion failed. Fred performed the minor miracle of passing the dish without dropping it or knocking anything over with it. He looked hopefully at Joanna, but she seemed to have relapsed into a state of catatonia.

Father Masterman said slowly, "Now I'm not sure I understand you, Tom. Let's get this straight. First off, the police is a public service, right?"

"Right."

"That means it's funded from the public purse, right?"

"Right."

"Which means taxes. And we pay our taxes, right?"

Tom didn't answer.

"Right, Tom?" insisted Father.

"To a certain extent," said Tom.

"To a hell of an extent!" exploded Father. "Have you ever seen our tax bill? Fred, you tell him. You know the figures. How much did we pay last year?"

For a moment panic pitted Fred's face like smallpox. Then he took a deep breath, let his lips move as though totting up columns of figures and said, "A hell of a lot."

"That's right," said Father. "A hell of a lot. So where's the problem, Tom?"

Time for evasion. Time to duck and weave. Time to kick Joanna under the table and hope she'd wake from some dream of Trevor's sexual inadequacy which she wished to share with the company.

But a vision of Miss bloody Muffet rose into his mind, the green-eyed Queen of Elfland offering him the apple with juice oozing out of the nick she'd made with those wicked white teeth.

He said, "The problem's what you want those taxes to be spent on. The problem's the kind of people you vote into power to spend those taxes. The problem's that you might pay a hell of a lot, but you slide out of paying a hell of a lot too."

"Tom!" exclaimed Mavis in outrage.

"No, let him speak," said Father. "What are you saying, Tom? That we cheat? Is that it?"

"Yes," sighed Tom thinking with regret of the sherry trifle. They did a very nice sherry trifle here and he'd been looking forward to it. But he had the feeling that he would be heading for bed without any pudding tonight.

"You'd better explain yourself, I think, Tom," said Trevor in his best senior management voice.

Tom pushed his plate away, saying goodbye to the rest of his roast beef too.

"All right," he said. "Take this dinner. You've got an arrangement with this restaurant, haven't you? They advertise Masterman's on the back of their menu. And the annual cost of that advert just happens to be whatever you spend on entertaining people here over the year. I've heard you boasting about the arrangement, Trev. So the cost of this meal will go down on your books as a tax-deductible advertising expense."

"Aye, that's right," said Father Masterman. "I thought that one up myself when they stopped business entertainment except for foreigners. Nothing wrong with keeping one step ahead of the game, is there, Tom?"

He smiled proudly as he spoke, and lowered his left eyelid in a man-of-the-world's knowing, conspiratorial wink.

"Oh no, nothing wrong," said Tom. "Except that it's a tax fiddle! No. Hear me out. Let's take those building workers you're always complaining of, the ones who are robbing you rotten. How many of them are working on the lump through so called subcontractors that in fact you run yourselves? That way, there's no records to keep, no National Insurance to pay, and you can get away with paying them under the odds, 'cos you know they need the work and they won't be filling in tax returns anyway. In other words you and others like you chicane your way out of paying millions of pounds to the Revenue every year, then you have the cheek to squeal, 'We're paying our taxes, aren't we?' The truth is, no, you're bloody well not! And until you do, you're not entitled to make cracks about an underfunded, overworked public service like the police!"

It must have been building up for some time, the way it gushed out in a swift unstoppable flow.

Some similar process must have been taking place inside Joanna, for suddenly she awoke, opened her eyes and her mouth very wide, said, "Oh dear," then her half-digested dinner gushed out in a swift unstoppable flow also.

Surely this would divert attention, if only temporarily, from his own disruptive outburst!

But no. Not even when Fred's attempt to dodge his sister-in-law's regurgitations sent him tumbling backwards in an explosion of splintering chair did the spotlight move from Tom.

"Now see what you've done!" cried Mavis. "You've ruined everything!"

And Father said, "You must hate us all very much, Tom, to go out of your way to destroy such a happy family occasion."

It was his pulpiteeringly self-righteous tone that finished Tom off.

"Happy family?" he cried. "Take a look at them. A limp dick, a fall-about drunk, a shambling wreck, a smelly mute, and a Michelin tyre advert! Charles Manson had a happier family than this!"

He headed for the door.

Mavis caught up with him as he paused to take in a deep breath of car park air.

He was already regretting the Michelin tyre crack. Nothing else, not yet. But that had been unforgivable.

He was right. She wasn't about to forgive him.

She said, "You bastard. That's it. I won't be home tonight. And when I do come, I don't want to find you there. I want you out, do you understand? Out! Or I'll get Daddy's solicitor to throw you out!"

She could do it too. The house, a Masterman "Georgian" villa, had been her father's wedding present and it was registered in her sole name.

He should have held out at the start, insisting that he didn't want a house he hadn't paid for. But he'd loved her too much then to believe it could be a problem. Loved her too much now to believe she meant what she was saying.

He said, "Mavis, I'm—" but was prevented from further explanation or apology by a round arm blow that sent him reeling.

She really was putting on weight. Last time she'd hit him she hadn't got punching power like this!

He wiped the blood off his lip and drove home.

There he sat and slowly worked his way down a bottle of Scotch which seemed to have lost its anaesthetising power. Eventually the bottom came in sight, but he was still cold sober.

He knew this because when the phone rang he had no difficulty in getting up and going to answer it.

"Hello?"

"Tom? Missendon here. Listen, I was just driving home from a speaking engagement when I caught a shout on my car radio that there was a barney at the Dog and Duck. It sounded serious."

Tom glanced at his watch. It was after midnight. It must have sounded very serious for the Chief Super to let a pub brawl keep him from his pit.

"You still there, Tom?"

"Yes sir."

"Well, listen, you'll love this. You know what was going on at the Dog? A private party to celebrate the release from custody of your old chum, Chuck Orgill. There's been a ruckus. And there's been some serious injuries, maybe worse. I'm on my way there now, and I thought, seeing who it is, you might like to join me."

Orgill. Where all this had started.

"Yes sir," said Tom. "Thank you, sir."

He climbed into his car and found he was still carrying the whisky bottle. Carefully he laid it on the passenger seat. Was he fit to drive? Legally, of course not. But he felt he could have walked a high wire with no problem. He started up.

There were lots of police cars round the Dog and Duck. Lots of people too, despite the hour. An ambulance came belling out of the forecourt and there was another one gently pulsating by the main door.

"Tom. There you are."

Missendon came towards him, smiling. He was still wearing his dinner jacket and looked like a head waiter welcoming a high-tipping diner.

Tom said, "Hello sir. What's the score?"

"One dead, two critical, four or five badly cut, a lot more gently bleeding. About par for the course when you let a mob like this loose among the bubbly."

"And Orgill?"

"The guest of honour? He's inside getting a couple of stitches in his face. He keeps shouting he wants to get off to the hospital but there's no way he's going out of my reach till I'm done with him."

"So who's dead?"

"Orgill's cousin, Jeff."

Tom whistled and said, "Someone's done us a favour, then. What happened?"

"Power struggle, from the sound of it. You know Jeff's been the heir apparent in the Orgill family for a long time. And when it looked like Chuck was going down for a stretch, he must have reckoned his hour had come. But little Miss Muffet changed all that. My reading is that once the booze loosened him up, he couldn't hide that he was less than happy to be welcoming Chuck back. Perhaps he even suggested that it was time for a change in the pecking order. Only he got pecked."

"By Chuck, you reckon? Now that would be nice. Got any witnesses?"

"Don't be silly, Tom," said Missendon. "In the first excitement, the barman rattled on about the two cousins having a bit of a barney, then all hell breaking loose. But once he had a chance to remember who he was talking about, he went amnesiac. The rest'll be the same, no matter whose side they were fighting on. There's only one boss now, and no one's going to risk crossing him."

As he spoke he led the way into the pub. Through the saloon door Tom saw a mixed bunch of men and women, most of them walking wounded, accompanied by half a dozen policemen noting names and addresses. Then Missendon ushered him into the public bar and he didn't need to ask where the fight had taken place. There was literally blood on the walls and the room was in such a state of chaos that amidst the confusion of broken glass and shattered furniture it took the eye a few moments to pick out the one piece of human wreckage.

"Stabbed?" said Tom approaching carefully to avoid treading on the blood which had gushed copiously out of the dead man's wounds.

"Three times by the look of it, maybe more. I just let the doc close enough to confirm death. I don't want anything moved in here till Forensic have gone over it with a fine-tooth comb."

"What're you hoping for?"

"Anything that will put Orgill in the dock for murder. He slipped away this morning, Tom. He's not going to do it again."

"It's going to be hard without witnesses," said Tom. "The kind of ruck that obviously went on here, it could have been anyone."

"You sound like Miss bloody Muffet. Look, there's a knife over there. Obviously got chucked when the first of our boys arrived. Could be the weapon. It'd be handy if it had Chuck's dabs on it. There's blood on Jeff's hand. With luck it'll match Chuck's that spurted out when Jeff shoved a glass in his face. And I've got Chuck's shirt. Covered in blood. I bet it'll turn out to be Jeff's group."

It was an empty optimism, thought Tom, because even if justified, what did it prove? For a start Chuck Orgill was blood group "O," the commonest. He knew this because he knew everything about the man. And chances were that Jeff was "O" or "A" like 90 per cent of the population. He could hear Sylvie Morphet's insidiously persuasive voice.

"How many people received injuries during this fracas, Inspector? Fifteen? Twenty? More? So there was a lot of blood around. And how many of those bleeding were groups 'A' or 'O'? *That* many? In which case how can you be certain . . ."

And so on.

"What's up son? You don't look happy," said Missendon sharply. "Spit it out. What's on your mind?"

"I was thinking you're clutching at straws, sir," said Tom baldly. "If the blood's all you've got to pin this on Orgill, Miss Muffet will have us dancing the polka. You'll need something a lot stronger than that to make this a runner."

"You think so, do you?" exclaimed Missendon angrily. "What's up, Tom? Miss Muffet got you scared?"

"You'd better believe it," said Tom. "Hello. What have we here?"

He squatted down close to the body and peered at the floor.

"What's up? You got something?"

"That shirt of Orgill's. Is there a button missing?"

Missendon joined him and peered down. About eighteen inches from the corpse's outstretched hand was a small mother-of-pearl button with thread and some fragments of cloth still attached, as though it had been forcibly ripped from its place.

"Hold on," said Missendon excitedly. "I'll take a look."

He left the room and returned a few seconds later with a sealed plastic evidence bag. Carefully, without opening the bag, he shook out the blood-stained shirt it contained.

"Tom, you're a genius," he said squatting down and displaying the garment.

The buttons were mother-of-pearl and the third one down in the shirt front had been ripped off.

"Now that could be the clincher," said Missendon. "Happy now?"

"It'll help," agreed Tom, rising. "But it's just another pointer. How many more buttons and bits of cloth do you think Forensic will find in this lot when they start looking? Now if it had been in Jeff's hand . . ."

"But it was," said Missendon in a surprised tone. "Don't you remember? Look."

He too stood up and stepped aside. Tom looked down at the corpse.

Almost concealed in the curled fingers of the outstretched right hand was the mother-of-pearl button.

"Grabbed the shirt as Orgill stabbed him, fell back and tore the button loose," said Missendon. "Even Forensic can't miss that."

"No, it was on the floor," said Tom stupidly.

"That's right. Jeff was on the floor and the button was in his hand," said Missendon. "You remember now, don't you?"

He was smiling, and as Tom met his gaze one eyelid dropped in a knowing, conspiratorial wink.

"You do remember, Tom, don't you?" repeated Missendon.

Tom didn't reply.

He thought of Orgill who, if there were justice in the world, should to-night have been starting a ten stretch.

He thought of Sylvie Morphet's secret smile, mocking his claim to be able to exist in a world of complete truthfulness.

He thought of the Mastermans' dinner and his ruined marriage.

He said, "No."

"Sorry?"

"No. I can't do that. I can't go along with a lie."

Missendon's face set hard as iron.

"What are you saying, Inspector?"

"I'm saying that, if asked, I'll tell the truth about where I found the button."

"Then it's just as well you never found it, isn't it? It's just as well you've no standing here. It's just as well you're going home now and your name's going to appear nowhere in this investigation. You've been working too hard, Tom. You've managed to cock up one case today from not being up to scratch . . ."

"That's bloody rubbish and you know it!" snarled Tom.

"Rubbish?" Missendon stepped up close to Tom and sniffed. "You've been drinking. Thought you must have had something to make you speak to me like that. How much have you had?"

"A bottle, but I'm not . . ."

"A bottle!" Missendon was genuinely amazed. "And you drove out here? Have you gone off your trolley or what? No wonder you don't know what you're doing. Now listen to this. You go near your car and I'll have you arrested, so help me God. I'll get someone to drive you home. And you can stay at home. Sick leave, till further notice, you understand me, Inspector?"

"Oh yes," said Tom. "I understand. But you'd better understand me, sir. If I'm asked . . ."

"If you're asked?" yelled Missendon. "Who the bloody hell's going to ask you anything?"

"I am!" cried Tom. "I am."

• • •

IT was ten to two by the old wall clock when Tom walked into the dining-room of the Green Tree.

Sylvie Morphet was at the same table, talking earnestly with Slime. Tom had no trouble guessing what they were talking about.

He approached and stood by the table till they looked up at him—the solicitor in surprise, the woman with that expression of secret amusement which was both irritating and beguiling.

"Inspector Tyler, you look tired," she said. "Burning the midnight oil in pursuit of justice, perhaps?"

"Something like that."

"But not very like it," she chided. "Mr. Lime's been telling me you've got poor Mr. Orgill banged up again. You don't waste time, do you?"

"Don't I?" he said. "Look, sorry to interrupt, but you did say two o'clock."

She looked puzzled, then smiled and said, "Of course. Excuse us, Mr. Lime, a little private wager. No, no need to go. It won't take a minute. Well, Inspector, how did it go? Have you come to tell me you've won and want to claim your prize?"

In fact, he didn't know why he had come, except that when he woke up, out of all the confusion of a life which seemed as complete a wreck as that bloodstained room in the Dog and Duck, only this appointment at two o'clock had remained as something solid to cling on to.

She was looking up at him expectantly, green eyes glinting like raindrops on spring foliage. Little white teeth gleaming behind soft red lips parted in a sympathetic smile, one blue-veined eyelid dropping in a knowing, con-spiratorial wink . . .

It came to him then that he had seen that expression before.

So Orgill had looked in his triumph at beating the rap. So Masterman had looked as he boasted of his tax fiddle. So Missendon had looked as he invited complicity in fixing the evidence.

Now here it was again, the same look, the same wink, on the face of the Queen of Elfland . . .

That was it! It came as no surprise. He'd known it all his adult life. These three—and God knows how many more like them—actually belonged to-gether, not in the ordinary workday human world, but in another shadowy country of hazy boundaries and shifting sands and swirling mists above rivers that ran red with blood . . .

And what did that make him?

Simple. He was a stranger in Elfland, and if he spoke out of turn, he might stay here for ever.

"Well?" she urged. "Did you win?"

He laughed and shook his head. He didn't know much, but he knew there was no way a mere human won bets with the Queen of Elfland.

"Don't be silly," he said easily. "Of course I didn't win. No chance. You always knew that. Now if you'll excuse me, I've got to go and meet my wife."

Oddly, that wasn't a lie. At least he hoped it wasn't.

The way he saw it was that by now Mavis would have had an evening of Tom-bashing with the whole family, carried on the good work over breakfast with her parents, sunk into soul-searching soliloquy during morning coffee with her silent sister, and was probably at this very moment having her future spelled out during the course of a long lunch with Trevor—on the firm, of course.

Now that, by the most conservative estimate, ought to be exposure enough. For Tom Tyler knew his wife's darkest secret.

Too much contact with her family got right up her nose. This was why the VSDs had to be so very perfect, to ease her guilt at neglecting them the rest of the time!

She would never admit it, of course, at least not more than the odd hint in those confidentially languorous moments which followed their lovemaking. But Tom felt sure that by the time lunch was over, Mavis would have had enough, and she'd make an excuse about needing to collect something, and head for home to get some time to herself.

Well, she was going to be out of luck. Or in it, depending how you looked at things. He would go a long way towards mending his bridges with the family. Not as far as working for them, no way! But a long way. And if she wanted evidence that he still loved her and found her irresistibly attractive, he didn't doubt he could supply testimony that would stand up to any examination.

As he reached the door, the clock began to strike two.

It occurred to him that this meant his lie about losing had fallen within the twenty-four hours, which meant he really had lost . . .

Except if he really had lost, then it wasn't a lie . . .

Which meant . . .

He shook his head ferociously. This was Elfland logic. He had done with all that.

Boldly he stepped out of the shadows of the Green Tree into the bright winter sunlight which had replaced yesterday's mists, and headed homeward to start reassembling the fragments of his truth-wrecked life.

MARKHEIM

Robert Louis Stevenson

"Yes," said the dealer, "our windfalls are of various kinds. Some customers are ignorant, and then I touch a dividend on my superior knowledge. Some are dishonest," and here he held up the candle, so that the light fell strongly on his visitor, "and in that case," he continued, "I profit by my virtue."

Markheim had but just entered from the daylight streets, and his eyes had not yet grown familiar with the mingled shine and darkness in the shop. At these pointed words, and before the near presence of the flame, he blinked painfully and looked aside.

The dealer chuckled. "You come to me on Christmas Day," he resumed, "when you know that I am alone in my house, put up my shutters, and make a point of refusing business. Well, you will have to pay for that; you will have to pay for my loss of time, when I should be balancing my books; you will have to pay, besides, for a kind of manner that I remark in you today very strongly. I am the essence of discretion, and ask no awkward questions; but when a customer cannot look me in the eye, he has to pay for it." The dealer once more chuckled; and then, changing to his usual business voice, though still with a note of irony, "You can give, as usual, a clear account of how you came into the possession of the object?" he continued. "Still your uncle's cabinet? A remarkable collector, sir!"

And the little, pale, round-shouldered dealer stood almost on tip-toe, looking over the top of his gold spectacles, and nodding his head with every mark of disbelief. Markheim returned his gaze with one of infinite pity, and a touch of horror.

"This time," said he, "you are in error. I have not come to sell, but to buy. I have no curios to dispose of; my uncle's cabinet is bare to the wainscot; even were it still intact, I have done well on the Stock Exchange, and should more likely add to it than otherwise, and my errand to-day is simplicity itself. I seek a Christmas present for a lady," he continued, waxing more fluent as he struck into the speech he had prepared; "and certainly I owe you every excuse for thus disturbing you upon so small a matter. But the thing was neglected yesterday; I must produce my little compliment at dinner; and, as you very well know, a rich marriage is not a thing to be neglected."

There followed a pause, during which the dealer seemed to weigh this statement incredulously. The ticking of many clocks among the curious lumber of the shop, and the faint rushing of the cabs in a near thoroughfare, filled up the interval of silence.

"Well, sir," said the dealer, "be it so. You are an old customer after all; and if, as you say, you have the chance of a good marriage, far be it from me to be an obstacle. Here is a nice thing for a lady now," he went on, "this hand glass—fifteenth century, warranted; comes from a good collection, too; but I reserve the name, in the interests of my customer, who was just like yourself, my dear sir, the nephew and sole heir of a remarkable collector."

The dealer, while he thus ran on in his dry and biting voice, had stooped to take the object from its place; and, as he had done so, a shock had passed through Markheim, a start both of hand and foot, a sudden leap of many tumultuous passions to the face. It passed as swiftly as it came, and left no trace beyond a certain trembling of the hand that now received the glass.

"A glass," he said hoarsely, and then paused, and repeated it more clearly. "A glass? For Christmas? Surely not?"

"And why not?" cried the dealer. "Why not a glass?"

Markheim was looking upon him with an indefinable expression. "You ask me why not?" he said. "Why, look here—look in it—look at yourself! Do you like to see it? No! nor I—nor any man."

The little man had jumped back when Markheim had so suddenly confronted him with the mirror; but now, perceiving there was nothing worse on hand, he chuckled. "Your future lady, sir, must be pretty hard favoured," said he.

"I ask you," said Markheim, "for a Christmas present, and you give me this—this damned reminder of years, and sins and follies—this hand-conscience! Did you mean it? Had you a thought in your mind? Tell me. It will be better for you if you do. Come, tell me about yourself. I hazard a guess now, that you are in secret a very charitable man?"

The dealer looked closely at his companion. It was very odd, Markheim did not appear to be laughing; there was something in his face like an eager sparkle of hope, but nothing of mirth.

"What are you driving at?" the dealer asked.

"Not charitable?" returned the other, gloomily. "Not charitable; not pious; not scrupulous; unloving, unbeloved; a hand to get money, a safe to keep it. Is that all? Dear God, man, is that all?"

"I will tell you what it is," began the dealer, with some sharpness, and then broke off again into a chuckle. "But I see this is a love match of yours, and you have been drinking the lady's health."

"Ah!" cried Markheim, with a strange curiosity. "Ah, have you been in love? Tell me about that."

"I," cried the dealer. "I in love! I never had the time, nor have I the time to-day for all this nonsense. Will you take the glass?"

"Where is the hurry?" returned Markheim. "It is very pleasant to stand here talking; and life is so short and insecure that I would not hurry away from any pleasure—no, not even from so mild a one as this. We should rather cling, cling to what little we can get, like a man at a cliff's edge. Every second is a cliff, if you think upon it—a cliff a mile high—high enough, if we fall, to dash us out of every feature of humanity. Hence it is best to talk pleasantly. Let us talk of each other: why should we wear this mask? Let us be confidential. Who knows, we might become friends?"

"I have just one word to say to you," said the dealer. "Either make your purchase, or walk out of my shop!"

"True, true," said Markheim. "Enough fooling. To business. Show me something else."

The dealer stooped once more, this time to replace the glass upon the shelf, his thin blond hair falling over his eyes as he did so. Markheim moved a little nearer, with one hand in the pocket of his greatcoat; he drew himself up and filled his lungs; at the same time many different emotions were depicted together on his face—terror, horror, and resolve, fascination and a physical repulsion; and through a haggard lift of his upper lip, his teeth looked out.

"This, perhaps, may suit," observed the dealer: and then, as he began to re-arise, Markheim bounded from behind upon his victim. The long, skewerlike dagger flashed and fell. The dealer struggled like a hen, striking his temple on the shelf, and then tumbled on the floor in a heap.

Time had some score of small voices in that shop, some stately and slow as was becoming to their great age; others garrulous and hurried. All these told out the seconds in an intricate chorus of tickings. Then the passage of a lad's feet, heavily running on the pavement, broke in upon these smaller voices and startled Markheim into the consciousness of his surroundings. He looked about him awfully. The candle stood on the counter, its flame solemnly wagging in a draught; and by that inconsiderable movement, the whole room was filled with noiseless bustle and kept heaving like a sea: the tall shadows nodding, the gross blots of darkness swelling and dwindling as with respiration, the faces of the portraits and the china gods changing and wavering like images in water. The inner door stood ajar, and peered into that leaguer of shadows with a long slit of daylight like a pointing finger.

From these fear-stricken rovings, Markheim's eyes returned to the body of his victim, where it lay both humped and sprawling, incredibly small and strangely meaner than in life. In these poor, miserly clothes, in that ungainly attitude, the dealer lay like so much sawdust. Markheim had feared to see it, and, lo! it was nothing. And yet, as he gazed, this bundle of old clothes and pool of blood began to find eloquent voices. There it must lie; there was none to work the cunning hinges or direct the miracle of locomotion— there it must lie till it was found. Found! ay, and then? Then would this dead flesh lift up a cry that would ring over England, and fill the world with the echoes of pursuit. Ay, dead or not, this was still the enemy. "Time was that when the brains were out," he thought; and the first word struck into his mind. Time, now that the deed was accomplished—time, which had closed for the victim, had become instant and momentous for the slayer.

The thought was yet in his mind, when, first one and then another, with every variety of pace and voice—one deep as the bell from a cathedral turret, another ringing on its treble notes the prelude of a waltz—the clocks began to strike the hour of three in the afternoon.

The sudden outbreak of so many tongues in that dumb chamber staggered him. He began to bestir himself, going to and fro with the candle, beleaguered by moving shadows, and startled to the soul by chance reflections. In many rich mirrors, some of home design, some from Venice or Amsterdam, he saw his face repeated and repeated, as it were an army of spies; his own eyes met and detected him; and the sound of his own steps, lightly as they fell, vexed the surrounding quiet. And still, as he continued to fill his pockets, his mind accused him with a sickening iteration, of the thousand faults of his design. He should have chosen a more quiet hour; he should have prepared an alibi; he should not have used a knife; he should have been more cautious, and only bound and gagged the dealer, and not killed him; he should have been more bold, and killed the servant also; he should have done all things otherwise: poignant regrets, weary, incessant toiling of the mind to change what was unchangeable, to plan what was now useless, to be the architect of the irrevocable past. Meanwhile, and behind all this activity, brute terrors, like the scurrying of rats in a deserted attic, filled the more remote chambers of his brain with riot; the hand of the constable would fall heavy on his shoulder, and his nerves would jerk like a hooked fish; or he beheld, in galloping defile, the dock, the prison, the gallows, and the black coffin.

Terror of the people in the street sat down before his mind like a be-sieging army. It was impossible, he thought, but that some rumour of the struggle must have reached their ears and set on edge their curiosity; and now, in all the neighbouring houses, he divined them sitting motionless and with uplifted ear—solitary people, condemned to spend Christmas dwelling alone on memories of the past, and now startingly recalled from that tender exercise; happy family parties, struck into silence round the table, the mother still with raised finger: every degree and age and humour, but all, by their own hearths, prying and hearkening and weaving the rope that was to hang him. Sometimes it seemed to him he could not move too softly; the clink of the tall Bohemian goblets rang out loudly like a bell; and alarmed by the bigness of the ticking, he was tempted to stop the clocks. And then, again, with a swift transition of his terrors, the very silence of the place appeared a source of peril, and a thing to strike and freeze the passer-by; and he would step more boldly, and bustle aloud among the contents of the shop, and imitate with elaborate bravado, the movements of a busy man at ease in his own house.

But he was now so pulled about by different alarms that, while one por-tion of his mind was still alert and cunning, another trembled on the brink of lunacy. One hallucination in particular took a strong hold on his cre-dulity. The neighbour, hearkening with white face beside his window, the passer-by arrested by a horrible surmise on the pavement—these could at worst suspect, they could not know; through the brick walls and shuttered windows only sounds could penetrate. But here, within the house, was he alone? He knew he was; he had watched the servant set forth sweet-hearting, in her poor best, "out for the day" written in every ribbon and smile. Yes, he was alone, of course; and yet, in the bulk of empty house above him, he could surely hear a stir of delicate footing—he was surely conscious, inex-plicably conscious of some presence. Ay, surely; to every room and corner of the house his imagination followed it; and now it was a faceless thing, and yet had eyes to see with; and again it was a shadow of himself; and yet again behold the image of the dead dealer, reinspired with cunning and hatred.

At times, with a strong effort, he would glance at the open door which still seemed to repel his eyes. The house was tall, the skylight small and dirty, the day blind with fog; and the light that filtered down to the ground storey was exceedingly faint, and showed dimly on the threshold of the shop. And yet, in that strip of doubtful brightness, did there not hang wavering a shadow?

Suddenly, from the street outside, a very jovial gentleman began to beat with a staff on the shop-door, accompanying his blows with shouts and railleries in which the dealer was continually called upon by name. Markheim, smitten into ice, glanced at the dead man. But no! he lay quite still; he was fled away far beyond earshot of these blows and shoutings; he was sunk beneath seas of silence; and his name, which would once have caught his notice above the howling of a storm, had become an empty sound. And presently the jovial gentleman desisted from his knocking and departed.

Here was a broad hint to hurry what remained to be done, to get forth from this accusing neighbourhood, to plunge into a bath of London multitudes, and to reach, on the other side of day, that haven of safety and apparent innocence—his bed. One visitor had come: at any moment another might follow and be more obstinate. To have done the deed, and yet not to reap the profit, would be too abhorrent a failure. The money, that was now Markheim's concern; and as a means to that, the keys.

He glanced over his shoulder at the open door, where the shadow was still lingering and shivering; and with no conscious repugnance of the mind, yet with a tremor of the belly, he drew near the body of his victim. The human character had quite departed. Like a suit half-stuffed with bran, the limbs lay scattered, the trunk doubled, on the floor; and yet the thing repelled him. Although so dingy and inconsiderable to the eye, he feared it might have more significance to the touch. He took the body by the shoulders, and turned it on its back. It was strangely light and supple, and the limbs, as if they had been broken, fell into the oddest postures. The face was robbed of all expression; but it was as pale as wax, and shockingly smeared with blood about one temple. That was, for Markheim, the one displeasing circumstance. It carried him back, upon the instant, to a certain fair-day in a fishers' village: a grey day, a piping wind, a crowd upon the street, the blare of brasses, the booming of drums, the nasal voice of a ballad singer; and a boy going to and fro, buried over head in the crowd and divided between interest and fear, until, coming out upon the chief place of concourse, he beheld a booth and a great screen with pictures, dismally designed, garishly coloured: Brownrigg with her apprentice; the Mannings with their murdered guest; Weare in the death-grip of Thurtell; and a score besides of famous crimes. The thing was as clear as an illusion; he was once again that little boy; he was looking once again, and with the same sense of physical revolt, at these vile pictures; he was still stunned by the thumping of the drums. A bar of that day's music returned upon his memory; and at that, for the first time, a qualm came over him, a breath of nausea, a sudden weakness of the joints, which he must instantly resist and conquer.

He judged it more prudent to confront than to flee from these considerations; looking the more hardily in the dead face, bending his mind to realise the nature and greatness of his crime. So little a while ago that face had moved with every change of sentiment, that pale mouth had spoken, that body had been all on fire with governable energies; and now, and by his act, that piece of life had been arrested, as the horologist, with interjected finger, arrests the beating of the clock. So he reasoned in vain; he could rise to no more remorseful consciousness; the same heart which had shuddered before the painted effigies of crime, looked on its reality unmoved. At best, he felt a gleam of pity for one who had been endowed in vain with all those faculties that can make the world a garden of enchantment, one who had never lived and who was now dead. But of penitence, no, not a tremor.

With that, shaking himself clear of these considerations, he found the keys and advanced towards the open door of the shop. Outside, it had begun to rain smartly; and the sound of the shower upon the roof had banished silence. Like some dripping cavern, the chambers of the house were haunted by an incessant echoing, which filled the ear and mingled with the ticking of the clocks. And, as Markheim approached the door, he seemed to hear, in answer to his own cautious tread, steps of another foot withdrawing up the stair. The shadow still palpitated loosely on the threshold. He threw a ton's weight of resolve upon his muscles, and drew back the door.

The faint, foggy daylight glimmered dimly on the bare floor and stairs; on the bright suit of armour posted, halbert in hand, upon the landing; and on the dark wood-carvings, and framed pictures that hung against the yellow panels of the wainscot. So loud was the beating of the rain through all the house that, in Markheim's ears, it began to be distinguished into many different sounds. Footsteps and sighs, the tread of regiments marching in the distance, the chink of money in the counting, and the creaking of doors held stealthily ajar, appeared to mingle with the patter of the drops upon the cupola and the gushing of the water in the pipes. The sense that he was not alone grew upon him to the verge of madness. On every side he was haunted and begirt by presences. He heard them moving in the upper chambers; from the shop, he heard the dead man getting to his legs; and as he began with a great effort to mount the stairs, feet fled quietly before him and followed stealthily behind. If he were but deaf, he thought, how tranquilly he would possess his soul! And then again, and hearkening with ever fresh attention, he blessed himself for that unresting sense which held the outposts and stood a trusty sentinel upon his life. His head turned continually on his neck; his eyes, which seemed starting from their orbits, scouted on every side, and on every side were half-rewarded as with the tail of something nameless vanishing. The four-and-twenty steps to the first floor were four-and-twenty agonies.

On that first storey, the doors stood ajar, three of them like three ambushes, shaking his nerves like the throats of cannon. He could never again, he felt, be sufficiently immured and fortified from men's observing eyes; he longed to be home, girt in by walls, buried among bedclothes, and invisible to all but God. And at that thought he wondered a little, recollecting tales of other murderers and the fear they were said to entertain of heavenly avengers. It was not so, at least, with him. He feared the laws of nature, lest, in their callous and immutable procedure, they should preserve some damning evidence of his crime. He feared tenfold more, with a slavish, superstitious terror, some scission in the continuity of man's experience, some wilful illegality of nature. He played a game of skill, depending on the rules, calculating consequence from cause; and what if nature, as the defeated tyrant overthrew the chess-board, should break the mould of their succession? The like had befallen Napoleon (so writers said) when the winter changed the time of its appearance. The like might befall Markheim: the solid walls might become transparent and reveal his doings like those of bees in a glass hive; the stout planks might yield under his foot like quicksands and detain him in their clutch; ay, and there were soberer accidents that might destroy him: if, for instance, the house should fall and imprison him beside the body of his victim; or the house next door should fly on fire, and the firemen invade him from all sides. These things he feared; and, in a sense, these things might be called the hands of God reached forth against sin. But about God Himself he was at ease; his act was doubtless exceptional, but so were his excuses, which God knew; it was there, and not among men, that he felt sure of justice.

When he had got safe into the drawing-room, and shut the door behind him, he was aware of a respite from alarms. The room was quite dismantled, uncarpeted besides, and strewn with packing cases, and incongruous furniture; several great pier-glasses, in which he beheld himself at various angles, like an actor on a stage; many pictures, framed and unframed, standing, with their faces to the wall; a fine Sheraton sideboard, a cabinet of marquetry, and a great old bed, with tapestry hangings. The windows opened to the floor; but by great good fortune the lower part of the shutters had been closed, and this concealed him from the neighbours. Here, then, Markheim drew in a packing case before the cabinet, and began to search among the keys. It was a long business, for there were many; and it was irksome, besides; for, after all, there might be nothing in the cabinet, and time was on the wing. But the closeness of the occupation sobered him. With the tail of his eye he saw the door—even glanced at it from time to time directly, like a besieged commander pleased to verify the good estate of his defenses. But in truth he was at peace. The rain falling in the street sounded natural and pleasant. Presently, on the other side, the notes of a piano were wakened to the music of a hymn, and the voices of many children took up the air and words. How stately, how comfortable was the melody! How fresh the youthful voices! Markheim gave ear to it smilingly, as he sorted out the keys; and his mind was thronged with answerable ideas and images; church-going children and the pealing of the high organ; children afield, bathers by the brookside, ramblers on the brambly common, kite-flyers in the windy and cloud-navigated sky; and then, at another cadence of the hymn, back again to church, and the somnolence of summer Sundays, and the high genteel voice of the parson (which he smiled a little to recall) and the painted Jacobean tombs, and the dim lettering of the Ten Commandments in the chancel.

And as he sat thus, at once busy and absent, he was startled to his feet. A flash of ice, a flash of fire, a bursting gush of blood, went over him, and then he stood transfixed and thrilling. A step mounted the stair slowly and steadily, and presently a hand was laid upon the knob, and the lock clicked, and the door opened.

Fear held Markheim in a vice. What to expect he knew not, whether the dead man walking, or the official ministers of human justice, or some chance witness blindly stumbling in to consign him to the gallows. But when a face was thrust into the aperture, glanced round the room, looked at him, nodded and smiled as if in friendly recognition, and then withdrew again, and the door closed behind it, his fear broke loose from his control in a hoarse cry. At the sound of this the visitant returned.

"Did you call me?" he asked, pleasantly, and with that he entered the room and closed the door behind him.

Markheim stood and gazed at him with all his eyes. Perhaps there was a film upon his sight, but the outlines of the newcomer seemed to change and waver like those of the idols in the wavering candlelight of the shop; and at times he thought he knew him; and at times he thought he bore a likeness to himself; and always, like a lump of living terror, there lay in his bosom the conviction that this thing was not of the earth and not of God.

And yet the creature had a strange air of the commonplace, as he stood looking on Markheim with a smile; and when he added: "You are looking for the money, I believe?" it was in the tones of everyday politeness.

Markheim made no answer.

"I should warn you," resumed the other, "that the maid has left her sweet-heart earlier than usual and will soon be here. If Mr. Markheim be found in this house, I need not describe to him the consequences."

"You know me?" cried the murderer.

The visitor smiled. "You have long been a favourite of mine," he said; "and I have long observed and often sought to help you."

"What are you?" cried Markheim: "the devil?"

"What I may be," returned the other, "cannot affect the service I propose to render you."

"It can," cried Markheim; "it does! Be helped by you? No, never; not by you! You do not know me yet; thank God, you do not know me!"

"I know you," replied the visitant, with a sort of kind severity or rather firmness. "I know you to the soul."

"Know me!" cried Markheim. "Who can do so? My life is but a travesty and slander on myself. I have lived to belie my nature. All men do; all men are better than this disguise that grows about and stifles them. You see each dragged away by life, like one whom bravos have seized and muffled in a cloak. If they had their own control—if you could see their faces, they would be altogether different, they would shine out for heroes and saints! I am worse than most; myself is more overlaid; my excuse is known to me and God. But, had I the time, I could disclose myself."

"To me?" inquired the visitant.

"To you before all," returned the murderer. "I supposed you were intel-ligent. I thought—since you exist—you would prove a reader of the heart. And yet you would propose to judge me by my acts! Think of it; my acts! I was born and I have lived in a land of giants; giants have dragged me by the wrists since I was born out of my mother—the giants of circumstance. And you would judge me by my acts! But can you not look within? Can you not understand that evil is hateful to me? Can you not see within me the clear writing of conscience, never blurred by any wilful sophistry, although too often disregarded? Can you not read me for a thing that surely must be common as humanity—the unwilling sinner?"

"All this is very feelingly expressed," was the reply, "but it regards me not. These points of consistency are beyond my province, and I care not in the least by what compulsion you may have been dragged away, so as you are but carried in the right direction. But time flies; the servant delays, looking in the faces of the crowd and at the pictures on the hoardings, but still she keeps moving nearer; and remember, it is as if the gallows itself was striding towards you through the Christmas streets! Shall I help you; I, who know all? Shall I tell you where to find the money?"

"For what price?" asked Markheim.

"I offer you the service for a Christmas gift," returned the other.

Markheim could not refrain from smiling with a kind of bitter triumph. "No," said he, "I will take nothing at your hands; if I were dying of thirst, and it was your hand that put the pitcher to my lips, I should find the courage to refuse. It may be credulous, but I will do nothing to commit myself to evil."

"I have no objection to a death-bed repentance," observed the visitant.

"Because you disbelieve their efficacy!" Markheim cried.

"I do not say so," returned the other; "but I look on these things from a different side, and when the life is done my interest falls. The man has lived to serve me, to spread black looks under colour of religion, or to sow tares in the wheat-field, as you do, in a course of weak compliance with desire. Now that he draws so near to his deliverance, he can add but one act of service—to repent, to die smiling, and thus to build up in confidence and hope the more timorous of my surviving followers. I am not so hard a master. Try me. Accept my help. Please yourself in life as you have done hitherto; please yourself more amply, spread your elbows at the board; and when the night begins to fall and the curtains to be drawn, I tell you, for your greater comfort, that you will find it even easy to compound your quarrel with your conscience, and to make a truckling peace with God. I came but now from such a deathbed, and the room was full of sincere mourners, listening to the man's last words: and when I looked into that face, which had been set as a flint against mercy, I found it smiling with hope."

"And do you, then, suppose me such a creature?" asked Markheim. "Do you think I have no more generous aspirations than to sin, and sin, and sin, and, at the last, sneak into heaven? My heart rises at the thought. Is this, then, your experience of mankind? or is it because you find me with red hands that you presume such baseness? and is this crime of murder indeed so impious as to dry up the very springs of good?"

"Murder is to me no special category," replied the other. "All sins are murder, even as all life is war. I behold your race, like starving mariners on a raft, plucking crusts out of the hands of famine and feeding on each other's lives. I follow sins beyond the moment of their acting; I find in all that the last consequence is death; and to my eyes, the pretty maid who thwarts her mother with such taking graces on a question of a ball, drips no less visibly with human gore than such a murderer as yourself. Do I say that I follow sins? I follow virtues also; they differ not by the thickness of a nail, they are both scythes for the reaping angel of Death. Evil, for which I live, consists not in action but in character. The bad man is dear to me; not the bad act, whose fruits, if we could follow them far enough down the hurtling cataract of the ages, might yet be found more blessed than those of the rarest virtues. And it is not because you have killed a dealer, but because you are Markheim, that I offer to forward your escape."

"I will lay my heart open to you," answered Markheim. "This crime on which you find me is my last. On my way to it I have learned many lessons; itself is a lesson, a momentous lesson. Hitherto I have been driven with revolt to what I would not; I was a bond-slave to poverty, driven and scourged. There are robust virtues that can stand in these temptations; mine was not so: I had a thirst of pleasure. But to-day, and out of this deed, I pluck both warning and riches—both the power and a fresh resolve to be myself. I become in all things a free actor in the world; I begin to see myself all changed, these hands the agents of good, this heart at peace. Something comes over me out of the past; something of what I have dreamed on Sabbath evenings to the sound of the church organ, of what I forecast when I shed tears over noble books, or talked, an innocent child, with my mother. There lies my life; I have wandered a few years, but now I see once more my city of destination."

"You are to use this money on the Stock Exchange, I think?" remarked the visitor; "and there, if I mistake not, you have already lost some thousands?"

"Ah," said Markheim, "but this time I have a sure thing."

"This time, again, you will lose," replied the visitor quietly.

"Ah, but I keep back the half!" cried Markheim.

"That also you will lose," said the other.

The sweat started upon Markheim's brow. "Well, then, what matter?" he exclaimed. "Say it be lost, say I am plunged again in poverty, shall one part of me, and that the worse, continue until the end to override the better? Evil and good run strong in me, haling me both ways. I do not love the one thing, I love all. I can conceive great deeds, renunciations, martyrdoms; and though I be fallen to such a crime as murder, pity is no stranger to my thoughts. I pity the poor; who knows their trials better than myself? I pity and help them; I prize love, I love honest laughter; there is no good thing nor true thing on earth but I love it from my heart. And are my vices only to direct my life, and my virtues to lie without effect, like some passive lumber of the mind? Not so; good, also, is a spring of acts."

But the visitant raised his finger. "For six-and-thirty years that you have been in this world," said he, "through many changes of fortune and varieties of humour, I have watched you steadily fall. Fifteen years ago you would have started at a theft. Three years back you would have blenched at the name of murder. Is there any crime, is there any cruelty or meanness, from which you still recoil?—five years from now I shall detect you in the fact! Downward, downward, lies your way; nor can anything but death avail to stop you."

"It is true," Markheim said huskily, "I have in some degree complied with evil. But it is so with all: the very saints, in the mere exercise of living, grow less dainty, and take on the tone of their surroundings."

"I will propound to you one simple question," said the other; "and as you answer, I shall read to you your moral horoscope. You have grown in many things more lax; possibly you do right to be so; and at any account, it is the same with all men. But granting that, are you in any one particular, however trifling, more difficult to please with your own conduct, or do you go in all things with a looser rein?"

"In any one?" repeated Markheim, with an anguish of consideration. "No," he added, with despair, "in none! I have gone down in all."

"Then," said the visitor, "content yourself with what you are, for you will never change; and the words of your part on this stage are irrevocably written down."

Markheim stood for a long while silent, and indeed it was the visitor who first broke the silence. "That being so," he said, "shall I show you the money?"

"And grace?" cried Markheim.

"Have you not tried it?" returned the other. "Two or three years ago, did I not see you on the platform of revival meetings, and was not your voice the loudest in the hymn?"

"It is true," said Markheim; "and I see clearly what remains for me by way of duty. I thank you for these lessons from my soul; my eyes are opened, and I behold myself at last for what I am."

At this moment, the sharp note of the door-bell rang through the house; and the visitant, as though this were some concerted signal for which he had been waiting, changed at once in his demeanour.

"The maid!" he cried. "She has returned, as I forewarned you, and there is now before you one more difficult passage. Her master, you must say, is ill; you must let her in, with an assured but rather serious countenance—no smiles, no over-acting, and I promise you success! Once the girl is within, and the door closed, the same dexterity that has already rid you of the dealer will relieve you of this last danger in your path. Thenceforward you have the whole evening—the whole night, if needful—to ransack the treasures of the house and to make good your safety. This is help that comes to you with the mask of danger. Up!" he cried; "up, friend; your life hangs trembling in the scales: up, and act!"

Markheim steadily regarded his counsellor. "If I be condemned to evil acts," he said, "there is still one door of freedom open—I can cease from action. If my life be an ill thing, I can lay it down. Though I be, as you say truly, at the beck of every small temptation, I can yet, by one decisive gesture, place myself beyond the reach of all. My love of good is damned to barrenness; it may, and let it be! But I have still my hatred of evil; and from that, to your galling disappointment, you shall see that I can draw both energy and courage."

The features of the visitor began to undergo a wonderful and lovely change: they brightened and softened with a tender triumph, and, even as they brightened, faded and dislimned. But Markheim did not pause to watch or understand the transformation. He opened the door and went downstairs very slowly, thinking to himself. His past went soberly before him; he beheld it as it was, ugly and strenuous like a dream, random as chance-medley—a scene of defeat. Life, as he thus reviewed it, tempted him no longer; but on the further side he perceived a quiet haven for his bark. He paused in the passage, and looked into the shop, where the candle still burned by the dead body. It was strangely silent. Thoughts of the dealer and the bell swarmed into his mind, as he stood gazing. And then the bell once more broke out into impatient clamour.

He confronted the maid upon the threshold with something like a smile. "You had better go for the police," said he: "I have killed your master."

EDWARD D. HOCH

Early in 1990, I was invited to write a story for a Mystery & Suspense issue of the literary quarterly Crosscurrents. I wanted to do a tale that was quite different from my usual efforts, yet still within the broad framework of the detective story. I think I achieved both goals with "The Detective's Wife." After I shamelessly reprinted the story in my own Year's Best anthology, it was reprinted by Ellery Queen's Mystery Magazine and then in Ed Gorman's The Year's 25 Finest Crime and Mystery Stories.

• • •

Though certainly not unknown, this 1958 gem by the late Stanley Ellin has not been reprinted nearly so much as many of his more famous stories. I believe it's one of the two or three best he ever wrote, and I think you'll find it makes a perfect companion piece to the story of mine which I selected. I had a high regard for Stanley's opinion, and I wish he'd been around to read my story when it appeared.

For those familiar with Stanley Ellin only through his short stories, let me direct your attention to The Key to Nicholas Street and The Eighth Circle, two of the very best mystery novels of the 1950s.

THE DETECTIVE'S WIFE

Edward D. Hoch

WHEN THEY WERE first married, before she realized what it would be like having a police detective for a husband, Jenny used to kid with him about his cases. Sometimes when he got home early enough for dinner he'd entertain her with accounts of the latest felonies around town. Most cases were solved by the testimony of eyewitnesses or the tips of informers, but once in a while there was the storybook crime that demanded a certain skill in the science of deduction.

It was these cases, especially, that Roger liked to explore with Jenny. He would go over the facts in careful detail; presenting what clues they'd been able to uncover, giving a brief account of suspects' testimony and alibis, if there were any ties, invariably, he would look at her and say, "You know my methods, Watson. Who is the guilty party?"

She almost never came up with the correct solution, but that didn't seem to matter. It was a game both of them enjoyed. She was Watson to his Holmes, and, "You know my methods, Watson," became their own private joke. Once when he spoke the line in bed during their lovemaking, she broke into a fit of giggles.

That was in the early years, when life was simpler for them both. As they passed into their thirties, still childless, something changed. "There's just more crime these days," Roger told her when she questioned him about his late hours.

"You never tell me about your cases any more."

He sighed and turned away. "What's there to tell about a drug dealer who gets cut up by an Uzi? It's the same thing every day, and I get tired of talking about it."

His words made sense, she knew. Other cops, friends of theirs, had gotten burnt out. It could happen to Roger too.

But there was more. The sex between them wasn't as good or as spontaneous as it had been during those first years. Sometimes she wondered if he had found someone else. She made a special effort to interest herself in his cases, and to act as his Watson once more.

"They can't all be drug killings, Roger," she argued one night. "Tell me something interesting."

"A bartender shot to death on the west side? Is that interesting?"

"Any motive?"

"Robbery, I suppose. It was after closing time when he was alone. The cash register wasn't touched but something might have scared the killer away. Or maybe there was another motive. Some seventeen-year-old kid he refused to serve goes home and gets his father's gun. The victim must have let the killer in, so he probably knew him."

That was in February, during the eighth year of their marriage.

• • •

JENNY worked in the production department of a small advertising agency downtown. Sometimes she had lunch with the other women in the office, but more often she ate a sandwich at her desk. Occasionally, if the weather was nice, she'd venture out on a summer's day to eat her sandwich in a little park across the street where the local utility company sponsored jazz concerts on Fridays. It was here that one of the agency's artists, a bearded young man named Carl, found her on a hot August afternoon. She'd heard he was leaving soon for a better job.

"How you doing, Jenny girl? Enjoying the music?"

"It's a break from the office," she told him with a smile. "I can just take so much of ordering typesetting and engravings and printing."

He sat down beside her on the smooth stone seat. "How's hubby?"

"Roger is fine," she answered defensively. The people at work, especially the men, seemed to treat him with thinly veiled disdain because of his position with the police.

"He catch any bad guys lately?"

"A drug dealer who—"

"What about the serial killer?" Carl asked, unwrapping a candy bar and starting to munch on it. "The one who's been shooting the bartenders."

It was true that three bartenders had been slain since February, at roughly two-month intervals. One paper had spoken of a serial killer, and there was a fear that August might bring a fourth killing. She'd spoken of it to Roger once or twice, but he preferred talking about the small everyday triumphs of his job. "I don't think he's working on that," she answered, though she knew he was in charge of it.

"That's the trouble with cops." He took a bite of his Mr. Smiley Nut Cluster. "They waste their time on unimportant crimes while the big stuff gets by them."

She suddenly felt the need to defend her husband. "Roger says most crimes are solved by informers. Someone like a serial killer acts alone. No one else knows about it, so no one can inform on him."

Carl finished his candy bar and leaned back, letting the music wash over him. Jenny recognized it as an old Duke Ellington tune, one that her father had liked to play when she was growing up. "I'll have to meet Roger sometime," Carl commented. "Why don't you ever bring him around to the office parties?"

"He works a lot of nights," she answered lamely. The truth of the matter was that she tried to keep her two lives separate. Roger wouldn't like the people she worked with, and they would have little respect for him. Many of them were artistic types, who wore torn jeans to work and thought of the police as right-wing oppressors.

"Yeah," Carl said, getting to his feet. "Well, I'll see you back at the office, Jenny girl. Hope you're coming to my party."

She watched him cross the little park and enter the side door of their building. He'd left the crumpled candy wrapper on the ground by their bench twisted into a knot.

• • •

ROGER was moody all through dinner that night. He picked at his food and didn't say much. She tried to ask him about the day's routine, about any new crimes, but he had nothing to contribute. Finally, over coffee, he said, "I was driving around downtown this noon. I passed your building."

"Oh? You should have stopped to see me. We could have had lunch together."

"I did see you, in that little park where they have the jazz concerts. You were with another man."

She had to laugh at this evidence of his jealousy. "That was just Carl, one of our artists. I don't take him too seriously—you shouldn't either."

"When I saw you from the car you looked like you were enjoying each other."

She could see he wasn't joking and this annoyed her. "If he bothers you, take heart. He's leaving in two weeks. He's found a better job in the art department at a printer."

"I was just *asking* for God's sake!"

"What's happening to you? What's happening to *us*? You used to talk about your job, about the cases you worked on. You made it sound like fun, like a game!"

"It isn't a game any more. After so many bodies it stops being a game."

Jenny tried to soothe him. "I just remember how you used to describe a case and give me the clues and let me try to solve it. You called me Watson."

"Yeah, I guess I did." He smiled at the memory.

A few nights later Roger surprised her with his suddenly buoyant spirits. He suggested they go out to dinner and took her to a neighborhood restaurant they'd frequented when they were first married. "I cracked a case today," he told her over drinks. "An interesting one I've been working on all week."

She knew he was going to tell her about it, and she felt a glow of anticipation. It was almost like the old days. "Do you have pictures?" she asked, remembering the large manila envelope he'd brought home earlier.

"Not before dinner. I'll show you back at the house."

"Tell me about it, at least."

"A man reported that his wife had committed suicide, hanged herself from a rafter in the garage."

"Did she leave a note?"

"No, which is one of the reasons we started investigating."

"What was the other reason?"

"Well, her car was outside in the driveway. Death by carbon monoxide is a lot tidier than hanging."

Their food arrived and the conversation shifted to pleasanter topics. She talked about the office, and some of the ad campaigns they were working on. It was the most pleasant dinner they'd enjoyed in months. Home was within walking distance, and the few blocks' stroll on a late summer evening was invigorating. The cool air against Jenny's face reminded her of the coming of autumn.

Back at the house he showed her the eight-by-ten glossies he'd brought from the office. The crime scene photographs were usually in color now, and she was thankful at least that there'd been no blood. The woman's stockinged feet dangled about two feet from the floor, next to an overturned crate of rough wood. "She climbed up on that and put the rope around her neck?"

"Apparently," Roger said with a slight smile. "Come on—you know my methods, Watson."

"First of all, the crate is too flimsy. I can see she's a good-sized woman. More important, in this shot of her from the rear, showing the bottoms of her feet, there are no snags in her stockings. She couldn't have climbed up on that flimsy crate in her stocking feet, adjusted the rope, and then kicked it away, all without getting a run or at least a snag from those wood splinters."

"Go to the head of the class! That's basically what I told her husband, and we had a confession within an hour."

"I'm glad," she whispered into his ear. She was glad he'd caught a murderer and glad he was back to the same old Roger she loved so much.

That night the serial killer struck again.

• • •

THE following evening he was worse than ever. "I told you the games were over and I meant it! My job's on the line now. Four killings of bartenders since February is too much for the city fathers to sit still for. If we don't make quick progress they're taking me off the case, and that means I can say good-bye to my chance of promotion. I'll be lucky if I'm not back giving traffic tickets."

"I didn't see the papers. Tell me about it. Was it like the others, in a restaurant?"

"This one was different. He was shot on his way home from work, around three in the morning. The killer apparently was waiting in an alley next to his apartment house."

"But he was a bartender?"

Roger nodded. "He was helping out at the Platt Street Bowling Lanes. Before that he worked at Max's Party House, the same place as victim number two."

"That might be a lead. Maybe they owed gambling debts to one of the customers. Or maybe someone owed them money. Maybe they were dealing drugs on the side."

"We checked all that out on the others. We'll try again but it doesn't look promising. The latest victim was a fill-in bartender. Granted, when he worked at Max's it was only when they needed extra people for a big party.

Victims two and four probably met, but they hardly knew each other, as near as we can tell."

"How about the other victims?"

"No connection."

"And it wasn't robbery?"

"His wallet wasn't touched."

"Could it be just a coincidence?"

Roger shook his head. "Ballistics says it was the same gun all four times—a nine millimeter automatic pistol."

He was glum for the rest of the night, and she could do nothing to shake him out of it. Finally she asked, "Did they give you any sort of deadline?"

"A week or two. They want some action."

"Maybe I can help."

He only sighed and walked away. As he'd told her earlier, the games were over.

• • •

ROGER didn't attend the office farewell party for Carl. She hadn't really expected that he would, and when she mentioned it he didn't even bother to reply. Most nights she ate alone, knowing it would be nine or ten or later before she saw him. She'd never thought it would be like this, being married to a detective.

The party, at one of downtown's fancier hotels, was a welcome relief. Carl himself hadn't had a drink in two years, since his wife was killed in an auto accident, but that didn't stop the rest of the staff from having a good time. Jenny's boss, the production manager, was a beefy man named Herb who imagined every young woman in the office to be fair game, married or not. At one point he had her pressed into a corner, but he was already too far gone to be a real threat. It was the president of the agency who suggested a bit later that perhaps Jenny could drive Herb home.

"He can't drive himself and I don't want another accident, Jenny. If I help you get him into the car could you take him home? It's less than a mile away."

"Certainly, Mr. Miller." She dreaded the idea, but she could hardly suggest that he call a cab for Herb. Miller didn't like anyone to know about drunken employees.

It wasn't till they were on the way that she remembered she hadn't even said good-bye to Carl.

Herb mumbled and snored all the way home, but he came awake as she brought the car to a stop in front of his apartment building and tried to make a pass without fully realizing who she was. She brushed his hand from her breast and he reached into his pocket for a handkerchief, pulling matches, gum and keys with it.

Jenny ran around to the passenger door and helped him out, retrieving his keys and whatever else she could find. The doorman at the building took charge then, betraying no surprise. Perhaps he'd seen Herb in this condition before.

When she got back to her own house, Roger was in the kitchen preparing a sandwich for himself. "I forgot you were going to be out tonight. How was the party?"

She shrugged, dropped her keys on the table. "The usual. My boss got drunk and I had to drive him home. How's the case coming?"

"It's not. Four murders now and we're no closer to an arrest than we were after the first one. My time is running out. The commissioner wants action before the November election."

"Won't you let me work on it with you?" she asked. "Bring home some of the pictures for me to look at. Remember, I spotted the clue in that hanging case right away."

"There's nothing in the pictures," he insisted. "I've been over them a dozen times."

The following morning she found an excuse to leave the office and do some library research. While there she checked the microfilmed copies of the daily papers and read about each of the earlier killings. There was nothing new, nothing to connect the four men except for their occupation. The second victim had worked exclusively at Max's Party House but the others had moved around, mostly filling in part-time at neighborhood places. The first victim had been the youngest, at twenty-six. The other three were all in their thirties or forties. They lived in different parts of the city and seemed to have been nothing more than passing acquaintances, if that much. Only one had been married at the time of his death. Two of the others were divorced. The youngest victim had never been married.

Was it a random thing she wondered, just killing bartenders? Or had these four been chosen for a reason?

That night Roger seemed more depressed than ever. He'd brought home some of the crime scene photographs but he never took them out of the envelope. He'd spent the entire day interviewing the girlfriends and ex-wives of the victims, and had nothing to show for it. "No girls in common, no jealous lovers."

Finally, just before bedtime, she asked, "Can I look at these pictures?"

"Go ahead. I have to take them back in the morning."

Jenny opened the clasp on the envelope and pulled out a dozen pictures of the various crime scenes. Bodies, four bodies. All shot at fairly close range. The first three were in the barrooms where the men had worked, as they prepared to close up for the night. The fourth was at the mouth of an alley where the killer had waited. One photo showed the cartridge case ejected from the killer's automatic pistol, lying amidst the dirt and trash of the alley.

An empty pack of cigarettes, a torn stub from a nearby movie, the spilled remains of a half-finished container of popcorn, the knotted wrapper off a candy bar, a broken piece of brick—

She went on to the next photo, then quickly turned back to the picture of the alley pavement. Where had she seen a candy wrapper tied in a knot like that? Was it something that people often did, or was it unique?

Then she remembered. Carl had dropped his candy wrapper on the ground that day they'd been listening to the jazz concert on the lunch hour. It was the same brand, Mr. Smiley Nut Cluster, and the wrapper had been twisted and knotted in the same manner.

Of course it proved nothing.

When she slid into bed next to Roger she said, "Those pictures gave me an idea. I want to check on something tomorrow."

"I need all the help I can get. I also need your car in the morning."

"How come?"

"The brakes aren't working on mine. I'll take it in over the weekend."

"You'll have to drop me off at work."

"Can you get home on your own?"

"Sue will give me a ride."

"Fine." He rolled over and was snoring within minutes.

• • •

JENNY searched through the newspaper files for an account of the accident that had killed Carl's wife two years earlier. She'd never heard the details of it, and it had happened before she came to the agency, but something Mr. Miller said—"I don't want another accident"—made her wonder if it might have happened after an office party. It took her a long time to find it, but there it was. Carl's wife had been hit by a truck as she pulled out of the parking lot at Max's Party House shortly after midnight. They'd come to the party in separate cars and he was still inside when it happened. Her blood alcohol level was extremely high at the time, and no charges were placed against the truck driver.

A later article talked about the liability of a place like Max's that continued serving someone who was obviously drunk. There was talk of a lawsuit and the owner stated that he was unable to determine which of the four bartenders on duty had been responsible.

Four bartenders.

Why hadn't they seen it? Why hadn't anyone seen it?

The answer to that was simple enough. They had approached the problem from the opposite direction, through the four victims. Jenny was approaching through Carl, and his dead wife, and the accident, and Max's Party House.

That had to be her next stop. Max's.

What a day for Roger to borrow the car!

Back at the office she arranged to take Sue's little Volvo. "I won't be more than an hour," she promised.

She struck it lucky at Max's Party House. Max himself was there, preparing for a big retirement dinner that evening. "Is this more about that lawsuit?" he asked when she told him what she wanted. "That whole thing was settled last January."

"The newspaper quoted you as saying there were four bartenders working the night of the accident. I want their names."

"Look, the case was settled out of court for a few thousand dollars. The husband's attorney convinced him he couldn't get any more than that. The only reason I paid anything was that she was hit driving out of our parking lot. As for the bartenders, I couldn't tell you if I wanted to. A couple of them were working off the books that night, to avoid paying taxes. It's not unusual in this business."

Jenny opened her purse and took out the list of names. "Just tell me one thing. Are these the four men?"

He glanced at it and then at her. "All right, those are the ones. A couple of them are dead now."

"You don't keep up with the papers. All four of them are dead now."

• • •

JENNY felt a rising excitement all the way home in the car with Sue. She barely heard her friend's chatter as she ran over the facts in her mind. Carl had settled the lawsuit in January, against his wishes, for a figure far less than he thought was justified. A month later, in February, the killings had begun, spaced two months apart in hopes no one would notice the connection right away. They had, of course, by the time of the third one, but then he only had to risk one more.

Four dead—one or more of them the ones who'd been directly responsible for his wife's tragic death. And he'd have gotten away with it if it hadn't been for that knotted candy wrapper dropped to the ground while he waited for the final victim to appear. How had he found out the identity of the four? Probably by getting friendly with the first victim and asking him in some innocent way. That helped explain how he came to be in the bar long after closing. He'd made friends with the first victim, and then killed him when he'd learned the names of the other three.

"Here we are," Sue said, pulling into her driveway. "Home at last. I don't see your car. Roger must be still working."

"He's been working every night lately. Thanks, Sue."

"See you in the morning."

Jenny hurried into the house and got out of her sweaty clothes, silently rehearsing how she'd tell Roger. She slipped into her robe and switched on the television, settling down opposite it without really seeing it.

Roger was very late that night and when he came in she could see that his mood was bad. He unbuckled his holster and tossed the gun onto a chair before he even spoke to her. "What does this mean, Jenny?" he said at last.

"What?" She tried to see what he was holding in his outstretched hand. "What is it?"

"A sealed packet containing an unused condom. I found it under the passenger seat of your car."

"I—"

"Do you have an explanation?"

Her mind was whirling. She could barely recognize this man standing before her. "Roger, let me think—I—"

"Make it good—for whatever it's worth."

"My God, Roger! You can't think I was making love to someone in my car!" Then suddenly it came to her. "Herb, my boss! I told you I drove him home from the party because he was drunk. When he got to his apartment he pulled out his handkerchief and a lot of things came with it. I picked them up but I must have missed this."

"Herb, your boss. Am I supposed to believe that?"

All at once the unfairness of his constant jealousy and suspicion moved her to a fury. "I don't give a damn what you believe!" She ripped open the top of her robe. "Here! Do you want to dust my breasts for fingerprints?"

That was when he slapped her. Hard.

• • •

JENNY slept that night curled up on the sofa, somehow protecting herself from further blows. When she awoke, just after dawn, it was raining. Roger came downstairs a little while later, and walked over to her. "I'm sorry about last night. This case has just got me down. I have to see the commissioner this morning and I've got nothing for him."

She got up, wrapping the robe around her, and started making breakfast. Later, while she was drinking her coffee, he remembered to ask, "Did you think of anything yesterday, about the killings?"

"No," she answered softly, staring straight ahead at the rainstreaked window. "Nothing at all."

YOU CAN'T BE A LITTLE GIRL ALL YOUR LIFE

Stanley Ellin

IT WAS THE silence that woke her. Not suddenly—Tom had pointed out
more than once with a sort of humorous envy that she slept like the dead—
but slowly; drawing her up from a hundred fathoms of sleep so that she lay
just on the surface of consciousness, eyes closed, listening to the familiar
pattern of night sounds around her, wondering where it had been disarranged.

Then she heard the creak of a floorboard—the reassuring creak of a
board under the step of a late-returning husband—and understood. Even
while she was a hundred fathoms under, she must have known that Tom
had come into the room, must have anticipated the click of the bed-light
being switched on, the solid thump of footsteps from bed to closet, from
closet to dresser—the unfailing routine which always culminated with his
leaning over her and whispering, "Asleep?" and her small groan which said
yes, she was asleep but glad he was home, and would he please not stay up
all the rest of the night working at those papers.

So he was in the room now, she knew, but for some reason he was not
going through the accustomed routine, and that was what had awakened
her. Like the time they had the cricket, poor thing; for a week it had relentlessly chirped away the dark hours from some hidden corner of the
house until she'd got used to it. The night it died, or went off to make a

cocoon or whatever crickets do, she'd lain awake for an hour waiting to hear it, and then slept badly after that until she'd got used to living without it.

Poor thing, she thought drowsily, not really caring very much but waiting for the light to go on, the footsteps to move comfortingly between bed and closet. Somehow the thought became a serpent crawling down her spine, winding tight around her chest. *Poor thing*, it said to her, *poor stupid thing—it isn't Tom at all!*

She opened her eyes at the moment the man's gloved hand brutally slammed over her mouth. In that moment she saw the towering shadow of him, heard the sob of breath in his throat, smelled the sour reek of liquor. Then she wildly bit down on the hand that gagged her, her teeth sinking into the glove, grinding at it. He smashed his other fist squarely into her face. She went limp, her head lolling half off the bed. He smashed his fist into her face again.

After that, blackness rushed in on her like a whirlwind.

• • •

SHE looked at the pale balloons hovering under the ceiling and saw with idle interest that they were turning into masks, but with features queerly reversed, mouths on top, eyes below. The masks moved and righted themselves. Became faces. Dr. Vaughn. And Tom. And a woman. Someone with a small white dunce cap perched on her head. A nurse.

The doctor leaned over her, lifted her eyelid with his thumb, and she discovered that her face was one throbbing bruise. He withdrew the thumb and grunted. From long acquaintance she recognized it as a grunt of satisfaction.

He said, "Know who I am, Julie?"

"Yes."

"Know what happened?"

"Yes."

"How do you feel?"

She considered that. "Funny. I mean, far away. And there's a buzzing in my ears."

"That was the needle. After we brought you around you went into a real sweet hysteria, and I gave you a needle. Remember that?"

"No."

"Just as well. Don't let it bother you."

It didn't bother her. What bothered her was not knowing the time. Things were so unreal when you didn't know the time. She tried to turn her head toward the clock on the night-table, and the doctor said, "It's a little after six: Almost sunrise. Probably be the first time you've ever seen it, I'll bet."

She smiled at him as much as her swollen mouth would permit. "Saw it last New Year's," she said.

Tom came around the other side of the bed. He sat down on it and took her hand tightly in his. "Julie," he said. "Julie, Julie, Julie," the words coming out in a rush as if they had been building up in him with explosive force.

She loved him and pitied him for that, and for the way he looked. He looked awful. Haggard, unshaven, his eyes sunk deep in his head, he looked as if he were running on nerve alone. Because of her, she thought unhappily, all because of her.

"I'm sorry," she said.

"Sorry!" He gripped her hand so hard that she winced. "Because some lunatic—some animal—!"

"Oh, please!"

"I know. I know you want to shut it out, darling, but you mustn't yet. Look, Julie, the police have been waiting all night to talk to you. They're sure they can find the man, but they need your help. You'll have to describe him, tell them whatever you can about him. Then you won't even have to think about it again. You understand, don't you?"

"Yes."

"I knew you would."

He started to get up but the doctor said, "No, you stay here with her. I'll tell them on my way out. Have to get along, anyhow—these all-night shifts are hard on an old man." He stood with his hand on the doorknob. "When they find him," he said in a hard voice, "I'd like the pleasure—" and let it go at that, knowing they understood.

• • •

THE big, white-haired man with the rumpled suit was Lieutenant Christensen of the police department. The small, dapper man with the mustache was Mr. Dahl of the district attorney's office. Ordinarily, said Mr. Dahl, he did not take a personal part in criminal investigations, but when it came to—that is, in a case of this kind special measures were called for. Everyone must cooperate fully. Mrs. Barton must cooperate, too. Painful as it might be, she must answer Lieutenant Christensen's questions frankly and without embarrassment. Would she do that?

Julie saw Tom nodding encouragement to her. "Yes," she said.

She watched Lieutenant Christensen draw a notebook and pad from his pocket. His gesture, when he pressed the end of the pen to release its point, made him look as if he were stabbing at an insect.

He said, "First of all, I want you to tell me exactly what happened. Everything you can remember about it."

She told him, and he scribbled away in the notebook, the pen clicking at each stroke.

"What time was that?" he asked.

"I don't know."

"About what time? The closer we can pin it down, the better we can check on alibis. When did you go to bed?"

"At ten thirty."

"And Mr. Barton came home around twelve, so we know it happened between ten thirty and twelve." The lieutenant addressed himself to the notebook, then pursed his lips thoughtfully. "Now for something even more important."

"Yes?"

"Just this. Would you recognize the man if you saw him again?"

She closed her eyes, trying to make form out of that monstrous shadow, but feeling only the nauseous terror of it. "No," she said.

"You don't sound so sure about it."

"But I am."

"How can you be? Yes, I know the room was kind of dark and all that, but you said you were awake after you first heard him come in. That means you had time to get adjusted to the dark. And some light from the streetlamp outside hits your window shade here. You wouldn't see so well under the conditions, maybe, but you'd see something, wouldn't you? I mean, enough to point out the man if you had the chance. Isn't that right?"

She felt uneasily that he was right and she was wrong, but there didn't seem to be anything she could do about it. "Yes," she said, "but it wasn't like that."

Dahl, the man from the district attorney's office, shifted on his feet. "Mrs. Barton," he started to say, but Lieutenant Christensen silenced him with a curt gesture of the hand.

"Now look," the lieutenant said. "Let me put it this way. Suppose we had this man some place where you could see him close up, but he couldn't see you at all. Can you picture that? He'd be right up there in front of you, but he wouldn't even know you were looking at him. Don't you think it would be pretty easy to recognize him then?"

Julie found herself growing desperately anxious to give him the answer he wanted, to see what he wanted her to see; but no matter how hard she tried she could not. She shook her head hopelessly, and Lieutenant Christensen drew a long breath.

"All right," he said, "then is there anything you can tell me about him? How big was he? Tall, short, or medium?"

The shadow towered over her. "Tall. No, I'm not sure. But I think he was."

"White or colored?"

"I don't know."

"About how old?"

"I don't know."

"Anything distinctive about his clothes? Anything you might have taken notice of?"

She started to shake her head again, then suddenly remembered. "Gloves," she said, pleased with herself. "He was wearing gloves."

"Leather or wool?"

"Leather." The sour taste of the leather was in her mouth now. It made her stomach turn over.

Click-click went the pen, and the lieutenant looked up from the notebook expectantly. "Anything else?"

"No."

The lieutenant frowned. "It doesn't add up to very much, does it? I mean, the way you tell it."

"I'm sorry," Julie said, and wondered why she was so ready with that phrase now. What was it that *she* had done to feel sorry about? She felt the tears of self-pity start to rise, and she drew Tom's hand to her breast, turning to look at him for comfort. She was shocked to see that he was regarding her with the same expression that the lieutenant wore.

The other man—Dahl—was saying something to her.

"Mrs. Barton," he said, and again, "Mrs. Barton," until she faced him. "I know how you feel, Mrs. Barton, but what I have to say is terribly important. Will you please listen to me?"

"Yes," she said numbly.

"When I talked to you at one o'clock this morning, Mrs. Barton, you were in a state—well, you do understand that I wasn't trying to badger you then. I was working on your behalf. On behalf of the whole community, in fact."

"I don't remember. I don't remember anything about it."

"I see. But you understand now, don't you? And you do know that there's been a series of these outrages in the community during recent years, and that the administration and the press have put a great deal of pressure—rightly, of course—on my office and on the police department to do something about it?"

Julie let her head fall back on the pillow, and closed her eyes. "Yes," she said. "If you say so."

"I do say so. I also say that we can't do very much unless the injured party—the victim—helps us in every way possible. And why won't she? Why does she so often refuse to identify the criminal or testify against him in cases like this? Because she might face some publicity? Because she might have started off by encouraging the man, and is afraid of what he'd say about her on the witness stand? I don't care what the reason is, that woman is guilty of turning a wild beast loose on her helpless neighbors!

"Look, Mrs. Barton. I'll guarantee that the man who did this has a police record, and the kind of offenses listed on it—well, I wouldn't even want to name them in front of you. There's a dozen people at headquarters right now looking through all such records and when they find the right one it'll lead us straight to him. But after that you're the only one who can help us get rid of him for keeps. I want you to tell me right now that you'll do that for us when the time comes. It's your duty. You can't turn away from it."

"I know. But I didn't see him."

"You saw more than you realize, Mrs. Barton. Now, don't get me wrong, because I'm not saying that you're deliberately holding out, or anything like that. You've had a terrible shock. You want to forget it, get it out of your mind completely. And that's what'll happen, if you let yourself go this way. So, knowing that, and not letting yourself go, do you think you can describe the man more accurately now?"

Maybe she had been wrong about Tom, she thought, about the way he had looked at her. She opened her eyes hopefully and was bitterly sorry she had. His expression of angry bewilderment was unchanged, but now he was leaning forward, staring at her as if he could draw the right answer from her by force of will. And she knew he couldn't. The tears overflowed, and she cried weakly; then magically a tissue was pressed into her hand. She had forgotten the nurse. The upside-down face bent over her from behind the bed, and she was strangely consoled by the sight of it. All these men in the room—even her husband—had been made aliens by what had happened to her. It was good to have a woman there.

"Mrs. Barton!" Dahl's voice was unexpectedly sharp, and Tom turned abruptly toward him. Dahl must have caught the warning in that, Julie realized with gratitude; when he spoke again his voice was considerably softer. "Mrs. Barton, please let me put the matter before you bluntly. Let me show you what we're faced with here.

"A dangerous man is on the prowl. You seem to think he was drunk, but he wasn't too drunk to know exactly where he could find a victim who was alone and unprotected. He probably had this house staked out for weeks in advance, knowing your husband's been working late at his office. And he knew how to get into the house. He scraped this window sill here pretty badly, coming in over it.

"He wasn't here to rob the place—he had the opportunity but he wasn't interested in it. He was interested in one thing, and one thing only." Surprisingly, Dahl walked over to the dresser and lifted the framed wedding picture from it. "This is you, isn't it?"

"Yes," Julie said in bewilderment.

"You're a very pretty young woman, you know." Dahl put down the picture, lifted up her hand mirror, and approached her with it. "Now I want to show you how a pretty young woman looks after she's tried to resist a man like that." He suddenly flashed the mirror before her and she shrank in horror from its reflection.

"Oh, please!" she cried.

"You don't have to worry," Dahl said harshly. "According to the doctor you'll heal up fine in a while. But until then, won't you see that man as clear as day every time you look into this thing? Won't you be able to point him out, and lay your hand on the Bible, and swear he was the one?"

She wasn't sure any more. She looked at him wonderingly, and he threw wide his arms, summing up his case. "You'll know him when you see him again, won't you?" he demanded.

"Yes." she said.

•   •   •

SHE thought she would be left alone after that, but she was wrong. The world had business with her, and there was no way of shutting it out. The doorbell chimed incessantly. The telephone in the hall rang, was silent while someone took the call, then rang again. Men with hard faces—police officials—would be ushered into the room by Tom. They would duck their heads at her in embarrassment, would solemnly survey the room, then go off in a corner to whisper together. Tom would lead them out, and would return to her side. He had nothing to say. He would just sit there, taut with impatience, waiting for the doorbell or telephone to ring again.

He was seldom apart from her, and Julie, watching him, found herself increasingly troubled by that. She was keeping him from his work, distracting him from the thing that mattered most to him. She didn't know much about his business affairs, but she did know he had been working for months on some very big deal—the one that had been responsible for her solitary evenings at home—and what would happen to it while he was away from his office? She had only been married two years, but she was already well-versed in the creed of the businessman's wife. Troubles at home may come and go, it said, but Business abides. She used to find that idea repellent, but now it warmed her. Tom would go to the office, and she would lock the door against everybody, and there would be continuity.

But when she hesitantly broached the matter he shrugged it off. "The deal's all washed up, anyhow. It was a waste of time. That's what I was going to tell you about when I walked in and found you like that. It was quite a sight." He looked at her, his eyes glassy with fatigue. "Quite a sight," he said.

And sat there waiting for the doorbell or telephone to ring again.

．　．　．

WHEN he was not there, one of the nurses was. Miss Shepherd, the night nurse, was taciturn. Miss Waldemar, the day nurse, talked.

She said, "Oh, it takes all kinds to make this little old world, I tell you. They slow their cars coming by the house, and they walk all over the lawn, and what they expect to see I'm sure I don't know. It's just evil minds, that's all it is, and wouldn't they be the first ones to call you a liar if you told them that to their faces? And children in the back seats! What is it, sweetie? You look as if you can't get comfy."

"I'm all right, thank you," Julie said. She quailed at the thought of telling Miss Waldemar to please keep quiet or go away. There were people who could do that, she knew, but evidently it didn't matter to them how anyone felt about you when you hurt their feelings. It mattered to Julie a great deal.

Miss Waldemar said, "But if you ask me who's really to blame I'll tell you right out it's the newspapers. Just as well the doctor won't let you look at them, sweetie, because they're having a party, all right. You'd think what with Russia and all, there's more worthwhile things for them to worry about, but no, there it is all over the front pages as big as they can make it. Anything for a nickel, that's their feeling about it. Money, money, money, and who cares if children stand there gawking at headlines and getting ideas at their age!

"Oh, I told that right to one of those reporters, face to face. No sooner did I put foot outside the house yesterday when he steps up, bold as brass, and asks me to get him a picture of you. Steal one, if you please! They're all using that picture from your high school yearbook now; I suppose they want something like that big one on the dresser. And I'm not being asked to do him any favors, mind you; he'll pay fifty dollars cash for it! Well, that was my chance to tell him a thing or two, and don't think I didn't. You are sleepy, aren't you, lamb? Would you like to take a little nap?"

"Yes," said Julie.

．　．　．

HER parents arrived. She had been eager to see them, but when Tom brought them into her room the eagerness faded. Tom had always despised her father's air of futility—the quality of helplessness that marked his every gesture—and never tried to conceal his contempt. Her mother, who had started off with the one objection that Tom was much too old for Julie—he was thirty to her eighteen when they married—had ultimately worked up to the point of telling him he was an outrageous bully, a charge which he regarded as a declaration of war.

That foolish business, Julie knew guiltily, had been her fault. Tom, who could be as finicking as an old maid about some things, had raged at her for not emptying the pockets of his jackets before sending them to the tailor, and since she still was, at the time, more her mother's daughter than her husband's wife, she had weepingly confided the episode to her mother over the telephone. She had not made that mistake again, but the damage was done. After that her husband and her parents made up openly hostile camps, while she served as futile emissary between them.

• • •

WHEN they all came into the room now, Julie could feel their mutual enmity charging the air. She had wistfully hoped that what had happened would change that, and knew with a sinking heart that it had not. What it came to, she thought resignedly, is that they hated each other more than they loved her. And immediately she was ashamed of the thought.

Her father weakly fluttered his fingers at her in greeting, and stood at the foot of the bed looking at her like a lost spaniel. It was a relief when the doorbell rang and he trailed out after Tom to see who it was. Her mother's eyes were red and swollen; she kept a small, damp handkerchief pressed to her nose. She sat down beside Julie and patted her hand.

"It's awful, darling," she said. "It's just awful. Now you know why I was so much against your buying the house out here, way at the end of nowhere. How are you?"

"All right."

Her mother said, "We would have been here sooner except for grandma. We didn't want her to find out, but some busybody neighbor went and told her. And you know how she is. She was prostrated. Dr. Vaughn was with her for an hour."

"I'm sorry."

Her mother patted her hand again. "She'll be all right. You'll get a card from her when she's up and around."

Her grandmother always sent greeting cards on every possible occasion. Julie wondered mirthlessly what kind of card she would find to fit this occasion.

"Julie," her mother said, "would you like me to comb out your hair?"

"No, thank you, mother."

"But it's all knots. Don't those nurses ever do anything for their money? And where are your dark glasses, darling? The ones you use at the beach. It wouldn't hurt to wear them until that discoloration is gone, would it?"

Julie felt clouds of trivia swarming over her, like gnats. "Please, mother."

"It's all right, I'm not going to fuss about it. I'll make up a list for the nurses when I go. Anyhow, there's something much more serious I wanted to talk to you about, Julie. I mean, while Dad and Tom aren't here. Would it be all right if I did?"

"Yes."

Her mother leaned forward tensely. "It's about—well, it's about what happened. How it might make you feel about Tom now. Because, Julie, no matter how you might feel, he's your husband, and you've always got to remember that. I respect him for that, and you must, too, darling. There are certain things a wife owes a husband, and she still owes them to him even after something awful like this happens. She's duty bound. Why do you look like that, Julie? You do understand what I'm saying, don't you?"

"Yes," Julie said. She had been chilled by a sudden insight into her parents' life together. "But please don't talk about it. Everything will be all right."

"I know it will. If we aren't afraid to look our troubles right in the eye they can never hurt us, can they? And, Julie, before Tom gets back there's something else to clear up. It's about him."

Julie braced herself. "Yes?"

"It's something he said. When Dad and I came in we talked to him a while and when—well, you know what we were talking about, and right in the middle of it Tom said in the most casual way—I mean, just like he was talking about the weather or something—he said that when they caught that man he was going to kill him. Julie, he terrified me. You know his temper, but it wasn't temper or anything like that. It was just a calm statement of fact. He was going to kill the man, and that's all there was to it. But he meant it, Julie, and you've got to do something about it."

"Do what?" Julie said dazedly. "What can I do?"

"You can let him know he mustn't even talk like that. Everybody feels the way he does—we all want that monster dead and buried. But it isn't up to Tom to kill him. He could get into terrible trouble that way! Hasn't there been enough trouble for all of us already?"

Julie closed her eyes. "Yes," she said.

• • •

DR. Vaughn came and watched her walk around the room. He said, "I'll have to admit you look mighty cute in those dark glasses, but what are they for? Eyes bother you any?"

"No," Julie said. "I just feel better wearing them."

"I thought so. They make you look better to people, and they make people look better to you. Say, that's an idea. Maybe the whole human race ought to take up wearing them permanently. Be a lot better for their livers than alcohol, wouldn't it?"

"I don't know," Julie said. She sat down on the edge of the bed, huddled in her robe, its sleeves covering her clasped hands, mandarin style. Her hands felt as if they would never be warm again, "I want to ask you something."

"All right, go ahead and ask."

"I shouldn't, because you'll probably laugh at me, but I won't mind. It's about Tom. He told mother that when they caught the man he was going to kill him. I suppose he was just—I mean, he wouldn't really try to do anything like that, would he?"

The doctor did not laugh. He said grimly, "I think he might try to do something exactly like that."

"To *kill* somebody?"

"Julie, I don't understand you. You've been married to Tom—how long is it now?"

"Two years."

"And in those two years did you ever know him to say he would do something that he didn't sooner or later do?"

"No."

"I would have bet on that. Not because I know Tom so well, mind you, but because I grew up with his father. Every time I look at Tom I see his father all over again. There was a man with Lucifer's own pride rammed into him like gunpowder, and a hair-trigger temper to set it off. And repressed. Definitely repressed. Tom is, too. It's hard not to be when you have to strain all the time, keeping the emotional finger off that trigger. I'll be blunt, Julie. None of the Bartons has ever impressed me as being exactly well-balanced. I have the feeling that if you gave any one of them enough motive for killing, he'd kill, all right. And Tom owns a gun, too, doesn't he?"

"Yes."

"Well, you don't have to look that scared about it," the doctor said. "It would have been a lot worse if we hadn't been warned. This way I can tell Christensen and he'll keep an eye on your precious husband until they've got the man strapped into the electric chair. A bullet's too good for that kind of animal, anyhow."

Julie turned her head away and the doctor placed his finger against her chin and gently turned it back. "Look," he said, "I'll do everything possible to see Tom doesn't get into trouble. Will you take my word for that?"

"Yes."

"Then what's bothering you? The way I talked about putting that man in the electric chair? Is that what it is?"

"Yes. I don't want to hear about it."

"But why? You of all people, Julie! Haven't you been praying for them to find him? Don't you hate him enough to want to see him dead?"

It was like turning the key that unlocked all her misery.

"I do!" she said despairingly. "Oh, yes, I do! But Tom doesn't believe it. That's what's wrong, don't you understand? He thinks it doesn't matter to me as much as it does to him. He thinks I just want to forget all about it, whether they catch the man or not. He doesn't say so, but I can tell. And that makes everything rotten; it makes me feel ashamed and guilty all the time. Nothing can change that. Even if they kill the man a hundred times over it'll always be that way!"

"It will not," the doctor said sternly. "Julie, why don't you use your head? Hasn't it dawned on you that Tom is suffering from an even deeper guilt than yours? That subconsciously he feels a sense of failure because he didn't protect you from what happened? Now he's reacting like any outraged male. He wants vengeance. He wants the account settled. And, Julie, it's his sense of guilt that's tearing you two apart.

"Do you know what that means, young lady? It means you've got a job to do for yourself. The dirtiest kind of job. When the police nail that man you'll have to identify him, testify against him, face cameras and newspapermen, walk through mobs of brainless people dying to get a close look at you. Yes, it's as bad as all that. You don't realize the excitement this mess has stirred up; you've been kept apart from it so far. But you'll have a chance to see it for yourself very soon. That's your test. If you flinch from it you can probably write off your marriage then and there. That's what you've got to keep in mind, not all that nonsense about things never changing!"

Julie sat there viewing herself from a distance, while the cold in her hands moved up along her arms turning them to gooseflesh. She said, "When I was a little girl I cried if anybody even pointed at me."

"You can't be a little girl all your life," the doctor said.

• • •

WHEN the time came, Julie fortified herself with that thought. Sitting in the official car between Tom and Lieutenant Christensen, shielded from the onlooking world by dark glasses and upturned coat collar, her eyes closed, her teeth set, she repeated it like a private *Hail Mary* over and over—until it became a soothing murmur circling endlessly through her mind.

Lieutenant Christensen said, "The man's a janitor in one of those old apartment houses a few blocks away from your place. A drunk and a degenerate. He's been up on morals charges before, but nothing like this. This time he put himself in a spot he'll never live to crawl away from. Not on grounds of insanity, or anything else. We've got him cold."

You can't be a little girl all your life, Julie thought.

The lieutenant said, "The one thing that stymied us was his alibi. He kept telling us he was on a drunk with this woman of his that night when it happened, and she kept backing up his story. It wasn't easy to get the truth out of her, but we finally did. Turns out she wasn't near him that night. Can you imagine lying for a specimen like that?"

You can't be a little girl all your life, Julie thought.

"We're here, Mrs. Barton," the lieutenant said.

The car had stopped before a side door of the headquarters building, and Tom pushed her through it just ahead of men with cameras who swarmed down on her, shouting her name, hammering at the door when it was closed against them. She clutched Tom's hand as the lieutenant led them through long institutional corridors, other men falling into step with them along the way, until they reached another door where Dahl was waiting.

He said, "This whole thing takes just one minute, Mrs. Barton, and we're over our big hurdle. All you have to do is look at the man and tell us yes or no. That's all there is to it. And it's arranged so that he can't possibly see you. You have nothing at all to fear from him. Do you understand that?"

"Yes," Julie said.

Again she sat between Tom and Lieutenant Christensen. The platform before her was brilliantly lighted; everything else was in darkness. Men were all around her in the darkness. They moved restlessly; one of them coughed. The outline of Dahl's sharp profile and narrow shoulders were suddenly etched black against the platform; then it disappeared as he took the seat in front of Julie's. She found that her breathing was becoming increasingly shallow; it was impossible to draw enough air our of the darkness to fill her lungs. She forced herself to breathe deeply, counting as she used to do during gym exercises at school. *In-one-two-three. Out-one-two-three.*

• • •

A door slammed nearby. Three men walked onto the platform and stood there facing her. Two of them were uniformed policemen. The third man—the one they flanked—towered over them tall and cadaverous, dressed in a torn sweater and soiled trousers. His face was slack, his huge hand moved back and forth in a vacant gesture across his mouth. Julie tried to take her eyes off that hand and couldn't. Back and forth it went, mesmerizing her with its blind, groping motion.

One of the uniformed policemen held up a piece of paper.

"Charles Brunner," he read loudly. "Age forty-one. Arrests—" and on and on until there was sudden silence. But the hand still went back and forth, growing enormous before her, and Julie knew, quite without concern, that she was going to faint. She swayed forward, her head drooping, and something cold and hard was pressed under her nose. Ammonia fumes stung her nostrils and she twisted away, gasping. When the lieutenant thrust the bottle at her again, she weakly pushed it aside.

"I'm all right," she said.

"But it was a jolt seeing him, wasn't it?"

"Yes."

"Because you recognized him, didn't you?"

She wondered vaguely if that were why. "I'm not sure."

Dahl leaned over her. "You can't mean that, Mrs. Barton! You gave me your word you'd know him when you saw him again. Why are you backing out of it now? What are you afraid of?"

"I'm not afraid."

"Yes, you are. You almost passed out when you saw him, didn't you? Because no matter how much you wanted to get him out of your mind your emotions wouldn't let you. Those emotions are telling the truth now, aren't they?"

"I don't know!"

"Then look at him again and see what happens. Go on, take a good look!"

Lieutenant Christensen said, "Mrs. Barton, if you let us down now, you'll go out and tell the newspapermen about it yourself. They've been on us like wolves about this thing, and for once in my life I want them to know what we're up against here!"

Tom's fingers gripped her shoulder. "I don't understand, Julie," he said. "Why don't you come out with it? He is the man isn't he?"

"Yes!" she said, and clapped her hands over her ears to shut out the angry, hateful voices clamoring at her out of the darkness. "Yes! Yes!"

"Thank God," said Lieutenant Christensen.

Then Tom moved. He stood up, something glinting metallically in his hand, and Julie screamed as the man behind her lunged at it. Light suddenly flooded the room. Other men leaped at Tom and chairs clattered over as the struggle eddied around and around him, flowing relentlessly toward the platform. There was no one on it when he was finally borne down to the floor by a crushing weight of bodies.

Two of the men, looking apologetic, pulled him to his feet, but kept their arms tightly locked around his. Another man handed the gun to Lieutenant Christensen, and Tom nodded at it. He was disheveled and breathing hard, but seemed strangely unruffled.

"I'd like that back, if you don't mind," he said.

"I do mind," said the lieutenant. He broke open the gun, tapped the bullets into his hand, and then, to Julie's quivering relief, dropped gun and bullets into his own pocket. "Mr. Barton, you're in a state right now where if I charged you with attempted murder you wouldn't even deny it, would you?"

"No."

"You see what I mean? Now why don't you just cool off and let us handle this job? We've done all right so far, haven't we? And after Mrs. Barton testifies at the trial Brunner is as good as dead, and you can forget all about him." The lieutenant looked at Julie. "That makes sense, doesn't it?" he asked her.

"Yes," Julie whispered prayerfully.

Tom smiled. "I'd like my gun, if you don't mind."

The lieutenant stood there speechless for the moment, and then laid his hand over the pocket containing the gun as if to assure himself that it was still there. "Some other time," he said with finality.

The men holding Tom released him and he lurched forward and caught at them for support. His face was suddenly deathly pale, but the smile was still fixed on it as he addressed the lieutenant.

"You'd better call a doctor," he said pleasantly. "I think your damn gorillas have broken my leg."

• • •

DURING the time he was in the hospital he was endlessly silent and withdrawn. The day he was brought home at his own insistence, his leg unwieldy in a cast from ankle to knee, Dr. Vaughn had a long talk with him, the two of them alone behind the closed doors of the living-room. The doctor must have expressed himself freely and forcefully. When he had gone, and Julie plucked up the courage to walk into the living-room, she saw her husband regarding her with the look of a man who has had a bitter dose of medicine forced down his throat and hasn't quite decided whether or not it will do him any good.

Then he patted the couch seat beside him. "There's just enough room for you and me and this leg," he said.

She obediently sat down, clasping her hands in her lap.

"Vaughn's been getting some things off his chest," Tom said abruptly. "I'm glad he did. You've been through a rotten experience, Julie, and I haven't been any help at all, have I? All I've done is make it worse. I've been lying to myself about it, too. Telling myself that everything I did since it happened was for your sake, and all along the only thing that really concerned me was my own feelings. Isn't that so?"

"I don't know," Julie said, "and I don't care. It doesn't matter as long as you talk to me about it. That's the only thing I can't stand, not having you talk to me."

"Has it been that bad?"

"Yes."

"But you understand why, don't you? It was something eating away inside of me. But it's gone now, I swear it is. You believe that, don't you, Julie?"

She hesitated. "Yes."

"I can't tell whether you mean it or not behind those dark glasses. Lift them up, and let's see."

Julie lifted the glasses and he gravely studied her face. "I think you do mean it," he said. "A face as pretty as that couldn't possibly tell a lie. But why do you still wear those things? There aren't any marks left."

She dropped the glasses into place and the world became its soothingly familiar, shaded self again. "I just like them," she said. "I'm used to them."

"Well, if the doctor doesn't mind, I don't. But if you're wearing them to make yourself look exotic and dangerous, you'll have to give up. You're too much like Sweet Alice. You can't escape it."

She smiled. "I don't tremble with fear at your frown. Not really."

"Yes, you do, but I like it. You're exactly what Sweet Alice must have been. Demure, that's the word, demure. My wife is the only demure married woman in the world. Yielding, yet cool and remote. A lovely lady wrapped in cellophane. How is it you never became a nun?"

She knew she must be visibly glowing with happiness. It had been so long since she had seen him in this mood. "I almost did. When I was in school I used to think about it a lot. There was this other girl—well, she was really a wonderful person, and she had already made up her mind about it. I guess that's where I got the idea."

"And then what happened?"

"You know what happened."

"Yes, it's all coming back now. You went to your first Country Club dance dressed in a beautiful white gown, with stardust in your hair—"

"It was sequins."

"No, stardust. And I saw you. And the next thing I remember, we were in Mexico on a honeymoon." He put his arm around her waist, and she relaxed in the hard circle of it. "Julie, when this whole bad dream is over we're going there again. We'll pack the car and go south of the border and forget everything. You'd like that wouldn't you?"

"Oh, very much." She looked up at him hopefully, her head back against his shoulder. "But no bullfights, please. Not this time."

He laughed. "All right, when I'm at the bullfights you'll be sightseeing. The rest of the time we'll be together. Any time I look around I want to see you there. No more than this far away. That means I can reach out my hand and you'll always be there. Is that clear?"

"I'll be there," she said.

So she had found him again, she assured herself, and she used that knowledge to settle her qualms whenever she thought of Brunner and the impending trial. She never mentioned these occasional thoughts to Tom, and she came to see that there was a conspiracy among everyone who entered the house—her family and friends, the doctor, even strangers on business with Tom—which barred any reference to the subject of Brunner. Until one evening when, after she had coaxed Tom into a restless sleep, the doorbell rang again and again with maddening persistence.

Julie looked through the peephole and saw that the man standing outside was middle-aged and tired-looking and carried a worn leather portfolio under his arm. She opened the door with annoyance and said, "Please, don't do that. My husband's not well, and he's asleep. And there's nothing we want."

The man walked past her into the foyer before she could stop him. He took off his hat and faced her. "I'm not a salesman, Mrs. Barton. My name is Karlweiss. Dr. Lewis Karlweiss. Is it familiar to you?"

"No."

"It should be. Up to three o'clock this afternoon I was in charge of the City Hospital for Mental Disorders. Right now I'm a man without any job, and with a badly frayed reputation. And just angry enough and scared enough, Mrs. Barton, to want to do something about it. That's why I'm here."

"I don't see what it has to do with me."

"You will. Two years ago Charles Brunner was institutionalized in my care, and, after treatment, released on my say-so. Do you understand now? I am officially responsible for having turned him loose on you. I signed the document which certified that while he was not emotionally well, he was certainly not dangerous. And this afternoon I had that document shoved down my throat by a gang of ignorant politicians who are out to make hay of this case!"

Julie said incredulously, "And you want me to go and tell them they were wrong? Is that it?"

"Only if you know they *are* wrong, Mrs. Barton. I'm not asking you to perjure yourself for me. I don't even know what legal right I have to be here in the first place, and I certainly don't want to get into any more trouble than I'm already in." Karlweiss looked over her shoulder toward the living-room, and shifted his portfolio from one arm to the other. "Can we go inside and sit down while we talk this over? There's a lot to say."

"No."

"All right, then I'll explain it here, and I'll make it short and to the point. Mrs. Barton, I know more about Charles Brunner than anyone else in the world. I know more about him than he knows about himself. And that's what makes it so hard for me to believe that you identified the right man!"

Julie said, "I don't want to hear about it. Will you please go away?"

"No, I will not," Karlweiss said heatedly. "I insist on being heard. You see, Mrs. Barton, everything Brunner does fits a certain pattern. Every dirty little crime he has committed fits that pattern. It's a pattern of weakness, a constant manifestation of his failure to achieve full masculinity.

"But what he is now charged with is the absolute reverse of that pattern. It was a display of brute masculinity by an aggressive and sadistic personality. It was the act of someone who can only obtain emotional and physical release through violence. That's the secret of such a personality—the need for violence. Not lust, as the Victorians used to preach, but the need for release through violence. And that is a need totally alien to Brunner. It doesn't exist in him. It's a sickness, but it's not his sickness!

"Now do you see why your identification of him hit me and my co-workers at the hospital so hard? We don't know too much about various things in our science yet—I'm the first to admit it—but in a few cases we've been able to work out patterns of personality as accurately as mathematical equations. I thought we had done that successfully with Brunner. I would still think so, if you hadn't identified him. That's why I'm here. I wanted to meet you. I wanted to have you tell me directly if there was any doubt at all about Brunner being the man. Because if there is—"

"There isn't."

"But if there is," Karlweiss pleaded, "I'd take my oath that Brunner isn't guilty. It makes sense that way. If there's the shadow of a doubt—"

"There isn't!"

"Julie!" called Tom from the bedroom. "Who is that?"

Panic seized her. All she could envision then was Brunner as he would walk down the prison steps to the street, as he would stand there dazed in the sunlight while Tom, facing him, slowly drew the gun from his pocket. She clutched Karlweiss's sleeve and half-dragged him toward the door. "Please, go away!" she whispered fiercely. "There's nothing to talk about. Please, go away!"

She closed the door behind him and leaned back against it, her knees trembling.

"Julie, who is that?" Tom called. "Who are you talking to?"

She steadied herself and went into the bedroom. "It was a salesman," she said. "He was selling insurance. I told him we didn't want any."

"You know I don't want you to open the door to any strangers," Tom said. "Why'd you go and do a thing like that?"

Julie forced herself to smile. "He was perfectly harmless," she said.

• • •

But the terror had taken root in her now—and it thrived. It was fed by many things. The subpoena from Dahl which Tom had her put into his dresser drawer for safekeeping and which was there in full view every time she opened the drawer to get him something. The red circle around the trial date on the calendar in the kitchen which a line of black crosses inched toward, a little closer each day. And the picture in her mind's eye which took many forms, but which was always the same picture with the same ending: Brunner descending the prison steps, or Brunner entering the courtroom, or Brunner in the dank cellar she saw as his natural habitat, and then in the end Brunner standing there, blinking stupidly, his hand moving back and forth over his mouth, and Tom facing him, slowly drawing the gun from his pocket, the gun barrel glinting as it moved into line with Brunner's chest—

The picture came into even sharper focus when Dr. Vaughn brought the crutches for Tom. Julie loathed them at sight. She had never minded the heavy pressure of Tom's arm around her shoulders, his weight bearing her down as he lurched from one room to another, hobbled by the cast. The cast was a hobble, she knew, keeping him tied down to the house; he struggled with it and grumbled about it continually, as if the struggling and grumbling would somehow release him from it. But the crutches were a release. They would take him to wherever Brunner was.

She watched him as he practised using the crutches that evening, not walking, but supporting himself on them to find his balance, and then she helped him sit down on the couch, the leg in its cast propped on a footstool before him.

He said, "Julie, you have no idea how fed up a man can get, living in pajamas and a robe. But it won't be long now, will it?"

"No."

"Which reminds me that you ought to give my stuff out to the tailor tomorrow. He's a slow man, and I'd like it all ready when I'm up and around."

"All right," Julie said. She went to the wardrobe in the hall and returned with an armful of clothing which she draped over the back of an armchair. She was mechanically going through the pockets of a jacket when Tom said, "Come here, Julie."

He caught her hand as she stood before him. "There's something on your mind," he said. "What is it?"

"Nothing."

"You were never any good at lying. What's wrong, Julie?"

"Still nothing."

"Oh, all right, if that's the way you want it." He released her hand and she went back to the pile of clothing on the armchair, sick with the feeling that he could see through her, that he knew exactly what she was thinking, and must hate her for it. She put aside the jacket and picked up the car coat he used only for driving. Which meant, she thought with a small shudder of realization, that he hadn't worn it since *that* night. She pulled the gloves from its pocket and tossed the coat on top of the jacket.

"These gloves," she said, holding them out to show him. "Where—?"

These gloves, an echo cried out to her. *These gloves,* said a smaller one behind it, and *these gloves, these gloves* ran away in a diminishing series of echoes until there was only deathly silence.

And a glove.

A gray suède glove clotted and crusted with dark-brown stains. Its index finger gouged and torn. Its bitter taste in her mouth. Its owner, a stranger, sitting on the couch, holding out his hand, saying something.

"Give that to me, Julie," Tom said.

She looked at him and knew there were no secrets between them any more. She watched the sweat starting from his forehead and trickling down the bloodless face. She saw his teeth show and his eyes stare as he tried to pull himself to his feet. He failed, and sank back panting.

"Listen to me, Julie," he said. "Now listen to me and take hold of yourself."

"You," she said drunkenly. "It was you."

"Julie, I love you!"

"But it was you. It's all crazy. I don't understand."

"I know. Because it was crazy. That's what it was, I went crazy for a minute. It was overwork. It was that deal. I was killing myself to put it across, and that night when they turned me down I don't know what happened. I got drunk, and when I came home I couldn't find the key. So I came through the window. That's when it happened. I don't know what it was, but it was something exploding in me. Something in my head. I saw you there, and all I wanted to do—I tell you I don't even know why! Don't *ask* me why! It was overwork, that's what it was. It gets to everybody nowadays. You read about it all the time. You know you do, Julie. You've got to be reasonable about this!"

Julie whispered, "If you had told me it was you. If you had only told me. But you didn't."

"Because I love you!"

"No, but you knew how I felt, and you turned that against me. You made me say it was Brunner. Everything you've been doing to me—it was just so I'd say it and say it, until I killed him. You never tried to kill him, at all. You knew I would do it for you. And I would have!"

"Julie, Julie, what does Brunner matter to anybody? You've seen what he's like. He's a degenerate. He's no good. Everybody is better off without people like that around."

She shook her head violently. "But you knew he didn't do it! Why couldn't you just let it be one of those times where they never find out who did it?"

"Because I wasn't sure! Everybody kept saying it was only the shock that let you blank it out of your mind. They kept saying if you tried hard enough to remember, it might all come back. So if Brunner—I mean, this way the record was all straight! You wouldn't have to think about it again!"

She saw that if he leaned forward enough he could touch her, and she backed away a step, surprised she had the strength to do it.

"Where are you going?" Tom said. "Don't be a fool, Julie. Nobody'll believe you. Think of everything that's been said and done, and you'll see nobody would even *want* to believe you. They'll say you're out of your mind!"

She wavered, then realized with horror that she was wavering. "They will believe me!" she cried, and ran blindly out of the house, sobbing as she ran, stumbling when she reached the sidewalk so that she fell on her hands and knees, feeling the sting of the scraped knee as she rose and staggered farther down the dark and empty street. It was only when she was at a distance that she stopped, her heart hammering, her legs barely able to support her, to look at the house. Not hers any more. Just his.

He—all of them—had made her a liar and an accomplice. Each of them for his own reason had done that, and she, because of the weakness in her, had let them. It was a terrible weakness, she thought with anguish—the need to have them always approve, the willingness to always say yes to them. It was like hiding yourself behind the dark glasses all the time, not caring that the world you saw through them was never the world you would see through the naked eye.

She turned and fled toward lights and people. The glasses lay in the street where she had flung them, and the night wind swept dust through their shattered frames.

CLARK HOWARD

It's been said, written, and taught that aspiring writers should write about what they know. Experiences. Memories. Events. Adventures.

A month after "The Last One to Cry" was published, a letter was forwarded to me by Ellery Queen Mystery Magazine from a retired lady who had once been an office worker at the Illinois State Training School. She was very moved by the story because while there she had once heard a rumor that a boy had died under circumstances similar to those in the story. She closed the letter with the words, "You were there. You know."

Yes, aspiring writers should write about what they know.

• • •

Back in the 1950s, when I returned from the Korean War and was discharged from the Marine Corps, I had already made up my mind that I was going to try to become a writer. Specifically, a short story writer. I had no ambition to write anything longer—just short stories, which I had always loved reading.

It was my practice in those days to buy, and read from cover to cover, every short story magazine published—and there were many of them: mystery, Western, romance, adventure. I learned to write by reading, studying, analyzing, the stories many other writers had written for these magazines. Soon, I began to have favorites, writers whose work I would look for every month. One favorite, probably the favorite I had in those days, was Jack Ritchie. He was a master of what some writers call the "hook." That was the ability to hook readers with the first several lines of a story—hook them so surely, so definitely, that they absolutely had to read the entire story. Along with the hook, Ritchie was a virtuoso of dialogue; the conversations of his characters was smooth, easy, effortlessly readable.

I studied the writing of Jack Ritchie as long as he lived, and became a better writer each time I read his work. The story that follows is the Edgar-winning "The Absence of Emily"—a flawless diamond among the many gems this fine short story writer mined.

THE LAST ONE TO CRY

Clark Howard

MARTIN COULDN'T BELIEVE what he saw when he got back to the personnel office after lunch. Sitting at the desk of one of the employment interviewers was the man who had killed Freddie Walsh more than twenty years ago.

Pausing in the doorway, Martin stared across the room at him. It was McKey, Martin was certain of it. It was Old Man McKey.

Going into his own glass-partitioned office, Martin sat down, aware that his hands were trembling slightly on top of his desk. He busied himself with a few papers, waiting. As personnel manager, he had to review every employment application, so it would only be a few minutes before he knew for sure whether it was really Old Man McKey or only someone who looked like him. In the meantime, not only Martin's hands were a problem but his mouth had gone dry and the sandwich he had eaten for lunch was doing something inside him.

Leaving his office, he went to the water cooler, drew a paper cup of ice water, and, back at his desk, dropped a single Alka-Seltzer in it. The tablet took forever to dissolve because the water was so cold, but finally Martin gulped it down just as the personnel interviewer brought him the application.

"He's applying for the night watchman's position at the plant," she said.

"Okay."

The interviewer left, knowing that Martin would buzz her to return after he had reviewed the application. He forced himself to wait until he was alone before letting his eyes move down to the name on the application.

Edward McKey.

Martin had never known Old Man McKey's first name. Was there a chance this was a brother or a cousin who looked like him? Martin opened the application to the page listing previous employers. The second one from the top was Illinois State Training School for Boys.

It was him. It was Old Man McKey.

The man who had killed Freddie Walsh.

• • •

THE trip from the Cook County Juvenile Detention Home was made in what looked like an ordinary school bus, except that it had a wire-grille separation between the driver's seat and the passenger section and an armed detention officer rode up front. Martin, who was twelve, sat next to a window and looked out at the countryside along the way. There were a dozen other boys on the bus—white, black, brown—all between twelve, the legal minimum, and sixteen, and they were all as tied up in frightened knots as Martin was, so there wasn't much conversation. None of them knew each other, except perhaps casually from holding-cells and dayrooms at the juvenile home, which didn't help any. For the most part, they were like strangers, all invited to a party to which none of them wanted to go but all of them had to.

The Illinois State Training School was located in St. Charles, Illinois, two counties west of Chicago on the highway to Iowa. It might as well have been in Asia, it was so completely foreign to Martin, who knew only the tenement streets of the city. While the color and terrain and natural beauty of the countryside stimulated a spark of fascination and appreciation deep inside him somewhere, at the same time his street instincts rose to exert immediate control over such thinking. It might be pretty, but how could one survive here? To survive, you needed doorways, alleys, rooftops.

A boy across the aisle moved over next to Martin. "You see them black-and-white cows back there?" he asked.

"Yeah," said Martin.

"I never knew there was black-and-white cows. I thought they was all brown."

Martin nodded his head. "Yeah—me, too." The boy was older than Martin, perhaps fourteen, and bigger, not quite as knotted with fear.

"Hey, where you from?" The question didn't mean from which city, it meant from which neighborhood—they were all from Chicago.

"West side," Martin answered. "Ashland and Van Buren."

"Yeah? I'm south side. Twenty-second and Sacramento. We weren't too far apart." He lowered his voice. "What they got you on?"

"I'm uncorrigible," Martin said. He was being sent to reform school for it, but didn't know what it meant and couldn't even pronounce it correctly. He supposed it had something to do with the fact that he had no father, his mother was a drug addict, he was a ward of the county, and he kept running away from every foster home they put him in.

"I'm down for burglary," the boy next to him said with an odd hint of mixed pride and fear. "Hey, my name's Freddie Walsh. What's yours?"

"Martin Howe."

Freddie studied him and grinned. "You sure do look young. I bet they call you Babyface."

Martin shrugged. "No."

"I think I'll call you that. Okay with you?"

Another shrug. "I guess so."

That's where Martin had gotten his reform-school nickname, from Freddie Walsh.

The kid Old Man McKey had killed.

• • •

AFTER Martin had studied Edward McKey's employment application, he buzzed the personnel interviewer and she returned to his office.

"Looks like he might do," Martin told her. "Run him through the routine."

The routine was the company's standard operating procedure for hiring new personnel. If an applicant, based on the information put in the application, appeared to fit the qualifications for a particular job, the person was told that they were being considered and would hear from the personnel office in a few days. The applicant's past employment, education, references, and other information were then checked by the personnel office, and if everything verified favorably the application was returned to Martin's desk for final scrutiny and hiring approval.

Martin had been personnel manager for two years, working his way up during a fourteen-year tenure from mailboy, office boy, clerk, interviewer, employment counselor, and, before his last promotion, assistant manager. The company, Wayne and Grayson, was a large paper-products firm specializing in flat stock for the printing of posters and outdoor billboards. It had plants in three states and a small national sales force. Martin was considered one of the bright young members of Wayne and Grayson's management team. He was dedicated, loyal, and ambitious. For nine years he had been attending university classes two nights a week, working toward a degree in business administration. He hoped to have that degree before he reached thirty-five.

In his office, after the interviewer took Edward McKey's application and returned to her desk, Martin continued to shift papers on his own desk, surreptitiously watching the man who had killed Freddie Walsh. McKey didn't appear to have changed much: he was still a sharp-edge-faced man with not quite a beak for a nose, hair combed straight back in a no-nonsense style, ears a touch too large for his skull. He seemed smaller to Martin, but that was simply perspective. When Martin had been twelve, McKey's angular body and solid, hairy arms had looked huge and intimidating. Now that Martin himself was a grown man, he realized that Edward McKey was no more than average size.

Martin watched the interviewer smile and shake hands with McKey and followed with his eyes as the older man left the office. McKey, he noted, still had the same loose-jointed, rolling-hip walk that Martin remembered from that first day in reform school.

• • •

ITS formal name was the Illinois State Training School for Boys, but because it was near the town of St. Charles, it had long before become known to the boys who passed in and out of it as "Charleytown." The term "training school" was a euphemism in every sense. Very little training was given, unless digging potatoes, cutting weeds, mopping floors, and the like was considered some kind of apprenticeship. And by no stretch of the imagination was it a school. It was a prison.

Martin, Freddie Walsh, and the others from the bus were processed into the Reception and Detention Unit, a separate barracks for new arrivals. They were stripped, their hair cut off down to the scalp, watched carefully while they scrubbed and rescrubbed with thick bars of brown laundry soap, and their heads, feet, armpits, and pubic areas were dusted with great clouds of yellow powder from a can powered by a rubber pressure ball, then made to stand under cold showers until everything was rinsed off. Only then were they given their reform-school-issue clothing: dark-blue-denim trousers, light-blue-denim shirts, white briefs and undershirts, heavy grey socks, and black, state-manufactured shoes unfinished on the insides.—No belts, because a belt with a buckle, wrapped around one's fist with four or five inches dangling, was an extremely dangerous weapon when used correctly. Belts had been banned at Charleytown after three boys in one year had an eye picked out in belt fights.

The length of stay in R-and-D was two weeks. The boys were confined to the barracks and to a small, cyclone-fenced exercise yard except when they were summoned individually for their appointments with various institution staff. Physical examinations were first. The doctors usually found nothing currently wrong with the new arrivals—street mongrels somehow managed to remain healthy, or reasonably so. Martin was found to have scar tissue on both lungs, which was first suspected to be tuberculosis but was not. "Multiple healed lung abscesses," the doctor determined after additional X-rays. "Probably a result of untreated staphylococcal pneumonia."

Freddie Walsh had healed scars also; strap marks on his buttocks and back. Another boy, Philly, had a severe speech impediment apparently due to an enlarged tongue. A boy nicknamed Wildcat because of a violent temper with a very short fuse was obviously of little higher intelligence than a moron but there was nothing to be done for him, either. The state didn't have a facility for mental deficients in his age group. An Italian boy named Joey Lupo, who was called Loop after the downtown section of Chicago, had a crooked right eye about which nothing was done. "Both eyes have to have amblyopia to qualify for corrective surgery," the doctor told him.

After medicals came dentals. There was one standard for everyone. Trench mouth was treated. Pyorrhea was treated. Ordinary cavities were let alone until they reached the pain threshold, then the tooth was extracted. Charleytown dentists didn't do fillings.

Psychological evaluations followed. All of them seemed to be sex-related. Look at this inkblot: does it remind you of a dirty picture? How many times a day do you masturbate? Have you ever had sex relations with a man? A relative? An animal? Draw a picture of a naked woman. The people asking the questions terrified most of the boys. They were all unsmiling, unblinking, softspoken, somehow threatening people whose very attitudes and demeanor seemed to scream: We know there's something terribly, terribly wrong with you! Mercifully, the evaluations were, for most new arrivals, brief. Only when a boy like Wildcat came along, a boy they could term a latent homicidal maniac or worse, was he resummoned again and again to be studied by the entire staff, his flaws discussed openly in front of him as if he were insensitive or deaf.

Job counseling, the biggest farce of all, was saved for last—probably, the boys decided, to give them a big laugh so they could be sent into the general population in a good frame of mind.

The counselor made checks on a printed form as he talked. "Ever had experience doing yard work?" he asked.

Yard work? Around Ashland and Van Buren? What the hell was a yard?

"Know anything about animals?" Yeah, sure. In the tenements, cats survived and dogs didn't.

"Ever worked as an office boy or messenger?" No.

"Ever worked as a busboy or kitchen helper?"

"I'm twelve, mister," Martin said. "You got to be sixteen to get a work permit."

The counselor's lips tightened. "All these questions are on the form. Just answer them."

When he got to the bottom of the form, the counselor asked the question Martin thought should have been on the top. "What kind of work, if any, *have* you done?"

"Pinboy in a bowling alley," Martin told him. After running away from his latest foster home, for a month before being caught and taken to juvenile hall, he had worked, and lived, in the Cascade Bowling Alley on West Madison Street. Spotting pins for two leagues a night, he'd earned enough to eat more or less regularly. He hid in the place until after it closed and slept on a divan in the ladies lounge. During the day, he wandered the streets or went to places where the juvenile officers never looked for runaways: the main library downtown, the museums, the art institute, the planetarium. When he needed clothes, he stole them from thrift shops—nobody expected you to steal secondhand clothes.

"That's all you've done, set pins?" The counselor smiled a humorless smile. "I guess this isn't your lucky day, then. When they built our recreation center, they left out a bowling alley. I'm assigning you to garbage detail. You won't need a work permit for that."

On their last day in R-and-D, Martin and the others were told to roll up their spare set of clothes and line up out front to be picked up by their house father. At Charleytown, the boys lived in barracks that were called "cottages" and were named after U.S. presidents. The man in charge of each cottage was a house father. Wildcat was assigned to Buchanan Cottage, which was for what the psychiatric staff referred to as "troubled inmates." Philly went to Grant Cottage. Martin, Freddie Walsh, and Loop went to Polk. The house father who came for them had a sharp face and a loose-jointed, rolling-hipped walk.

• • •

MARTIN remained in his office a few minutes after five. When his staff was gone, he found Edward McKey's employment application and made a copy of it on the Xerox machine.

When he got home, Kevin, his eight-year-old, was waiting on the porch with his fielder's mitt and a ball. "Be out as soon as I change, Kev," Martin told his son. It was Kevin's first year in Little League and Martin gave him half an hour of practice every evening.

In the kitchen, Martin's wife, Peg, was basting a pork roast. With an oven mitt on one hand, ladle in the other, she was defenseless, so Martin set his briefcase down and proceeded to fondle her from behind.

"If you make me burn myself, Martin—"

"Hi, Daddy," said Ellie, their five-year-old, coming into the kitchen. She looked up at her parents with gap-toothed curiosity.

Martin let Ellie carry his briefcase into the master bedroom and sit on what she called "the big bed" while Martin changed into some scruffy clothes. Listening to her tales of the day, which included preschool, a spilt glass of Gatorade, and helping Mommy replant a flowerbox, Martin delighted that she was so much like Peg. Coming from the same tenements that Martin had, Peg, too, had grown up knowing the harsh side of life: an alcoholic father, a mother without happiness or hope, two brothers who became hoodlums, a sister who started prostituting under the stairs when she was fourteen. Peg had gone a different way, living by her own rules and standards, much as Martin had. Now, as a woman, she remembered the things she had missed as a child, and gave those things to Ellie. Because she and Ellie were so much alike, it was as if Peg were raising *herself*, and that delighted Martin. Just as it delighted Peg that Martin was doing the same thing with Kevin.

When Martin was ready, he said, "Want to come practice catching with your brother and me?"

"I already had my bath," Ellie said. "If I play baseball, will I have to take another one?"

"Probably."

"Then I don't want to."

Martin and Kevin had their practice session, then showered and dressed for supper. Afterward, the kids watched television while their parents cleaned up the kitchen. Then, as they did three nights a week, they had family hour, the four of them alternating at selecting the activity, which ranged from playing Hide-the-Button, Ellie's usual choice, to naming animals, articles of clothing, etc., which started with each letter of the alphabet, a game Martin had created. Sometimes the activity was simply going for a walk.

In bed later that night, Martin asked, "Did I ever tell you about a kid I knew in Charleytown named Freddie Walsh?"

"I don't remember," Peg said drowsily. She liked to float in and out of sleep after they made love—she called it her afterglow. "You've told me about so many."

"This kid died in there."

"I don't think you ever told me about anybody who died." She drifted for a moment, then came back. "Why?"

"Nothing, really. I was just reminded of him today." He pulled the sheet over her shoulder. "Go on to sleep, honey," he said quietly.

After Peg's breathing became even, Martin remained awake for a long time, staring at a memory as vivid in his mind as if it had happened that day.

• • •

"My name is Mr. McKey," the edge-faced man said. "I'm your house father. You will always address me and refer to me as 'Mister' and you will always say 'sir' when speaking to me. Any time you fail to do so will result in your receiving a demerit. Ten demerits will result in punishment."

McKey's eyes swept the six faces before him: Martin, Freddie, Loop, and three others. "Form a single-file line and follow me," he ordered. "No talking."

McKey led them to the cottage. In an anteroom just inside the double-doored entrance, he had them stop and directed their attention to a small bulletin board. On it was thumbtacked a newspaper clipping with a headline that read: BILLY McKEY MAKES ALL-STATE. There was a photo in the clipping of a handsome, smiling boy of fourteen, wearing a football helmet.

"My son Billy," said McKey. "He made the varsity team his first year in high school. He was the only freshman ever named to an all-state football team. I put news about Billy on this board to show the boys in my cottage what a decent kid does with his life. Might encourage some of you to change your ways." McKey's eyes narrowed slightly. "It is a requirement of this cottage that you read everything I put on the board about Billy. I sometimes ask questions about it. Anyone who can't answer correctly is given a demerit."

From the anteroom, McKey took them into the dormitory, assigned each of them a cot, and demonstrated how it was to be made up. "Improperly made cots get you a demerit." Each boy was given a locker. McKey showed them how their spare clothing and towel were to be placed. "Failure to keep your locker neat gets a demerit." He showed them the shower room. "Wasting soap gets a demerit. Not turning the water off all the way gets a demerit."

At one point, when McKey's back was turned, Freddie Walsh whispered to Martin, "Breathing too much air gets a demerit."

McKey's head snapped around in time to catch the last movement of Freddie's lips. "Whispering behind a house father's back gets a demerit," he said, taking a small spiral notebook and pencil from his shirt pocket. "Walsh, isn't it?"

Freddie would soon learn, as would Martin, Loop, and the other new-comers, that life at Charleytown was a never-ending, usually futile effort to avoid demerits. It was practically impossible to do—there were too many pitfalls. An unbuttoned shirt collar got a demerit. Raising your voice got a demerit. Failure to clean your tray in the dining hall got a demerit—as did not being where you were supposed to be when the whistle was blown, looking at the body of a female staff member, walking on the wrong side of a sidewalk, any kind of horseplay, communicating with boys from another cottage, stepping on the grass, spitting, closing a door too loudly. A shirttail hanging out, even an expression on your face that the house father didn't like resulted in demerits, as did a multitude of other indiscretions, most of them committed innocently, carelessly, thoughtlessly, or playfully. Most of the kids sent to Charleytown were old beyond their years to begin with. At Charleytown, they got much older.

Martin, Freddie, and Loop decided to stick together for their mutual protection. Freddie, a little older and a lot tougher, was the natural leader of the trio. Because he had red hair, and because he was hard, he got the nickname Brick. It soon became common knowledge in Polk Cottage that anybody who messed with Babyface or Loop messed with Brick. And any-body Brick couldn't handle by himself Babyface and Loop would help him with. And anybody the three of them couldn't handle behind the barracks in the daytime they could always get in the middle of the night, because even the toughest kid had to sleep sometime.

The actual boss of the cottage was Lightning, a handsome black kid with corded muscles and extraordinarily fast hands—hence his nickname. He left Babyface, Brick, and Loop alone because it wasn't worth his while to do otherwise. None of them got an allowance from home, and only Loop got food packages on visiting day, the first Sunday of every month. Freddie's mother never brought him anything and Martin never had a visitor. For Lightning to have hassled three guys for a share of one box of food a month—Italian food at that—would have been stupid.

While Freddie went out on the field crew every day to hoe weeds and Loop reported to the institution laundry to operate a hand-cranked wringer, Martin rode the big garbage truck that came through the gate twice a day to collect all kitchen waste and shop trash. He hung onto the rear of the truckbed with a black kid, Jazz, so named because he was always jiving and shucking. At every stop they hopped off, hoisted the fifty-five-gallon drums of garbage, and emptied them into the truckbed.

The driver, a townsman who contracted the work, said the same thing to them at every stop: "Come on, you punks, snap it up! I ain't got all day!" Jazz and Babyface never varied their speed. At the end of every day, when the truck dropped them back at Polk Cottage, Mr. McKey would ask the driver how the two boys had performed and the driver would also give a variation of the same reply: "Slow. I could get outta here half an hour earlier if they was to work faster. They're just too lazy to do it. I can see why they're where they are." Every day, McKey would give each of them a demerit.

Just working on the garbage truck got them enough demerits to qualify for punishment three times a month.

• • •

"I'D like to drive down and see Loop in the morning," Martin told Peg on Friday night. "You didn't have anything planned for me, did you?"

"We promised to take the kids to that carnival at the mall, but that's not until midafternoon. You'll be back by then, won't you?"

"Sure."

"Don't forget to take the kids' new school pictures," Peg reminded him. "You know how he likes to watch them grow up."

"I've already got them in my wallet," Martin said.

He got up early Saturday and drove down to Stateville, the maximum-security penitentiary north of Joliet. At the visitor entrance, he filled out a short form and gave it to a corrections officer at the counter. The officer keyed the name "Lupo, Joseph Angelo" and his inmate number into a computer terminal. After verifying that Martin's name was on the inmate's approved visitor list, Martin was passed into a second room, where the contents of his pockets were scrutinized and where, as usual, his key ring had to be left behind because his briefcase key was too similar in design to a handcuffs key. He then went through a metal detector, was given a visitor pass, and let inside.

The visiting room was long and narrow, divided by an anchored table running from one end to the other. A white line was painted down the middle of the table and officers sat on elevated chairs at either end to make certain that nothing ever crossed that line. When Martin entered his side of the room, he gave the school photos of Kevin and Ellie to an officer to be given to Loop.

As Loop entered his side of the room, he waved, winked his still-crossed right eye at Martin, and broke into a delighted grin when the guard handed him the photos. On their respective sides of the table, he and Martin moved to the middle of the room, putting themselves as far from each officer as possible.

"Jeez, Babyface, these kids look great," Loop said as he sat down, holding a photo in each hand. "Kevin looks just like you used to. And this Ellie, is she gonna be a heartbreaker. Look at that smile. I can't believe how fast they're growing up. Jeez." Loop had never seen Martin's children in person. He had been in prison since before they were born and knew them only through photographs and spoken and written description. Peg, whom he had also never met, wrote him a chatty letter once a month. Martin visited him half a dozen times a year and they put what they could afford into his commissary account. It was understood between them, without being discussed, that Martin would never bring his family to the prison.

Loop put the photos aside and the two men discussed generalities for a while—how the Cubs and White Sox were doing, the ridiculous mess the heavyweight division was in, whether Martin would buy a car now or wait for the new models, the lack of rain throughout the Midwest, Loop's job in the prison bindery where state schoolbooks were bound, Martin's job in the personnel office.

Finally Martin lowered his voice almost to a whisper and said, "Loop, where can I get a piece that can't be traced?"

The convict frowned. "Where can—? What the hell for?" he asked, his voice even lower than Martin's, his lips barely moving.

"I need one," Martin said.

"I asked what for," Loop repeated. His expression hardened. "Don't play no games with me, Babyface," he said firmly.

Martin swallowed dryly. "Remember Old Man McKey?"

"The Charleytown screw? Sure. Who could forget that bum?"

"He came into my office the other day for a night watchman's job."

Loop's mouth dropped open in surprise. "I'll be damned," he said incredulously.

The two men locked eyes as they remembered a promise they had made to each other long ago.

• • •

PUNISHMENT in Polk Cottage was administered every night at seven-thirty. Any boy who had accumulated ten demerits was called into the anteroom by Mr. McKey, who returned from his home in town after supper each evening to personally supervise the punishment period. When punishment was over and the boys all locked in the dormitory, McKey would then leave, turning the cottage over to a night orderly who stayed on duty in the office until the house father returned the following morning.

There was hardly a boy who didn't receive demerits for failing to answer questions McKey would randomly ask, without warning, about items he had put on the bulletin board regarding his son Billy. Not only sports items (BILLY McKEY CATCHES WINNING PASS, BILLY McKEY LEADS VARSITY TO BASKETBALL TOURNAMENT, BILLY McKEY SETS NEW STATE REC-ORD FOR 100-YARD DASH), but items from a Boy Scout newsletter (BILLY McKEY EARNS 15TH MERIT BADGE), a Presbyterian Church bulletin (BILLY McKEY SELECTED AS VACATION BIBLE SCHOOL TEACHER FOR YOUNGER CHILDREN), a high-school newspaper (BILLY McKEY NEW R.O.T.C. LIEUTENANT, BILLY McKEY ELECTED SOPHOMORE CLASS PRESIDENT), and a National Honor Society magazine (BILLY McKEY EARNS 4.0 SCHOLASTIC AVERAGE FOR THIRD STRAIGHT YEAR).

It wasn't that the kids in Polk Cottage didn't read everything Mr. McKey tacked up—they did. It was just that they were unable to understand most of it, couldn't individually identify with it and therefore were unable to remember it. They knew nothing about the Boy Scouts, the R.O.T.C., or the National Honor Society. Most of the time the news they read of All-American boy Billy McKey was simply a lot of words that didn't register. And that was how McKey caught them.

"You there, Walsh," he would challenge, "name the softball team that my boy Billy pitched a shutout against last week."

Freddie thought and shrugged. "I can't remember, Mr. McKey, sir."

Out came the spiral notebook. "That's a demerit, Walsh."

And: "You, Lupo. When Billy won the high-school debating contest, what subject did he debate?"

Loop's expression twisted into a squinting frown. "What does 'subject' mean, Mr. McKey?"

"It means another demerit for you, Lupo."

Or: "You, Howe. What organization wrote about my boy's perfect grade average?"

"The National Grade Society," Martin tried.

"Close, Howe, but not close enough. One demerit. Pay more attention to what you read next time."

Punishment varied. Pushups were the most common for the younger kids. Those a little older were made to hold their arms straight out in front of them, palms down, with a length of two-by-four wood laid across the backs of their hands. Within minutes it made them feel as if their arms were being torn out of their sockets and their necks were going to burst.

There was also the Spot, a white circle on the floor near the wall in which a kid had to stand, looking at a white line on the wall. Freddie Walsh set the record for standing on the Spot: eleven hours and twenty minutes before he dropped. Most kids fainted long before that.

And there was Old Faithful—Mr. McKey's leather strap. Old Faithful was optional. Instead of pushups, the two-by-four, or the Spot, Mr. McKey occasionally let a boy choose a predetermined number of strokes with the strap. The licks had to be taken in undershorts, without trousers, while leaning over a straight chair.

The worst punishment by far was the fire hose. It hung rolled up in a wooden box on the wall of the anteroom, connected to a large faucet next to the box. Long enough to stretch far into the dormitory, it also could stretch down a short flight of stairs to the basement of the cottage. The basement was empty except for the furnace that heated the cottage in winter. There was a brick wall near the bottom of the steps and Martin's second summer at Charleytown McKey came up with the idea of making the boys with enough demerits line up naked in front of the wall. He would drag the fire hose down the stairs, have the night orderly turn on the faucet, and blast the line of boys with the spray. The force of the water drove them back against the rough wall and made them double up in protective crouches on the floor.

As soon as their faces contorted in pain and they began to cry and plead, McKey would let them out of the basement, one by one, to half run, half stumble back upstairs to their cots, gasping for breath, drenched, pitiful. The last one to cry, the one who took the hose blast the longest, the one who took the most punishment, the one who was the toughest, the biggest hardhead was always the last one to be let go.

It was usually Freddie Walsh.

The thing about Freddie that rankled Old Man McKey the most was that sometimes Freddie refused to cry at all, refused to plead. Sometimes Freddie got it into his head that he would take whatever McKey handed out, all of it, without backing down. Times like that, he would curl his naked body into a ball on the floor next to the brick wall and let McKey hit him with the fire-hose spray for long minutes after all the other boys had been allowed upstairs. With one shoulder and one hand protecting his ears, the other hand protecting his testicles, Freddie would press against the floor and the wall his eyes shut tightly, his jaw clenched between gasps of air, making McKey stand there until his arms ached from holding the heavy, bucking hose. The house father would direct the blast of water at Freddie's head, neck, shoulders, back, buttocks—any part that was exposed. When the pain of the water's impact became too much on one spot, Freddie would shift position and McKey would select a new target on the boy's body. He soon learned that the most vulnerable places seemed to be the lower back just above the hipbone on either side. The more he could hit Freddie there, the quicker Freddie was likely to cry.

McKey usually won the battles of will between them. Only on a few rare occasions did he yell up to have the hose turned off before Freddie conceded to his pain and pleaded for relief. On those occasions, Old Man McKey would be glowering darkly when he left for the night.

The last night that Freddie outlasted the Old Man, he did it because he passed out. He was unconscious when the water stopped. The boys in the dorm watched out the windows as Freddie was taken to the infirmary on a stretcher. They never saw him again. McKey announced a couple of days later that Freddie was all right and had been transferred to another cottage. Babyface and Loop found out differently. They managed to slip over to Roosevelt Cottage, where the infirmary workers were quartered, and talked to one of the boys there.

"He wasn't transferred, man," the boy told them in confidence. "That kid died. His kidneys quit working. The docs couldn't figure out why."

Late that night, crying together in the cottage shower room in the dark, Babyface and Loop made their promise to each other. Somehow, sometime, one or both of them would kill Old Man McKey.

• • •

"You're crazy," Loop muttered across the visiting-room table. "You're out of your goddamned skull if you think I'm gonna put you onto a piece. You don't owe Freddie nothing."

"We took an oath, Loop," Martin reminded him.

"That was kid stuff. We ain't kids any more."

"Someone's got to get even for what McKey did." Martin's tone was becoming as determined as his friend's.

"Get *even*? Christ, you sound like half the guys in the joint here. There's no such thing as getting even, kid. You're lucky in life if you just *break* even." Loop leaned forward as far as the white line would permit. His voice became softer but more urgent. "Listen to me," he said. "You're one of the lucky ones, one of the very few who were able to crawl up out of the sewer and live in the sunshine. You've got a sweet wife, two great kids, a house, a decent job. Don't you know what that's *worth?*" He sat back and began silently drumming his fingertips on the tabletop, his patience ebbing.

"Look at me, kid. I'm only a couple of years older than you but I look ten years older. I'm doing life as a habitual criminal. Remember Philly, the kid with the big tongue who couldn't talk right? He got blown away in a liquor-store holdup. The owner's wife came out of the back room and plowed him under with a four-ten shotgun. Remember Wildcat, the little punk with the bad temper? He's on Death Row out in California—killed a highway patrolman who pulled him over for speeding. A *traffic ticket*, for God's sake, and the guy's sweating out the gas chamber.

"Remember Jazz, the black kid you worked with on the garbage truck? He turned into a junkie and died in a doorway from an OD of heroin. And Lightning, the big black kid that ran the cottage? Know what he is today? The leader of a gang of strongarmers around Twelfth and Kedzie that call themselves the Ebony Stallions and shake down their own people for a living."

The convict took a quick breath and stopped drumming his fingers. His hard, criminal eyes fixed on Martin like cannon directed at an enemy.

"If you think you owe Freddie Walsh anything, you're a goddamned fool. Freddie got off easy. He wouldn't have been like you, he would have been like *us*. Me and Philly and Jazz and the rest. He would've stayed in the sewer all his life." Loop shook his head. "I won't tell you where to get a gun. 'Cause I won't help you kill yourself. And that's what you'd be doing if you killed Old Man McKey—killing yourself."

Martin shielded his eyes with one hand and stared at the table. Loop put both hands flat on his side of the line and did the same. A heavy silence fell between them, awkward, uncomfortable, unfamiliar to both of them after so many friendly, easy visits. A minute seemed like ten, then Martin took his hand down and nodded slowly.

"You're right, Loop," he said quietly, forcing a weak smile. "I guess I just needed somebody to remind me of that. Thanks. I owe you one."

Loop shrugged. "You don't owe me nothing. It's them you owe," he said, bobbing his chin at the school photos of Martin's children.

A corrections officer came over and put a slip of paper on the table in front of Loop, indicating that the time allowed for the visit was up. Martin and Loop walked along their respective sides to the officer at the entrance, where Loop gave him the photos to pass back to Martin.

"So long, Loop," said Martin. "Thanks."

The convict winked his bad right eye again. "Take care, kid."

Martin left the prison and crossed the visitor parking lot, Loop's words rebounding in his mind. The one thing that never occurred to Martin was that Loop would decline to stand by his promise. Loop was the one person he had been sure would understand and help. Freddie Walsh had been their friend, at times he had been their protector. He had come from the same streets they had—been kicked in the teeth by the same society, judged by the same establishment, condemned by the same authority. But most of all, Freddie had always been the last one to cry. For that, if nothing else, he deserved to be avenged.

And Loop, although he did not realize it, *had* told Martin where to get a gun to do it.

• • •

THE drive into Chicago took an hour. On the way, Martin stopped at a branch of the bank with which he did business and at an automatic teller machine withdrew three hundred dollars with his bank card. When he reached the city, he headed for the heart of the southwest side. It was all black now; there wasn't a white face in sight as he guided the car along Kedzie Avenue. Some of the people on the sidewalk glared at him as he drove past—wondering what I am, Martin thought: bill collector, parole officer, slum landlord. Simply by his color he was an alien here, an enemy. And he felt it—by the time he got to Twelfth Street, his shirt was wet with perspiration halfway down the sleeves.

He had anticipated problems once he got to the neighborhood, but his anxiety was alleviated as soon as he turned the corner into Twelfth. A few doors from the intersection he saw a storefront building with its windows painted black and a sign reading: THE EBONY STALLIONS CLUB. In smaller letters it advised MEMBERS ONLY. Martin let out a sigh of relief. But he kept sweating.

Parking, he got out and locked his car, wondering if he would make it across the sidewalk where several unsmiling youths were regarding him ominously. Tough and bluff, Martin remembered from his own youth. Never show fear. Walking around his car, he gave the youths a cursory glance and went past them as if they weren't there. He heard some obscene comments behind his back and ignored them as a terrifying thought entered his mind: if the door to the Ebony Stallions Club was locked—

It wasn't. Inside, the place was arranged like a neighborhood lounge: bar, booths, a few tables, postage-stamp dance floor. There were a dozen men, several women, and a bartender in the place. When Martin entered, they all looked at him as if they couldn't believe their eyes. Not even white *cops* walked into the Ebony Stallions Club. Several of the men rose and stood threateningly. The bartender came to the end of the bar, staring.

Martin walked over to him.

"I'm looking for a man called Lightning," he said.

They all kept staring at him. No one spoke.

"I don't know him by any other name," Martin said. "I only know him as Lightning."

Still the stares, still the silence.

"I'm a friend of his," Martin said, not very convincingly.

The bartender smirked. "One thing Lightning ain't got is no white friends."

A couple of the men who had stood up now began moving slowly toward the bar. Tough and bluff, Martin thought again. He put one hand under the front of his coat as if he might be armed. "You'd better let Lightning decide whether I'm a friend or not," he told the bartender curtly. "Just say Babyface is here. From Charleytown."

They all studied Martin for a moment longer, then one of the men nodded and the others sat back down and resumed drinking. The man who had nodded strode to the front door and left. Martin took his hand from under his coat.

The bartender pondered for a moment, then asked, "You want a drink?"

Martin had never wanted one more badly. "Vodka on the rocks," he said.

He had half the drink inside him a few minutes later when the man who had left returned with a tall, handsome, immaculately groomed black man who, unlike Loop, did not look as if he had aged five years in the twenty since Charleytown.

"Well, well," said Lightning, "Babyface."

Smiling, he held out a hand.

• • •

AN hour later, Martin was driving back downstate. In the glove compartment of his car, with the copy of Edward McKey's employment application, was a loaded .380 automatic.

"It's as cold as a piece can be," Lightning had told him. "Made illegally in Italy, smuggled in through Haiti, never registered in the U.S. Doesn't even have a manufacturer's name or serial number on it—and no ballistics record anywhere. Absolutely no way it can be traced."

Lightning had refused to take Martin's money. He seemed genuinely pleased that Martin lived inside the law and had a family, and talked about his own two sons, both illegitimate by different women, both on the streets, one on drugs, but apparently some hope for the other one. "The boy likes classical music," Lightning revealed, as if it were some strange miracle. "I've told him I'll get him into the London Conservatory if he stays in line and finishes high school."

Lightning hadn't asked why Martin wanted the cold gun and Martin hadn't volunteered the information. His street instincts, never dormant, told him that the fewer people who could connect him with McKey's killing the better.

Martin got back home in time to take Peg and the kids to the carnival.

"You were gone longer than usual," Peg said. "Anything the matter?"

"The car stalled on me a couple of times," Martin told her. He detested having to lie to Peg, but it fit in with his alibi for getting out of the house that night. "After supper, I think I'll run it over to Mac's all-night garage and have it checked. The carburetor probably needs cleaning."

The carnival was fun for Peg and the kids, and Martin managed to give the impression he was enjoying himself. His only bad moment came at the shooting gallery where he was trying to win a kewpie doll for Ellie. All the targets looked like Old Man McKey and Martin's hands sweat so much he couldn't control the pellet rifle. "We'll try again next time there's a carnival, honey," he told the little girl. She was disappointed only as far as the cotton-candy stand.

After the carnival, they went to a Pizza Hut to eat. It was eight o'clock when they finally got home. "I'll run the car over while you put the kids to bed," Martin said as casually as he could. "I shouldn't be more than an hour or so."

On his way out, he went through the garage and picked up a pair of cotton work gloves. They would alleviate his sweating palms and prevent fingerprints. Lightning, holding the pistol in a handkerchief, had shown Martin how to jack a round into the chamber and set the safety, then he had wiped off the weapon carefully and wrapped it in the handkerchief.

When Martin had gotten back to town that afternoon he had driven past Edward McKey's house before going home, so he knew exactly where it was. All he had to do now, he thought as he got in his car, was go over there and kill the son of a bitch.

• • •

MARTIN parked half a block away, around the corner from an alley that ran behind McKey's house. Pulling on the cotton gloves, he unwrapped the gun and put it in his windbreaker pocket. Leaving his car unlocked, he walked away from McKey's street. A few feet past the alley, he stepped into the shadows next to a tree. For a few moments he stood there, eyes and ears measuring the dark little street. All was quiet.

Moving out of his concealment, he entered the alley and hurried along behind the houses on McKey's street.

McKey lived in the fifth house from the corner. Martin had been surprised earlier that day to find that it was a tacky little place in a rundown neighborhood. He had always imagined McKey living in the kind of home he used to see in Andy Hardy movies.

Martin counted backyard gates as he moved along the alley, which was darker than the street had been. At the fifth gate, he stopped and scrutinized what he could see across the yard. There was one light on in the rear of the house, probably the kitchen—nothing else. With one hand, he rattled the gate very quietly to see if there might be a dog in the yard. All remained quiet.

Carefully opening the gate, he entered and walked stealthily up to the back porch. The steps were wooden, so he used the inside edge where they were less likely to creak, testing each one before putting his entire weight on it. Odd, he thought, how some things you never forgot.

Peering in the window, Martin saw a cluttered little kitchen, with someone in a wheelchair, back to the window, pushed up to a table. He frowned. He couldn't see all of the kitchen, but there was another window to the other side of the kitchen door through which he might. He started toward it.

The porch light suddenly came on, the back door opened, and Edward McKey stepped out with a sack of garbage in one hand. He and Martin saw each other and each stepped back, startled.

"Who are you?" McKey asked fearfully. "What do you want?"

There's a witness, Martin thought tensely. The person in the wheelchair.

"Mr. McKey," Martin said in a controlled voice, "I'm the personnel manager over at Wayne and Grayson, where you applied for the night watchman's job. I happened to be driving by and thought I'd stop in for a minute. I knocked at the front door but I guess you didn't hear me."

"Guess I didn't," McKey said. He put the sack in a garbage can on the porch. "Come in," he said, "Mr.—"

"Howe. Martin Howe."

The name didn't seem to register on McKey. Martin followed him into the kitchen.

"Excuse the mess," McKey said. "My missus passed away a few years ago. There's just me and the boy here." He gestured toward the wheelchair. "I'm not much of a housekeeper."

Martin looked at the figure in the wheelchair. Not a boy at all, but a young man two years older than Martin, with a face that Martin still recognized from the many pictures he had seen of it on the Polk Cottage bulletin board. Billy McKey. His head slumped slightly to one side. There was a line of spittle drooling from the corner of his mouth and his eyes stared unblinkingly at nothing.

No witness, after all.

Martin put his hand on the gun in his pocket.

"I guess it's too much to hope that you stopped by to tell me I got the job," McKey half stated, half inquired. "I sure do need it because of the boy here. I have to work nights because it costs too much to hire somebody to look after him during the day, when he needs a lot of tending to. But a widow lady next door has agreed to stay over nights while he's sleeping. If I can just get a good night job, things ought to work out good for us."

"What's the matter with your son, Mr. McKey?" Martin asked. He had to be sure there was no witness.

McKey shrugged self-consciously and looked away. "Drugs. He got mixed up with them in college. He had everything in the world going for him: looks, personality, intelligence, athletic ability. Threw it all away for drugs. He used too much of that angel-dust stuff one night and went into a coma. When he came out of it, he was the way you see him now—a vegetable."

"Can't talk or anything?" Martin asked.

McKey shook his head. "He can't even think."

Martin slipped the safety off the pistol. His eyes flicked from McKey to Billy and back to McKey. His finger tightened on the trigger a fraction.

"Why *did* you stop by, Mr. Howe?" McKey asked, squeezing his son's shoulder.

Martin gazed at the tense hand on the shoulder, then relaxed his own hand and put the safety back on. "To tell you that you got the job," he said. "Come by the personnel office Monday morning. Ask for me."

McKey swallowed with difficulty. "You don't know what this means to me," he said, almost choking on the words. "We've had it pretty hard, me and the boy—"

"I'm sure things will be better for you now," Martin told him encouragingly. "See you Monday. Goodnight."

He left as he had come in, by the back door. Passing the window, he glanced in and saw McKey on his knees, face buried in the blanket on Billy's lap, sobbing. And Martin thought, Freddie Walsh hadn't been the last one to cry, after all.

THE ABSENCE OF EMILY

Jack Ritchie

THE PHONE RANG and I picked up the receiver. "Yes?"

"Hello, darling, this is Emily."

I hesitated. "Emily who?"

She laughed lightly. "Oh, come now, darling. Emily, your wife."

"I'm sorry, you must have a wrong number." I hung up, fumbling a bit as I cradled the phone.

Millicent, Emily's cousin, had been watching me. "You look white as a sheet."

I glanced covertly at a mirror.

"I don't mean in actual *color*, Albert. I mean figuratively. In attitude. You seem frightened. Shocked."

"Nonsense."

"Who phoned?"

"It was a wrong number."

Millicent sipped her coffee. "By the way, Albert, I thought I saw Emily in town yesterday, but, of course, that was impossible."

"Of course it was impossible. Emily is in San Francisco."

"Yes, but *where* in San Francisco?"

"She didn't say. Just visiting friends."

"I've known Emily all her life. She has very few secrets from me. She doesn't *know* anybody in San Francisco. When will she be back?"

"She might be gone a rather long time."

"How long?"

"She didn't know."

Millicent smiled. "You have been married before, haven't you, Albert?"

"Yes."

"As a matter of fact, you were a widower when you met Emily?"

"I didn't try to keep that fact a secret."

"Your first wife met her death in a boating accident five years ago? She fell overboard and drowned?"

"I'm afraid so. She couldn't swim a stroke."

"Wasn't she wearing a life preserver?"

"No. She claimed they hindered her movements."

"It appears that you were the only witness to the accident."

"I believe so. At least no one else ever came forward."

"Did she leave you any money, Albert?"

"That's none of your business, Millicent."

Cynthia's estate had consisted of a fifty-thousand-dollar life insurance policy, of which I was the sole beneficiary, some forty-thousand dollars in sundry stocks and bonds, and one small sailboat.

I stirred my coffee. "Millicent, I thought I'd give you first crack at the house."

"First crack?"

"Yes. We've decided to sell this place. It's really too big for just the two of us. We'll get something smaller. Perhaps even an apartment. I thought you might like to pick up a bargain. I'm certain we can come to satisfactory terms."

She blinked. "Emily would never sell this place. It's her home. I'd have to hear the words from her in person."

"There's no need for that. I have her power of attorney. She has no head for business, you know, but she trusts me implicitly. It's all quite legal and aboveboard."

"I'll think it over." She put down her cup. "Albert, what did you do for a living before you met Emily? Or Cynthia, for that matter?"

"I managed."

When Millicent was gone, I went for my walk on the back grounds of the estate. I went once again to the dell and sat down on the fallen log. How peaceful it was here. Quiet. A place to rest. I had been coming here often in the last few days.

Millicent and Emily. Cousins. They occupied almost identical large homes on spacious grounds next to each other. And, considering that fact, one might reasonably have supposed that they were equally wealthy. Such, however, was not the case, as I discovered after my marriage to Emily.

Millicent's holdings must certainly reach far into seven figures, since they require the full-time administrative services of Amos Eberly, her attorney and financial advisor.

Emily, on the other hand, owned very little more than the house and the grounds themselves and she had borrowed heavily to keep them going. She had been reduced to two servants, the Brewsters. Mrs. Brewster, a surly creature, did the cooking and desultory dusting, while her husband, formerly the butler, had been reduced to a man-of-all-work, who pottered inadequately about the grounds. The place really required the services of two gardeners.

Millicent and Emily. Cousins. Yet it was difficult to imagine two people more dissimilar in either appearance or nature.

Millicent is rather tall, spare, and determined. She fancies herself an intellect and she has the tendency to rule and dominate all those about her, and that had certainly included Emily. It is obvious to me that Millicent deeply resents the fact that I removed Emily from under her thumb.

Emily. Shorter than average. Perhaps twenty-five pounds overweight. An amiable disposition. No claim to blazing intelligence. Easily dominated, yes, though she had a surprising stubborn streak when she set her mind to something.

When I returned to the house, I found Amos Eberly waiting. He is a man in his fifties and partial to gray suits.

"Where is Emily?" he asked.

"In Oakland." He gave that thought.

"I meant San Francisco. Oakland is just across the bay, isn't it? I usually think of them as one, which, I suppose, is unfair to both."

He frowned. "San Francisco? But I saw her in town just this morning. She was looking quite well."

"Impossible."

"Impossible for her to be looking well?"

"Impossible for you to have seen her. She is still in San Francisco."

He sipped his drink. "I know Emily when I see her. She wore a lilac dress with a belt. And a sort of gauzy light-blue scarf."

"You were mistaken. Besides, women don't wear gauzy light-blue scarves these days."

"Emily did. Couldn't she have come back without letting you know?"

"No."

Eberly studied me. "Are you ill or something, Albert? Your hands seem to be shaking."

"Touch of the flu," I said quickly. "Brings out the jitters in me. What brings you here anyway, Amos?"

"Nothing in particular, Albert. I just happened to be in the neighborhood and thought I'd drop in and see Emily."

"Damn it, I told you she isn't here."

"All right, Albert," he said soothingly. "Why should I doubt you? If you say she isn't here, she isn't here."

It has become my habit on Tuesday and Thursday afternoons to do the household food shopping, a task which I preempted from Mrs. Brewster when I began to suspect her arithmetic.

As usual, I parked in the supermarket lot and locked the car. When I looked up, I saw a small, slightly stout woman across the street walking toward the farther end of the block. She wore a lilac dress and a light-blue scarf. It was the fourth time I'd seen her in the last ten days.

I hurried across the street. I was still some seventy-five yards behind her when she turned the corner.

Resisting the temptation to shout at her to stop, I broke into a trot.

When I reached the corner, she was nowhere in sight. She could have disappeared into any one of a dozen shop fronts.

I stood there, trying to regain my breath, when a car pulled to the curb. It was Millicent. "Is that you, Albert?"

I regarded her without enthusiasm. "Yes."

"What in the world are you doing? I saw you running and I've never seen you run before."

"I was *not* running. I was merely trotting to get my blood circulating. A bit of jogging is supposed to be healthy, you know."

I volunteered my adieu and strode back to the supermarket.

The next morning when I returned from my walk to the dell, I found Millicent in the drawing room, pouring herself coffee and otherwise making herself at home—a habit from the days when only Emily occupied the house.

"I've been upstairs looking over Emily's wardrobe," Millicent said. "I didn't see anything missing."

"Why should anything be missing? Has there been a thief in the house? I suppose you know every bit and parcel of her wardrobe?"

"Not every bit and parcel, but almost. Almost. And very little, if anything, seems to be missing. Don't tell me that Emily went off to San Francisco without any luggage."

"She had luggage. Though not very much."

"What was she wearing when she left?"

Millicent had asked that question before. This time I said, "I don't remember."

Millicent raised an eyebrow. "You don't remember?" She put down her cup. "Albert, I'm holding a séance at my place tonight. I thought perhaps you'd like to come."

"I will not go to any damn séance."

"Don't you want to communicate with any of your beloved dead?"

"I believe in letting the dead rest. Why bother them with every trifling matter back here?"

"Wouldn't you want to speak with your first wife?"

"Why the devil would I want to communicate with Cynthia? I have absolutely nothing to say to her anyway."

"But perhaps she has something to say to you."

I wiped my forehead. "I'm not going to your stupid séance and that's final."

That evening, as I prepared for bed, I surveyed the contents of Emily's closet. How would I dispose of her clothes? Probably donate them to some worthy charity, I thought.

• • •

I was awakened at two A.M. by the sound of music.

I listened. Yes, it was plainly Emily's favorite sonata being played on the piano downstairs.

I stepped into my slippers and donned my dressing robe. In the hall, I snapped on the lights.

I was halfway down the stairs when the piano-playing ceased. I completed my descent and stopped at the music room doors. I put my ear to one of them. Nothing. I slowly opened the door and peered inside.

There was no one at the piano. However, two candles in holders flickered on its top. The room seemed chilly. Quite chilly.

I found the source of the draft behind some drapes and closed the French doors to the terrace. I snuffed out the candles and left the room.

I met Brewster at the head of the stairs.

"I thought I heard a piano being played, sir," he said. "Was that you?"

I wiped the palms of my hands on my robe. "Of course."

"I didn't know you played the piano, sir."

"Brewster, there are a lot of things you don't know about me and never will."

I went back to my room, waited half an hour, and then dressed. In the bright moonlight outside, I made my way to the garden shed. I unbolted its door, switched on the lights, and surveyed the gardening equipment. My eyes went to the tools in the wall racks.

I pulled down a long-handled irrigating shovel and knocked a bit of dried mud from its tip. I slung the implement over my shoulder and began walking toward the dell.

I was nearly there when I stopped and sighed heavily. I shook my head and returned to the shed. I put the shovel back into its place on the rack, switched off the lights, and returned to bed.

The next morning, Millicent dropped in as I was having breakfast.

"How are you this morning, Albert?"

"I have felt better."

Millicent sat down at the table and waited for Mrs. Brewster to bring her a cup.

Mrs. Brewster also brought the morning mail. It included a number of advertising fliers, a few bills, and one small blue envelope addressed to me.

I examined it. The handwriting seemed familiar and so did the scent. The postmark was torn.

I slit open the envelope and pulled out a single sheet of notepaper.

Dear Albert:

You have no idea how much I miss you. I shall return home soon, Albert. Soon.

Emily

I put the note back into the envelope and slipped both into my pocket.

"Well?" Millicent asked.

"Well, what?"

"I thought I recognized Emily's handwriting on the envelope. Did she say when she'd be back?"

"That is *not* Emily's handwriting. It is a note from my aunt in Chicago."

"I didn't know you had an aunt in Chicago."

"Millicent, rest assured. I *do* have an aunt in Chicago."

That night I was in bed, but awake, when the phone on my night table rang. I picked up the receiver.

"Hello, darling. This is Emily."

I let five seconds pass. "You are *not* Emily. You are an imposter."

"Now, Albert, why are you being so stubborn? Of course this is me, Emily."

"You couldn't be."

"Why couldn't I be?"

"*Because.*"

"Because why?"

"Where are you calling from?"

She laughed. "I think you'd be surprised."

"You couldn't be Emily. I *know* where she is and she couldn't—*wouldn't*—make a phone call at this hour of the night just to say hello. It's well past midnight."

"You think you know where I am, Albert? No, I'm not there anymore. It was so uncomfortable, so dreadfully uncomfortable. And so I left, Albert. I left."

I raised my voice. "Damn you, I can *prove* you're still there."

She laughed. "Prove? How can you prove anything like that, Albert? Good night." She hung up.

I got out of bed and dressed. I made my way downstairs and detoured into the study. I made myself a drink, consumed it slowly, and then made another.

When I consulted my watch for the last time it was nearly one A.M. I put on a light jacket against the chill of the night and made my way to the garden shed. I opened the doors, turned on the lights, and pulled the long-handled shovel from the rack.

This time I went all the way to the dell. I paused beside a huge oak and stared at the moonlit clearing.

I counted as I began pacing. "One, two, three, four—" I stopped at sixteen, turned ninety degrees, and then paced off eighteen more steps.

I began digging.

• • •

I had been at it for nearly five minutes when suddenly I heard the piercing blast of a whistle and immediately I became the focus of perhaps a dozen flashlight beams and approaching voices.

I shielded my eyes against the glare and recognized Millicent. "What the devil is this?"

She showed cruel teeth. "You had to make sure she was really dead, didn't you, Albert? And the only way you could do that was to return to her grave."

I drew myself up. "I am looking for Indian arrowheads. There's an ancient superstition that if one is found under the light of the moon it will bring luck for the finder for several weeks."

Millicent introduced the people gathered about me. "Ever since I began suspecting what really has happened to Emily you've been under twenty-four-hour surveillance by private detectives."

She indicated the others. "Miss Peters. She is quite a clever mimic and was the voice of Emily you heard over the phone. She also plays piano. And

Mrs. McMillan. She reproduced Emily's handwriting and was the woman in the lilac dress and the blue scarf."

Millicent's entire household staff seemed to be present. I also recognized Amos Eberly and the Brewsters. I would fire them tomorrow.

The detectives had brought along their own shovels and spades, and two of them superseded me in my shallow depression. They began digging.

"See here," I said, exhibiting indignation. "You have no right to do that. This is *my* property. At the very least you need a search warrant."

Millicent found that amusing. "This is *not* your property, Albert. It is *mine*. You stepped over the dividing line six paces back."

I wiped my forehead. "I'm going back to the house."

"You are under arrest, Albert."

"Nonsense, Millicent. I do not see a *proper* uniformed policeman among these people. And in this state private detectives do not have the right to arrest anyone at all."

For a moment she seemed stymied, but then saw light. "You are under *citizen's* arrest, Albert. Any citizen has the power to make a citizen's arrest and I am a citizen."

Millicent twirled the whistle on its chain. "We knew we were getting to you, Albert. You almost dug her up last night, didn't you? But then you changed your mind. But that was just as well. Last night I couldn't have produced as many witnesses. Tonight we were ready and waiting."

The detectives dug for some fifteen minutes and then paused for a rest. One of them frowned. "You'd think the digging would be easier. This ground looks like it's never been dug up before."

They resumed their work and eventually reached a depth of six feet before they gave up. The spade man climbed out of the excavation. "Hell, nothing's been buried here. The only thing we found was an Indian arrowhead."

Millicent had been glaring at me for the last half hour.

I smiled. "Millicent, what makes you think that I *buried* Emily?"

With that I left them and returned to the house.

• • •

WHEN had I first become aware of Millicent's magnificent maneuverings and the twenty-four-hour surveillance? Almost from the very beginning, I suspect. I'm rather quick on the uptake.

What had been Millicent's objective? I suppose she envisioned reducing me to such a state of fear that eventually I'd break down and confess to the murder of Emily.

Frankly, I would have regarded the success of such a scheme as far-fetched, to say the least. However, once I was aware of what Millicent was attempting, I got into the spirit of the venture.

Millicent may have initiated the enterprise, the play, but it is I who led her to the dell.

There were times when I thought I overdid it just a bit—wiping at non-existent perspiration, trotting after the elusive woman in the lilac dress, that sort of thing—but on the other hand I suppose these reactions were rather expected of me and I didn't want to disappoint any eager watchers.

Those brooding trips to the dell had been quite a good touch, I thought. And the previous night's halfway journey there, with the shovel over my shoulder, had been intended to assure a large audience at the finale twenty-four hours later.

I had counted eighteen witnesses, excluding Millicent.

I pondered. Defamation of character? Slander? Conspiracy? False arrest? Probably a good deal more.

I would threaten to sue for a large and unrealistic amount. That was the fashion nowadays, wasn't it? Twenty million? It didn't really matter, of course, because I doubted very much if the matter would ever reach court.

No, Millicent wouldn't be able to endure the publicity. She couldn't let the world know what a total fool she'd made of herself. She couldn't bear to be the laughingstock of her circle, her peers.

She would, of course, attempt to hush it up as best she could. A few dollars here and a few there to buy the silence of the witnesses. But could one seriously hope to buy the total silence of eighteen individual people? Probably not. However, when the whispers began to circulate, it would be a considerable help to Millicent if the principal player involved would join her in vehemently denying that any such ridiculous event had ever taken place at all.

And I would do that for Millicent. For a consideration. A *large* consideration.

At the end of the week, my phone rang.

"This is Emily. I'm coming home now, dear."

"Wonderful."

"Did anyone miss me?"

"You have no idea."

"You haven't told anyone where I've been these last four weeks, have you, Albert? Especially not Millicent?"

"Especially not Millicent."

"What *did* you tell her?"

"I said you were visiting friends in San Francisco."

"Oh, dear. I don't *know* anybody in San Francisco. Do you suppose she got suspicious?"

"Well, maybe just a little bit."

"She thinks I have absolutely no willpower, but I really have. But just the same, I didn't want her laughing at me if I didn't stick it out. Oh, I suppose going to a health farm is cheating, in a way. I mean you can't be tempted because they control all of the food. But I really stuck it out. I could have come home any time I wanted to."

"You have marvelous willpower, Emily."

"I've lost *thirty* pounds, Albert! And it's going to *stay* off. I'll bet I'm every bit as slim now as Cynthia ever was."

I sighed. There was absolutely no reason for Emily to keep comparing herself to my first wife. The two of them are separate entities and each has her secure compartment in my affections.

Poor Cynthia. She had insisted on going off by herself in that small craft. I had been at the yacht-club window sipping a martini and watching the cold gray harbor.

Cynthia's boat seemed to have been the only one on the water on that inhospitable day and there had apparently been an unexpected gust of wind. I had seen the boat heel over sharply and Cynthia thrown overboard. I'd raised the alarm immediately, but by the time we got out there it had been too late.

Emily sighed too. "I suppose I'll have to get an entire new wardrobe. Do you think we can really afford one, Albert?"

We could now. And then some.

EVAN HUNTER

When Playboy published "The Interview," they retitled it "The Sardinian Incident." I always preferred my original title. In fact, when I learned that Playboy was buying it, I hoped they would title it "The Playboy Interview" and run it as if it were a genuine celebrity interview. The story was first published in 1971. This was eight years after my working relationship with Alfred Hitchcock on The Birds and Marnie came to an end, and twelve years after I'd been hired to adapt Robert Turner's story.

• • •

"Eleven O'clock Bulletin" was first published in Bluebook in 1955. Four years later I got a call from Alfred Hitchcock. He had bought the story for his television show and wanted to know if I'd do a teleplay based on it. He later told me he'd chosen me for the job because of the story's "internal" nature. This meant that much of the story took place inside the protagonist's head. In Hollywood jargon, the story needed "opening up." Two years after I finished the teleplay, Hitch called again, this time to ask if I would like to do the screenplay for The Birds, a Daphne DuMaurier novella that also needed "opening up." I shall always believe that if Robert Turner hadn't written his intense little story, I never would have been hired to write The Birds.

THE INTERVIEW

Evan Hunter

SIR, EVER SINCE the Sardinian accident, you have refused to grant any interviews. . . .

I had no desire to join the circus.

Yet you are not normally a man who shuns publicity.

Not normally, no. The matter on Sardinia, however, was blown up out of all proportion, and I saw no reason for adding fuel to the fire. I am a creator of motion pictures, *not* of sensational news stories for the press.

There are some "creators of motion pictures" who might have welcomed the sort of publicity the Sardinian . . .

Not I.

Yet you will admit the accident helped the gross of the film.

I am not responsible for the morbid curiosity of the American public.

Were you responsible for what happened in Sardinia?

On Sardinia. It's an island.

On Sardinia, if you will.

I was responsible only for directing a motion picture. Whatever else happened, happened.

You were there when it happened, however. . . .

I was there.

So certainly . . .

I choose not to discuss it.

The actors and technicians present at the time have had a great deal to say about the accident. Isn't there anything you'd like to refute or amend? Wouldn't you like to set the record straight?

The record is the film. My films are my record. Everything else is meaningless. Actors are beasts of burden and technicians are domestic servants, and refuting or amending anything either might care to utter would be a senseless waste of time.

Would you like to elaborate on that?

On what?

On the notion that actors . . .

It is not a notion, it is a simple fact. I have never met an intelligent actor. Well, let me correct that. I enjoyed working with only one actor in my entire career, and I still have a great deal of respect for him—or at least as much respect as I can possibly muster for anyone who pursues a profession that requires him to apply makeup to his face.

Did you use this actor in the picture you filmed on Sardinia?

No.

Why not? Given your respect for him . . .

I had no desire to donate fifty percent of the gross to his already swollen bank account.

Is that what he asked for?

At the time. It may have gone up to seventy-five percent by now, I'm sure I don't know. I have no intention of ever giving a plowhorse or a team of oxen fifty percent of the gross of a motion picture *I* created.

If we understand you correctly . . .

You probably don't.

Why do you say that?

Only because I have never been quoted accurately in any publication, and I have no reason to believe your magazine will prove to be an exception.

Then why did you agree to the interview?

Because I would like to discuss my new project. I have a meeting tonight with a New York playwright who will be delivering the final draft of a screenplay upon which we have labored long and hard. I have every expectation that it will now meet my requirements. In which case, looking ahead to the future, this interview should appear in print shortly before the film is completed and ready for release. At least, I hope the timetable works out that way.

May we know who the playwright is?

I thought you were here to talk to *me*.

Well, yes, but . . .

It has been my observation that when Otto Preminger or Alfred Hitch-cock or David Lean or even some of the fancy young *nouvelle vague* people give interviews, they rarely talk about anyone but themselves. That may be the one good notion any of them has ever contributed to the industry.

You sound as if you don't admire too many directors.

I admire some.

Would you care to name them?

I have admiration for Griffith, DeMille, Eisenstein, several others.

Why these men in particular?

They're all dead.

Are there no living directors you admire?

None.

None? It seems odd that a man known for his generosity would be so chary with praise for other acknowledged film artists.

Yes.

Yes, what?

Yes, it would seem odd, a distinct contradiction of personality. The fact remains that I consider every living director a threat, a challenge, and a competitor. There are only so many motion picture screens in the world, and there are thousands of films competing to fill those screens. If the latest Hitchcock thriller has them standing on line outside Radio City, the chances are they *won't* be standing on line outside *my* film up the street. The theory that an outstanding box-office hit helps *all* movies is sheer rubbish. The outstanding hit helps only itself. The other films suffer because no one wants to see them; they want to see only the big one, the champion, the one that has the line outside on the sidewalk. I try to make certain that all of my films generate the kind of excitement necessary to sustain a line on the sidewalk. And I resent the success of any film but my own.

Yet you have had some notable failures.

Failures are never notable. Besides, I do not consider any of my films failures.

Are we talking now about artistic failures or box-office failures?

I have never made an artistic failure. Some of my films were mildly dis-appointing at the box office. But not very many of them.

When the Sardinian film was ready to open last June . . .

July. It opened on the Fourth of July.

Yes, but before it opened, when

That would have been June, yes. July is normally preceded by June.

There was speculation that the studio would not permit its showing.

Rubbish.

The rumors were unfounded? That the studio would suppress the film?

The film opened, didn't it? And was a tremendous success, I might add.

Some observers maintain that the success of the film was due only to the publicity given the Sardinian accident. Would you agree to that?

I'll ask *you* a question, young man. Suppose the accident on Sardinia had been related to a film called *The Beach Girl Meets Hell's Angels,* or some such piece of trash? Do you think the attendant publicity would have insured the success of *that* film?

Perhaps not. But given your name and the stellar quality of it . . .

You can stop after my name. Stars have nothing to do with any of my pictures. I could put a trained seal in one of my films, and people would come to see it. I could put *you* in a film, and people would come to see it.

Don't you believe that films are a collaborative effort?

Certainly not. I tell the script writer what I want, and he writes it. I tell the set designer what to give me, and he gives it to me. I tell the cameraman where to aim his camera and what lens to use. I tell the actors where to move and how to speak their lines. Does that sound collaborative to you? Besides, I resent the word "effort."

Why?

Because the word implies endeavor without success. You've tried to do something and you've failed. None of my films are "efforts." The word "effort" is like the word "ambitious." They both spell failure. Haven't you seen book jackets that proudly announce "This is So-and-So's most ambitious effort to date"? What does that mean to you? To me, it means the poor bastard has set his sights too high. And failed.

Are you afraid of failure?

I cannot abide it.

Do you believe the Sardinian film was a success? Artistically?

I told you earlier . . .

Yes, but many critics felt the editing of the film was erratic. That the sequences filmed before the drowning were inserted piecemeal into . . .

To begin with, whenever critics begin talking about editing or camera angles or dolly shots or anything technical, I instantly fall asleep. They haven't the faintest notion of what filmmaking is all about, and their pretentious chatter about the art may impress maiden ladies in Flushing Meadows, but it quite leaves me cold. In reality, *none* of them know what's going on either behind the camera or up there on the screen. Do you know what a film critic's sole requirement is? That he has seen a lot of movies, period. To my way of thinking, *that* qualifies him as an expert on popcorn, not on celluloid.

In any event, you were *rather limited, were you not, in editing the final portion of the film?*

Limited in what way?

In terms of the footage you needed to make the film a complete entity?

The film *was* a complete entity. Obviously, I could not include footage that did not exist. The girl drowned. That was a simple fact. We did not shoot the remainder of the film as originally planned; we *could* not. But the necessary script revisions were made on the spot—or rather in Rome. I flew to Rome to consult with an Italian screenwriter, who did the work I required.

He did not receive credit on the film.

He *asked* that his name be removed from the picture. I acceded to his wishes.

But not without a struggle.

There was no struggle.

It was reported that you struck him.

Nonsense.

On the Via Veneto.

The most violent thing I've ever done on the Via Veneto was to sip a Campari-soda outside Doney's.

Yet the newspapers . . .

The Roman press is notoriously inaccurate. In fact, there isn't a single good newspaper in all Italy.

But, sir, there was some dispute with the screenwriter, wasn't there? Surely, the stories about it couldn't all have been . . .

We had some words.

About what?

Oh my, we *must* pursue this deadly dull rot, mustn't we? All right, all right. It was *his* allegation that when he accepted the job, he had no idea the publicity surrounding the girl's death would achieve such hideous proportions. He claimed he did not wish his good Italian name—the little opportunist had written only one film prior to my hiring him, and that an Italian Western starring a second-rate American television actor—did not wish his name associated with a project that had even a *cloud* of suspicion hanging over it. Those were his exact words. Actually, quite the opposite was true. Which is why I resisted his idiotic ploy.

Quite the opposite? What do you mean?

Rather than trying to *avoid* the unfortunate publicity, I felt he was trying to capitalize on it. His move was really completely transparent, the pathetic little bastard. I finally let him have his way. I should have thought he'd be proud to have his name on one of my pictures. As an illuminating sidelight, I might add he did *not* return the five thousand dollars a week I'd paid for the typing he did. Apparently, my *money* did not have a similar "cloud of suspicion" hanging over it.

"Typing," did you say?

Typing. The ideas for changing the script to accommodate the . . . to allow for a more plausible resolution were all mine.

A resolution to accommodate the drowning?

To explain the absence of the girl in the remainder of the film. I'm reluctant to discuss this, because it has a ghoulish quality I frankly find distasteful. The girl *did*, after all, drown; she *did* die. But that was a simple fact, and we must not lose sight of another simple fact. However cold-blooded this may sound, and I am well aware that it may be an unpopular observation, there had already been an expenditure of three million dollars on that film. Now I'm sure you know that leading players *have* taken ill, *have* suffered heart attacks, *have* died during the filming of other pictures. To my knowledge, such events have never caused a picture to halt production, and neither do I know of a single instance in which a film was entirely scrapped, solely because of the death of one of the leading players. Yet this was the very pressure being brought to bear on me immediately following the drowning, and indeed up to the time of the film's release.

Then the studio did try to suppress the film?

Well . . . at first, they only wanted to stop production. I refused. Later, when they saw the rough cut—this was when all the publicity had reached its peak—they sent in a team of strong-armed executive producers, and production chiefs, and what-have-you, all know-nothings with windy titles, who asked me to suppress the film. I told them exactly where to go. And then later on, when the film had been edited and scored, the same thing happened. I finally threatened suit. My contract called for a large percentage of the gross of that film, and I had no intention of allowing it to crumble unseen in the can.

You did not feel it was a breach of good taste to exhibit the film?

Certainly not. The girl met with an accident. The accident was no one's fault. She drowned. If a stunt man had died riding a horse over a cliff, would there have been all that brouhaha about releasing the film? I should say not.

But you must agree the circumstances surrounding the drowning . . .

The drowning was entirely accidental. We were shooting in shallow water.

The reports on the depth of the water vary from ten feet to forty feet. Neither of which might be considered shallow.

The water was no higher than her waist. And she was a tall girl. Five feet seven, I believe. Or eight. I'm not sure which.

Then how did she drown, sir?
I have no idea.
You were there, were you not?
I was on the camera barge, yes.
Then what happened?

I suppose we must set this to rest once and for all, mustn't we? I would much rather discuss the present and/or the future, but apparently we cannot do that until we've dealt *ad nauseam* with the past.

As you wish, sir.

I wish the accident had never happened, sir, that is what *I* wish. I also wish I would not be pestered interminably about it. The Italian inquest determined that the drowning was entirely accidental. What was good enough for the Italian courts is damn well good enough for me. But there is no satisfying the American appetite for scandal, is there? Behind each accident or incident, however innocuous, however innocent, the American public *must* insist upon a plot, a conspiracy, a cabal. Nothing is permitted to be exactly what it appears to be. Mystery, intrigue must surround everything. Nonsense. Do you think any of us *wanted* that girl to drown? I've already told you how much money we'd spent on the picture before the accident. I would estimate now that the delay in completion, the cost of revisions, the necessity for bringing in a second girl to resolve the love story added at least a million dollars to the proposed budget. No one wanted the drowning. If for business reasons *alone*, no one wanted it.

Yet it happened.
It happened.
How?
The exact sequence of events is still unclear to me.
Your assistant director . . .
Yes.
Testified at the inquest . . .
Yes, yes.
That the girl pleaded not to go into the water.

The water was unusually cold that morning. There was nothing we could do about *that*. It was a simple fact. The light was perfect, we had our setup, and we were prepared to shoot. Actors are like children, you know. If I had allowed her to balk at entering the water, the next thing I knew she'd have balked at walking across a lawn.

The writer of the original screenplay claims that the scene you were shooting that morning . . .

Where the girl swims in to the dock? What about it?

He claims he did not write that scene. He claims it was not in the original script.

Well, let him take that up with the Writers Guild.

Was it in the original script?

I have no idea. If there were no innovations during the shooting of a film . . . really, does anyone expect me to follow a script precisely? What then is my function as director? To shout "louder" or "softer" to an actor? Let the writers direct their own scripts, in that case. I assure you they would not get very far.

Was *the scene an innovation? The scene in the water?*

It might have been. I can't recall. If it was not in the original shooting script, as our Hollywood hack claims, then I suppose it *was* an innovation. By definition, yes, it would have been an innovation, isn't that so?

When was it added to the script?

I don't recall. I will sometimes get ideas for scenes the night before I shoot them. In which case, I will call in the technicians involved and describe the setup I will need the next day, and I will have it in the morning. If there is additional dialogue involved, I'll see to it that the actors and the script girl have the necessary pages, and I'll ask the actors to study them overnight. If there is no additional dialogue . . .

Was there any dialogue in this scene?

No. The girl was merely required to swim in to the dock from a speedboat.

What do you do in such a case? In an added scene where there's no dialogue?

Oh, I'll usually take the actor aside and sketch in the scene for him. The gist of it. This was a particularly simple scene. She had only to dive over the side of the boat and swim in to the dock.

In shallow water?

Well, not so shallow that she was in any danger of hitting the bottom, if that's what you mean.

Then perhaps the estimates of the water's depth . . .

The water's depth was no problem for anyone who knew how to swim.

Did the girl know how to swim?

Of course she did. You certainly don't think I'd have allowed her to play a scene in water . . .

I merely wondered if she was a good swimmer or . . .

Adequate. She was neither Eleanor Holm nor Esther Williams, but the part didn't call for an Olympic champion, you know. She was an adequate swimmer.

When did you explain the gist of the scene to her?

That morning, I believe. If memory serves me . . . yes, I believe the idea came to me the night before, and I called in the people involved and told them what I would need the following morning. Which is when I explained the scene to her. At least, that's usually the way it works; I assume it worked the same way concerning this particular scene.

You explained that she would have to dive over the side of the boat and swim in to the dock?

Which is all she had to do.

Did she agree to do this?

Why, of course. She was an inexperienced little thing; this was her first film. Of course, she agreed. There was never any question of her *not* agreeing. She'd been modeling miniskirts or what-have-you for a teenage fashion magazine when I discovered her. This was an enormous opportunity for her, this film. Look at the people I surrounded her with! Do you know what we had to pay her leading man? Never mind. It still irritates me.

Is it true he threatened to walk off the picture after the girl drowned?

He has said so in countless publications across the length and breadth of the world. I'm surprised he hasn't erected a billboard on the moon, but I imagine he's petitioning NASA for the privilege this very moment.

But did *he threaten to walk off?*

He did. I could not allow it, of course. Neither would his contract allow it. An actor will sometimes be deluded into believing he is something more than a beast of the field. Even with today's largely independent production structure, the studio serves as a powerful steamroller flattening out life's annoying little bumps for any second-rate bit player who's ever seen his own huge face grinning down idiotically from a screen. The *real* head sometimes gets as big as the fantasy head up there. Walk off the picture? I'd have sued his socks from under him.

Why did he threaten to walk off?

We'd had difficulty from the start. I think he was searching for an excuse, and seized upon the girl's drowning as a ripe opportunity.

What sort of difficulty?

I do not believe I need comment on the reputation of the gentleman involved. It has been adequately publicized, even in the most austere family publications.

Is it true, then, that a romance was developing between him and the girl?

I have never yet worked on a film in which a romance did not develop between the girl and her leading man. That is a simple fact of motion-picture production.

Was it a simple fact of this motion picture?

Unfortunately, yes.

Why do you say "unfortunately"?

The girl had a brilliant career ahead of her. I hated to see her in a position that . . . I hated to see her in such a vulnerable position.

Vulnerable?

The Italian press would have enjoyed nothing better than to link her romantically with someone of his reputation. I warned her against this repeatedly. We'd spent quite a lot of money grooming this girl, you know. Stardom may happen overnight, but it takes many *days* of preparation for that overnight event.

Did she heed your warnings?

She was very young.

Does that mean to say . . . ?

Nineteen, very young.

There were, of course, news stories of a developing romance between them. Despite your efforts.

Yes, despite them. Well.

Yes?

The young are susceptible. And yet, I warned her. Until the very end, I warned her. The night before she drowned, there was a large party at the hotel, given in my honor. We had seen the rushes on the shooting we'd done the day before, and we were all quite pleased, and I, of course, was more than ever certain that the girl was going to be a tremendous smash. That I had found someone, developed someone, who would most certainly become one of the screen's enduring personalities. No question about it. She had . . . she had a luminous quality that . . . it's impossible to explain this to a layman. There are people, however, who are bland, colorless, insipid, until you photograph them. And suddenly, the screen is illuminated with a life force that is positively blinding. She had that quality. And so I told her again, that night of the party, I took her aside, and we were drinking quietly, and I reminded her of what she had been, an unknown model for a juvenile fashion magazine, and of what she would most certainly become once this film was released, and I begged her not to throw this away on a silly flirtation with her leading man, a man of his reputation. The press was there, you know, this was quite an occasion—I had met the host on the Riviera, oh, years ago, when I was doing another film, and this was something of a reunion. Well. Well, I suppose none of it matters quite, does it? She's dead. She drowned the next day.

What happened? At the party?

They managed to get some photographs of her. There is a long covered walk at the hotel, leading to the tower apartments that overlook the dock. The *paparazzi* got some pictures of the two of them in a somewhat, shall we say, compromising attitude. I tried to get the cameras, I struggled with one of the photographers. . . .

Were these the photographs that were later published? After the accident?

Yes, yes. I knew even then, of course. When I failed to get those cameras, I knew her career was ruined. I knew that everything I'd done, all the careful work, the preparation—and all for *her*, you know, all to make the girl a *star*, a person in her own right—all of it was wasted. I took her to her room. I scolded her severely, and reminded her that makeup call was for six A.M.

What happened the next morning?

She came out to the barge at eight o'clock, made up and in costume. She was wearing a bikini, with a robe over it. It was quite a chilly day.

Was she behaving strangely?

Strangely? I don't know what you mean. She seemed thoroughly chastised, as well she might have. She sat alone and talked to no one. But aside from that, she seemed perfectly all right.

No animosity between you?

No, no. A bit of alienation perhaps. I had, after all, been furious with her the night before and had soundly reprimanded her. But I *am* a professional, you know, and I *did* have a scene to shoot. As I recall, I was quite courteous and friendly. When I saw she was chilled, in fact, I offered her my Thermos.

Your Thermos?

Yes. Tea. A Thermos of tea. I like my tea strong, almost to the point of bitterness. On location, I can never get anyone to brew it to my taste, and so I do it myself, carry the Thermos with me. That's what I offered her. The Thermos of tea I had brewed in my room before going out to the barge.

And did she accept it?

Gratefully. She was shivering. There was quite a sharp wind, the beginning of the mistral, I would imagine. She sat drinking the tea while I explained the scene to her. We were alone in the stern; everyone else was up forward, bustling about, getting ready for the shot.

Did she mention anything about the night before?

Not a word. Nor did I expect her to. She only complained that the tea was too bitter. I saw to it that she drank every drop.

Why?

Why? I've already told you. It was uncommonly cold that day. I didn't want to risk her coming down with anything.

Sir . . . was there any other *reason for offering her the tea? For making certain that she drank every drop?*

What do you mean?

I'm only reiterating now what some of the people on the barge have already said.

Yes, and what's that?

That the girl was drunk when she reported for work, that you tried to sober her up, and that she was still drunk when she went into the water.

Nonsense. No one drinks on my sets. Even if I'd worked with W. C. Fields, I would not have permitted him to drink. And I respected him highly. For an actor, he was a sensitive and decent man.

Yet rumors persist that the girl was drunk when she climbed from the camera barge into the speedboat.

She was cold sober. I would just love to know how such rumors start. The girl finished her tea and was sitting *alone* with me for more than three hours. We were having some color difficulty with the speedboat; I didn't like the way the green bow was registering, and I asked that it be repainted. As a result, preparation for the shot took longer than we'd expected. I was afraid it might cloud up and we'd have to move indoors to the cover set. The point is, however, that in all that time not a single soul came anywhere near us. So how in God's name would anyone know whether the girl was drunk or not? Which she wasn't, I can definitely assure you.

They say, sir ...

They, they, who the hell are *they*?

The others on the barge. They say that when she went forward to climb down into the speedboat, she seemed unsure of her footing. They say she appeared glassy-eyed ...

Rubbish.

... that when she asked if the shooting might be postponed ...

All rubbish.

... her voice was weak, somehow without force.

I can tell you definitely and without reservation, and I can tell you as the single human being who was with that girl from the moment she stepped onto the barge until the moment she climbed into the speedboat some three and a half hours later that she was at all times alert, responsive, and in complete control of her faculties. She did not want to go into the water because it was cold. But that was a simple fact, and I could not control the temperature of the ocean or the air. Nor could I reasonably postpone shooting when we were in danger of losing our light, and when we finally had everything including the damn speedboat ready to roll.

So she went into the water. As instructed.

Yes. She was supposed to swim a short distance underwater, and then surface. That was the way I'd planned the scene. She went into the water, the cameras were rolling, we ... none of us quite realized at first that she was taking an uncommonly long time to surface. By the time it dawned upon us, it was too late. *He*, of course, immediately jumped into the water after her. . . .

He?

Her leading man, his heroic move, his hairy-chested *star* gesture. She was dead when he reached her.

What caused her to drown? A cramp? Undertow? What?

I haven't the foggiest idea. Accidents happen. What more can I say? This was a particularly unfortunate one, and I regret it. But the past is the past, and if one continues to dwell upon it, one can easily lose sight of the present. I tend not to ruminate. Rumination is only stagnation. I plan ahead, and in that way the future never comes as a shock. It's comforting to know, for example, that by the time this appears in print, I will be editing and scoring a film I have not yet begun to shoot. There is verity and substance to routine that varies only slightly. It provides a reality that is all too often lacking in the motion-picture industry.

This new film, sir . . .

I thought you'd never ask.

What is it about?

I never discuss the plot or theme of a movie. If I were able to do justice to a story by capsulizing it into three or four paragraphs, why would I then have to spend long months filming it? The synopsis, as such, was invented by Hollywood executives who need so-called "story analysts" to provide simple translations because they themselves are incapable of reading anything more difficult than "Run, Spot, run."

What can *you tell us about your new film, sir?*

I can tell you that it is set in Yugoslavia, and that I will take full cinematic advantage of the rugged coastal terrain there. I can tell you that it is a love story of unsurpassing beauty, and that I have found an unusually talented girl to play the lead. She has never made a film before; she was working with a little theater group in La Cienaga when I discovered her, quite by chance. A friend of mine asked me to look in on an original the group was doing, thought there might be film possibilities in it, and so forth. The play was a hopeless botch, but the girl was a revelation. I had her tested immediately, and the results were staggering. What happens before the cameras is all that matters, you know, which is why some of our important stage personalities have never been able to make a successful transition to films. This girl has a vibrancy that causes one to forget completely that there are mechanical appliances such as projectors or screens involved. It is incredible; it is almost uncanny. It is as though her life force transcends the medium itself, sidesteps it so to speak; she achieves direct uninvolved communication at a response level I would never have thought existed. I've been working with her for, oh, easily six months now, and she's remarkably receptive, a rare combination of intelligence and incandescent beauty. I would be foolish to make any sort of prediction about her future, considering the present climate of Hollywood, and the uncertain footing of the entire industry. But if this girl continues to listen and to learn, if she is willing to work as hard in the months ahead as she has already worked, then given the proper vehicle and the proper guidance—both of which I fully intend to supply—I cannot but foresee a brilliant career for her.

Is there anything you would care to say, sir, about the future of the industry in general?

I never deal in generalities, only specifics. I feel that so long as there are men dedicated to the art of making good motion pictures—and I'm not talking now about pornography posing as art, or pathological disorders posing as humor—as long as there are men willing to make the sacrifices necessary to bring quality films to the public, the industry will survive. I intend to survive along with it. In fact, to be more specific, I intend to endure.

Thank you, sir.

ELEVEN O'CLOCK BULLETIN

Robert Turner

THERE WAS THE kind of heat where you lie on your back and don't move—hardly breathe, even—and still you sweat. I was in my room just lying there, staring at the ceiling and listening to the old lady clanking pots and pans around out in the kitchen when the thing began to slip up on me again. It was like a pulse beating in my mind: *Tonight*, it said, *Tonight, Tonight, Tonight*.

Lying around doing nothing wasn't any good.

I got up and walked to the dresser mirror and looked into it. I wanted to make sure I didn't look sick or nervous or anything—I didn't want to get the old lady upset. It was bad enough for her.

It seemed I looked a little bit older than 18 tonight, but maybe it was because I always tried to look tough and tense when I looked into a mirror and because I had a pretty heavy beard for my age; I'd started shaving when I was 15. But I didn't look sick or nothing. I looked all right.

Out in the kitchen there was the smell of something baking. It smelled good but at the same time it made me a little upset in the stomach. The old lady was hunkered in front of the oven and she was pulling a pie out of the thing. The crust was crinkled around the edges and nicely browned. She looked up at me and poked out her lower lip and blew at a wisp of hair over her sweat-beaded forehead.

"Apple, Davie," she said. "It came out nice, too. Your favorite, a nice apple pie."

"Hey, that's swell," I told her. I guess maybe I didn't sound too enthusiastic, though, because she flashed me a funny look.

"You want to set the table, we're ready to eat," she said.

I got out the silver and stuff and set it around and sat down and she put a big dish of franks and beans on the table. I got a knot in my stomach, looking at them. I got kind of like a sore throat. I looked up at the clock and saw that it was 7:30. I didn't mean to do that because I'd promised myself I wouldn't look at any clocks, but I just sort of did it without thinking.

Then I got up from the table and walked out of the kitchen. I went over by the window in the living room and looked down onto the street. It was summer and still light out. The window was open and I could hear as well as see the little kids playing stickball down on the street. They ran around like crazy down there and there didn't seem to be any pattern to it but there was, of course. I knew that. I used to do it myself, over in the old neighborhood where we lived. Only remembering it, it seemed as though it wasn't really me but somebody else way back then.

When I looked up, I saw Mary Polaff in a window across the street, leaning out and looking over here. She's only a kid but she's got a shape on her already. I started to wave and yell something when I saw her quickly draw back out of the window. She thought I couldn't see her and she turned and called to somebody back in the room behind her and then her fat old lady came over to her and the two of them stood back a little from the window, looking out over here, and they probably thought I couldn't see them there, but I could.

• • •

I knew what they were staring at, what they were talking about. I shouldn't have done it but I got sore; you know how it comes over you quick and later you get ashamed but at the time you don't even know its happening. I leaned out the window and I could feel veins bulging at my neck and temples. I yelled:

"What the hell are you peekin' at, nosy? Go ahead and look! Take a good look, why don't you?"

Then I pulled back in and turned around and the old lady had come out of the kitchen. She looked like she wanted to cry but couldn't, and she said: "Davie! Please, Davie, please, darling!"

I turned away from her and stood there feeling dopey and weak with the anger gone out of me. She came over and put her arm around my shoulders.

She said: "Come on out and eat, Davie. Please. We've got to keep control, son. Remember what we decided. We aren't going to think about it. Please."

"Yeah," I said. "Only what the hell were they lookin' at? Do I look like I'm different from anybody else, a freak or something?"

I pulled out from under her arm. I said: "I guess I ain't hungry. I forgot to tell you, I had a hamburger late this afternoon, so I don't want anything right now. I'll see you later."

I walked toward the door and she sounded sort of panicky as she called: "Where are you going, son? What are you going to do?"

"I don't know," I said. "Going for a walk, maybe. I don't know."

She didn't say anything else but I knew she wanted to. She wanted to ask me what about the movie we were going to see, the musical down at the Parkside, the nice dopey musical that wouldn't have any crime stuff in it or anything, that she thought would be nice if we could see, but she didn't do that.

I felt pretty sorry for the old lady. I felt lousy walking out on her, but she was going to get on my nerves bad if I stuck around and I'd end up saying something to hurt her. So I got out. Maybe I'd get a grip on myself later and come back. I didn't know.

Outside on the street the heat was still coming up from the pavement and bouncing off the apartment houses even though the sun was almost gone down. I felt like I was going to suffocate. I walked fast away from the house, not looking at the people sitting out on the stoops. Some of the kids playing stickball yelled something at me but I didn't hear what it was and I didn't pay any attention.

After awhile I was at the 181st Street IRT subway entrance and without thinking about it or why or where I was going, I went in and downstairs. It should have been cool down there but it wasn't. It was hotter than the street. I took a downtown express. Those big crazy overhead fans in the subway car whirled and made a wind that mussed your hair up and all and blew pieces of newspaper around but they didn't make you any cooler. I sat right under one. There was about a dozen people in the car with me. It seemed every time I looked at one of them they were staring at me with a funny look but that wasn't really so; I knew I just thought that.

When we got to Times Square I got out and went upstairs. Broadway was jammed with people walking around, looking in windows and yammering at one another the way it always is on a hot summer night in New York. Up near the top of that screwy little triangle-shaped Times Tower building electric bulbs blinked out the time: 8:32 P.M.

I swore at the clock and at myself for looking at it and my throat began to hurt again. I couldn't seem to swallow at all for a few moments.

The first bar I came to, I turned in. I started to go right out again when I saw it was mobbed with service guys, Army guys and sailors in summer whites and a couple of Air Force guys, but then I figured maybe it'd do me good to get into a fight. Maybe knocking the crap out of some guy or vice versa, would help. So I went in and pushed into the bar between a sailor whose whites were too tight across his big can and a stocky-looking paratrooper. I didn't beg anybody's pardon for crowding in. They both turned too quick and looked at me but they didn't say anything. They just made room for me.

The back-bar mirror had a fishnet draped across it, supposed to make the place look cooler or something and when you saw yourself through the holes in the net you looked at one feature at a time. I saw I had a pretty big nose and I had one eyebrow higher than the other. I always thought I looked like Jeff Chandler, a little, only I didn't tonight. Not through that fishnet. I just looked like some ordinary jerk who was mad about something.

I had $3.50 in my pocket. I had a shot and a beer chaser and that was half a buck, so I knew I was good for seven rounds, anyhow.

It was a noisy place, with all the service guys talking it up and the juke box turned up loud so you could hear it out on the street and running without stopping. But nobody knew me here; nobody paid any attention. After a couple of drinks I got to kind of like it. I didn't hardly feel the first three drinks at all or at least I didn't notice it, but then something happened, I knew I was getting a little tight. I don't get a muscle on over nothing at all unless I'm a little greased.

The big swabbie next to me asked the bartender what time it was and the bartender turned and looked up at an electric clock on the wall down at the end of the bar. I hadn't noticed it before. I hadn't thought about the time since I'd come into the place; I swear I hadn't. But now I looked up at the clock, too, and it was 9:30 already and now it was only an hour-and-a-half off and I guess suddenly realizing it was that close, I got kind of uncorked. I turned to the sailor.

"If the time means so much to you, why don't you buy yourself a damned watch? They pay you in the Navy, don't they?"

As soon as I said it I knew I was going to get broken in half. The guy was big enough to do that. But I didn't care. It wasn't that I was brave or tough or anything; it just didn't seem to matter. But the Navy guy just turned around, looking kind of surprised. He said, quietly:

"You ought to take it easy, Mac. What's eatin' on you, anyhow?" He had one of those slow Southern accents.

• • •

I told him it wasn't any of his business what was eating on me and he looked me over carefully and shook his head sadly and said it was too bad he had a date and he was so late already. I agreed with him but he just looked back at the clock again and left the bar. I felt funny about that—kind of let-down, like; kind of disappointed. I looked both ways along the bar, waiting for somebody else to have something to say but nobody was paying any attention.

I had one more drink and then a blowzy old blonde hustler came in with some guy who wasn't so stiff he couldn't navigate but he must've been pretty well laced to be giving this bag any time at all. It was plain she was mining him and making time like anything. As soon as they got into a booth they started smooching it up. It was kind of disgusting at their age.

I was standing sideways to the bar, with my back turned to that clock at the other end, and I couldn't help watching this pair. Then, I don't know whether it was the drinks or what, but the blonde bindle began to look like my old lady. I mean like the old lady might look in a few years, maybe 10, if she dyed her hair. It was crazy and I don't know what it was about the blonde that reminded me of the old lady because she didn't really *look* like her, but it was something. It got me. It made me think about the old lady and what the hell good was I doing her or myself, even, laying one on like this, feeling sorry for myself. I thought that it still wasn't too late to take her to the show.

• • •

So I left the place. It was dark out now—as dark as it ever gets in Times Square, that is—and a little cooler. You come out onto Broadway at night and it kind of shocks you no matter how used to it you are. There's something about it. Like a world where nothing's real and you forget everything except you want to have a big time, a hell of a time; and if you're alone or even with some guys, you want a girl bad, real, real bad. It was like that with me, tonight.

It felt so good I walked down to 42nd and then up to 50th, stalling off going home for awhile, and then walked over to Eighth Avenue to take the Independent subway up to Washington Heights.

That was a bad deal. Eighth Avenue was empty and sad even though it, too, was all lit up. There's something about Eighth Avenue; it'll never get anywhere. In some other town it'd be the big deal, the Main Drag. But it's too close to Times Square, here. It's like a dirty, beat up old floozy walking beside a pretty young showgirl and they're both dressed the same but that's the end of it. It gave me the real glooms.

It made the thing I'd been trying not to think about all night, all day, begin to press on my mind again like a thumb in a wound. I couldn't let it. Once I let go and really thought about it I wouldn't be able to stop. I all at once felt all alone, walking along Eighth there, like that, and about four inches high and trembling scared and I had to do something fast. I went into another creep joint.

This one was bird. I hadn't noticed the name of it but the minute I went in I knew it was called Paddy's Shamrock Bar or something. It was one of those saloons that cater to professional Irishmen. They had a raft of crazy-shaped shillelaghs hanging back of the bar and some brown derbys and they still had dirty green bunting and decorations from St. Patrick's Day draped across the mirror here in August, for crying out loud. But it wasn't very crowded and they had a big 30-inch TV set going and I didn't see any clock in the place. So I bellied up to the bar, like they say in the Westerns.

The TV had one of those situation-comedy things on, all about a dumb blonde and her roommate, only the blonde's dumbness didn't get on your nerves because she was kind of cute about it and what she had in front, it didn't make much difference how dumb she was. It didn't break me up or give me convulsions or anything but it was something to watch that put you in a kind of vacuum and the dozen or so Countycorkmen in the joint got such a root out of it, it was contagious. I even laughed, once.

I had two more boilermakers while that was on and was on the seventh, the last one I could pay for, when the thing ended. The stuff had taken hold by this time, too, though not as good as I wanted. All I had was a kind of loose, tingle-fingered, putty-like looseness all over and everything was too sharply focused like in 3-D or something. I knew it was one of those times like I'd heard older guys talk about where no matter how much you lapped up, you didn't get really drunk.

While I sipped the last drink the commercial came on and the guys at the bar stopped staring at the TV like they'd never seen one before and got back to doing some serious drinking and talking. It was one of those places where everybody knew everybody else and calls them by the first name and everybody pleasantly insults everybody else and calls them gutter names and nobody gets sore. Nobody paid any attention to me. I began to feel like the invisible man from Mars. That was all right. That was about like I wanted it.

• • •

THEN a big beetle-browed guy with a soup-bowl haircut that looked as if he gave it to himself and with his blue workshirt sleeves rolled up over arms that were big as my thighs, started *shushing* everybody, trying to stop the talk that had busted out along the bar.

As it quieted down I heard him say: "Shhhhh, shut up, now, and be listenin' to the news. The news! The news!" He kept saying that one word over and over.

I looked up at the TV and there was a serious-faced college-grad type sitting behind a desk with a globe map on it and a can of motor oil and he was yakking at us with his very sincere, serious voice.

As though the big guy had waved a magic wand, everybody in the joint shut up now and went back to staring at the TV. I heard the newscaster say: "—but first, the eleven o'clock local news, straight from the wire services of the. . . ."

I didn't hear the rest of it. All I heard was somewhere in my mind, the guy's voice saying over and over again. "The news! The news!" and the announcer's voice saying, "the eleven o'clock . . . the eleven o'clock . . . the eleven o'clock. . . ." like a record that had broke and stuck there.

Eleven o'clock. In another three minutes. . . .

What I should have done was get out of there. I didn't have to listen to the newscast. The part I didn't want to hear would not come on until near the end, anyhow, maybe in a special bulletin or something, if they put it out over this one at all. I had plenty of time. I didn't have to hear it. But I didn't even think about that, then. I didn't think about anything.

• • •

I kept looking at the newscaster's sincere, serious face in closeup now, filling the whole screen and listening to the even, cultured tone of his voice and I could feel my fingers squeezing the heavy-bottomed shot glass on the bar in front of me until I thought I'd never get them unstuck.

I heard myself saying like it was somebody else, very loud, almost hysterical: "Shut it off! Shut that thing off!"

All the heads along the bar swung around toward me as though they were on a wire. They looked at me like I'd suddenly cursed aloud in the middle of Mass. I didn't care. That voice was going on and on and it was going to say something I didn't want to hear.

"Are you going to shut that damn guy off?" I shouted.

They weren't. I could tell. I knew. But I couldn't let him keep talking up there. I probably couldn't have done it again in a million years if I'd wanted to, if I tried, but this time it was easy. I picked up the shot glass. It was at least 40 feet down to that TV set and it was on a shelf 10 feet from the floor but I hit the screen dead center and the glass went right through the picture tube and one second there was this big bright shot of the newscaster and the sound of his voice and then there was nothing but some jagged glass in the front of the set and the most silence you ever heard.

I saw the big shave-necked Irishman coming toward me. His face was the color of the bricks he probably laid all day and his eyes were too little and too bright, way back in his head. But I couldn't seem to move.

"And why did you do that?" He sounded hurt. He didn't sound mad at all. "Have you gone daft, boy? Why did you do that?"

He didn't wait for me to answer even if I could have. He started slapping me and I can't stand anyone slapping me and I guess that was when you could say I flipped a little. There was still some beer in my big glass and it splashed back on me when I swung it off the bar and hit him in the forehead with it. It was good glass. It didn't break even when it slipped from my hand and fell to the floor. Then I hit him in the belly with my fist.

The rest of it's not too clear. It seemed like a hundred guys came at me all at once only it couldn't have been because there was only a dozen or so in the place. And that was all right with me. I wanted them to. The bartender, who looked too fat to move if his pants were on fire, came over the bar like a gazelle. He had a big knobby-looking blackthorn shillelagh in his fist.

It was a ball for awhile because they all tried to get to me at once and were like a herd of hogs trying to squeeze through a narrow gate. They were climbing all over each other to get to me, and I kept pumping punches fast as I could move my arms and I hit the first three flush in the face. I felt the gristle in somebody's nose go. I felt the sickening shifting softness of an eyeball under my fist. Then something hit me in the cheek and it didn't hurt too bad but it made my ears ache and somebody grabbed my arm and took it and twisted it some crazy way and I felt something snap and I screamed. Then it was like a brick wall was falling down on me and wouldn't ever stop, even after I was all covered with it so that I couldn't see and everything was dark. . . .

I was in an ambulance, only it took me awhile to figure that out, even though the sound of the whining siren was right in my ears and I saw two guys in white jackets and the cop, sitting across from me. My face didn't feel like a face. It felt like one of those big throbbing, slithering masses of goo that comes out of the sea to invade the earth like in horror stories. I moved and that made my arm one big electric shock that hurt like hell. That reminded me.

I said: "What time is it?"

The cop and the two ambulance guys just sat there and looked at me. I had the crazy notion that they hadn't heard me, that no matter how loud I talked they wouldn't ever hear me; they'd just sit there like that forever, staring at me.

Then the baldheaded ambulance guy looked at a wrist-watch and said: "Eleven-twenty." He had a funny voice, sort of thick and gargly.

• • •

I lay there and didn't move any more on account of my arm and I began to think and now there didn't seem to be any reason not to do that. What harm could it do, now? It was over. It was forever over and 17 minutes ago they'd shot the big juice through him and he'd jumped and strained against the strap like I'd heard that they do but the lights didn't dim all over the place at the time because I'd heard that didn't really happen any more. And then maybe three, four or was it five minutes and he'd been still. He hadn't moved any more.

Even though they'd had his head covered I could see what he looked like. He had that same expression on his face I'd seen once when I was about 10 and he took me on a hike over to the Palisades and a copperhead bit his leg. He sat right down and lit a match to my Boy Scout knife and after tying a handkerchief real tight above it. He was awful pale and looking the closest to crying I'd ever seen him but looking more mad than hurt and his big, even white teeth showing in a grin or a grimace or something.

That's what he'd looked like tonight when they did that to him, I knew.

I don't know how long I'd been crying before I realized it, but I was really tearing it off. Bawling like a baby. I thought: *But it isn't for you, up there, you hear that? I wouldn't cry for you or be sorry for you for no money, because you stopped being my old man five years ago when you ran off with her and left me and the old lady. Because when we knew you weren't coming back we agreed to pretend like you were dead and never talk about you and we did that; it wasn't so hard after awhile. And I ain't crying for me and the old lady because we got along all right. We both work and we've done all right.*

Only why did you have to catch the lousy little tramp with somebody else, finally, and kill her and make all that big stink in the newspapers and the trial and all and they had to execute you tonight at eleven-o-three? Pop, why did you have to do that?

And I thought: *So to hell with you, it ain't because of you I'm bawling, it's because of this arm, the way it's killing me, hurting. That's all. You understand that?*

Then I must have tried to get up because the two ambulance guys and the cops pounced on me and held me down and one of them stuck a needle into my good arm and that was all I knew. . . .

STUART KAMINSKY

Sarasota, Florida, where I live, is a small jewel of culture—theaters, an opera company, a performing arts center, luxury homes on the offshore keys, a new library, an orchestra, a jazz club. Our beaches, broad, long and blanketed with cool, white sand, are covered with retirees and tourists from all over the world. But there is a dark side here as there is everywhere, parts of the city that are not talked about where people are lost or hide and live on a thin thread.

Lew Fonesca is neither tall, nor strong, nor ambitious. He is not even a detective. He is a process server, a finder of people. Lew has an affinity for those who are lost, those who live on the dark side and those who search for wives, sisters, sons and daughters lost in the darkness. Lew will always find those lost, but he will not always be able to save them. There are so many Adeles. There is too much darkness.

● ● ●

"The Death of Colonel Thoureau" appeared in The Knickerbocker or New York Monthly Magazine in September 1861. I have no idea who wrote it. I would guess it has appeared nowhere else but that issue. I have a passion for going through the cracking and crumbling pages of old magazines, reading the lost poems, the passionate essays, the forgotten stories.

This mystery was written during the Civil War. Its unknown author only hints at the conflict and the issue of slavery. Instead he concentrates on the murder of a military man in a tale that says a great deal, probably without intending to do so, about death, race and attitudes toward women more than a century ago. It is written in the style of its time. It rings of the idiom of Poe without, perhaps, the quality. It is an example of a thriving post-Poe genre of which we know little or nothing. Oh, and if for no other reason, could one not be intrigued by a mystery in which the protagonist's employer is the Volcano Life-Insurance Company?

ADELE

Stuart M. Kaminsky

"Hot in here."

She looked around my tiny office trying not to show uncertainty and disapproval.

"Air conditioner doesn't work," I said.

"Then why do you leave it on?"

"Fan makes the air move a little. Your daughter is missing?"

She nodded.

So far all I had from her was that her daughter Adele was missing and that the woman's name was Beryl Fitztown. Beryl was about fifty, dark hair cut short, on the thin side, wearing a serious but slightly shabby loose-fitting blue dress with a belt and no style. She kept her purse on her knees and her knees tight and together. She had nice blue eyes and had once probably been very pretty. She also had a blue-yellow bruise on her cheek the size of a large peach.

"I have a picture," she said opening her purse.

I waited. The air conditioner buzzed and I pretended it wasn't hot.

"Here."

She handed me a little photograph that looked as if it were taken in one of those automatic camera booths you find in malls.

The girl was definitely pretty. She was blonde, straight hair, wearing a green sweater and a fine set of white teeth.

"Adele," Beryl said looking toward the window as if her daughter might suddenly appear.

It was my turn to nod.

"How'd you get hurt?"

She touched the bruise on her cheek and said, "Fell in the bathroom of the motel."

"Tell your story, Miss . . ."

"Mrs.," she corrected looking down at her purse. "Husband died when Adele was little. Tree."

"His name was 'Tree'?"

"No," she said with a sigh. "His name was Dwight. Tree trimmer and landscape gardener. Fell out of a big oak."

"Sorry," I said.

"I raised Adele alone. Not much to do for a child in Brisbane, Kansas, while I worked days and a lot of nights at the restaurant, Jim and Ella's Good Food. Truckers welcome. Most nights Adele would watch the TV, look out the window of the apartment at the oil rigs in the field. At least till she got older and got in with the crowd."

"Bad crowd?" I asked.

"Only crowd in Brisbane, if you count four or five kids as a crowd."

"Go on."

"Not much more to tell. She wasn't much of a student in high school. Got into a little trouble. She's got a temper like Dwight, her pa."

"The tree trimmer," I said.

"Got on the cheerleaders but didn't go to practice and they cut her," said Beryl with a sigh. "In a couple of school plays. One she had a lot of things to say. How do they remember all those things to say?"

I ignored the sweat on my scalp.

"I don't know," I said.

"Well," Beryl Fitztown went on. "Life is a puzzle."

"Yes," I said.

"She ran away a little over three months ago. Just packed up and left a message taped to the TV saying she was going and she would call. I told Josh Hamilton, the sheriff, that she had run and he took a picture just like the one you're holding and said he'd follow up and maybe get her on milk cartons and paper bags if she didn't show up in a few weeks.

"She didn't show up. Josh suggested I get one of those things you put on your phone that shows the number someone is calling you from. I did, but no call from Adele till two weeks ago. I wrote down the number. Adele sounded bad, scared. Wouldn't tell me why. I told her to come home. She said she couldn't, that she'd be all right. Call came from right here, Sarasota, Florida."

Beryl Fitztown reached into her purse and came up with a sheet of paper. She handed it to me. It had an 813 area code number.

"I called her back," Beryl said fingering the little silver latch on her purse. "Called back maybe fifteen times. No answer. Little over a week ago a man answered, said I was calling a pay phone outside a motel on Tamiami Trail. I got a ride from Ella to Wichita, bus here. Adele is sixteen, just barely. She's pretty, none too bright and in trouble. I've been wandering around for the last week looking for her, but I don't know how to do it or what to ask."

"Did you go to the police?"

"Yes," she said. "First thing. They took my only other nearly grown-up picture of Adele and the phone booth number and said they'd look into it. Nice man, a sergeant, said he would get it posted and go in the computer. I got the feeling Adele was going in a big box with a hundred or more other lost children."

"I think you're right."

I placed the phone number right next to the photograph of the smiling girl on my desk.

"Anything else?" I asked.

"Yes," she said. "Who are you?"

"My name is Lewis Fonesca. I used to work for the State Attorney's office in Cook County, Illinois. Investigations. One morning my wife took the car to work. She died in a car accident on Lake Shore Drive. It was winter. I wasn't going any further up in my job and I'm not ambitious. I was cold and too many places and people reminded me of my wife. Am I telling you too much?"

"No," she said.

"How did you find me?"

"Man at the Dairy Queen," she said nodding at the door beyond which was a concrete landing overlooking a Dairy Queen on Route 301, which was also Washington Street, though in my six months in town I never heard anyone call it anything but 301. They also called Bahia Vista, Baya Vista, and Honore Street was usually referred to as Honor Street.

She looked at me for about the third time and saw a forty-one-year-old man with rapidly thinning hair, reasonable dark looks and a short-sleeved button-down blue shirt and grey jeans.

"You're a detective, like on television," she said. "Rockford."

"More like Harry Orwell," I said. "I'm not a detective. I don't have a license in this state. But any citizen can make inquiries. That's what I do. I make inquiries."

"You ask questions."

"I ask questions."

"What do you charge?"

"Fifty dollars a day, plus expenses."

"Expenses?"

"Phone calls. Gas. Things like that. I report to you every day. You can stop my services any time before the next day. My guess is I'll find Adele in two or three days or tell you she's not in Sarasota."

"O.K.," she said, opening her purse once again and pulling out a wallet from which she extracted five tens. "I will need a receipt."

I took the money, found a pad of yellow legal-sized paper and wrote out a receipt. She took it and said, "I'm staying at the Best Western behind the car wash. I'm in Room 204."

"Well," I said handing her my card. "You can call me here day or night."

Beryl Fitztown took my card, looked at it, put it in her purse, stood up, and snapped her purse closed. I stood up too.

"I am not a warm woman," she said. "I do not show my affections. I did not do so with Adele, but I do love her and I think she knows that. Please find her."

"I will," I said.

And she was gone.

I pulled some Kleenex from my drawer, wiped my head, face and neck and threw the used tissues into my Tampa Bay Buc's wastebasket. My shirt was sweat-blotched and clinging wet to my back. It was a hot December day in Sarasota, probably about 93 degrees and humid, hot for winter, but not unheard of. It was the middle of the snow bird season. Tourists and winter residents rented or owned overpriced houses and apartments on the mainland in Bradenton and Sarasota. The winter crowd with real money were in the resorts and condos on the beaches of Longboat and Siesta Key. All in all, about two hundred thousand people in Manatee and Sarasota counties combined during The Season.

In Sarasota, south of the airport, there was a strip of low-cost motels on Tamiami Trail stretching for a couple of miles to downtown and the theater district. The primary residents of the motels were prostitutes, though in the winter French and German tourists wandered in. This was where I'd start looking for Adele's phone booth. If that failed, I'd go South of Bayfront park and downtown and start my search among the malls, restaurants and shops. Sarasota has hundreds of restaurants catering to retirees, tourists and full-time working residents. It could be a long day or two of work.

However, I didn't think Adele would be that tough to find, and I needed the fifty dollars. If I'd known that I was going to be dealing with two murders . . . Hell, I probably would have taken the job anyway.

I was living in my office. My sleeping bag, a pillow and my clothes were in the closet near the window across from my desk. Next to the closet was a slightly brown-stained sink where I brushed my teeth, washed and tried not to look at myself in the mirror above it when I shaved. Almost every day I drove to the Y.M.C.A. where I worked out on the machines, swam and took a long, hot shower.

When I first came to town, I made the rounds of lawyers in Sarasota and Bradenton, offering my services at a price substantially lower than they were paying to licensed investigators. I was starting to pick up some business from law firms and some significant hostility from licensed private investigators, but was within the law as long as I simply asked questions and brought the information to whoever hired me.

I knew Sarasota and Bradenton reasonably well now. They were still small towns where a pretty young girl might be remembered. The first thing to do was check the telephone numbers in phone booths on Tamiami Trail. There was a chance that Adele had used a phone near where she was staying.

I put Adele's photo and the phone booth number in my wallet, put on my Chicago Cub's baseball cap and went down to the Dairy Queen where my car was parked.

It was almost ten at night. I was hungry. I bought a large chocolate-covered cherry Blizzard and a deluxe burger and thanked Dave for sending me a client.

"Lady needs help," he said. "Kid running away like that."

Dave was probably around my age, but years in the sun working on boats in the bay had turned his skin to dark, dry leather. His body was still hard and strong, but his face had gone to sun-fried hell.

"I think I can find her," I said while he prepared the burger and shake.

"Kids," Dave said with a shake of the head.

When my order came up I showed Adele's photograph to Dave. He looked at it for a while and squinted in thought.

"I don't think I've seen her," he said, "but who knows? She cuts her hair, maybe dyes it, puts on a lot of makeup, orders a Dilly bar and off she goes. Who knows?"

"Thanks, Dave," I said taking my Blizzard and burger.

"Who knows?" he repeated. "You know what I mean?"

"I know," I said.

I ate in my '85 Cutlass with the motor running and the air conditioner on full blast. I had paid $500 for the car when I had hit town. I had put another $300 in repair work within two months. It was running and the air conditioning worked.

The dividing line between Bradenton and Sarasota is just north of New College and the Asolo Center for Performing Arts. Sarasota is a Culture town. Capital 'C' in Culture. An art museum, five equity theaters including one that only does musicals, a massive concert hall, two ballet companies and an opera company.

There wasn't much that could be considered big-C culture near the first phone booth outside the Warm Breeze Motel across from the Harcourt Inn. The number was wrong. There was another phone booth on the wall of the Warm Breeze Motel. I checked that one. The number was the same as the one Beryl Fitztown had given me.

I turned around and found myself facing a prostitute who took me for a Mister Right.

"Want some company?" she asked.

She was a washed-out brunette with sad eyes, rough skin and almost no breasts.

"No, thanks, but I'd like to know if you recognize this girl."

I took out my wallet and handed Adele's photograph to the hooker, who didn't look much older than the girl she was looking at.

"Nice looking kid," she said flatly and handed the picture back. "You a cop? I thought I knew all the cops in town. New?"

"I'm not a cop," I said. "I'm just trying to find a missing girl and ask her some questions."

"Thought you were a cop. Lots of cops last week or so."

"Why?"

"John got killed at the Yellow Sun, across the street there. Cops marched all the girls in, asked questions, found nothing."

Traffic whizzed by. A car slowed down. A dirty-blond kid with a big, round face stuck his head out of the window and in a red-neck voice called, "That the best you can do, man? You are really sorry."

And the car sped up.

The girl clenched her teeth, took a breath and tried to jump back in the game.

"What else you got in the wallet?" she said.

"Five dollars if you know the girl in the picture and can tell me something about her."

"Five bucks," she moaned.

"Hard times," I said.

"I'll take it," she said. "Before I talk."

I handed her a five and put the wallet back in my pocket.

"Her name's Suzanne," the girl said, folding her arms across her chest. "Worked from the Linger Longer."

She nodded over her shoulder. Two motels down was a tired neon sign with a flashing arrow pointing the way to the Linger Longer Motel.

"And?" I asked.

"Then she was gone," the girl said with a shrug.

"Who was working her?"

The girl shrugged again and looked across the busy street at nothing.

"That wasn't worth five dollars," I said.

"All you're getting," she said. "Hard times."

It was my turn to shrug. I moved past her and headed for the Linger Longer. I had a start. Pay dirt on my second phone booth. Adele's local name and the place she stayed.

The glass door on the Linger Longer Motel office said that American Express, MasterCard, Visa, and Discover were welcome and that German, Spanish and French were spoken. It also said that the clerk kept no cash. I pushed the door open. There was no lounge, no chair and not much room. A coffeepot sat half full with foam cups next to it. Behind the low counter a kid sat reading *Principles of Economics*. He put the book down and said, "Can I help you?"

He took off his big glasses and stood up with a polite smile.

I took out my wallet and the photograph of Adele and handed it to him. He put his glasses back on.

"Suzanne," he said. "Stayed here . . . oh, a couple of months back. Why?"

"Her mother's looking for her," I said.

He cocked his head to one side and looked at the photograph again before handing it back to me.

"You're not a cop. If you're a private investigator, show your card."

"I'm not a private investigator," I said. "I just ask questions for people. Suzanne have a last name?"

The kid thought for a while, thumped his right hand softly on the counter, sighed deeply and said, "I think she was one of those chanteuses in a club down in Port Charlotte."

"You get a lot of one-name chanteuses staying here?"

"A surprisingly large number," the kid said. "You a Cub fan?"

The cap. "Yeah."

I took off the cap and wiped the sweat band with a tissue from a box on the counter.

"Covers the lack of hair," the kid observed as I put the cap back on and dropped the tissue in the wastebasket.

"You like Suzanne?" I said, getting back to the subject. "I mean what you saw of her?"

"She didn't talk much. Some of our chanteuses like to talk. Some of them could drive a person nuts. She had a temper, but yeah, I liked her."

I just stood there waiting while he considered what to do next.

"Look," he said lowering his voice though there was no one there but us. "I'm a student over at New College. This job pays well and I get to read, do my homework and once in a while practice my Spanish, German or French with tourists who don't know what kind of motel they've wandered into."

This time the pause was very long. He looked out the window at the passing traffic.

"Would five bucks help you decide?" I asked.

He shook his head no and said, "She worked for Tilly. Room 5 in the corner. If he asks you how you found him, tell him you tracked down a girl named Elspeth, tall bleached blonde, short hair, big lips, average breasts. Elspeth ducked on Tilly three weeks ago and headed back to San Antonio."

"Thanks," I said.

"I hope you find her," the kid said. "She reminded me of a beautiful crippled kingfisher my sister and I took in when I was a kid."

I went across the cement parking area toward the corner of the L-shaped motel. There were two cars parked, one, a little blue Fiat in front of Room 5.

"Who?" A voice came from inside the room when I knocked.

"My name's Seymour."

"Seymour what?"

"Just Seymour," I said. "I'm a chanteuse."

An eye peered through the tiny, thick-glass peephole.

"You a cop?" he asked.

"Everyone asks me that," I said. "No, I'm not a cop. I just have a couple of questions to ask you."

"About what? Why?"

"About Suzanne," I said. "Her mother's looking for her."

"So am I," he said, opening the door.

"Tilly?"

"Come in," he said.

I went into the motel room and he closed the door. He was a lean, handsome black man about six feet tall and wearing a pair of clean jeans and neatly ironed button-down white shirt. He couldn't have been more than twenty-five.

I looked around. The room was motel tacky. It didn't look like home.

"I don't live here," he said, reading my mind. "Why are you looking for Suzanne?"

"Her mother's here. Wants to take her home."

"Home? Mother? She's got no mother, no home. She said she ran from a bitch of an aunt and uncle back in L.A."

"Adele's got a mother and she's not from L.A."

"She lied," he said, shaking his head. "Want a drink? Don't drink myself, but I keep a fridge for guests and visitors."

"No thanks," I said.

"Suit yourself," he said and went to the small brown refrigerator in the corner of the room. He pulled out a can of Mountain Dew and went to sit on the worn-out rust-colored two-seat sofa. I remained standing.

"Adele ran out on you," I said.

He laughed and took a sip of Mountain Dew.

"They don't run out on me," he said. "Once in a while I might ask a young lady to leave, but they don't want to go. I take a fair split and I never raise a hand. And I don't get tired. You understand?"

"I understand. Elspeth," I said. "She ran away."

"She say that? I threw her out. She had a bad attitude as her heading you to me proves. Elspeth. God-awful name, but she wouldn't let me give her another."

"Suzanne," I said.

"Good kid. A little too sad in the eyes, but a good worker and she didn't complain. Had a temper, though. Gave me this."

He rolled up his right sleeve. A deep red gash was starting to form a scar.

"Not bad to have a few battle marks in my business," he said rolling his sleeve back down.

"You know where she is?"

He touched the can of Mountain Dew to his forehead and closed his eyes. Someone opened the door with a key. A heavily made-up woman in a short, tight black dress stepped in, smiled at me and looked at Tilly, who still hadn't opened his eyes.

"Go get a cup of coffee, Francine," he said. "Make it a big cup."

Francine's smile disappeared on her very red lips and she eased out of the room and closed the door.

"What the hell," Tilly said, opening his eyes and sitting up with his arms spread over the back of the sofa. "I'll tell you something if you give me your word that you won't tell where you got it."

"Why would you take my word?" I asked

"I wouldn't, man," he said with exasperation. "I think it would be just fine if you found Adele and took her home with her mama. I think it would really piss off a couple of people who I'd like to see pissed off. You follow?"

"Blindly," I said.

"Mr. John Pirannes," Tilly said with contempt. "Big operator out of the Beach Tide Resort on Longboat. Services tourists, mostly rich old men. Picked out Adele when she wasn't here for a week. Came to me with the usual backup, a top-heavy Haitian with bad skin. Mr. Pirannes made me an offer, a piece-of-shit offer. I took it with a smile."

"People selling's a tough job," I said.

"Hey, I just gave you free, key information. Don't stand there trying to give out trips to Guilt Town."

He emptied the can of Mountain Dew and placed the can on the small white table in front of him. I had to give him credit. He didn't crush the can and shoot it toward the wastebasket near the refrigerator.

"You're right," I said. "Thanks."

"Hey," he said clicking on the television with a little black remote. "I told you. I'm doing you no favors. Getting Adele away from Mr. John Pirannes won't be a run to the 7-Eleven, if you know what I mean. Now if you'll just move out. You're blocking the screen."

"Last question," I said.

He hit the mute button and the voice of a vaguely familiar woman stopped behind me.

"Last question," he said.

"How did you know her name was Adele, not Suzanne?"

"You called her . . ." he started and then paused. "You know that mailbox about a half block down?"

"Yeah."

"She wrote a postcard to a friend somewhere in Kansas, said she was fine, had a job as a secretarial trainee and loved Sarasota."

"You broke into the mailbox?"

"That's another question, and you're all out. I'm trying to be polite, but you are worrying me."

I walked to the door and the woman's voice came out of the television set. I glanced at the screen just before I left. Mary Tyler Moore was trying to explain something to Ed Asner.

Francine was just inside the motel office when I passed. She was smoking and doing what she was told, having a cup of coffee. I pointed back at the room to show that it was all hers. The kid behind the counter looked my way and I nodded to show that everything had gone well with Tilly.

The evening was young, and I had work to do. There was still an hour left before the Selby Public Library closed. I went down Tamiami Trail to the Boulevard of the Arts, parked in front of the Hyatt, left my Cub cap on the front seat and walked to the library, where I went through microfilm of the *Sarasota Herald-Tribune* looking for a mention of Mr. John Pirannes. I scan fast, learned it working for the State's Attorney's office. No Pirannes, no mention of the Beach Tides Resort other than some ads that looked the same for all the other hotel resorts on the island. I did come across an item about a Canadian tourist who had been murdered at the Yellow Sun Motel. Story suggested that he had probably caught a thief in his room and paid with his life. The prostitute at the phone booth had told me the dead guy was a John, a customer. The newspaper hadn't chosen to dig into this one.

I hadn't expected to find much. I went to the librarian's desk.

The woman behind the desk had long, dark hair and a pleasant smile.

"You ever hear of a man named John Pirannes?" I asked.

The woman kept smiling and said, "I beg your pardon."

"You're a librarian," I said.

"I've been aware of that for several decades," she said.

"Librarians, I've found, are good sources for local . . ."

"Gossip," she said, still not losing her smile.

"Information," I said.

I showed her Adele's photograph. It rang no bell. I told her my story and she listened without asking a question.

Four people were lined up behind me now to check out books before the library told them to go home.

"We're closing in five minutes," the librarian said. "I'll meet you across the street in the Hyatt bar."

I got out of the line and headed for the Hyatt. The night had brought no relief from the heat, and though it was only a little over a football field away, I was sweating as the hotel's chill hit me.

At the bar I listened to a conversation between two guys about some movie. The bartender took my order, a Bass Ale, and I considered showing him Adele's photograph. I thought better of it and sat nursing my ale and listening to movie talk while I waited for the librarian.

She showed up about fifteen minutes later, white silk blouse, colorful skirt with a lot of red and yellow in it.

"Sorry," she said sitting next to me on the stool. "Took me a little longer than I thought."

"Worth waiting for," I said hoisting my glass of ale to her.

"I was right," she said. "You were trying to pick me up."

I hadn't been, but since she let the door open. . . .

"And I was trying to get information on John Pirannes."

"Usual, Rhonda?" the bartender asked.

Rhonda the Librarian nodded and the bartender asked if I wanted another ale. I said yes.

"I have twenty minutes," she said, checking her watch. "I'm meeting a friend for a movie."

"Man?"

"I was trying to give that impression, but no, a woman. So, why are you asking questions about John Pirannes?"

"I do it for a living. Young girl may be with him. Girl's mother wants to find her and get her back to Kansas."

"I see," she said, accepting a glass of dark iced amber from the bartender.

"You're together?" the bartender asked.

"On my check," I said.

Rhonda toasted me and took an I-needed-that sip of her drink.

"John Pirannes," she said, putting the glass down and looking at me, "likes to wear white, combs his dark hair straight back and has nicely capped teeth and a decent vocabulary. Word is that he has all his money tied up in cash. Been here five years. Very, very high-class call girl operation. Reputation for angry public outbursts, usually with one of his girls. Always with a little guy named Tony Spiltz who works out every day at the Y."

"Little guy with a shaved head?" I asked.

"That's him," Rhonda confirmed.

"I see him at the Y when I get there early in the morning. Man of few words."

"But he reads a lot," she said. "A man who loves books, particularly the classics. My take on Tony?"

"Sure."

"He spent a lot of time somewhere where there wasn't much to do but read," she said, going back to her drink.

"O.K., so we have a dangerous man with a bodyguard ex-con," I said. "That helps."

"Good," she said, looking at her watch again. "Look, I've got to go. You know where to find me. Thanks for the drink."

She touched my hand. I liked it, and then she was gone. I settled the bill, nodded at the bartender like we were old friends and headed for the nearest telephone. In less than half a day, I had done what I had been hired to do by Beryl Fitztown. The next illogical step would have been for me to go out to Lido to look for her. Logic prevailed. I called the Best Western Motel and asked for Room 204.

"Yes," Mrs. Fitztown said.

I could see her sitting, fully clothed, legs together, on the bed watching PTL and waiting for my call.

"This is Lew Fonesca. I found Adele. I mean I know where she is and who she's with."

"Where?"

"I'll tell you if you promise me to go to the police and ask them to help you. You'll know where she is. It'll be hard for them to say no."

"Please tell me now where Adele is."

"She's with a man named Pirannes, John Pirannes at the Beach Tides Resort on Longboat Key."

She repeated everything I had said and asked me to spell "Pirannes." I did.

"Thank you," she said. "I'll give you any additional money I owe you in the morning."

"We're even, Mrs. Fitztown. Just go to the police with this information. You'll never get Adele to go with you on your own."

"I'm not afraid of whoremongers, Mr. Fonesca," she said. "I've come to understand that if the Lord is at your side, you have nothing to fear."

"A big cop with a gun on your other side's not a bad idea either," I said. And she hung up.

I had cleared a few dollars, not enough to fix the air conditioner maybe, but enough to keep me in burgers and shakes, gas and oil and a large load at the Bee Ridge Laundromat. I decided I needed a television set and wondered what a small black and white would go for at the Goodwill.

I laid out my sleeping bag, took off my pants and shirt and turned off the light. I listened to traffic zipping down 301 and heard a few voices raised and a little laughter from Dairy Queen. I was almost asleep. Then I thought of something Beryl Fitztown had said.

I got up, adjusted my underwear and turned on the lights. The phone was waiting for me on the desk. I called the police.

"Officer Scott," came a solid man's voice. "Can I help you?"

"Woman named Beryl Fitztown come in tonight to the po-lice?" I said in my best rural Alabama.

"Yes?" Scott said.

"Well, I wondered if maybe like you could check to be sure she showed up, filled out one of them complaints."

"Who are you to Ms. Fitztown?" Scott asked.

"Brother, Orel Bass, live out near Myakka. I'm sure worried 'bout her, officer."

"Who was the complaint against?"

"Well sir, she's mostly lookin' for her missing daughter, my niece, Adele, who's sixteen, and she thinks she knows where she is. I'm more'n a might scared she'd go lookin' for Adele herself in the wrong places."

Long, long pause.

"I'm checking," Scott said. And then, "No complaint tonight from a Mrs. Beryl Fitztown. One wife abused in a bar by her husband, man who claims his house was broken into."

"Much obliged," I said, hanging up before he could ask any more questions.

Beryl Fitztown had said that she and the Lord could take care of Johnny Pirannes or any whoremonger. What made her think Johnny was a whoremonger? I hadn't said anything. He could as well have been a boyfriend or kindly old dentist who cared for runaways. Of course, Beryl Fitztown could have considered anyone with her daughter a whoremonger, but it didn't sound that way.

I was dressed and out of the office in three minutes. Traffic was light. I went up to Fruitville, turned left and drove to the Trail where I turned left and then made the right past Denny's to head over the bridge to Bird Key and then again over the causeway to St. Armand's. The bay was dark and glittering with boat lights, and St. Armand's Circle was alive with tourists. I swerved to avoid hitting a horse-drawn tourist carriage and then headed toward Longboat Key, over another bridge and down Gulf of Mexico Drive, the only road on the five-mile-long island.

Longboat is money. Resorts and high-rise beach condos on my left, very private home developments on my right. Wealthy French and Germans lived here in the winter. Movie stars had million-dollar retreats and Johnny Pirannes and others operated quietly.

I pulled up to the guard gate at the Beach Tides Resort, rolled down my window and smiled.

"Mr. Pirannes is expecting me," I said.

The guard was old but he wasn't stupid. He looked at my beat-up car and went into his glassed-in hut to call. He was out in about thirty seconds.

"No answer," he said. "Sorry."

"I just have a . . ."

"Sorry," the guard said as if he were truly sorry.

I backed up, turned around and went back out on Gulf of Mexico Drive where I did what I should have done in the first place. I drove to the small shopping mall a quarter of a mile down, pulled in and parked. Not much was open, but there were other cars. I walked back to the Beach Tides Resort, hoping a cop wouldn't stop me and ask questions. I kept close to the trees and found a hole in the shrubs I could get through. Security at the resorts was fine as long as you tried to get through the front gate, but none of the resorts had fences all the way around them. With the help of the moonlight and the lights from the high-rise condo next to the Beach Tides, I stumbled through a pond, almost stepped on a dozing white crane and bumped my knee on a brick barbecue pit. When I reached the beach, I took off my shirt, slung it over my shoulder and sauntered down the soft white sand past others on late-night strolls. At the Beach Tides I walked around the lighted pool where a single old man treaded water and nodded to me as I passed. I tried three buildings, checking names in the lobby, avoiding the security people who rode around on little golf carts. In the third building, I found a J. Pirannes and pushed the button.

No answer.

I pushed again. This time a girl answered and said, "Hello."

"John Pirannes please," I said.

"He can't come to the phone now."

"Why?"

"I think he's dead," the girl said.

"Is this Adele?"

"Yes."

"Push the button and let me in," I said.

"Button?"

"On the phone, near the door, somewhere."

"Who are you, the police?"

"Good guess," I said. "The door."

I heard her put down the phone and I waited, phone in hand, watching the driveway outside for the golf cart patrol. Then, a buzz. I hung up the phone and went into the lobby. Pirannes's apartment was on the sixteenth floor. I was up and running down the corridor in about twenty seconds. The door to Pirannes's room was locked. I knocked. I knocked again.

"Who is it?" a familiar voice asked.

"Lew Fonesca," I said.

The door opened and I found myself facing Beryl Fitztown. In her left hand was her purse. In her right was a gun pointing at my chest. The bruise on her cheek had turned puffy and purple.

"Please close the door," she said.

I closed the door.

Sprawled on the sofa behind Beryl Fitztown was a burly man with dark hair combed straight back and a large bullet hole oozing blood in the center of his chest.

"Where's Adele?" I asked looking around.

"Gone," she said. "She answered the phone, pushed a button and ran out of here."

"Maybe we should go find her?" I said.

She shook her head no and motioned for me to sit in a flower-print soft chair across from the corpse. I sat. She kept standing.

"What happened?" I asked.

"Came here in a cab, tried to talk to him. Adele said she'd go with me. He said no, hit me, told me to leave. I shot him."

"And the tourist earlier this week," I said. "You walked in on your daughter and a client. He tried to stop you from taking Adele. That's how you got that bruise on your cheek. You shot him and . . ."

"Adele ran away from me. I searched, asked and then I gave up and found you."

Beryl Fitztown sank into the sofa next to the body. He bounced a little. She didn't notice.

"Tony Spiltz took her away, didn't he?" I asked.

She shrugged, kept the gun pointed at me.

"Where did they go?"

No answer, and then a deep sigh.

"We will sit here for an hour or two, overnight maybe," she said, "and then we will call the police."

"And you'll confess to two murders?"

"I will," she said.

I sat back and yawned. I was sleepy. There was a creep of stubble on my chin.

"You didn't kill either of them, did you, Beryl?" I asked.

"Killed them both," she said, holding up the gun.

"You tracked down Adele after you came to town, found her at the motel with the tourist. Guy tried to throw you out. He hit you. Adele had a gun hidden in the room for protection. She got it out, shot the tourist. You were ready to take a fall on that one to protect Adele, but she left you in the room, maybe telling you she was going for the police. She left and took the gun with her. Am I close?"

She didn't answer. I was close.

"So, you came to me, gave me this story about a phone call and a number," I went on. "I had no trouble finding the booth right next to the hotel where our tourist was shot. I asked around, found Adele, told you about Johnny Pirannes, and you made the mistake of calling him a whoremonger. You knew what your daughter was."

Beryl Fitztown looked at the dead man and shook her head. I wasn't sure what it meant.

"You came here, went through pretty much the same scene you'd gone through with the tourist. Pirannes told you to get lost. Adele saw you getting pushed around again. She went for the gun and boom, one less whoremonger."

She didn't answer.

"Mrs. Fitztown, Beryl?"

"You are wrong," she said firmly. "I shot and killed both men and will so tell the police."

"Suit yourself," I said. "Meanwhile, Adele is on the road with a half-mad ex-con with a shaved head. And I have the feeling that Adele pulls out guns and uses them just a mite hastily. Who's she going to shoot next, Beryl?"

"She didn't shoot anybody," the woman said firmly.

"Nope," I said. "She didn't kill anybody. I think I'll leave you and Pirannes's corpse here alone for a nice long talk before you call the police. Let's make a deal. I don't run out and call the police, and you don't mention to them that I've been here."

She laughed. Not much of a laugh and not a healthy one, but a laugh.

I got up slowly, gave her a little smile and started moving for the door.

"Last suggestion," I said. "Turn her in. Get her some help."

"Man who took her had a pile of money. Said he'd take care of her."

"You believe that?"

"Not much choice," she said with a shrug.

I was at the door now.

"Beryl . . ."

"She looked so pretty, Mr. Fonesca," she said with a distant smile. "Not decked and painted like on television. She's a lost child, Mr. Fonesca. She needs a guiding hand."

"And Tony Spiltz is just the guy to give it to her?"

"She's my baby," Beryl said, looking at me for understanding.

I left the apartment and closed the door slowly behind me.

The night was hot and I still had to duck the old security guards and make my way back to where I hoped my car was still sitting in the parking lot.

I tried not thinking about Beryl Fitztown sitting next to the corpse of Johnny Pirannes and deciding when she should call the police. I tried not to think of Adele sitting next to Tony Spiltz barreling up I-75 toward Tampa or down I-75 on the way to Miami. I tried not to think. I'm not good at it. I'd been a failure at meditation. If I got any sleep tonight, I knew I'd dream about Beryl Fitztown and the girl named Adele whom I had never met.

I headed for an all-night bar in Bradenton where they had a two-for-one special after midnight.

THE DEATH OF COLONEL THOUREAU

Anonymous

I AM A Northern man by birth; a lawyer by profession; and reside and have a tolerable practice in a Southern city, which must be nameless here, but which is not more than a thousand miles from Charleston, S.C.

So much of myself I have thought it proper to state, by way of introduction to the singular story I am about to relate.

Three years ago the present month of August, I found time to make a visit to the home of my childhood in Massachusetts. Sojourning some days in Boston, I was one day in the office of an old school-mate and fellow-graduate—Mr. Richards let us call him—a lawyer already of some note as a counsellor, and occupying the responsible position of confidential adviser to the most solid Life-Insurance Company in New-England's capital.

"You are just here in time," said R. to me; "I have a matter submitted to me, in which you can, perhaps, give me some information."

Thereupon he proceeded to tell me that the Volcano Life-Insurance Company had but that morning received a proposal for effecting an insurance upon the life of a Colonel Thoureau resident in the city of which I also was an inhabitant. The proposition had come directly to the Company in Boston, not, as usual, through their local agent. It was accompanied with the necessary medical and other certificates as to health, habits, etc.; and so far, was perfectly regular. The amount desired to be insured alone caused hesitation on the part of the Directors. Colonel T., who was already forty years of age, desired to secure to his legal heirs the sum of $25,000.

The Company, R. informed me in confidence, had recently sustained some severe losses by the unexpected demise of persons insured to considerable amounts. At least one of these deaths had excited suspicion of foul play on the part of claimants; and it was determined, while investigating the causes of past losses, to be extremely guarded in the future.

"Now, our correspondent is a townsman of yours: can you not give me some information concerning him?"

I knew Colonel T. by sight. He boarded at a hotel where I lived; and I had noticed him there chiefly on account of his partiality for a game of chess, and his generally quiet and unobtrusive manners. He was a moderately stout, hale-looking man, with slightly gray hair, erect carriage, and good complexion. This was all I could say of him; and this—so far as it went—looked quite favorable.

"When you return, I wish you would ascertain something of this gentleman for me. We shall hold his proposal under consideration for some weeks. The risk is too large to act precipitately."

Two weeks thereafter I was back in my office. I lost no time in making such quiet inquiries among my friends concerning Colonel T. as I thought would elicit the information desired by R. I could learn, however, but very little. In fact, there seemed but little to be known. The Colonel—so I was told—was a Louisianian, of French descent. He had been a planter, but had some years before, for what reason no one knew, sold out his plantation and negroes, and removed to New-York, where he spent a winter, and then removed to his present place of residence. He had brought his wife with him; but during the first year of their residence here, they had disagreed, and separated in a very quiet way. For the last three and a half years the Colonel had lived alone in a quiet but pleasant part of the city, occupying the first floor of a small house, having but one hired servant, an old negro woman, who was lodged in the attic; and taking his meals, as I before mentioned, at an hotel in the neighborhood. In his habits he was reputed simple and regular. He made much use of cold and shower-baths; played at chess more or less every day, and was somewhat curiously given to mathematical studies. He had no regular employment, but was a gentleman of leisure. As for his means of subsistence, no one could give me any information. Only, that his income was sure and sufficient, seemed certain from the fact that his wife lived handsomely, at the other extreme of the town, and there appeared to be no debts. I ought to have mentioned before that they had no children.

All this seemed satisfactory, and I lost no time in communicating these details to my friend R. in Boston.

To my surprise, the Directory did not find them so full as I had thought. Their local agent, a young legal friend of mine, received directions to communicate with me on the subject, with the request that I lend my aid to its further elucidation. It was thought especially desirable to ascertain something about the actual pecuniary circumstances, and the family affairs of the Colonel.

I counselled Willard, the agent, to put these remaining questions frankly at once to Colonel T. himself. He did so, and received for reply that his wife was his only heir, that though unfortunately separated from her, he desired to provide for her in case of his sudden death; that his property was so tied up, that though it would keep him and her while he lived, it might not serve her after death. All this was communicated to Willard with such an air of frankness and honesty, that he was induced to counsel the Directory to close with the proposal; and when the resident-physician of the Company, Dr. Evarts, had again instituted a most careful examination of the Colonel's physical condition, and pronounced also a favorable opinion, the Directory in Boston no longer hesitated, but sent on the necessary documents; and on presentation of the insurance policy, Colonel T. at once handed over the amount of the premium and other charges.

It was quite natural that, having had so much to do with this affair, Colonel T., the chief party in it, should have henceforth more interest in my eyes than hitherto. In fact, my curiosity had been excited—as much by what had not been ascertained concerning the man, as by what had—and when we met, as we did daily, either after dinner in the reading-room of our hotel, or in the evening on the promenade, I looked curiously at the somewhat inscrutable face, and sought—but vainly—to cast some momentary glance into the soul which I was soon convinced used these features to conceal rather than to display the emotions by which it was stirred. I am a man of regular habits myself—a bachelor—and Colonel T. soon became, so to speak, a part of my daily life. I looked for him in his usual haunts each day, and was at rest if he were there—or felt uneasy if, perchance, my eye did not rest upon his manly figure during my evening walk; or if his quiet corner on the hotel verandah was without him.

As for the Colonel himself, he exchanged but few words with any one. Every body knew him—by sight, that is—and so he passed current in our society. He seemed essentially a solitary man. Not misanthropic, but simply solitary. And this, at least, was so plainly written upon his face, that he was not troubled by social appeals on the part of those among whom he moved, but was left to pursue his pleasures unmolested.

To be sure, once in a while some new-comer among us would ask, "Who is Colonel T.?" and we, shrugging our shoulders, would repeat the question, by way of answer, and ourselves wonder who he was. But then, he dressed well, was civil to every body, and was evidently a man of the world; and one soon loses curiosity about people who have no striking peculiarity to distinguish them from the mass.

Yet I could not help watching the Colonel. And so much did my interest in him increase, by reason of his taciturnity, I suppose, that I finally determined at all hazards to approach him and seek his acquaintance. It was already late in autumn, when I proceeded one afternoon, as usual, on my daily promenade, thinking that when I met the object of my speculations, I would make some occasion for addressing him. But he was not there.

In vain I walked and looked. I walked on, and had already continued my promenade much farther along the sea-shore than I had intended, when I was suddenly made aware, by a few big premonitory drops, that a rain-cloud was about to burst over-head. I had on light summer clothing, and, fearful of taking cold, looked hastily about for a shelter. At a little distance, I saw an unfinished house, and within its walls I found shelter from the rain, which soon began to pour down in right earnest. The clouds had shortened the twilight, and it was now quite dark.

Presently I became aware that I was not the only occupant of the shelter. I heard voices, seemingly at but little distance. I was enabled to distinguish two; both base, but one evidently belonging to a young man, the other, the deeper and energetic tones of an older man.

The rain ceased as suddenly as it had begun. As I was preparing to step forth from my place of shelter, the owners of the voices approached. I stepped back involuntarily, when the tones of the elder struck my ear familiarly.

"You have all, now?" asked he.

"Yes, all," was the answer of the younger, in a somewhat excited tone.

"And you recollect your oath?"

"Yes, Sir; you may depend upon me."

"Neither sooner nor later; let nothing prevent you. You know the house. You will surely go?"

"Punctually, Sir."

"Well, you may remain now, and let me pass on in advance. Remember your reward. Good-by till to-night."

"Till to-night; I will not forget, Sir."

The steps approached the doorway near which I had taken shelter. I stepped back silently, and peered out at the speaker, who walked swiftly by. As he passed, the sky brightened a little and I beheld—certainly, and beyond the shadow of a doubt—my mysterious friend, the Colonel. He walked at speed; and ere I had recovered from my surprise, was lost to sight in the gloom.

Singular, thought I, as I walked along homeward. It was certainly the Colonel. But what was he doing here? And who was the young person whom he adjured to "remember his oath"? And what about to-night?

The next morning I was sitting in my private office, busily studying up an important case, for which I had to prepare the papers, when I heard my copyist denying admittance to some one who evidently desired to see me. I recognized the voice of my friend W., the insurance-agent, and willing to be excused from even him, listened to hear him go down-stairs again.

"I *must* see him," said he. "It is important to me. Just announce my name; and say I will not stay more than five minutes."

I flung open my door, and greeted W., saying that business of pressing importance forced me to deny myself to every body for some hours.

"But what is the matter? You look agitated."

"Why, yes," said he; "it is a misfortune, so to speak. You remember Colonel T.?"

"Certainly; what of him?" said I quickly—remembering also the incident of the previous evening.

"He is dead. He was found dead in bed this morning—his throat cut. I have just seen the corpse."

He continued, after a pause: "You can see how unpleasant this is for me, when you bear in mind the large risk taken on his life, and that it was at my advice it was taken."

I still stared him in the face in vacant surprise. The news was so unexpected.

"Tell me," said I, "how it was."

"The negro woman who took care of the Colonel's rooms, had gone as usual about nine o'clock to clear them up for the day. She had found the outer door fastened; had knocked repeatedly, and, not receiving any answer, had informed her master, who lived near by. A lock-smith was called to open the door, and behold a tragedy! In the inner room they had found the Colonel lying upon the bed, dead, and in a pool of blood."

"In what condition were the rooms?"

"The inner communicating doors were wide open. The windows of the sleeping apartment were open, they opened upon the street. The furniture was in perfect order. The Colonel's gold watch and purse lay upon a toilet-stand near the head of the bed. There was some disarrangement of the bed-clothes, but not much—apparently the result of the struggles of the death-agony. Aside from this, no article of apparel or furniture in the room seemed in the slightest degree disarranged. Life had evidently fled some hours ago. The corpse of the unhappy man was stiff and cold. A razor lay on the floor, at the bedside, as though it had fallen out of his hands."

"And no sign of outside violence?" I asked.

"Not the least. Clearly a case of suicide; and I am not going to let our Company suffer for such a rascally proceeding," said the irate Willard, who evidently regarded the deceased Colonel as one who had designs upon the coffers of the Volcano Life-Insurance Company.

"Of course the coroner has the matter in hand?"

"Yes."

"Well, telegraph immediately to Boston," said I, after momentary consideration. "In two hours I will meet you at Colonel T.'s rooms."

When I arrived upon the scene of the tragedy, Dr. Davis, the coroner, had already impannelled a jury, and examined the other residents of the house. My head full of the strange colloquy to which I had been an unwilling listener the previous evening, and mystified by this far more than any of the others, I listened eagerly to the evidence.

The ground-floor of the house was occupied as a dry-goods store. Its owner slept elsewhere. The floor above the Colonel's apartments was rented by an invalid with her servant. The attic was occupied by the negro woman who attended the Colonel's rooms, and by a negro laundress.

The lock of the outer door of the Colonel's apartments had not been tampered with. The key was found under the pillow, in the bed. The window, as before mentioned, was found open; but a close scrutiny of the wall, outside and in, and of the window-sill, revealed no marks of unlawful entrance.

On the floor lay the mystery! From the bed-side, where a little pool of blood had gathered on the floor, to the door, *and one step beyond, on the outside of the room,* there were the tracks of a human foot! *tracked in blood!* Only once was the impression of the whole foot given; the other tracks were as of one walking on his toes. All were of a bare foot.

The dead man's feet were bare; but they were bloodless. Moreover, on comparing, his foot was not quite so large as that which had made the track. So said one of the persons who measured. But the doctor, who examined all very carefully, was of opinion that the Colonel's bare and living foot would have left just such a track.

So far, those present were about equally divided between the two suppositions: *murder* and *suicide.*

"Why should he be murdered? He was not robbed," said one jury-man to another.

"Why should he commit suicide; and why go out of the door after he had cut his throat; and how get back?" was asked in answer.

Several persons were now examined. A night-watchman deposed to seeing a light in the Colonel's room till about ten o'clock the previous night.

The lady who resided above, had heard, between two and three o'clock in the morning, a noise as of one hastily throwing open a door, in the Colonel's room.

The woman-servant of the invalid lady had seen the Colonel going up-stairs to his room about nine the previous evening. She noticed no change from his usual appearance, but thought he walked slower than in general.

The laundress, being interrogated, stated that she was awakened about three o'clock, by a noise as of a door or window being opened. That, having to go early to work, she presently arose, dressed, and sallied out into the street. That she found the street-door simply latched—not locked—though the key hung up upon its usual hook upon the back of the door. Finally, that as she emerged into the street, she saw a man stooping down, on the other side of the street. Hearing her step, he got up hurriedly, but slowly walked away. Owing to the darkness, she could not distinguish his features; but he was short, stout, and dressed loosely, somewhat like a sailor.

Just at this stage of the proceedings, a carriage stopped before the house. "Here is Mrs. T.," said Doctor Davis.

She had been sent for. As she was ushered into the sitting-room, the Doctor advanced to meet her; the rest of us remained in the adjoining room. I looked through the door-crack, and beheld a slender form, a face showing traces of suffering, but also traces of a beauty now in its decline.

After some words of respectful condolence upon the sad occasion which drew her hither, the coroner proceeded to ask her some questions as to the deceased.

"How long is it, Madam, since you last saw your husband?"

Her tears fell fast, and a heavy sob interrupted her as she essayed to answer—at last:

"I have not spoken to him for nearly four years," said she in a voice still broken with emotion.

"Would you like to see him?"

She was led into the next room, and there left alone with the corpse. She sank upon her knees at the bed-side, yet without touching the corpse, and wept silently, her whole body heaving convulsively with the violence of her grief.

When she returned, the coroner again interrogated her.

"Was your husband given to fits of melancholy, Madam?"

"No, Sir."

"Were his circumstances embarrassed?"

"So far as I know, they were not, Sir."

"Did he ever speak of committing suicide, in your hearing?"

She buried her face in her hands, and trembled in silent agony, for a while, ere she could answer, with much hesitation: "He did, Sir; but only once."

"I told you so," whispered the suicidal juryman, to his murderous fellow.

"Will you explain the occasion of that, Madam?"

After consideration, the lady looked up, with a somewhat stern, composed face, and said calmly: "No, Sir, I would rather not. It has nothing—" and than stopped abruptly.

There was a little consultation among the lawyers and the coroner, and the latter asked again:

"I am sorry to put the question, but it is necessary, Madam: do you know any circumstances which would elucidate the mystery of your husband's death?"

Again she covered her face with her hands, and wept and trembled in that dreadful agony of spirit which seemed to seize her, but when she could speak, answered with a tolerably clear voice, and certainly a truthful look: "No, Sir, I know nothing."

"We shall not need you more for the present, Madam," said the coroner presently.

The lady retired, casting a last and seemingly almost despairing look of sorrow toward the corpse, and even making a step toward the bed, as though she would catch the hand of the deceased in hers. But she refrained.

The waitress was recalled, and asked if she missed any accustomed object about the room. She said no. The fire-place, which was protected by a tight-fitting screen, was exposed. There was no mark of an extraordinary advent or exit in this direction. Finally, I related what had occurred to me the preceding evening. My statement, as may be readily conceived, excited the liveliest attention. But it had no real bearing upon the mystery of the Colonel's death. I could not even depose certainly that it was the Colonel I saw. And if it was he, the circumstance by no means cleared up the case. It rather complicated it. The more we heard the deeper the mystery became. The jury agreed to suspend their verdict; indeed, they were so divided between suicide and murder, and there were so many floating theories and suppositions, that a verdict was an impossibility. The coroner thought it a case of suicide. Willard, the agent, thought it a complicated case of conspiracy to defraud his company, and desired to have Mrs. T. arrested as a leader in the plot. The jurymen were wise, as all jurymen are. But whatever they guessed, they knew so little that, as I have said, they finally agreed to suspend the verdict and await the possible developments of the day. Meantime, the papers of the deceased were being looked over. Every thing was in apple-pie order, as a fruit-seller on the jury observed. But they shed no light upon the mystery. There was no will found; of silver, ready money and jewelry, there was absolutely scarce a trace. This was astonishing in one of the Colonel's habits and means. Willard remarked that it strengthened him in the belief that the man had committed suicide with felonious intents upon the Volcano; while a keen-scented juryman thought he smelled a robbery, perhaps a murder.

We were about to retire, when entered a gentleman who claimed to be a friend of the deceased, and whom I recognized immediately as a person with whom he sometimes played chess. Captain Snyder, so he gave his name, appeared astonished and grieved at the sudden death, but could give no information. He had just received a note from Mrs. T., asking him to attend on her part to the obsequies, etc., and now offered to take charge of any thing not in the hands of the authorities.

"By the way, Doctor," he remarked to the coroner, as we were going out, "I would like very much to have a remembrance of my deceased friend. If the effects are sold, I desire to purchase for myself a set of silver chess-men, with the help of which he and I have passed so many pleasant hours, and also, I would like to have a St. George's sovereign, which my friend used to carry in his pocket as a pocket-piece."

"You say there was a set of silver chess-men?"

"Yes; you will probably find them in this little table. You see the top is thrown over in this way"—performing the action—"and you have then a chess-board. But the chess-men are not here!"

Nor were they to be found. Nor was the St. George's sovereign any where to be discovered.

Here was evidence of a robbery!

The Captain assured us that he had played at chess with his deceased friend on Tuesday morning, that is, two days preceding the night in which he died.

This discovery gave a new turn to the affair. If robbed, why, then, there was either murder or a most strange coincidence between an accident and a crime. At any rate, there was now something to be traced up, and a prospect of arriving, by the discovery of the lost property, at some clue to the singular complication. A description of the missing articles was at once made out and sent to the police, who were requested to make earnest search in pawnbrokers' shops and other localities for them. The room of the Colonel's waitress was searched, but ineffectually, and the honest negress shed tears at thought that she was suspected of having robbed a master who had always treated her with kindness.

The police gained no clue to the lost articles. It became highly probable that the thief had melted up the valuable silver chess set. As for the sovereign, it might circulate unsuspected, and might possibly have gone through many hands without being remarked. For in so considerable a sea-port, foreign coins excite but little attention; and the only peculiarity of this sovereign was one so far common that a dozen like it might be in circulation in the city at the same time. It was, namely, a coin of the last century, having upon one of its sides a device of St. George and the Dragon, whereas sovereigns of a later date bear a bust of the reigning sovereign instead. The old sovereigns are worth some cents more than the newer ones, and have consequently been nearly all called in or melted up. Yet are they not so scarce that the possession of one of these old coins could be called remarkable.

More than two weeks passed without a clue to the mystery; the matter was already dropped from the papers; and as neither Mrs. T. nor any one else had laid claim to the insurance, Willard was more than ever convinced that the deceased Colonel was a rascal, when one day a new development really promised, or half promised, a denouement. The wife of the chief of police, settling a grocery bill, received in change for a bill an English sovereign. On handing the change to her husband in the evening, he at once perceived that this sovereign was of the identical coinage with that which had so mysteriously disappeared from the Colonel's pocket. He immediately made inquiries of the owner of the grocery-store, and succeeded in tracing the coin to the possession of a small dealer near the water-side. This man stated that he received it some days ago, perhaps ten, perhaps more, of a man whom he did not know, but who was dressed as a common seaman. He had purchased an article of clothing from the general assortment, had received his purchase and the required small change, and was gone— whither no one knew. The dealer described his person, but the description was little worth as a clue.

A few days thereafter, however, happening into this small dealer's shop, an individual was pointed out to the chief, quietly, as the one who had paid out the sovereign.

"You are sure?" asked he of the dealer.

"Yes, Sir, I remember him very well."

The man was about going out. The official approached him, and placing his hand upon his shoulder, said: "Where did you stow the silver chess-men and the money you stole at Colonel T.'s house?"

The man turned pale, trembled violently, and finally when he had partially recovered his self-possession, vehemently protested entire ignorance of that with which he was charged. He even denied all knowledge of the sovereign he was said to have paid out; but afterward admitted that part of the charge against him, alleging that in his fear at so unexpected an accusation he had been led to deny every thing, and that his embarrassment was the result only of his utter innocence of the evil with which he was charged. He gave himself out to be a ship's carpenter, out of employment; had been in the city but a few weeks, having travelled overland from New-Orleans, where he found it difficult to procure employment; had lived at eating-houses, and slept in different places while in the city, having no regular stopping-place; had no friends to vouch for his character, which he violently maintained to be irreproachable, and begged with tears that he might be let go. Though the suspicions were slight, he was locked up; and it was determined to examine him thoroughly the next day. Pending which, I was curious enough to call and see him, in company with Willard, who wanted to talk to him. The prisoner's voice seemed strangely familiar to me, but I could not remember having ever seen him before. But being informed that I was a lawyer, he insisted upon my "taking care of him to-morrow," as he termed it, and begged this so piteously, that, not believing him to have any concern with the Colonel's death, I consented. He assured me of his innocence of the slightest wrong, and repeated the story told already to the Chief.

The examination came on. The lodging-house keeper where George Gordon (this was the name of the prisoner) had slept deposed that he saw him to his room at or about eleven o'clock on the night in question, and that he came down from his room to breakfast about seven the next morning. The prisoner maintained that he had not quitted the room in the intervening period. The testimony of the laundress pointed to the hour of two as that when the robbery most likely took place. The District-Attorney being called upon, was unable to prove even that the suspicious coin which had caused the prisoner's arrest, was the identical one owned by the Colonel. Strangely enough Captain S., the witness whose testimony was most necessary to identify this coin, was missing. When inquiry was made for him, it appeared that he had suddenly left town, for New-Orleans apparently, but even of this no reliable information could be obtained. When the District-Attorney mentioned the unaccountable absence of Captain S., the prisoner's face brightened up, and he leaned over the dock and whispered to me: "They will have to clear me now. They can bring no proof against my alibi."

The lodging-house keeper was recalled. He was sure that it was eleven o'clock, perhaps a little later, when the prisoner came in. He (the prisoner) had originally maintained that he was in bed by ten.

"Where were you before eleven?" the District-Attorney asked. "It was quite possible that this robbery should be committed at an early hour of the evening."

"You need not answer this question if it will criminate you," said I to him, by way of caution.

"Will I certainly be discharged if I can give a satisfactory account of myself for the earlier hours of the evening?" he asked me eagerly.

I said, as matters looked then, it was almost certain.

"Then," said he, with a sudden resolve, "I will tell you. I was at Mrs. Thoureau's house!"

"At Mrs. Thoureau's, the widow of the deceased?" said I, looking aghast. The whole court was electrified at the announcement.

"If you will send for the lady she will doubtless bear witness to the fact."

Mrs. T. was immediately sent for. Meantime, my client, in answer to interrogations from the Court, stated that he had been employed in the house of Mrs. T. to repair and polish some pieces of furniture; that the lady had learned something of his poverty, and had kindly given him good advice and means to supply his most pressing necessities, and that on that evening he had called there to get some money due him, and had remained until his return to his lodgings.

Mrs. T. was announced. She corroborated the story of the prisoner in every particular.

"One more question, Mrs. T.," said the District-Attorney. "Have you never perchance, in the prisoner's presence, made any allusion to the circumstances and mode of life of your deceased husband?"

"Never, Sir."

"Do you know if the prisoner was acquainted with Col. T., and familiar with his location and habits?"

"On the contrary, I know that he did not know Col. T., and I don't think he ever saw him."

There was a silence of a minute's duration. The prisoner looked hopeful. The District-Attorney, who had for some minutes been studying first the face of Mrs. T., and then that of the prisoner, turned suddenly upon the former, and asked: "What relation does George Gordon, the prisoner, bear to you, Madam?"

The face of the witness flushed up for a moment, then grew ashy pale. She essayed to speak, but her lips moved without producing any sound. She grasped the table for support, then sank lifeless to the floor. The fainting woman was quickly borne into the fresh air. A physician was called. He

ordered her to be conveyed to her home, and pronounced her to be attacked with paralysis. Her presence in court was therefore impossible.

"It was not certain, even, that the poor lady would survive the night
through," said the physician, hastening away after his patient.

"My mother! my poor mother! I killed you!" cried out the prisoner, wring-
ing his hands with anguish, and losing at last all self-control.

His mother? Here was a new complication.

The session of court was adjourned; the prisoner was remanded to his
cell. We who had become interested in the case were more puzzled than
ever. Was Mrs. Col. T. concerned in the crime which seemed to have been
committed? She looked too honest to be aught else than an honest woman.
Beside, had she not denied all claim to the estate of the deceased? And
yet—

The first news I heard when I arose the following morning, was that my
client, the prisoner, had made his escape the previous night, disguised in
the garments of one of the jailer's assistants, whom he had overpowered
when he was locking him in for the night. The escape was not known until
some hours after, and I may as well mention here that the poor fellow
concealed himself on board a vessel just sailing for Curaçao, and successfully
evaded pursuit. He left a note for me, which was slipped under my office-
door during the night. In this he promised a full account of his share in
the mysterious transaction as soon as possible, making at the same time most
solemn asseverations of his entire innocence of the supposed murder, and
stating that he never knew Col. T. as such, or by any other name, having
only on two occasions accidentally met him, one of these being on the
evening of the rain. Hence I recollected his voice.

Two days thereafter we were agreeably surprised at the reappearance of
the missing Captain Snyder. From him was now obtained finally an explanation of the mystery which had so long excited the attention of the few
who knew of it. I will give the Captain's account in as few words as possible:

Mrs. Thoureau was the daughter of a Louisiana planter. She was educated
at a Northern boarding-school. Being of a romantic temperament, at the
age of seventeen, she fell in love with an individual who occupied in the
institution in which she found a home, the post of instructor in rhetoric.
This man was possessed of a showy figure and considerable personal grace,
but was at the same time entirely devoid of principle. Seeing the artless
young girl's infatuation, he pretended to return her affection. The result of
the amour was a child, born but a month before its mother was to leave her
school for home. Her shame was known to but three persons—the seducer,
who fled when the fruits of his crime became apparent, and the two maiden

ladies who owned and carried on the school. Alarmed at the consequences to their establishment should Emily's misfortune become known, they aided her in concealing her shame, and when she was safely delivered of a male child, provided a home for that in a distant farm-house, where its origin would not be inquired into so long as the means for its support were forthcoming. The poor mother asked vainly for her infant. It was only upon her solemn promise never to seek for it in any manner, that the two maiden principals of the academy consented to preserve inviolate the secret of her shame.

When fully recovered, she returned to her Southern home. Here, after five years spent in quiet repentance and the exemplary performance of the real duties of life—for the young girl had sinned through weakness, not for love of sin—she met Col. Thoureau. There was a mutual attraction. He saw in her quiet, grave but kindly demeanor and the conscientious rectitude of all her actions the embodied ideal of his soul. She found in the frank, noble gentleman all those real qualities whose sham semblance had deceived her young heart to so fatal an error. Fancy her anguish when the Colonel spoke his love, and asked her to return it. Her eyes brightened for a moment, but in the next appeared before her mind's eye her sin and shame, and with tears and sobs she hurried unanswering from the presence of her lover.

Could she tell him all? Him who had loved her as a being all purity and innocence. And yet dared she wed herself to any one, keeping to herself that dread secret which drove happiness away from her? What bitter struggles, what vain resolves, what tears and prayers were hers it were vain here to attempt to tell. Suffice it that, submitting to her lover's persistent entreaties, she became his—but without that frank confession of her single error, which might have made her a happy woman, and would certainly have made her an honest one.

The marriage was a happy one. Emily—now Mrs. Col. T.—had been informed that the fruit of her error had disappeared—was probably dead. Her seducer was a wandering profligate, living in a distant part of the country. Was she not safe? She thought so; and ventured to enjoy a few years of truest bliss. Her father died. Her mother was long since dead. Of brothers or sisters she had none. Her husband was all to her, and she devoted herself to his happiness.

Who knows the abyss upon whose brink he stands! Emily's seducer, ever going down-hill on the broad road of vice, was mastered by necessities which must be supplied at all hazards. He applied by letter to his former victim, coolly stating his needs, and desiring relief at her hands. The wretched lady was forced to parley with the villain, and from her own means satisfy his demands, vainly hoping and entreating that she might be left in peace.

Vain hope it was! So good an opportunity for spoils was not to be given up. Again and again she submitted to his demands, enforced by threats of exposure. And when at last, rendered desperate by the growing audacity of the villain, she refused to hold further communication with him, there came one day, directed to her husband, a package containing old letters and tokens, which proved but too clearly the guilt which the sender alleged.

At this time the unhappy pair were residing in our city, whither Mrs. T. had induced her husband to remove, in the vain hope of eluding the clutches of the villain who was torturing her. The Colonel, who tenderly loved his wife, compromised with the quondam Professor on such terms as were likely to insure his future silence, then made separate provision for his wife, and thus they parted, both unhappy.

Anxious to secure from want the woman whom he still loved, the Colonel had finally hit upon the expedient of insuring his life, determined while he lived to have her comfort looked after, and by securing her a sum after his death, to place her beyond necessities of any kind. He effected the insurance in good faith. But a month thereafter he was once more made unhappy by a threatening letter from the brute who had destroyed his peace. This affected him much. He wrote to the wretch—who shall be nameless here—and by dint of a considerable sum of money, gained from him a written obligation to leave America, never to return. But to complete the Colonel's distress, the sum he had payed his persecutor was spent at the gambling-table, and the miscreant now refused to depart without an additional subsidy.

Meantime, Emily's son had grown up to be a stout young man. He was apprenticed to a steam-boat builder, on one of the Western rivers. His foster-mother died, and on her death-bed revealed to him the secret of his birth, and the place of residence of his mother. Animated by a desire to see her to whom he owed his life, he raked together his little means and at once proceeded to C—. He called upon Mrs. T., and upon telling the poor lady his story, was received by her with a joy and love which he little expected. Both felt the necessity of preserving secret the bond existing between them; and the poor mother never, even to her son, revealed those particulars of her life, which we have but just glanced at. He thought her a widow; and little suspected that her husband lived in the same city with her.

Now, on his first coming to the city, (he had actually come around by ship from New-Orleans, instead of over-land, as he asserted on his trial,) he had fallen among thieves, and was robbed and nearly murdered by a part of his former ship-mates. Col. T. coming up just as he was about to be overcome by his assailants, had dispersed these and taken the poor lad home to dress his bruises, little suspecting the tragic connection of their fates.

"A few days thereafter," continued Captain Snyder, who, I must admit, proved himself an acute and courageous man on this occasion, and who had brought all parts of this strange story together, "Jeremiah Randall, the Professor before mentioned, made another demand upon Colonel Thoureau. He was desperate. So was the poor Colonel. He had seen a considerable part of his fortune slip into this miscreant's hands, to be wasted in all manner of low dissipation. He lived in abject terror of this fellow's indiscretions. Many a time must the poor hunted Colonel have thought longingly of the gallows which was waiting for this "Professor," and through all it seems certain that the good gentleman loved with his whole heart his unfortunate wife. If only he had had the wisdom to own this love, to take her to his bosom, and to fly with her out of reach of this defamer! But it was not to be so.

"What I am now about to relate," continued Captain Snyder, "I have literally choked out of the infernal rascal whom I caught so snugly in Poydras-street, New-Orleans, and who is now lodged in the tightest cell in our prison. Blast him! I did not want to forestall the hangman, or my hands would have held him till his wind was gone!" And the Captain showed a hand which I should not like to feel at my throat. "You must know, then, that my poor friend appointed a meeting for that fatal Thursday night, when he and the "Professor" were to have a final settlement. As the hour was a late one, he sent to the "Professor" the key of the house and a duplicate night-key, and at eleven Randall came up silently and found the Colonel waiting for him. He says the Colonel cursed him, which I can believe; and threatened his life, which is a cowardly lie; and that while they talked, suddenly there was a scuffle, in which he got Thoureau down. That then he (Randall) felt that blood was about to be spilled. He looked for a pistol and did not see one. He had only a piece of stout packing-twine in his pocket, and he owned to me, the infernal scoundrel!" hissed Snyder in our horrified ear, "that he tied the Colonel's feet as he held him down, then his arms, gagged him, and then laying him upon the bed, deliberately cut his throat with his own razor! After which he took three hours of moon-light to arrange the room, whose general disposition he well knew, for he had received money there frequently, and then he went out bare-footed. But taking a last look at his victim, now lying upon the bed, his feet got inadvertently into the pool of blood, and hence the tracks, which ceased at the outside of the door, where he first discovered them. And the coward did not dare to return to the room after the door was once closed behind him to erase these fatal tracks."

"And the negro laundress saw him putting on his shoes on the other side of the street, as she came out of the street-door?" I queried.

"Exactly," said Snyder. "Poor Mrs. Thoureau, whom I have known and respected for a long time, called for me after the Colonel's burial, and with many tears, told me not only her own sad story, but also her suspicions as to the author of her husband's death. She put me upon the track to find him, and I scarce slept till I had him before a revolver, with part of a confession upon his cowardly lips. Thank the Devil! they hang people for murder in this State. If they didn't, I should have killed this brute myself."

And that was the solution of a mystery which had puzzled us all a good deal.

Professor Jeremiah Randall was hanged. I saw him swing. I shall never go to see another man hanged. It is too horrid.

Poor Mrs. Thoureau lingered on for a few weeks, but her system, enfeebled by much mental distress, finally succumbed to paralysis, and she died before Randall was hung. Her ill-fated son I have never seen since. Three days ago I received a note inclosing a hundred dollars, and a few words, saying: "Once you defended me when I had no friends. Many thanks." This brought the story to my mind which is told above. Names and dates are somewhat altered, but for the rest, any lawyer of ten years' standing, in our district, will tell you of the remarkable murder of Colonel Thoureau.

SHARYN McCRUMB

I know about bullies. Every neighborhood seems to have one, and as a shy only child I was the natural target of the roaring lout on Jackson Drive. I was four years old. Every afternoon, my mother would send me out to play, only to have me return an hour later, dirt-streaked and sobbing—the victim of the neighborhood bully.

Finally, one day in exasperation, she said to me, "The next time you come home crying, I'm going to spank you a lot harder than that boy hit you." She would have, too. My parents were not the doting Ward and June Cleaver types. They used green switches. It would never have occurred to my mother to confront the boy's parents on my behalf. Childhood was a war, and I was in country alone.

The next day I walked out of the house in frozen terror. First the bully would thrash me, and then my mother would beat me again. I felt that all the escape holes had been blocked—and a cornered animal is a dangerous one.

I found the Jackson Drive bully at the top of the hill, talking to the other big boys. He was totally ignoring me for once, but I knew that state of affairs was too good to last. Before he could catch sight of me, I picked up an iron pipe lying in the grass, raised it as high as I could, and brought it down across the back of his head. The bully went down like a pole-axed steer, and I went home and told my mother, "It's okay now. I killed him."

I hadn't killed him, but he got a trip to the emergency room. He never came near me again.

In my short story "Foggy Mountain Breakdown" I tapped into my own feelings of being the victim to tell the story of a shy young boy in the east Tennessee of my father's generation. The boy deals with the same sort of swaggering bully I faced, but with a more subtle and ironic form of revenge. The bully's own cruelty is his undoing.

• • •

I found echoes of my story, and of my solitary childhood, in the life of H. H. Munro, the English short story writer who published under the name of Saki. His childhood tormentor was a maiden aunt with whom he lived while his father, a British soldier, was stationed in India. In his wonderfully evocative story "Sredni Vashtar," Saki imagines a terrible revenge against the hateful guardian who deprives him of his pet, his only friend.

"Foggy Mountain Breakdown" is based on an actual incident— only the final revenge is invented. I am convinced that this is also true of the situation in Saki's story—a real injury toward a beloved pet is turned by the writer into a triumph of revenge. Writing has many joys—settling scores without going to jail is not the least of them.

FOGGY MOUNTAIN BREAKDOWN

Sharyn McCrumb

THAT AFTERNOON THE Haskell girls came by collecting money for a funeral wreath. Davy gave them a nickel and ten pennies from the baking powder can in the pantry. Mama would probably have given them a quarter, since Dad was working a couple of days a week at the railroad shop now, but she was visiting over at the Kesslers, talking about the accident. All the mothers in the community would be talking about the tragedy, with their eyes red from crying, because, as the preacher said, death is always a pang of sorrow no matter who is taken, but sooner or later, every one of them would say, "It might have been my boy." It wasn't one of their boys, though; it was Junior Mullins. Fifteen cents was enough for Junior Mullins, Davy thought.

The money collected from the twenty-three families living back in the hollow of Foggy Mountain would be enough for a decent bunch of store-bought flowers from the shop in Erwin. One of the Haskell girls would write every family's name on the card to be given to Junior's parents. There would probably be bigger, fancier wreaths from Mr. Mullins's fellow managers at the railroad, maybe even one from the president of the railroad himself, considering the circumstances, but the neighbors would want to send one anyway, to show that their thoughts and prayers were with the family in this time of sorrow.

Davy was still in mourning for his bicycle. Nobody was collecting flowers for it. Two dollars it had cost. Two dollars earned in solitary misery with sweat and briar-pricks, picking blackberries in the abandoned fields, and selling them door to door at ten cents a gallon. It takes a lot of blackberries to make a gallon. Getting two dollars' worth of dimes had cost Davy two precious weeks of summer—two weeks of working most of the day dragging a gallon bucket through the briars, sidestepping snakes and poison oak, while everybody else went swimming or played ball at the old gravel pit. Two weeks without candy, soda pop, or Saturday matinees.

Saturday afternoons were the hardest. Davy would be alone in a field of brambles, so hot that the air was wavy when you looked into the distance, with the mountains shutting him in like the green walls of an open air prison. Somewhere on the other side of that ridge, his friends were having fun. Hour after hour he stooped over blackberry thickets, and to keep his mind off his sore back and his stuck fingers he'd try to imagine what was playing at the picture show. The cowboys, like Buck Jones or Tom Mix and his horse Tony, were his favorite, but he went every Saturday he could afford, no matter what was playing. When you're eleven years old and home seems duller than ditch water, anything on the screen is better than real life. You had to want something real bad to miss the movies on account of it. Right now the movie house was showing *Hills of Peril*: Buck Jones helps a young woman save her gold mine from outlaws. The pictures were silent, but the dialogue was printed on cards that were projected onto the screen. Davy reckoned most of the boys in the county had learned more about reading at the picture show than they had in the schoolhouse. At Saturday matinees, with all those boys reading the lines out loud as they flashed on the screen, the theater hummed with a steady drone that sounded like the Johnsons' beehives at swarm time.

Davy'd missed most of the Phantom serial. He'd had to make do with a summary of the story from Johnny Suttle, who forgot bits of the story and kept repeating the parts he liked. But Davy didn't care. There'd be other movies, and his reward for missing this one was his very own bicycle. He had done it.

His hard-earned two dollars bought one bicycle frame with no accessories: no tires, no brakes, no pedals. He had made tires for the wheels himself, with a little help from Old Lady Turner's yard. She had never missed that twelve feet of red rubber garden hose, and the tires he made from them were the perfect width and strength for the homemade bike. He'd caught hell, though, for cutting Mama's clothesline and taking the galvanized wire to run through the four lengths of garden hose so that he could fasten them around the wheel rims. The beating he got for taking the clothesline had been worth it, though. Now he was riding.

Davy's two-dollar bike had cast-off railroad spikes for pedals, and the Morris coaster brakes didn't work, but that didn't matter. He was riding. Dad had brought home an almost-empty can of blue paint from one of the railroad shops, and Davy had painted his bike so that from a distance it looked almost store-bought.

Up and down the gravel pit he wheeled and turned, dipping into the chug-holes and jumping out on the far side high enough to clear an upright Quaker Oats box set there as an obstacle. If he needed to stop the bike, he pressed his foot on the front wheel. That worked fairly well for solitary riding, but when he wanted to get into the bicycle polo games in Well's pasture, he needed something more reliable.

Bicycle polo was played with an old softball and croquet mallets that one of the boys had scrounged from somebody's trash pile. They would divide up into teams and race up and down the pasture on their bikes, swatting at the softball. You needed brakes, though, to keep from crashing into your teammates, or so that you could change directions suddenly when the ball was intercepted by the other team and swatted off in the other direction. After a few hours of tinkering, he had repaired the Morris coaster brakes with a brake drum fashioned from a Coca-Cola bottle cap. After two or three hours of hard riding, the cap would grind up, leaving him brakeless again, but by then the polo game would be over, and he could go home and make repairs for the next match.

He had been able to hold his own just fine on his jerry-rigged bike—that is, until Junior Mullins showed up for the game, riding piggyback on Charlie Bestor's motorcycle. Davy thought Junior and Charlie were two of a kind: big arrogant bully, little arrogant bully. Charlie was a high school senior who had been going to ROTC Camp at Fort Oglethorpe, Georgia, every summer. On the last trip he had brought home the motorcycle, and now he roared up and down the paved roads, promising his toadies rides on his motorcycle, and lording it over every other boy around.

Junior Mullins was the kind of big, loud kid that other boys hate but nobody stands up to. His father was a manager down at the railroad, working steady, so Junior had clothes that weren't hand-me-downs, and meat sandwiches and an apple or an orange in his lunch box, while everybody else had corn bread and a cold potato. Junior Mullins had a store-bought bike, a shiny red one, brand-new, that his dad had bought in Johnson City for his birthday. Junior thought that he was better than the other boys in the neighborhood because his father was the boss of everybody else's father, because the Mullins family lived in a brick house, and because Junior got a toy truck and a model airplane for Christmas, instead of just an orange, a stick of rock candy, and a new pair of shoes. Junior enforced his superiority with the ruthless cruelty of a ten-year-old tyrant. His weapons were scorn, derision, taunting, and, as a last resort, his fists. Davy tried to stay out of his way, and most of the time he succeeded, but nobody could escape Junior Mullins's notice forever.

Davy's turn came in Well's pasture, when Junior Mullins showed up just as the boys were starting a game of polo. Charlie Bestor stopped the motorcycle a few yards away from the group, and Junior climbed down, his red face curled into its usual sneer. He was wearing a pair of blue dungarees without a single patch on them and a leather jacket. "You babies still riding bikes?" he said. "We've got a real set of wheels." He jerked his thumb toward the motorcycle.

Charlie Bestor patted his motorcycle and called out, "You fellows want to race?"

Johnny Suttle scuffed the toe of his shoe in the dirt. "We were just fixing to play polo," he mumbled.

Junior Mullins hooted. "Hear that, Charlie? They were fixing to play polo! You sissies don't know how to play polo," he announced, swaggering over to the gaggle of bikers. "I reckon I'll just have to teach you."

"You can't play without a bike," Dewey Givens pointed out. As soon as the words were out of his mouth, he wished he hadn't said them, because Junior's face lit up with spiteful glee, and he stepped back to survey the taut faces of his victims. He was showing off for his big-shot friend now, which would make him more vicious than ever. He let the boys squirm in silence while he pretended to consider the matter.

"I believe you're right about that, Dewey," Junior said at last. "Yep. I got to agree with you. I sure can't play polo without no bike, now can I? I reckon I'll just have to borrow me one." He surveyed the knot of squirming boys, each one carefully looking anywhere except in Junior Mullins's face.

When he couldn't stand the suspense anymore, Davy spoke up. "You could go home and get yours," he said.

Even Charlie Bestor laughed at that. Everybody knew that Junior Mullins wouldn't risk scratching up his brand-new bike in a rough-and-tumble game like polo, where crashing your bike into the other players' mounts was inevitable. All the other boys had beat-up second-hand bikes, or scrounged homemade ones. His was store-bought, too good for the likes of them. Junior grinned at Davy. "No. I think I'll just borrow one," he said. He eyed the polished blue bike at Davy's side. "Yours is new, isn't it? You make it yourself?"

Davy nodded, proud of himself, despite the threat of Junior Mullins, looming within punching distance and sneering at him like he was a night crawler in a fishing bucket. Junior made a great show of examining Davy's bike, inspecting the garden-hose tires, the flawless paint job, the Coca-Cola cap brakes. *Maybe he'll see how much pride I took in it, and he'll leave it be,* Davy thought, hoping that respect would win him what mercy could not.

"Nice job," drawled Junior, fingering the railroad-spike pedals. He glanced back to make sure that Charlie Bestor was watching. "For a home-made bike, that is. It looks sturdy enough. I guess I'll try it out for you so we can see what kind of job you did."

Davy gripped the handlebars tighter. "You're too big for it, Junior," he said. "You'd break it."

Junior's face turned a deeper shade of red. He was a stocky boy, verging on fat, and he didn't like comments about his size, however innocuously intended. He jerked the bike out of Davy's hands. "We'll just have to risk it, won't we. I've got a polo match to play." He snatched up a croquet mallet, hoisted his bulk onto the smaller boy's bicycle, and teetered off into the center of the pasture. "Let's get this show on the road!" he yelled to the other boys.

One by one they wheeled their bikes onto the playing field. Some of them gave Davy a look of apology or commiseration as they went past, but Davy didn't care what the other boys thought of Junior or how sorry they were that he had been singled out as victim. He wanted his bike, and nobody was going to help him get it back. If he tried to fight Junior on his own, he would end up with a bloody nose and a torn shirt, and Junior would destroy the bike.

He stood on the sidelines with clenched fists, watching as the teams pedaled up and down the pasture, swatting the softball back and forth. Above the thwack of the wooden mallets hitting the ball, and the shouts of the players, Davy thought he could hear the creaking of his overloaded bike. Junior Mullins was playing with a vengeance, going out of his way to collide with the other boys, whether they were close to the ball or not. He seemed to have no interest in scoring goals or in affecting the outcome of the game. For Junior the polo match was an excuse to hit something. Davy winced at every crash, thinking of the dents Junior was putting in the bike, and the scratches scoring the new paint job. A few yards away Charlie Bestor leaned his motorcycle against a tree and watched the game with the wry amusement of a superior being, sometimes shouting encouragement to Junior, and egging him on to more reckless playing.

After nearly an hour Junior tired of the game. He threw Davy's bike down in the weeds at the far end of the pasture, and loped back to Charlie Bestor's motorcycle. "Let's get out of here!" he said. "It's no fun playing with this bunch of babies."

As Junior climbed into the saddle behind the grinning Charlie Bestor, he called out to Davy, "Nice bike! Maybe I'll try it again sometime."

It was more than a threat. It was a promise.

Davy waited until the motorcycle roared out of sight, over the railroad track, and around the first curve, and then he hurried across the field to inspect the damage to his bike. The other boys hung back. One by one they drifted away from the pasture, and Davy was alone.

He reached into the briar-laced grass and pulled on the handlebars to his bike. After a few tugs, he was able to jerk it free. He set it down in the dirt, and ran his fingers along the shredded length of garden hose that had been the front tire. The frame was scratched and dented, and the handle-bars were twisted out of alignment where the collisions and Junior's weight had combined to overstress the metal. Long gashes scarred the bike's paint-work, and the battered brakes needed much more than a bottle cap to repair them. Davy wheeled his wrecked creation home, across the empty pasture, half carrying it across the rocky creek, picking his way along the rougher parts of the path. Davy's face was pinched, and his jaw was set tighter than a bulldog's, but his eyes had a faraway look as if he was some-where other than the road to Foggy Mountain. He never once cried.

• • •

No one saw Davy from that Saturday until the next. Nobody stopped by to see how he was doing, because they knew how he was doing, and there wasn't anything anybody could say. Best to let him be for a while. He'd come back when he was over it, and things would go on as before.

Davy stayed in the smokehouse in the backyard, working as long as it was light. He scrounged, and tinkered, and sanded, and hammered, and painted, and tinkered some more, until the bike looked almost the way it had before. It would never be as good, of course. He couldn't get the handlebars completely straight, and the deeper scars showed through the new paint job, but the bike was fixed. It had brakes again. He could ride it.

When Mama asked him what happened to his bike, Davy told her that he'd tried to take it down too steep a hill, and that he'd wrecked on a hidden tree root. She had looked at him for a long minute, as if she was fixing to say more, but finally she shrugged and went back into the house. There wasn't any point in telling his folks about Junior Mullins, whose dad was a boss down at the railroad shop. No point at all.

He practiced riding the bike on Friday night, up and down the road in front of the house until the fireflies lit up the yard and Mama called him in. He found that he could maneuver pretty well. With a few minor adjustments the bike would be ready to go.

• • •

ON Saturday morning he set off early, before Dad could catch him with a list of chores or Mama could set him to work weeding the corn. His sneakers were still damp from dew when he heard shouting from up the dirt road past the quarry. He found the gang at the usual congregating place, Wells's pasture. This time, though, no game was in progress. Five boys had pulled their bikes into a circle, and now they were arguing about what to do on a long Saturday morning. Davy looked at them: Johnny Suttle, Dewey Givens, Jack Howell, Bob Miller, and Junior Mullins. Davy walked his bike across the expanse of field, and slid silently into place between Johnny and Bob.

"Polo is a sissy game!" Junior was saying.

This declaration was followed by a doubtful silence. The younger boys looked at one another. Finally Bob Miller said, "How 'bout we jump potholes in the quarry?"

"*How 'bout we jump potholes in the quarry?*" said Junior, changing his voice to a mocking whine.

More silence.

"Anybody want to play pony express?" said Junior. "Or are you boys too yellow?"

Johnny Suttle whistled. "Chase a freight train on our bikes? My mama would skin me alive if she found out I was doing that."

Several of the others grunted in agreement.

"How's she going to find out?" said Junior.

"When I come home with my bike all tore up," said Johnny.

Junior shrugged. "Not if you do it right. The only tricky part is when you grab onto the ladder of the boxcar and kick the bike away. But if we find a place where there's a grassy slope alongside the track, it shouldn't hurt the bike too much when it falls down the embankment.

"It's dangerous," said Davy softly.

"I've done it before," said Junior. "It's a great ride. When the freight train slows down to take the curve, you catch up to it, swing up on the ladder, and ride the rails until you find a nice soft jumping-off place. Don't tell me you sissies have never tried it?"

Junior looked at each one in turn, daring somebody to admit he was scared. The five Foggy Mountain boys stared back, wide-eyed, and redder than their sunburns, but nobody objected and nobody looked away.

"It's settled then," said Junior. "I know just the place."

The five boys followed him out to the dirt road, riding slowly along in single file up the hill until they reached the place where the railroad tracks crossed the road. Junior led the way on his store-bought red beauty, sitting tall in the saddle and signaling with an outstretched forearm, as if he were a cavalry officer in the matinee.

"We'll follow the tracks to the right!" he shouted to his troops.

They turned on command and dismounted, wheeling their bikes along the gravel shoulder of the railroad tracks, while Junior inspected the terrain. "We need a long straightaway where we can build up speed, but it has to be just after a curve, so that the train will be slow enough for us to catch up with it."

Nobody bothered to answer him. He was thinking out loud.

Johnny Suttle, following close behind Davy, was bringing up the rear. "He's not looking at the embankment like he said he would. He's not looking for a grassy place. There's rocks all the way down this slope."

"He doesn't care," said Davy.

They both knew why.

The solemn procession followed the tracks up the steep grade that would send the train up and over the mountain in a series of spirals. The fields below glistened green in the July sunshine, and the Nolichucky River sparkled as brightly as the railroad tracks that ran alongside it for the length of the valley. Here the gravel berm was two feet wide, and just beyond it the ground fell away into a steep slope of clay and loose rocks.

Johnny Suttle touched Davy's arm. "We could turn back," he said.

Davy shook his head. You couldn't chicken out on a dare. That was part of the code. If you showed that you were afraid, you were out of the group, and Junior Mullins would hunt you like a rabbit from there on out.

They trudged on, past two more curves that Junior judged unsuitable for their purpose, and then they rounded the sharpest curve, midway up the mountain, and saw that there was nearly a hundred yards of straightaway before the tracks started up another incline. Junior turned and nodded, pointing to the ground. "Here!"

It was a good place. There was a thicket of tall laurels on the edge of the embankment that would hide them from the view of the engineer. Once the locomotive hurtled past their hiding place, they could give chase, and they had a hundred yards to build up speed and grab for the boxcar ladder

Junior motioned the pack under the laurels. "Should be a freight train along any minute now," he said, squinting up at the sun. He had sweated so much that his shirt stuck to his back, making the bulges show even more. He wiped his brow with a sweaty forearm, and surveyed the track. "This will do," he said. "There's just one more thing." He set his red bicycle carefully against the trunk of the laurel, and stared at the gaggle of boys. He was grinning.

Everybody looked away except Davy.

"I'll need to borrow a bike."

"I just fixed mine," said Davy quietly. He wasn't pleading or whining about it, just stating a fact that ought to be taken into consideration.

"That's real good," said Junior. "I'm glad you got it working again. I wouldn't want to borrow no *sorry* bike." He gripped the newly repaired bike with one hand, and shoved Davy out of the way with the other. "You can watch, kid," he said.

Davy shrugged. It wouldn't do any good to argue with Junior Mullins. Things went his way or not at all. Everybody knew that. Complaining about the unfairness of his action would only get Davy labeled a crybaby.

Johnny Suttle looked at the railroad track, and then at his own battered bicycle. "Here, Junior. Why don't you take mine?"

"That beat-up old thing? Naw. I want a nice blue one. I'm kinda used to Davy's anyhow."

Davy knelt down in the shade of the laurels next to Junior's bike. "Okay," he said.

Junior stepped forward, ready with another taunt, but a faint sound in the distance made him stop. They listened for the low whine, echoing down the valley, a long way off.

Train whistle.

"Okay," said Junior, turning away as if Davy were no longer there. "Mount up, boys. I lead off. You wait till the coal car has gone past us, and then you count to five, and you start riding. Got that? When you get up alongside the boxcar, grab the ladder with both hands, and pull yourself up off the saddle. Then kick the bike away with both feet. Got it?"

They nodded. Another blast of the train whistle made them shudder.

"Won't be long now," said Junior.

It seemed like an eternity to Davy before the rails shook and the air thickened with the clatter of metal wheels against track, and finally the black steam locomotive thundered into view. They hunkered down under the laurels, close enough to see the engineer's face, and to feel the gush of wind as the train swept past.

"Now!" screamed Junior above the roar. He took a running start out of the hiding place, and leaped onto Davy's bike in midstride, pedaling furiously in an effort to stay even with the train. The other boys climbed onto their own mounts and sped off after him, whooping like the marauding

Indians who attacked trains in the Buck Jones westerns down in the movie house.

Davy watched them go.

Junior kept the lead, leaning almost flat across the handlebar in a burst of speed that kept pace with the rumbling freight train. Fifty yards across the straightaway, he was nearly even with the ladder on the third boxcar.

What happened next seemed to take place in slow motion. The home-made bike seemed to pull up short, and wobble back and forth for one endless, frozen moment. Then, before Junior could scream or anyone else could blink, the bike crumpled and pitched to the left. It, and Junior, vanished beneath the wheels of the train. To Davy, despite the thunderous clatter of the boxcars, it all seemed to happen in perfect silence.

• • •

THE oldest Haskell girl lingered in the doorway. She fingered the collection can with the words JUNIOR MULLINS printed in black capitals around the side. The funeral was tomorrow. Closed casket, they said. "You were there when it happened, weren't you?" she said.

Davy nodded.

She leaned in so close to him that he could see her pores and smell the mint on her breath. "What was it like?" she whispered.

"He just fell."

"I hear you couldn't even tell who he was—after."

"No." The bike was unrecognizable, too. Just a tangle of metal caught underneath the boxcar and dragged another fifty yards down the track. Dad had told him how the workmen cut the bits of it away from the underside of the train. Out of consideration for the Mullins family, they hosed it down before they threw it in the scrap heap.

"You won't be getting it back," his father said. "Seems a shame, you losing your friend and your bike, too. It was a good bike. I know you worked a long time on it."

Davy nodded. He had worked a long time. He had built it twice, almost from scratch, and he had been proud of it. On the night before the pony express game, the last thing he had done was to file through one link of the bicycle chain, so that when any stress was put on it, the chain would break, throwing the bike off balance.

"It's all right, Dad," said Davy. "It's all right."

SREDNI VASHTAR

Saki

CONRADIN WAS TEN years old, and the doctor had pronounced his professional opinion that the boy would not live another five years. The doctor was silky and effete, and counted for little, but his opinion was endorsed by Mrs. De Ropp, who counted for nearly everything. Mrs. De Ropp was Conradin's cousin and guardian, and in his eyes she represented those three-fifths of the world that are necessary and disagreeable and real; the other two-fifths, in perpetual antagonism to the foregoing, were summed up in himself and his imagination. One of these days Conradin supposed he would succumb to the mastering pressure of wearisome necessary things—such as illnesses and coddling restrictions and drawn-out dullness. Without his imagination, which was rampant under the spur of loneliness, he would have succumbed long ago.

Mrs. De Ropp would never, in her honestest moments, have confessed to herself that she disliked Conradin, though she might have been dimly aware that thwarting him "for his good" was a duty which she did not find particularly irksome. Conradin hated her with a desperate sincerity which he was perfectly able to mask. Such few pleasures as he could contrive for himself gained an added relish from the likelihood that they would be displeasing to his guardian, and from the realm of his imagination she was locked out—an unclean thing, which should find no entrance.

In the dull, cheerless garden, overlooked by so many windows that were ready to open with a message not to do this or that, or a reminder that medicines were due, he found little attraction. The few fruit-trees that it contained were set jealously apart from his plucking, as though they were rare specimens of their kind blooming in an arid waste; it would probably have been difficult to find a market-gardener who would have offered ten shillings for their entire yearly produce. In a forgotten corner, however, almost hidden behind a dismal shrubbery, was a disused tool-shed of respectable proportions, and within its walls Conradin found a haven, something that took on the varying aspects of a playroom and a cathedral. He had peopled it with a legion of familiar phantoms, evoked partly from fragments of history and partly from his own brain, but it also boasted two inmates of flesh and blood. In one corner lived a ragged-plumaged Houdan hen, on which the boy lavished an affection that had scarcely another outlet. Further back in the gloom stood a large hutch, divided into two compartments, one of which was fronted with close iron bars. This was the abode of a large polecat-ferret, which a friendly butcher-boy had once smuggled, cage and all, into its present quarters, in exchange for a long-secreted hoard of small silver. Conradin was dreadfully afraid of the lithe, sharp-fanged beast, but it was his most treasured possession. Its very presence in the tool-shed was a secret and fearful joy, to be kept scrupulously from the knowledge of the Woman, as he privately dubbed his cousin. And one day, out of Heaven knows what material, he spun the beast a wonderful name, and from that moment it grew into a god and a religion. The Woman indulged in religion once a week at a church near by, and took Conradin with her, but to him the church service was an alien rite in the House of Rimmon. Every Thursday, in the dim and musty silence of the tool-shed, he worshipped with mystic and elaborate ceremonial before the wooden hutch where dwelt Sredni Vashtar, the great ferret. Red flowers in their season and scarlet berries in the winter-time were offered at his shrine, for he was a god who laid some special stress on the fierce impatient side of things, as opposed to the Woman's religion, which, as far as Conradin could observe, went to great lengths in the contrary direction. And on great festivals powdered nutmeg was strewn in front of his hutch, an important feature of the offering being that the nutmeg had to be stolen. These festivals were of irregular occurrence, and were chiefly appointed to celebrate some passing event. On one occasion, when Mrs. De Ropp suffered from acute toothache for three days, Conradin kept up the festival during the entire three days, and almost succeeded in persuading himself that Sredni Vashtar was personally responsible for the toothache. If the malady had lasted for another day the supply of nutmeg would have given out.

The Houdan hen was never drawn into the cult of Sredni Vashtar. Conradin had long ago settled that she was an Anabaptist. He did not pretend to have the remotest knowledge as to what an Anabaptist was, but he privately hoped that it was dashing and not very respectable. Mrs. De Ropp was the ground plan on which he based and detested all respectability.

After a while Conradin's absorption in the tool-shed began to attract the notice of his guardian. "It is not good for him to be pottering down there in all weathers," she promptly decided, and at breakfast one morning she announced that the Houdan hen had been sold and taken away overnight. With her short-sighted eyes she peered at Conradin, waiting for an outbreak of rage and sorrow, which she was ready to rebuke with a flow of excellent precepts and reasoning. But Conradin said nothing: there was nothing to be said. Something perhaps in his white set face gave her a momentary qualm, for at tea that afternoon there was toast on the table, a delicacy which she usually banned on the ground that it was bad for him; also because the making of it "gave trouble," a deadly offence in the middle-class feminine eye.

"I thought you liked toast," she exclaimed, with an injured air, observing that he did not touch it.

"Sometimes," said Conradin.

In the shed that evening there was an innovation in the worship of the hutch-god. Conradin had been wont to chant his praises, tonight he asked a boon.

"Do one thing for me, Sredni Vashtar."

The thing was not specified. As Sredni Vashtar was a god he must be supposed to know. And choking back a sob as he looked at the other empty corner, Conradin went back to the world he so hated.

And every night, in the welcome darkness of his bedroom, and every evening in the dusk of the tool-shed, Conradin's bitter litany went up: "Do one thing for me, Sredni Vashtar."

Mrs. De Ropp noticed that the visits to the shed did not cease, and one day she made a further journey of inspection.

"What are you keeping in that locked hutch?" she asked. "I believe it's guinea-pigs. I'll have them all cleared away."

Conradin shut his lips tight, but the Woman ransacked his bedroom till she found the carefully hidden key, and forthwith marched down to the shed to complete her discovery. It was a cold afternoon, and Conradin had been bidden to keep to the house. From the furthest window of the dining-room the door of the shed could just be seen beyond the corner of the shrubbery, and there Conradin stationed himself. He saw the Woman enter,

and then he imagined her opening the door of the sacred hutch and peering down with her short-sighted eyes into the thick straw bed where his god
lay hidden. Perhaps she would prod at the straw in her clumsy impatience.
And Conradin fervently breathed his prayer for the last time. But he knew
as he prayed that he did not believe. He knew that the Woman would come
out presently with that pursed smile he loathed so well on her face, and
that in an hour or two the gardener would carry away his wonderful god, a
god no longer, but a simple brown ferret in a hutch. And he knew that the
Woman would triumph always as she triumphed now, and that he would
grow ever more sickly under her pestering and domineering and superior
wisdom, till one day nothing would matter much more with him, and the
doctor would be proved right. And in the sting and misery of his defeat, he
began to chant loudly and defiantly the hymn of his threatened idol:

> Sredni Vashtar went forth,
> His thoughts were red thoughts and his teeth were white.
> His enemies called for peace, but he brought them death.
> Sredni Vashtar the Beautiful.

And then of a sudden he stopped his chanting and drew closer to the
window-pane. The door of the shed still stood ajar as it had been left, and
the minutes were slipping by. They were long minutes, but they slipped by
nevertheless. He watched the starlings running and flying in little parties
across the lawn; he counted them over and over again, with one eye always
on that swinging door. A sour-faced maid came in to lay the table for tea,
and still Conradin stood and waited and watched. Hope had crept by inches
into his heart, and now a look of triumph began to blaze in his eyes that
had only known the wistful patience of defeat. Under his breath, with a
furtive exultation, he began once again the pæan of victory and devastation.
And presently his eyes were rewarded: out through that doorway came a
long, low, yellow-and-brown beast, with eyes a-blink at the waning daylight,
and dark wet stains around the fur of jaws and throat. Conradin dropped
on his knees. The great polecat-ferret made its way down to a small brook
at the foot of the garden, drank for a moment, then crossed a little plank
bridge and was lost to sight in the bushes. Such was the passing of Sredni
Vashtar.

"Tea is ready," said the sour-faced maid; "where is the mistress?"

"She went down to the shed some time ago," said Conradin.

And while the maid went to summon her mistress to tea, Conradin fished
a toasting-fork out of the sideboard drawer and proceeded to toast himself
a piece of bread. And during the toasting of it and the buttering of it with

much butter and the slow enjoyment of eating it, Conradin listened to the noises and silences which fell in quick spasms beyond the dining-room door. The loud foolish screaming of the maid, the answering chorus of wondering ejaculations from the kitchen region, the scuttering footsteps and hurried embassies for outside help, and then, after a lull, the scared sobbings and the shuffling tread of those who bore a heavy burden into the house.

"Whoever will break it to the poor child? I couldn't for the life of me!" exclaimed a shrill voice. And while they debated the matter among themselves, Conradin made himself another piece of toast.

JOYCE CAROL OATES

"Lover" sprang out of a nightmare vision of a harsh, wetly sunny Easter Sunday in New Jersey. I was driving on Route 1 (in the story, Route 11) having turned up from Princeton Junction (Pelham Park) and on my way home some miles to the south. A strangeness of the light made me "see" the traffic on all sides in a kind of holding pattern. I could "see" individuals in their vehicles, each bent upon an intense, perhaps obsessive secret agenda. It swept over me—what destruction we could wreak upon one another, if we wished. If we simply crossed out of our lanes, braked or swerved erratically, rammed our front fenders against others' rear fenders . . . and so forth. The vision seemed to me hellish, while at the same time utterly natural. Why doesn't this sort of thing happen all the time? Civilization is such a frail vessel, containing and protecting us. Here we are hurtled along in our cars, at high speeds, taking for granted the essential sanity of our fellow citizens.

In "Lover," the betrayed woman's private revenge is perfectly logical to her, as it would be, perhaps, to us in her place. There is a certain inevitability about revenge, a sense of primal justice. The usual sexual duel is reversed here, for the woman is the hunter and the man, her ex-lover, is the prey. She hasn't got him quite yet—but we know that she will, soon. Her Saab is her accomplice, a sleek, powerful, amoral machine built to do her bidding, finely tuned for precise movements at dangerously high speeds.

I wanted to celebrate here, too, the strange, unnameable romance of driving, through our new city-worlds of suburban high-rise office buildings and corporate "parks," expressways, clover leafs, "exit-only" lanes, and the terrifying intimacy of speed. Though I am the author of this story, I read it with a quickened sense of adventure as if not knowing the outcome. I can't help but side with the betrayed woman, and want her to send the Mercedes careening off the road. . . .

Well, maybe not. And in any case it's only a lurid female fantasy.

• • •

"The Black Cat" is one of Edgar Allan Poe's several masterpieces, along with "The Tell-Tale Heart" and "The Fall of the House of Usher." Like these dreamlike, surreal narratives, "The Black Cat" evokes images of primitive horror: the terror of destroying that which is dear to us, as a way of destroying our own deranged selves; and the terror of being "walled up"—"buried alive." As the doomed narrator says, "This dread was not exactly a dread of physical evil." Invariably in Poe, the fundamental dread is that of losing one's sanity, for if sanity is relaxed even for a brief moment, evil springs forth.

There are literally two cats in "The Black Cat." Yet, symbolically, there is only one. Somehow, mysteriously, this cat is also the narrator's wife, an uncontrollable female principle that eludes comprehension. Unfettered by the restrictions of realism, Poe typically strikes straight to the heart: when his wife intervenes, meaning to save the life of her cat, the narrator responds,

> *Goaded by the interference into a rage more than demoniacal, I withdrew my arm from [my wife's] grasp and buried the axe in her brain. She fell dead upon the spot without a groan.*

So easy! In Poe, murder is always astonishingly easy, executed with cartoonlike swiftness. (The old man with the blue eye in "The Tell-Tale Heart" dies just as easily, crushed beneath a bed.) It's the aftermath of murder that is hard. Where Dostoyevsky dealt at considerable length with Raskolnikov's guilt, which is to say his unexpected crisis of conscience, Poe again moves in swiftly to the issue at hand, dramatizing guilt and the punishment of conscience in virtually the same succinct space. If the murderer's own amplified heartbeat doesn't betray him to the police, the wailing of a walled-up cat will. The conclusion of "The Black Cat" links female and cat in a single demonic image, as visually arresting as a nightmare. After police tear down the cellar wall, there is revealed

> *The corpse, already greatly decayed and clotted with gore, stood erect before the eyes of the spectators. Upon its head, with red extended mouth and solitary eye of fire, sat the hideous beast whose craft had seduced me into murder. . . . I had walled the monster up within the tomb.*

The reader knows that no one "seduced" the narrator into murder except himself, and that the only monster is the narrator. Poe's genius is the ability to portray deranged states of mind as if they were utterly natural . . . in fact, identical to our own.

LOVER

Joyce Carol Oates

YOU WON'T KNOW me, won't see my face. Unless you see my face. And then it will be too late.

Now the spring thaw had begun at last, now her blood, too, began to beat again. The earth melting into rivulets eager and sparkling as wounds.

Since the man who'd been her lover would have recognized her car, she acquired another.

Not one you know, or would expect but of a make she'd never before owned, never driven nor even ridden in—an elegant yet not conspicuous Saab sedan. It was not a new model but appeared, to the eye, pristine, newly minted, inviolate. In bright sunshine it gleamed the beautiful liquidy green of the ocean's interior and in clouded, impacted light it gleamed a subtler, perhaps more beautiful dark, steely gunmetal grey. Its chassis was strongly built to withstand even terrible collisions. It had a powerful transmission that, as she drove, vibrated upward through the soles of her sensitive feet, through her ankles, legs, belly and breasts; through her spinal column, into her brain. *This is a car you will grow into,* the Saab salesman was saying. *A car to live with.* She felt the reverberations from the car's murmurous hidden machinery as of an intense, fearful excitement too private to share with any stranger.

It was the weekend of Palm Sunday.

So now in the thaw. Miles of puddled glistening pavement, staccato dripping. Swollen, bruised clouds overhead and a pervasive odour as of un-washed flesh, a fishy odour of highway exhaust, gases like myriad exhaled breaths of unspeakable intimacy. In this car that responded so readily to her touch as no other car she'd ever driven.

She was patient and she was methodical. Taking the route her former lover took on the average of five evenings a week from his office building in the suburb of Pelham Junction to his home in the suburb of River Ridge; three miles along a highway, Route 11, and five-and-a-half miles along an expressway, I-96. Memorizing the route, absorbing it into her very skin. *Unless you see my face. And then it will be too late.* She smiled, she was a woman made beautiful by smiling. Gleam of perfect white teeth.

And her ashy pale hair dyed now a flat matt black. Swinging loose about her face. And sunglasses, lenses tinted nearly black, disguising half her face. Would she be willing to die with him? That was the crucial, teasing question. She'd kick off her shoes in the car, liking the feel of her stockinged feet, the sensitive soles of her feet, against the Saab's floor and pedals.

Sometimes, pressing her foot against the gas pedal, feeling the Saab so instantly, it seemed simultaneously, respond to her lightest touch, she experienced a sharp, pleasurable stab in her groin, like an electrical current.

How many times she would drive the complete route, exiting for River Ridge and returning on southbound I-96, like a racing driver preparing for a dangerous race, rehearsing the race, in full ecstatic awareness that it might be the final, lethal race of his life, she would not know; would not recall. Sometimes by day, but more often by night, when she could drive unimpeded by slow-moving traffic, the Saab like a captive beast luxuriating in release, yearning for higher speeds. Like one transfixed, she watched as the speedometer needle inched beyond seventy-five toward eighty, and beyond eighty, risking a traffic ticket in a sixty-five-mile zone. *At high speeds, unhappiness is slightly ridiculous.*

It was in the second week of her preparation, near midnight on Saturday, that she passed her first serious accident site in the Saab. On southbound I-96, near the airport exit, four lanes funnelled to one, traffic backed up for a mile. As she approached, she saw two ambulances pulling away from the concrete, glass- and metal-littered median, sirens deafening; saw several squad cars surrounding the smoking wreckage, revolving red lights, blinding red flares set in the roadway. Yet, as soon as the ambulances were gone, an eerie silence prevailed. What had happened, who had been injured? Who had died? The Saab, sober now, was one of a slow and seemingly endless stream as of a funeral procession of mourners. Strangers gazing in silence at the wreckage of strangers. Only death, violent and unexpected and spectacular death, induces such silence, sobriety. She did not believe in God, nor in any supernatural intervention in the plight of mankind, yet her lips moved in prayer, as if without volition. *God, have mercy!*

The Saab's driver's window was lowered. She hadn't recalled lowering it but was leaning out, staring at the wreckage, sniffing, her sensitive nostrils stung by a harsh yet exhilarating odour of gasoline, oil, smoke; she was appalled and fascinated, seeing what appeared to be three vehicles mangled together, luridly illuminated by flares and revolving red lights. Two cars, of which one appeared to have been a compact foreign car, possibly a Volvo, and the other a larger American car, both crushed, grilles and windshields and doors shoved in; the cars looked as if they'd been flung together from a great height with contempt, derision, supreme cruelty by a giant-child. The third vehicle, an airport limousine, was less damaged, its stately chrome grille crumpled and discoloured and its windshield cracked like a cobweb; its doors flung open crudely, like exclamations. She was disappointed that the accident victims had all been taken away, no one remained except official, uniformed men sweeping up glass and shattered metal, calling importantly to one another, taking their time about clearing the accident site and opening the expressway again. The Saab was moving forward at five miles an hour, a full car length behind the car that preceded it, as if reluctant to leave the accident site, though a police officer was brusquely waving her on, and, behind her, an impatient driver was tapping his horn.

The sleek black stretch limo was one of a kind in which her former lover frequently rode on his way to and from the airport, on the average of three times a month; several times, in the early days of their relationship, she'd ridden with him, the two of them intimate and hidden in the plush back seat, shielded by dark-tinted windows, whispering and laughing together, breaths sweetened with alcohol, hands moving freely over one another. How eagerly, how greedily touching one another. *If it had happened then. If, the two of us. Then.* She could have wept, that opportunity lost.

• • •

NEXT day she slept late, waking dazed at noon. Bright and chill and fresh, and the sun glaring in the sky like a beacon. It was Easter Sunday.

The man who'd been her lover, and whom she had loved, was an executive with an investment firm whose headquarters were in a corporate park off Route 11. Beautifully landscaped, like a miniature city, this complex of new office buildings glittered like amber Christmas-tree ornaments. It had not existed five years before. In the bulldozed, gouged and landscaped terrain of Route 11, northern New Jersey, new lunar-looking cities arose every few months, surrounded by inlets of shining, methodically parked automobiles.

She'd visited her former lover in his office suite on the top, eighth floor of his gleaming glass-and-aluminum building; she'd memorized her way through the maze of the corporate park, past clover leaves, past a sunken pond and Niobe willows—she could not attract the unwanted scrutiny of any security guard. For in her beautiful sleek Saab, in her good clothes, styled hair and sunglasses, with her imperturbable intelligent face, her poise, she looked the very model of a female inhabitant of Pelham Park, a young woman office manager, a computer analyst or perhaps an executive. She would have her own parking space, of course. She would know her destination.

Her former lover's reserved parking space was close by his office building. She hadn't had to worry that, like her, he might have acquired a new car, for his car was identifiable by the reserved space; in any case, she'd memorized his licence-plate number.

His telephone number, too, she'd memorized. Yet had never once dialled since he'd sent her away. Pride would never allow her to risk such hurt, guessing he'd changed the number.

You won't see my face. But you will know me.

Weekdays he left his office sometime after six-fifteen p.m. and before seven p.m., crossing briskly to his car, which was a silvery-grey Mercedes, and departing on his north-northwest drive to River Ridge. (Except for the days he was travelling. But she could tell at a glance when he was away, of course.) The Mercedes aroused in her a wave of physical revulsion; it was a car she knew well, had ridden in many times. The sight of it made her realize, as she hadn't quite realized until then, that he, her former lover, had not felt the need to alter anything in his life since sending her away; his life continued as before, his professional life, his family life in River Ridge in a house she had never seen, and would not see; nothing had been altered for him, above all nothing had been altered in his soul, except the presence of her from whom he'd detached himself like one shrugging off a coat. A coat no longer fashionable, desirable.

Circling the parking lot, which was divided into sectors, each sector bounded by strips of green, bright and fine-meshed as artificial grass though in fact it was real, and vivid spring flowers. Waiting at a discreet distance. Knowing he would come, must come. And when he did, quite calmly following him in the Saab, giving herself up to the instincts of the fine-tuned motor, the dashboard of gauges that glowed with its own intelligence, volition. *You will know me. You will know.* The first time she followed him only on Route 11, as far as the exit for I-96; she was several cars behind him, unnoticed by him of course. The second time she followed him on to I-96, which was trickier, again keeping several vehicles between them, and on the expressway the Saab had quickly accelerated, impatient with holding back; moving into the outer, fast lane and passing the Mercedes (travelling at approximately the speed limit, in a middle lane) and continuing on, at a gradually reduced speed, past Exit 33 where he departed for River Ridge; again he hadn't noticed her of course, for what reason could he have had to notice her? Even had he seen her in the swift-moving Saab he could not have identified her in her new matt-black hair, her oversized dark glasses.

The third time she followed him was in a sudden, pelting April rain that turned by quick degrees to hail, hailstones gaily bouncing on the pavement like animated mothballs, bouncing on the silver hood and roof of the Mercedes, bouncing on the liquidy-dark hood and roof of the Saab. She'd wanted to laugh, excited, exhilarated as a girl, daring, on the expressway, to ease up behind him, directly behind him in a middle lane, following him unnoticed for five-and-a-half dreamlike miles at precisely, teasingly, his speed, which was sixty-nine miles an hour; when he exited for River Ridge, the Saab had been drawn in his wake, and she'd had to tug at the steering wheel to keep from following him on to the ramp. *You never knew! Yet—you must know.*

Sometimes cruising the expressway after he'd left. For she was so strangely, unexpectedly happy. Strapped into the Saab's cushioned dove-grey seat, a band across her thighs, slantwise between her breasts, tight, as tight as she could bear, holding her fast, safe. It was at the wheel of the Saab, passing a second and a third accident site, she'd understood that there are no accidents, only destiny. What mankind calls accident is but misinterpreted destiny.

Naked inside her clothes, now the days were warmer. Now the thaw had come at last, the earth glistened with melting, everywhere shining surfaces, oil-iridescent puddles like mirrors. *So happy! You can't know.* She surmised that her former lover might be thinking that she'd disappeared or was dead. He'd expressed concern that she was "suicidal"—with what disdain he'd uttered the word, as if its mere syllables offended—and now he would be thinking, quite naturally he would be thinking she was dead. If he thought of her at all.

Naked inside her clothes, which were loose-fitting yet clinging, sensuous against her skin. Her buttocks pressed into the cushioned driver's seat, her thighs carelessly covered by the thin, silky synthetic material of her skirts. (For always she wore skirts or dresses, never trousers.) And her legs bare, pale from winter but smooth, slender and graceful, like the sleek contours of the Saab's interior. She kicked off her high-heeled shoes, placed them on the passenger seat, liking to drive barefoot, liking the intimacy of her skin against the Saab's gas and brake pedals. Sometimes at night truckers pulled up alongside her, even if she was travelling in the outer, fast lane, these strangers in their high, commanding cabs, not readily visible to her, maintaining a steady speed beside her for long tension-filled minutes, peering down at her, at what they could see of her slender body, her bare ghostly-glimmering legs in the dashboard light of the Saab, they were talking to her of course, murmuring words of sweet, deranged obscenity which she could not hear and had no need of hearing to comprehend. *Not now, not yet! And not you.*

. . .

ONCE, sobbing in the night. Her knuckles muffling the sound. And the pillow dampened with her saliva. And she'd felt his hands on her. In his sleep, his hands groping for her. Not knowing who she was, perhaps. Her exact identity, as in the depths of sleep, in even the most intimate sleep, lying naked beside another we sometimes forget the identity of the other. Yet he'd sensed her presence, and his hands had reached for her to quiet her, to subdue. To cease her sobbing.

. . .

WEEKS after Palm Sunday and the Saab entering her life. A mild, misty evening of a month she could not have named.

By this time she'd memorized the route, every fraction of every mile of the route, absorbed it into her brain, her very skin. The precise sequence of exit ramps, the succession of overhead signs she might have recited like a rosary, stretches of median which were made of concrete and stretches of median which were weedy grass; how beyond Exit 23 of I-96 there was, on the highway's shoulder, a litter of broken glass like fine-ground gems, part of a rusted bumper, twisted strips of metal that looked like the remains of a child's tricycle. And in a railroad underpass near Exit 29 a curious disfigured hubcap like a skull neatly sheared in half. By day you could see secreted on certain stretches of pavement, on both Route 11 and I-96, hieroglyphic stains, a pattern of stains, oil or gasoline or blood or a combination of these, baked into the concrete, discernible as coded messages to only the sharpest eye. And there was Exit 30 where you turned in a tight hairpin, scary and exhilarating as a carnival ride if your car was moving above twenty miles an hour, circling a marshy area of starkly beautiful six-foot reeds and cat's-tails, at its core pools of stagnant water, black and viscous as oil on the sunniest days. How drawn she was, how unexpected her yearning, to such rare remaining pockets of "nature"—relics of the original landscape where, in theory, perhaps in fact, a body might be secreted for years; a body quietly decomposing for years, never discovered though passed each day by hundreds, thousands of people. For in such a no man's land, at the very core of the complex highway system, no pedestrians ever ventured.

From six p.m. onward she waited until, at six-fifty p.m., her former lover appeared. Carrying his attaché case, walking quickly to his car. Unseeing. As she sat in the Saab, motor off, some fifty yards away, calmly smoking a cigarette, betraying no agitation, nor even alert interest; knowing herself perfectly disguised, her sleekly styled matt-black hair covering part of her face. Her makeup was flawless as a mask, her mouth composed, eyes hidden by dark glasses. Her nails were filed short but fastidiously manicured, polished a dark plum shade to match her lipstick. Calmly, in no haste, turning the key in the ignition, feeling the quick, stabbing response of the Saab's motor waking, leaping to life.

Yes, now. It's time.

An insomniac night preceding, a night of cruising I-96, and yet she felt fully rested, restored to herself. Tightly strapped into the driver's seat like a pilot at the controls of a small plane, yet controlled by the plane; secured in place, trusting to fine-tuned, exquisitely tooled machinery.

At a careful distance she followed her former lover through the winding lanes of Pelham Park. Waited a beat or two to allow him to ease into traffic on northbound Route 11. Then following, with utter casualness. Once on the highway, a mile or so after entering, the Saab demanded more mobility, more speed, so she shifted into the outer, fast lane; she'd lowered both the windows in the front, her hair whipped in the gassy, sulphurous air, and she'd begun to breathe quickly. Now there was no turning back, the Saab was aimed like a missile. The Mercedes was travelling at about sixty-five miles an hour in a middle lane; her former lover would be listening to a news broadcast, windows shut, air-conditioning on. It was a hazy evening; overhead were massed, impacted storm clouds like wounds; at the western horizon, brilliant shafts of fiery, corrupt sun the colour of a rotted orange; the industrial-waste sky was streaked with beauty of a kind, as a girl living elsewhere, he'd never seen. By degrees the misty air turned to a light feathery rain, the Saab's windshield wipers were on at the slowest of three tempos; a caressing, stroking motion; hypnotic and urgent. Now she was rapidly overtaking the Mercedes and would exit close behind it for I-96; once on I-96 she would swing out again into the fast lane to pass slower vehicles including the Mercedes, one of a succession of vehicles, at which she need not glance. She had five-and-a-half miles in which to make her move.

How many times she'd rehearsed, yet, on the road, in the exhilaration of the Saab's speed and grace, she would trust to instinct, intuition. Keeping the silvery, staid-looking car always in sight in her rear-view mirror even as she maintained her greater speed; hair blowing about her heated face, strands catching in her mouth. Her eyes burnt like headlights; there was a roaring in her that might have been the coursing of her own fevered blood, the sound of the Saab's engine. *At high speeds, unhappiness is not a serious possibility.*

He hadn't loved her enough to die with her; now he would pay. And others would pay.

The glowing speedometer on the Saab's elegant dashboard showed seventy-two miles an hour; the Mercedes, two cars behind, was travelling at about the same speed. She would have wished a higher speed, eighty at least, but hadn't any choice; there was no turning back. Pinpoints of sweat were breaking out on her tense body, beneath her arms, in the pulsing heat between her legs, on her forehead and upper lip. She was short of breath as if she were running or in the throes of copulation.

Switching lanes, shifting the Saab into the next lane to the right, so abruptly she hadn't time to use her turn signal, and the driver of a car in that lane protested, sounding his horn. But she knew what she meant to do and would not be dissuaded, allowing two cars to pass her in the Mercedes's lane; then moving back into that lane, so that now she was just ahead of the Mercedes, by approximately two car lengths. Rain fell more forcibly now. The Saab's windshield wipers were moving faster, in swift, deft, percussive arcs, though she didn't recall adjusting them. In sensuous snaky patterns rain streamed across the curved glass. In the rear-view mirror the Mercedes was luminous with rain and its headlights were aureoles of dazzling light, and staring at its image she felt a piercing sensation in her groin. She believed she could see, through the rain-streaked windshield, the pale oval of a man's face; a frowning face; the face of the man who'd been her lover for one year, eleven months and twelve days; yet perhaps she could not have identified the face; perhaps it was a stranger's face. Yet the Saab propelled her onward and forward; she could almost imagine that the Saab was propelling the Mercedes forward as well. She was bemused, wondering: how like high-school math: if the Saab suddenly braked, causing the Mercedes to ram into its rear, with what force would the Mercedes strike? Not the force of a head-on collision, of course, since both vehicles were speeding in the same direction. Would both swerve into another lane, or lanes? And which other vehicles would be involved? How many individuals, at this moment unknown to one another, would be hurt? How many injuries, how many fatalities? Out of an infinity of possibilities, only one set of phenomena could actually happen. The contemplation of it left her breathless, giddy; she felt as if she were on the edge of an abyss gazing blindly out—where?

It was then that she saw, in the rainwashed outside mirror, another vehicle rapidly approaching at the rear. A motorcycle! A Harley-Davidson, by the look of it. The cyclist was a hunched figure in black leather, his head encased in a helmet and shining goggles; he seemed oblivious of the rain, weaving through lanes of traffic, boldly, recklessly, now cutting in front of a delivery van, provoking an outraged response of horn-blowing, now weaving out again, into the lane to the Saab's right, just behind the Saab. She pressed down quickly on the gas pedal to accelerate, to allow the cyclist to ease in behind her if he wished; there was no doubt in her mind he would do so, and he did; bound for the outer, fast lane in a breathtaking display of driving skill and bravado. And in the rain! *Because he doesn't care if he dies. Because there is no other way.*

She felt a powerful sexual longing for him, this hunched, bearded stranger in his absurd leather costume; this stranger she would never know.

Acting swiftly then, intuitively. For Exit 31 was ahead, with its two exit-only lanes; many vehicles on I-96 would be preparing to exit, shifting their positions, causing the constellation of traffic to alter irrevocably. Within seconds the cyclist would have roared ahead, gone. In the dreamy space of time remaining she felt a rivulet of moisture run down the left side of her face, like a stream of blood she dared not wipe away, gripping the steering wheel so hard her knuckles ached. She saw admiringly that the Saab was free of human weakness; its exquisite machinery was not programmed to contain any attachment to existence, any terror of annihilation; for time looped back upon itself at such speeds and perhaps the Saab and its entranced driver had already been annihilated in a multi-vehicular crash involving the Harley-Davidson, the Mercedes and other vehicles; perhaps it was a matter of indifference whether the cataclysm had happened yet, or was destined to happen within minutes; or, perversely, not to happen at all. But her bare foot was pressing on the brake; her toes that were icy with fear, pressing on the Saab's brake as a woman might playfully, tauntingly press a bare foot against a lover's foot; a quick pressure, but then a release; and another quick pressure, and a release; jockeying for position, preparing to move into the left lane, the cyclist might not have noticed, for a low-slung sports car was approaching in that lane out of a tremulous glimmer of headlights, quite fast, possibly at eighty miles an hour, lights blinding in the rain; the cyclist was rapidly calculating if he had time to change lanes, or had he better wait until the sports car passed; he was distracted, unaware of the Saab's erratic behaviour only a few yards ahead of him; and a third time, more forcibly, she depressed the brake pedal, unmistakably now, the Saab jerked in a violent rocking motion, and there was a shriek of brakes that might have been the Saab's, or another's; the Harley-Davidson braked,

MASTER'S CHOICE VOLUME II   279

skidded, swerved, seemed to buckle and to right itself, or nearly; she had a glimpse of the bearded man's surprisingly young face, his incredulous eyes widened and wondering inside the goggles, in her rear-view mirror, in the very fraction of an instant the Saab was easing away, like a gazelle leaping away from danger. Within another second the Saab was gone, and in its wake a giddy drunken skidding, swerving, a frantic sounding of horns; faint with excitement she held the gas pedal to the floor racing the Saab to eighty, to eighty-five, the car's front wheels shuddering against the rain-slick pavement yet managing to hold the surface, while behind her it appeared that the motorcycle had swerved into the outer lane, and the sports car had swerved to avoid a direct collision yet both vehicles careened on to the median, and there they did collide and crash; at the same time the Mercedes, close behind the motorcycle, had turned blindly into the lane to its right, and what appeared to be a delivery van had narrowly managed to avoid hitting it. The Mercedes and the van and a string of dazed, stricken vehicles were slowing, braking like wounded beasts, passing the flaming wreckage that would be designated the accident site. She saw this spectacle in miniature, rapidly shrinking in her rear-view mirror and in her outside mirror; by this time the Saab itself was exiting the expressway, exhausted, safe; she was trying to catch her breath, laughing, sobbing, finally rolling to a stop in a place unknown to her, near a culvert or an underpass smelling of brackish water and bordered by wind-whipped thistles, and her spinal cord was arched like a bow in a delirium of spent pleasure and depletion; her fingers rough between her legs trying to contain, to slow, the frantic palpitations.

Next time, she was consoled. Next time.

THE BLACK CAT

Edgar Allan Poe

FOR THE MOST wild yet most homely narrative which I am about to pen, I neither expect nor solicit belief. Mad indeed would I be to expect it, in a case where my very senses reject their own evidence. Yet, mad am I not—and very surely do I not dream. But to-morrow I die, and to-day I would unburden my soul. My immediate purpose is to place before the world, plainly, succinctly, and without comment, a series of mere household events. In their consequences, these events have terrified—have tortured—have destroyed me. Yet I will not attempt to expound them. To me, they have presented little but horror—to many they will seem less terrible than *baroques*. Hereafter, perhaps, some intellect may be found which will reduce my phantasm to the commonplace—some intellect more calm, more logical, and far less excitable than my own, which will perceive, in the circumstances I detail with awe, nothing more than an ordinary succession of very natural causes and effects.

From my infancy I was noted for the docility and humanity of my disposition. My tenderness of heart was even so conspicuous as to make me the jest of my companions. I was especially fond of animals, and was indulged by my parents with a great variety of pets. With these I spent most of my time, and never was so happy as when feeding and caressing them. This peculiarity of character grew with my growth, and, in my manhood, I derived from it one of my principal sources of pleasure. To those who have cherished an affection for a faithful and sagacious dog, I need hardly be at the trouble of explaining the nature or the intensity of the gratification thus derivable. There is something in the unselfish and self-sacrificing love of a brute, which goes directly to the heart of him who has had frequent occasion to test the paltry friendship and gossamer fidelity of mere *Man*.

I married early, and was happy to find in my wife a disposition not uncongenial with my own. Observing my partiality for domestic pets, she lost no opportunity of procuring those of the most agreeable kind. We had birds, gold-fish, a fine dog, rabbits, a small monkey, and a *cat*. ·

This latter was a remarkably large and beautiful animal, entirely black, and sagacious to an astonishing degree. In speaking of his intelligence, my wife, who at heart was not a little tinctured with superstition, made frequent allusion to the ancient popular notion, which regarded all black cats as witches in disguise. Not that she was ever *serious* upon this point—and I mention the matter at all for no better reason than that it happens, just now, to be remembered.

Pluto—this was the cat's name—was my favorite pet and playmate. I alone fed him, and he attended me wherever I went about the house. It was even with difficulty that I could prevent him from following me through the streets.

Our friendship lasted, in this manner, for several years, during which my general temperament and character—through the instrumentality of the Fiend Intemperance—had (I blush to confess it) experienced a radical alteration for the worse. I grew, day by day, more moody, more irritable, more regardless of the feelings of others. I suffered myself to use intemperate language to my wife. At length, I even offered her personal violence. My pets, of course, were made to feel the change in my disposition. I not only neglected, but ill-used them. For Pluto, however, I still retained sufficient regard to restrain me from maltreating him, as I made no scruple of maltreating the rabbits, the monkey, or even the dog, when, by accident, or through affection, they came in my way. But my disease grew upon me—for what disease is like Alcohol!—and at length even Pluto, who was now becoming old, and consequently somewhat peevish—even Pluto began to experience the effects of my ill temper.

One night, returning home, much intoxicated, from one of my haunts about town, I fancied that the cat avoided my presence. I seized him; when, in his fright at my violence, he inflicted a slight wound upon my hand with his teeth. The fury of a demon instantly possessed me. I knew myself no longer. My original soul seemed, at once, to take its flight from my body;

and a more than fiendish malevolence, gin-nurtured, thrilled every fibre of my frame. I took from my waistcoat-pocket a penknife, opened it, grasped the poor beast by the throat, and deliberately cut one of its eyes from the socket! I blush, I burn, I shudder, while I pen the damnable atrocity.

When reason returned with the morning—when I had slept off the fumes of the night's debauch—I experienced a sentiment half of horror, half of remorse, for the crime of which I had been guilty; but it was, at best, a feeble and equivocal feeling, and the soul remained untouched. I again plunged into excess, and soon drowned in wine all memory of the deed.

In the meantime the cat slowly recovered. The socket of the lost eye presented, it is true, a frightful appearance, but he no longer appeared to suffer any pain. He went about the house as usual, but, as might be expected, fled in extreme terror at my approach. I had so much of my old heart left, as to be at first grieved by this evident dislike on the part of a creature which had once so loved me. But this feeling soon gave place to irritation. And then came, as if to my final and irrevocable overthrow, the spirit of PERVERSENESS. Of this spirit philosophy takes no account. Yet I am not more sure that my soul lives, than I am that perverseness is one of the primitive impulses of the human heart—one of the indivisible primary faculties, or sentiments, which give direction to the character of Man. Who has not, a hundred times, found himself committing a vile or a stupid action, for no other reason than because he knows he should *not*? Have we not a perpetual inclination, in the teeth of our best judgment, to violate that which is *Law*, merely because we understand it to be such? This spirit of perverseness, I say, came to my final overthrow. It was this unfathomable longing of the soul *to vex itself*—to offer violence to its own nature—to do wrong for the wrong's sake only—that urged me to continue and finally to consummate the injury I had inflicted upon the unoffending brute. One morning, in cold blood, I slipped a noose about its neck and hung it to the limb of a tree;—hung it with the tears streaming from my eyes, and with the bitterest remorse at my heart;—hung it *because* I knew that it had loved me, and *because* I felt it had given me no reason of offence;—hung it *because* I knew that in so doing I was committing a sin—a deadly sin that would so jeopardize my immortal soul as to place it—if such a thing were possible—even beyond the reach of the infinite mercy of the Most Merciful and Most Terrible God.

On the night of the day on which this most cruel deed was done, I was aroused from sleep by the cry of fire. The curtains of my bed were in flames. The whole house was blazing. It was with great difficulty that my wife, a servant, and myself, made our escape from the conflagration. The destruction was complete. My entire worldly wealth was swallowed up, and I resigned myself thenceforward to despair.

I am above the weakness of seeking to establish a sequence of cause and effect, between the disaster and the atrocity. But I am detailing a chain of facts—and wish not to leave even a possible link imperfect. On the day succeeding the fire, I visited the ruins. The walls, with one exception, had fallen in. This exception was found in a compartment wall, not very thick, which stood about the middle of the house, and against which had rested the head of my bed. The plastering had here, in great measure, resisted the action of the fire—a fact which I attributed to its having been recently spread. About this wall a dense crowd were collected, and many persons seemed to be examining a particular portion of it with very minute and eager attention. The words "strange!" "singular!" and other similar expressions, excited my curiosity. I approached and saw, as if graven in *bas-relief* upon the white surface, the figure of a gigantic *cat*. The impression was given with an accuracy truly marvelous. There was a rope about the animal's neck.

When I first beheld this apparition—for I could scarcely regard it as less—my wonder and my terror were extreme. But at length reflection came to my aid. The cat, I remembered, had been hung in a garden adjacent to the house. Upon the alarm of fire, this garden had been immediately filled by the crowd—by some one of whom the animal must have been cut from the tree and thrown, through an open window, into my chamber. This had probably been done with the view of arousing me from sleep. The falling of other walls had compressed the victim of my cruelty into the substance of the freshly-spread plaster; the lime of which, with the flames, and the *ammonia* from the carcass, had then accomplished the portraiture as I saw it.

Although I thus readily accounted to my reason, if not altogether to my conscience, for the startling fact just detailed, it did not the less fail to make a deep impression upon my fancy. For months I could not rid myself of the phantasm of the cat; and, during this period, there came back into my spirit a half-sentiment that seemed, but was not, remorse. I went so far as to regret the loss of the animal, and to look about me, among the vile haunts which I now habitually frequented, for another pet of the same species, and of somewhat similar appearance, with which to supply its place.

One night as I sat, half stupefied, in a den of more than infamy, my attention was suddenly drawn to some black object, reposing upon the head of one of the immense hogsheads of gin, or of rum, which constituted the chief furniture of the apartment. I had been looking steadily at the top of this hogshead for some minutes, and what now caused me surprise was the fact that I had not sooner perceived the object thereupon. I approached it, and touched it with my hand. It was a black cat—a very large one—fully as large as Pluto, and closely resembling him in every respect but one. Pluto had not a white hair upon any portion of his body; but this cat had a large, although indefinite splotch of white, covering nearly the whole region of the breast.

Upon my touching him, he immediately arose, purred loudly, rubbed against my hand, and appeared delighted with my notice. This, then, was the very creature of which I was in search. I at once offered to purchase it of the landlord; but this person made no claim to it—knew nothing of it—had never seen it before.

I continued my caresses, and when I prepared to go home, the animal evinced a disposition to accompany me. I permitted it to do so; occasionally stooping and patting it as I proceeded. When it reached the house it domesticated itself at once, and became immediately a great favorite with my wife.

For my own part, I soon found a dislike to it arising within me. This was just the reverse of what I had anticipated; but—I know not how or why it was—its evident fondness for myself rather disgusted and annoyed me. By slow degrees these feelings of disgust and annoyance rose into the bitterness of hatred. I avoided the creature; a certain sense of shame, and the remembrance of my former deed of cruelty, preventing me from physically abusing it. I did not, for some weeks, strike, or otherwise violently ill use it; but gradually—very gradually—I came to look upon it with unutterable loathing, and to flee silently from its odious presence, as from the breath of a pestilence.

What added, no doubt, to my hatred of the beast, was the discovery, on the morning after I brought it home, that, like Pluto, it also had been deprived of one of its eyes. This circumstance, however, only endeared it to my wife, who, as I have already said, possessed, in a high degree, that humanity of feeling which had once been my distinguishing trait, and the source of many of my simplest and purest pleasures.

With my aversion to this cat, however, its partiality for myself seemed to increase. It followed my footsteps with a pertinacity which it would be difficult to make the reader comprehend. Whenever I sat, it would crouch beneath my chair, or spring upon my knees, covering me with its loathsome caresses. If I arose to walk it would get between my feet and thus nearly throw me down, or, fastening its long and sharp claws in my dress, clamber, in this manner, to my breast. At such times, although I longed to destroy it with a blow, I was yet withheld from so doing, partly by a memory of my former crime, but chiefly—let me confess it at once—by absolute *dread* of the beast.

This dread was not exactly a dread of physical evil—and yet I should now be at a loss how otherwise to define it. I am almost ashamed to own—yes, even in this felon's cell, I am almost ashamed to own—that the terror and horror with which the animal inspired me, had been heightened by one of the merest chimeras it would be possible to conceive. My wife had called my attention, more than once, to the character of the mark of white hair, of which I have spoken, and which constituted the sole visible difference between the strange beast and the one I had destroyed. The reader will remember that this mark, although large, had been originally very indefinite; but, by slow degrees—degrees nearly imperceptible, and which for a long time my reason struggled to reject as fanciful—it had, at length, assumed a rigorous distinctness of outline. It was now the representation of an object that I shudder to name—and for this, above all, I loathed, and dreaded, and would have rid myself of the monster *had I dared*—it was now, I say, the image of a hideous—of a ghastly thing—of the GALLOWS!—oh, mournful and terrible engine of Horror and of Crime—of Agony and of Death!

And now was I indeed wretched beyond the wretchedness of mere Humanity. And *a brute beast*—whose fellow I had contemptuously destroyed— *a brute beast* to work out for *me*—for me, a man fashioned in the image of the High God—so much of insufferable woe! Alas! neither by day nor by night knew I the blessing of rest any more! During the former the creature left me no moment alone, and in the latter I started hourly from dreams of unutterable fear to find the hot breath of *the thing* upon my face, and its vast weight—an incarnate nightmare that I had no power to shake off— incumbent eternally upon my *heart*!

Beneath the pressure of torments such as these the feeble remnant of the good within me succumbed. Evil thoughts became my sole intimates— the darkest and most evil of thoughts. The moodiness of my usual temper increased to hatred of all things and of all mankind; while from the sudden, frequent, and ungovernable outbursts of a fury to which I now blindly abandoned myself, my uncomplaining wife, alas, was the usual and the most patient of sufferers.

One day she accompanied me, upon some household errand, into the cellar of the old building which our poverty compelled us to inhabit. The cat followed me down the steep stairs, and, nearly throwing me headlong, exasperated me to madness. Uplifting an axe, and forgetting in my wrath the childish dread which had hitherto stayed my hand, I aimed a blow at the animal, which, of course, would have proved instantly fatal had it descended as I wished. But this blow was arrested by the hand of my wife. Goaded by the interference into a rage more than demoniacal, I withdrew my arm from her grasp and buried the axe in her brain. She fell dead upon the spot without a groan.

This hideous murder accomplished, I set myself forthwith, and with entire deliberation, to the task of concealing the body. I knew that I could not remove it from the house, either by day or by night, without the risk of being observed by the neighbors. Many projects entered my mind. At one period I thought of cutting the corpse into minute fragments, and destroying them by fire. At another, I resolved to dig a grave for it in the floor of the cellar. Again, I deliberated about casting it in the well in the yard—about packing it in a box, as if merchandise, with the usual arrangements, and so getting a porter to take it from the house. Finally I hit upon what I considered a far better expedient than either of these. I determined to wall it up in the cellar, as the monks of the Middle Ages are recorded to have walled up their victims.

For a purpose such as this the cellar was well adapted. Its walls were loosely constructed, and had lately been plastered throughout with a rough plaster, which the dampness of the atmosphere had prevented from hardening. Moreover, in one of the walls was a projection, caused by a false chimney, or fireplace, that had been filled up and made to resemble the rest of the cellar. I made no doubt that I could readily displace the bricks at this point, insert the corpse, and wall the whole up as before, so that no eye could detect any thing suspicious.

And in this calculation I was not deceived. By means of a crowbar I easily dislodged the bricks, and, having carefully deposited the body against the inner wall, I propped it in that position, while with little trouble I relaid the whole structure as it originally stood. Having procured mortar, sand, and hair, with every possible precaution, I prepared a plaster which could not be distinguished from the old, and with this I very carefully went over the new brick-work. When I had finished, I felt satisfied that all was right. The wall did not present the slightest appearance of having been disturbed. The rubbish on the floor was picked up with the minutest care. I looked around triumphantly, and said to myself: "Here at least, then, my labor has not been in vain."

My next step was to look for the beast which had been the cause of so much wretchedness; for I had, at length, firmly resolved to put it to death. Had I been able to meet with it at the moment, there could have been no doubt of its fate; but it appeared that the crafty animal had been alarmed at the violence of my previous anger, and forbore to present itself in my present mood. It is impossible to describe or to imagine the deep, the blissful sense of relief which the absence of the detested creature occasioned in my bosom. It did not make its appearance during the night; and thus for one night, at least, since its introduction into the house, I soundly and tranquilly slept; aye, *slept* even with the burden of murder upon my soul.

The second and third day passed, and still my tormentor came not. Once again I breathed as a freeman. The monster, in terror, had fled the premises for ever! I should behold it no more! My happiness was supreme! The guilt of my dark deed disturbed me but little. Some few inquiries had been made, but these had been readily answered. Even a search had been instituted— but of course nothing was to be discovered. I looked upon my future felicity as secured.

Upon the fourth day of the assassination, a party of the police came, very unexpectedly, into the house, and proceeded again to make rigorous investigation of the premises. Secure, however, in the inscrutability of my place of concealment, I felt no embarrassment whatever. The officers bade me accompany them in their search. They left no nook or corner unexplored. At length, for the third or fourth time, they descended into the cellar. I quivered not in a muscle. My heart beat calmly as that of one who slumbers in innocence. I walked the cellar from end to end. I folded my arms upon my bosom, and roamed easily to and fro. The police were thoroughly satisfied and prepared to depart. The glee at my heart was too strong to be restrained. I burned to say if but one word, by way of triumph, and to render doubly sure their assurance of my guiltlessness.

"Gentlemen," I said at last, as the party ascended the steps, "I delight to have allayed your suspicions. I wish you all health and a little more courtesy. By the bye, gentlemen, this—this is a very well-constructed house," (in the rabid desire to say something easily, I scarcely knew what I uttered at all),— "I may say an *excellently* well-contructed house. These walls—are you going, gentlemen?—these walls are solidly put together"; and here, through the mere frenzy of bravado, I rapped heavily with a cane which I held in my hand, upon that very portion of the brickwork behind which stood the corpse of the wife of my bosom.

But may God shield and deliver me from the fangs of the Arch-Fiend! No sooner had the reverberation of my blows sunk into silence, that I was answered by a voice from within the tomb!—by a cry, at first muffled and broken, like the sobbing of a child, and then quickly swelling into one long, loud, and continuous scream, utterly anomalous and inhuman—a howl—a wailing shriek, half of horror and half of triumph, such as might have arisen only out of hell, conjointly from the throats of the damned in their agony and of the demons that exult in the damnation.

Of my own thoughts it is folly to speak. Swooning, I staggered to the opposite wall. For one instant the party on the stairs remained motionless, through extremity of terror and awe. In the next a dozen stout arms were toiling at the wall. It fell bodily. The corpse, already greatly decayed and clotted with gore, stood erect before the eyes of the spectators. Upon its head, with red extended mouth and solitary eye of fire, sat the hideous beast whose craft had seduced me into murder, and whose informing voice had consigned me to the hangman. I had walled the monster up within the tomb.

IAN RANKIN

I like the main character in "Adventures in Babysitting," I like the set-up, and I had a lot of fun writing it. I've always been fascinated by the movies, and by the monster that is Hollywood. There's not much of a film industry here in the U.K., and I thought it would be interesting to juxtapose some big Hollywood actor and his entourage with a savvy English "minder." I'd read an article in a British film mag about these minders and the kinds of thing they have to put up with. But the polyp, I can assure you, is all mine own.

• • •

Mat Coward writes terrific short stories, but has yet to produce a novel. As a short-story writer, he remains too little known. He has a tremendous range of styles and subjects, and "No Night by Myself" is a good example of the way he can mix humor and horror to exemplary effect. It's the ultimate middle-class nightmare: Christmas, and a singular Madness has just entered your home. But because it's done from the point of view of the intruder, Coward engenders sympathy as well as tension. We don't know whose side we're on. This is fiction that makes you think as well as feel.

ADVENTURES IN BABYSITTING

Ian Rankin

I THOUGHT IT was the hotel's fire alarm at first, and shot out of bed to hide my clothes.

Then I remembered: I wasn't in the same hotel as the talent. Panic over, I slumped back on the bed.

To explain: I was once staying in the same hotel as the talent, and some-one in the talent's entourage decided to set off the hotel's smoke detectors. This was one in the morning. Sprinklers came on all over the sixth floor. People were stumbling from their bedrooms soaking wet and screaming and swearing. The film company was inundated with compensation claims, not least from the hotel itself. I think it was the Fairmount in Glasgow. Nice hotel. I'd only just unpacked my suitcase; my clothes were ruined. Though the film company tried to put up the shutters, the story made several tab-loids. Obviously someone had phoned the papers, probably anonymously. The talent lost a couple of big parts with Paramount after that . . .

My phone was ringing, that's what it was. Not a fire alarm; my phone. I picked up the receiver, knowing who'd be on the other end.

"Hello?"

I could hear sounds of a party in progress, then a voice. "Jenny? Jenny, I need a big favour?"

Another big favour.

"What is it, Mr. Claymore?"

"Todd, I told you, call me Todd."

Todd. That's what the world called him. Todd Terrific. Todd-ally Tremendous. The new Stallone, Arnie with feelings. Todd Claymore, hunky but sensitive, loved by men and women. But to me, Mr. Claymore.

"What is it?" I repeated.

He launched straight in, while a female squealed behind him, then burst out laughing. I knew who *that* laugh belonged to: Claymore's new wife, Sherilynne Tamasco. The one and only. "A bow," Todd Claymore was saying. "I need a bow."

"You mean like for your hair?"

"Hell no, I mean a *crossbow.*"

"Three in the morning and you want a crossbow?"

I'd turned on the bedside lamp and reached for my cigarette packet. Some people would think this scene surreal, but I'd experienced worse. I was a professional babysitter after all. That's what film publicists call it; we say we're babysitting the talent. And Todd Claymore was A-list, definitely not someone I wanted crying back to the producers and the company.

"See," he was saying, "here we are in *Notting*ham . . . ?"

"Yes?"

"Home of Robin Hood . . ."

"Ye-ess?"

"So I need a goddamned crossbow, Jenny!"

"Why exactly?"

"So I can shoot the damned apple off Sherry's beautiful head!"

More laughter behind him, pitched towards the hysterical. They were a noisy couple, Todd and Sherilynne, always to be placed in the middle suite—other members of the entourage either side to muffle them from other hotel rooms, other guests.

"Mr. Claymore," I said calmly, "Robin Hood didn't shoot apples off anybody's head. That was William Tell. And Robin Hood wouldn't have used a crossbow, he'd have used a longbow."

"Well get me a longbow then," he snapped. Todd Claymore didn't like to be corrected, and he *definitely* didn't like not having his requests complied with immediately and to his full satisfaction. He was Californian, his parents had spoiled him, and now he was A-list, a financial hot property—he simply wasn't used to being denied.

He was recent A-list, and those are the worst. He was just learning to throw his weight around. He'd become A-list after the belated success—sleeper hit of the year—of his thriller *Untold Passion.* He was in the UK to promote the follow-up, *Crime Yellow*. We were in Nottingham because he was guest of honour at a festival which was about to have its UK-premiere, *Crime Yellow*. I'd tried briefing him in the limo on the way up from London, but his mind was on more important questions. Sample dialogue:

"Ever met Bruce Willis, Jenny?"

"Yes." And the name's Jennifer.

"Tell me," leaning forward, showing bulgy stomach and pecs which looked bigger on the screen, "when he's in England, is his limo the same size as this . . . or is it *bigger*?"

"Same size."

"Yeah, but how does he get here? Private jet, right?"

"I'm not sure." Second lie.

Todd Claymore explodes. "Well *I* know, baby. He flies private, and *I* have to fly public! Me, Todd Claymore!"

By "public" he means Concorde, of course.

"And how big's his per diem, huh?"

And so it goes.

Cut to Nottingham, and Todd and his wife, plus his brother, a bodyguard, Sherilynne's dresser and make-up artist, their joint manager and a representative from Todd's Hollywood agent: they're all booked into the city's best hotel, while I settle for a three-star hovel a short distance away, guessing—wrongly—that if I kept my distance I might catch a full night's sleep.

"A longbow then," Todd Claymore was saying. "Yeah, like Kevin used in the movie. Jesus, they should've tested me for that."

"You'd have been beyond belief," I said, thinking if I did a bit of strategic toadying, maybe he'd—

"Hey," he roared suddenly, "I *want* a crossbow!"

I rubbed my face with my free hand. "Crossbow or longbow?"

"Whatever Kevin used. Yeah, we'll take a car out to Sherwood Forest, do some arching."

In an hour, I knew he wouldn't want to do that at all. In an hour, he'd have forgotten all about his request. He'd be asleep in his wife's arms, two babes together between the satin sheets Todd's agent had requested. Flashback: a sheaf of faxes from Hollywood—"My client Todd Claymore requests . . ."—a fantasy list, everything from his favoured brand of mineral water (Calistoga, cherry flavour) to a daily diet of black satin sheets.

"Don't piss me off," Todd was saying now. My hackles rose and I slammed down the phone.

So who else could I phone but Bunny? Bunny who knows everybody, who can put his hands on *any*thing. Harrods incarnate. And—final blessing—an insomniac. So he sounded alert when he picked up the receiver in his Clapham three-storey.

"Bunny, it's Jennifer."

"Jennifer Juniper," he sang quietly. "That was before your time, right?"

"Right."

"Don't tell me another of your charges has woken you up with a teeny-tiny request?"

"He wants a longbow."

Bunny didn't flinch. "Who does?"

"Todd Claymore."

"Hot Toddy himself, I'm impressed. I hear Disney is about to sign him for that new fantasy film."

Bunny loved the business. "It's called *Armour World*," I confided. "If Claymore signs on the line, he makes three and a half."

As in, 3.5 million dollars. Hollywood figures made me queasy.

"I think I know a guy," Bunny was saying. "Lives in Nottingham. Runs an archery club."

"Perfect." I was no longer amazed at the stuff Bunny knew. I pulled a pad of paper on to my lap. "Give me his phone number."

And Bunny, dear Bunny, reeled it off.

• • •

AN hour and a half later I was at Todd's hotel, knocking on his suite door. The chauffeur was outside with the limo. Hey, if you're having a shitty night, spread it around, right? The chauffeur had taken me all round the city till we found the right address, Mr. Archery guiding us in, me on the cellphone passing his directions to the driver. Then back to the hotel with the longbow, at six feet high a full foot taller than me. Plus a dozen arrows in a mock-leather quiver. The whole package costing a cool grand. Mr. Archery's out-of-hours fee.

I knocked on the suite door. I waited. I knocked again. I looked up and down the hallway. I swore. As I was walking away, I heard a roar from one of the other rooms. I followed the sound, longbow in hand, and knocked loudly. The door was hauled open by Todd Claymore, his teeth bared in a snarl. His face was puce with anger, beads of sweat on his high, tanned forehead. He wasn't acting.

"This whole damned thing is off!" he yelled. Then he pushed past me and stalked to his room.

I walked through the open door as Todd's door slammed shut. This was Chris Klamowski's room, Chris being Todd's brother—Klamowski being

Todd's real surname. I liked Chris. He was young, goofy and enjoying the ride without thinking he could take too many liberties. Still, he was a Hollywood hanger-on, and therefore not to be trusted. Maybe his *niceness* was part of an act. They all had an act: the agents, producers, managers, accountants. They all had a face.

Chris was standing by his window. On the bed sat Sherilynne. She was in tears, her legs tucked beneath her. She wore a white towelling robe and looked to die for. Matthieu Preene, the agent, handed her a box of tissues he'd brought from the bathroom. At this same time of night, Preene still wore his suit, a three-piece at that. But he'd taken off his tie and undone the top button of his shirt. In his books this probably counted as "casual." I'd take bets Matthieu wasn't spelt that way on his birth certificate.

Standing near the bed was Chuck, the Claymore-Tamasco bodyguard. Usually Todd and his bride were inseparable, which made Chuck's job a cinch. But now he didn't know where he should be. He cracked his knuckles and belched. Like most men who spend time in gymnasia, Chuck possessed the social grace of a lipid.

Seated at a table was the last member of the group, the Claymore-Tamasco joint manager, "Howie" Malamud. Like Chuck, Howie didn't know where to be: here, comforting Sherilynne (who might soon sign opposite Sly in next year's high-tech, low-IQ blockbuster), or by Todd's anguished side, protecting the Disney deal?

At our first meeting, Howie had pulled me to one side and told me he hoped together, as a team, acting in the best interest of everyone, we could keep Todd out of trouble. Press stories had to be OK'd before publication. Ditto photos. And any unseemly scenes were to be kept under wraps. Howie was small and fat and hairy with a perspiration problem.

I knew why he was sweating. Disney's contract would allow them to pull out should the talent cause embarrassment to the company in any way. This meant: no drugs, no boozing, no extramarital rumpy . . . not in the public domain.

"Well," I said, beaming a smile to the assembly, "the gang's all here. Suppose you tell me what's going on?"

"What the hell is that?" Chuck asked. "That" was the longbow. I rested it against the wall. A cool grand of the film company's cash. I laid the quiver of arrows on the floor.

"Could we do with some coffee?" I suggested. The group perked up at that, and Chris called room service. Requests flew at him. Cream   low-fat sweetener . . . ice (Howie was nursing a whisky from the suite's fridge) . . . some sandwiches, ham and French mustard . . . Finally, he was able to put the receiver down.

"So?" I hinted.

"So," Matthieu Preene said, "there has been a robbery."

"Jesus, Matthieu," Howie Malamud interjected, "we haven't even searched his room yet."

"Todd says he's turned that room upside down."

Oh great. "What's missing?"

Everyone looked to Sherilynne, who sniffed and knew what was expected of her. She took a deep breath.

"His lucky mascot. He never goes anywhere without it."

"Well, can we replace it?"

She shook her perfect locks. The room watched her hair move like they'd paid for the privilege. In front of men—especially *Hollywood* men—Sherilynne did her act. But it *was* an act. We'd had a ten-minute conversation in London, just the two of us, and she'd been very different, cool and sussed. Flashback:

"You and me," she'd told me, "we're alike in a lot of ways." Like, we were both in our twenties and blonde . . . "Me," she said, "I'm playing the system the only way they'll let me. Let's face it," running her fingers through her insured tresses, "I'm never going to be cast as the rocket scientist. As long as I look like this and want to be in movies, I'll be the villain's babe or the easy lay next door . . ."

Cut to a hotel suite in Nottingham:

"Do you mind me asking what exactly this memento is?" I was thinking of Bunny, of replacing the item without Todd ever knowing the truth.

Sherilynne took another exquisite deep breath. "It's a polyp," she said.

I kissed the notion of Bunny goodbye.

• • •

WE finally got Todd to open his door and initiated a search of the room, which looked like a tornado had been through it. Todd refused to help. He glared at everyone in turn and wouldn't take a ham sandwich.

"It was in the drawer of the bedside cabinet," he told me, like he was explaining something to a child. "I put it there myself. Then Sherry and me went to dinner, came back, invited everyone in for a drink."

"I heard on the telephone."

"Yeah, and just after I phoned you, that's when I pulled open the drawer, wanted to show Chuck . . . and it wasn't there. So some asshole's taken it, and it must be one of you!" He pointed his finger at all of us. "And you," he spat at me, "you're supposed to look after me!"

To which I should have replied: "But not your polyp."

This was no polyp *ordinaire*. It had been removed from Todd's father's rump during extended surgery in Our Lady of Aloysius General Hospital in Eureka. I got the details from Chris as we stood in the hallway.

"And he kept it?" I asked.

"Had it preserved in formaldehyde in a little glass phial," Chris confirmed. "When the old guy died, it was all Todd wanted by way of a keepsake. He said it would remind him of the motivation that had taken him out of Eureka and into the movies."

"And what motivation was that?"

Chris sniffed. "Our father," he said, "was a royal pain in the ass."

Back in Todd and Sherilynne's bedroom, I noticed two things. One, that it was growing light outside. The other was that there was someone missing.

Ludmilla, Sherilynne's dresser and makeup woman.

• • •

WE knocked on her door, but got no response, then tried rousing her by telephone. We summoned the night manager, who was polite but looked as sorely pressed as if we'd put his legs into a Corby. Finally, he agreed to unlock Ludmilla's door.

She lay on her bed, fully dressed and pretty well dead.

An ambulance rushed her to hospital. The prognosis was not great: if I didn't keep this out of the papers, I might not keep my job.

We were eating breakfast in the hotel restaurant when Howie came with the news.

"They think there may be brain damage. Lack of oxygen or something." He took off his glasses and wiped them. His eyes were red-rimmed. Our large table was the only one occupied at this hour. Normally, breakfast started at seven, but hotel kitchens made allowances for talent.

"What had she taken?"

Howie smoothed his hairy arms. "Cocaine maybe, and some tablets—amphetamines."

"Was Ludmilla at the party?" I asked Todd. He nodded. Sherilynne was clinging to his arm and crying softly. She'd dehydrate soon, the liquid she was losing.

"Drinking heavily," Chris added.

"She left early though," Matthieu Preene said. He was the only one at the table managing a cooked breakfast. He'd put his tie back on.

"This is a nightmare," Todd groaned.

"Don't worry," Howie said, patting his shoulder, "we'll keep the lid on it." He looked at me. "Right, Jennifer?"

I excused myself and went back up to the suites floor. I had to get that damned bow back by nine A.M. or there'd be another day to pay on it. Plus I wanted to telephone my boss in private.

Chuck was coming out of Ludmilla's room.

"Hi," I said, "lose something?"

His face reddened, an actor with no cue-board. "Can you keep a secret?"

"Usually."

He looked down at the floor. "Ludmilla and me, we . . . you know, had something going."

"Nice," I said. It hadn't stopped him propositioning me that first night in London.

"But I swear I didn't know she did drugs. Thing is, if the police start asking questions, I don't want them to know about Ludmilla and me."

My mind clicked. "You take drugs?" I examined his physique: made by chemists.

"Only," Chuck said, "I ain't sure what's legal in this country and what ain't."

I nodded. "You were checking there was nothing of yours in Ludmilla's room?"

"Hey," he growled, "I'm sorry she's dead and all, but I've my career to think of."

"Don't we all," I said, making for Chris's room and the longbow.

• • •

"If this gets out," Todd Claymore said, "I can kiss Disney goodbye."

We were in conference in his suite, just the two of us, despite Matthieu Preene's protests.

"I'll do my best."

His face darkened. "But I mean it about that polyp. As long as it's missing, that's it, tour over. This is non-negotiable, understand?"

"Any idea *why* someone would want to steal it?"

He shook his head. "Not a damned clue. But you can forget England, you can forget France."

France: after the English tour, Todd and his retinue were flying to Bordeaux, another film festival, another premiere. Only this time he was joint guest of honour with his musclebound *arriviste* rival, Jeremiah Tang. Tang was an American with a Hong Kong mother, and boasted martial arts training to make up for lack of acting ability. Todd Claymore, it was accepted, could act Tang off any film set. But Tang, one-time video star, had yet to make a film which didn't recoup its cost ten times over. Age twenty-five, Todd Claymore could hear the youngster's footsteps taking the stairs two at a time towards the A-list.

I wasn't accompanying Todd and Co. to France, my boss was. Sore point.

I'd spoken to my boss in London. He'd been in the bathtub and furious. So now I was trying to keep the media away from Ludmilla, and track down the missing polyp. I even considered visiting the hospital, not to see Ludmilla but to talk to staff about the possibility of purchasing a small lump of extraneous gristle, preferably in formaldehyde, money no object.

But I had to keep close to Todd. We had a press conference in the ballroom at eleven, then a TV interview at three, and selected individual media interviews from five till seven. The premiere was at nine. Always supposing Todd deigned to go. I had Matthieu and Howie pressuring him to carry out his prescribed duties. He'd signed up to everything, and if he backed out, there'd be a financial penalty. It was in neither man's interest to have *that* happen.

"Hey," Hairy Howie said, pointing a small, fat finger, "much as I like you, Jennifer, if anything screws up around here, I'll see to it that the closest you ever get to the industry again is renting a video."

Matthieu Preene nodded, checking his cufflinks.

"I admire your candour, gentlemen," I said, standing up, head high as I walked away. It felt like a move from an old film.

• • •

CHRIS was in the lounge, reading a comic book. It could be boring, touring with talent. I sat down and asked him what he thought of Ludmilla.

"I guessed she was on dope," he confessed, "I just couldn't figure *what.* I mean, she never spoke much, kept herself to herself except when she was in Sherry's room. She'd be in there for *hours.*"

"What about Ludmilla and Chuck? Weren't they . . . ?"

He snorted. "Are you kidding? She couldn't stand him. I think he was putting the make on her again last night, that's why she left the party early. Maybe she went out to get away from him."

"Went out?"

Chris had rolled the comic into a cylinder, and peered down it at me before panning the lounge. "I had to go to my room to get something. I saw her disappear into the elevator."

I left Chris and went to speak to the day manager. He was dubious about giving me the names of the night staff, never mind home telephone numbers. I dug into the dwindling film company pot and salved his professional conscience.

Five calls later, I knew that Ludmilla had come down to the lobby. She'd been drunk, or acting drunk, weaving from wall to wall, looking for the bar. When told it was closed, she demanded it reopen. The night manager explained that room service would be pleased to furnish her with any refreshments. She'd remonstrated, stumbled, knocked a wastebin over, and eventually retreated to the elevator.

And presumably to an accidental overdose.

I checked the ballroom and saw that the press conference was going ahead. Preene and Malamud flanked their property, both men with mobile phones on the desk in front of them. There was no sign of Sherilynne, but Chuck—liar and phony—was seated off to one side, arms prodigiously folded. There was a good crowd, including a few foreign journalists. I recognized one from Denmark who always asked the talent the same question: "What in particular greatness are you thinking merits of that actor is Robert deNiro?"

While answers varied, the most frequent was "Excuse me?"

I went to talk to the cleaning staff, but first I phoned Bunny and managed to set something up. He made me promise it wasn't for my own personal use. After talking to the cleaners, I went up to my room and changed into my scruffiest clothes, then went back down to help sift last night's cleaning-bags.

I needed a shower after that. Everyone was lunching in the dining room, tab to be picked up by the film company. They invited me to join them, but I shook my head, giving my professional smile. I said I had somewhere to be.

"Just don't go talking to any damned journalists," Preene warned. Most of the ones from the press conference were still in the hotel bar.

Todd was chewing bread and staring at the walls from behind tortoise-shell Ray-Bans.

"You know," he said, "I really want to work with Quentin. Quentin *knows* actors."

"Well, he knows a few," I said into the silence. "By the way, I'll have that polyp for you this evening. I'll hand it over at the premiere."

Then I turned and walked away, knowing I look good from the back.

• • •

I visited a flat on one of the city's less salubrious schemes, then got my driver to stop outside a video rental shop, and had the pale-faced teenage manager do some cross-referencing for me. Cut to: the hotel, where Sherilynne was casting prospective replacements for Ludmilla. It was short notice, and the contenders milling in the hallway looked unconvincing. I knocked and entered her suite. A girl with pink dreadlocked hair and several nose studs was just leaving.

"I'm exhausted," Sherilynne said.

"You must be."

She looked up at me, studied my face, then narrowed her eyes. For a second, we knew one another, and then she twitched and showed me the fingers of her left hand.

"I had that last one give me a manicure and varnish. Painful *and* amateurish."

I stuck the phial in front of her nose and she flinched.

"Look what Ludmilla dropped in the foyer," I said. "And guess who had to sift a dozen hoover bags to find it?"

Sherilynne's face had gone so pale I could make out the individual specks of make-up.

"Do you want me to give this to Todd?" I asked.

"Of course," she said, not at all convincingly.

"That line doesn't fit the script, Sherry." I sat on a chair. "You took the polyp from the drawer and told Ludmilla to get rid of it, or maybe just to hold on to it. She didn't have any reason to steal it for herself. Then she OD'd, and you didn't know what she'd done with it, so you talked Chuck into searching her room—not hard to sweet-talk Chuck, is it?"

"I don't know what you're . . ." She corpsed, and took a moment to compose herself. Maybe she was switching to another act, but I didn't think so.

"I don't want us to go to Bordeaux," she said.

"I know." Her eyes widened. "When we spoke in London, you mentioned the kinds of roles you were given, including a villain's babe. But you've only once played that role. *The Knife That Bled*. It went direct to video and from there to the Dumpster."

"You've seen it?" She sounded amazed.

"I love films, Sherry. There was a time I rented maybe fifteen a week. I had a vague memory of *The Knife That Bled*. Your boyfriend the bad guy was a then unknown called Jerry Tang. So I put two and two together . . ."

Her voice was dry and quiet. "It only lasted the length of shooting, maybe three weeks. Nobody knew except for the cast and crew, and they've been surprisingly reticent. But I just know that when Todd and Jerry . . . I know that if they get into some macho I-can-beat-you bullshit, then Jerry will use his ultimate weapon." She looked up with wet eyes. "Me. And Todd will hate me for that, I know it."

I got up to leave. I didn't like seeing this woman in front of me, the one with tears streaming down her face. I didn't like the bruised, frightened voice. I like her better bold and bitchy, with a snarling comeback line in almost every scene she played.

"What will you do?" she said.

"Todd's bound to find out. You two are so big now . . . eventually some-one will talk, either for money or just from jealousy." But she knew that already. She just wanted more time, real time. "You know, I could have lost my job over this," I told her.

"I'm sorry." But she wasn't.

"I'll see you at the premiere," I said. "And Sherry, you won't be going to Bordeaux." I winked at her. "Trust me."

• • •

THERE was a big crowd on the pavement outside the theatre, with crash barriers and police to keep them in check. They didn't pay me much atten-tion as I walked up the red carpet and through the doors. They were waiting for a Hollywood couple. I wondered why. I wondered what the attraction really was. But then some people like to visit zoos, too.

There was a standing ovation as Todd and his glittering wife entered the auditorium. They were late, and had arrived by limo despite their hotel being next door to the theatre. They walked hand in hand, waving to the fans. Todd pecked Sherry on the cheek to cheers and renewed applause.

When Todd saw me, he squeezed Sherilynne's hand and came over. She stood frozen as I handed over the phial. He checked it before slipping it into his pocket. Then he gave me his big, warm, film-star smile and hugged me, whispering, "You did all right, Jenny. You did all right."

Caught in his cologne embrace, I slipped something into his other pocket, then watched him take his seat.

• • •

THE film was no more enjoyable for me fourth time round. The holes in the plot gaped wider, a change of takes in the middle of one scene screamed from the screen, and the dialogue was all paste and scissors.

There was another standing ovation at the end, and a rush of autograph hunters. But Todd and Sherilynne couldn't hang around. They had a pri-vate plane to catch. It was taking them to Paris, where my boss would join them for the trip down to Bordeaux.

Their bags had already been packed, and the retinue proceeded straight to the airport from the theatre. Nobody said goodbye to me, or thanks or anything. Not even Chris. I returned to my hotel, undressed and lay on the bed. I was returning to London in the morning. By train. Second class. I picked up the telephone and dialled the number I'd been given, the one for Customs & Excise. Using a voice from my repertoire I told them that the actor Todd Claymore would be attempting to carry cocaine into France.

I knew the message would be passed along, and that the drugs squad would be waiting. I'd slipped just enough coke into Todd's pocket for there to be embarrassment, disquiet, a certain *interest* in the event.

My second call was to a stringer on the *Sun*. Now he owed me *two* favours. The exposure would be bad for Todd. Disney would not be amused. Malamud and Preene would be *extremely* unamused. And my boss's Bordeaux trip would be cancelled. I didn't know if Hollywood would rate that a happy ending.

Closing credits.

NO NIGHT BY MYSELF

Mat Coward

"I'VE GOT TO go into hospital straight after Christmas."

"Shit," says Diplomacy. "Sorry to hear that, mate."

"Yeah. Royal Free, second day after Boxing Day. For tests."

"I'm really sorry to hear that, mate."

"Mind you," I say. "Tests—they're test-mad these days, aren't they? I mean, you go to the doc with a mouth ulcer these days, they send you down the hospital for tests."

"That's true," says Diplomacy, sipping the top off his pint. "There again, my brother-in-law had a mouth ulcer, wouldn't clear up, they sent him down the Free for tests, and we buried him six months later."

What's so funny about that is, the actual reason they call him Diplomacy is because he used to be a chauffeur for some foreign bloke, some Arab who lived on Ambassadors' Row. That's what's so funny about that.

"And I'll tell you what," says Diplomacy, "he must've been a good ten years younger than you, my brother-in-law. Mid-thirties, he was."

"Well, anyway," I say. "I haven't got a mouth ulcer."

"So what you doing for Christmas, Madness?" he says. "Usual is it, going over your gran's, as per?"

I shake my head. Not like *no*; more like *slightly annoyed*. "Gran died, yeah? In the summer."

"Oh Christ," says Diplomacy. "Sorry mate, of course. I hadn't really forgotten, you did tell me. I just wasn't thinking. Sorry mate. June, wasn't it? Only I remember, because Wimbledon was on, Cherry watches it on the telly. So what you got lined up, then? Hotel room full of teenage nymphos, yeah?"

"I don't know," I say. "Nothing, really."

Diplomacy wipes his hand across his mouth, picks up his lager and finishes it. Right down the hatch, fast as you like. He stands up to go. "Well, whatever you do, I hope you have a good one, mate. Look, I got to be going. Wife, etc. Christmas Eve, you know—last-minute instructions and what have you." He claps a hand on my shoulder, picks up his lighter and some small change off the counter. "Be seeing you, Madness. Have fun, yeah? And don't get caught!"

And he's gone.

So has almost everybody by now, it's getting late. Few faces I half know over the other side of the bar, younger than me, they're getting ready to go, too. Buying bottles to take out.

I call over to them. "Having a party, lads?"

They make out they haven't heard me. If they are having a party, it's not one I'm invited to.

There's never been a Christmas in my life I didn't spend with my gran. I've been inside a few times, yeah, but even then, as it happened, I was never inside at Christmas. Always at my gran's.

The boys go off to their party or whatever, and it's just me and the Paddy barman. He sees me still sitting there and brings over a parcel, a heavy cardboard box tied up with string.

"Jim said to give you this," he says, putting it on the counter. I pick it up and put it down by my feet.

"Oh yeah, cheers son. I was expecting it."

"Right," says the barman, polishing the counter, collecting empty glasses.

"Jim say anything about it, did he?"

"No," he says, "only that you'd know what it was about."

"Yeah, that's all right," I say. "I know about it."

"Which I don't," says the barman. "OK? I don't know anything about it."

I finish my drink, and I'm about to see what the chances are of getting another when the barman takes the glass from me and says, "Right, cheers then, Madness. Mind how you go."

He's in a rush. Not working tomorrow, wants to get over his girlfriend's for Christmas.

"Yeah, fair enough mate," I say. "Let me get a couple of bottles to take out, right?"

"No problem," says the barman. "What's your pleasure?"

A couple of bottles—Jesus. I have *never* spent Christmas on my own, not ever. Never alone.

• • •

I'M walking through Golders Green, walking home to my room, thinking maybe there'll be a message on the board by the pay phone in the entrance hall—"So-and-so rang while you were out, can you come for Xmas dinner?"—but really, I can't think of anyone who might leave a message like that. If there is anyone, I've already rung them.

And all the time I'm walking, my mind keeps going: "Never alone, never alone, *never* alone."

The parcel the barman gave me is awkward to carry, and the bag with the bottles in it is clanking against my leg, so I stop for a moment, put everything down, light a fag.

I'm stretching my arms and I look round, and I'm standing right outside this really nice house. I've walked down this road thousands of times, and it is a nice road, all the houses look like quality. Detached, big garage to the side, an in-and-out gravel drive with a rose bush or something in a brown earth island in the middle of a tiny front lawn. The windows have that lead stuff on them, like old-fashioned houses, but they're not, they're younger than me, these houses. I remember when they went up.

They always look nice, but tonight, Christmas Eve, this particular house looks *really* nice. They've got a holly wreath on the door with a bright red bow on it, and I can see all lights through the windows, and a paper-chain. So I pick up Jim's parcel and the bag of booze and scrunch my way up the drive and knock on the door. I have to use my knuckles, because the actual knocker is covered by the holly.

It's gone midnight now, and I'm thinking maybe it's too late, maybe I shouldn't be knocking so late at night, everyone might be in bed. But almost immediately the door opens, opens wide and welcome, and I walk in.

"Hello?" says the woman who's opened the door. Pleasant-looking woman, very white cheeks with red dots on them and light, thin hair. Just a few years younger than me, I reckon. Wearing a dress, quite smart, and some tiny pearls round her neck.

"*Excuse* me," she says, still holding the front door open. Then she forgets the door and calls out: "Tony!"

Meanwhile, I'm opening a door off the hall, on the left, peering into a room which at first I think, from the smell of it, is empty, unused. A spare room downstairs—well, when you've got this many rooms, why not? No point heating them all up just for the sake of using them. But when I turn the light on I see a big, green-topped desk with a computer screen on it, and there's a swivel chair and a filing cabinet and that. Like an office at home. In case you get snowed in or something, I suppose.

"Excuse me?"

I look round. There's a man standing there, late thirties, bald at the front, wearing suit trousers and a striped, ironed shirt, but without the jacket, and no tie. I switch the light off in the spare office, close the door behind me and slip past the man—not pushing, not roughly—because I've just caught sight of the living room across the hall.

The man, the husband obviously, pinches at my sleeve as I walk into the big room—light's already on in here—and says: "I *said*, excuse me! Do I know you? Can I help you?" The wife's standing behind him, the red spots on her cheeks getting bigger.

Beautiful room. Very good quality furniture, wallpaper, all that. Very warm, from an artificial coal fire at the far end. Really nice room. These people have got taste, not just money. Little framed pictures on the walls, of country scenes. No telly—they probably keep that in another room, a special TV room—but a huge Christmas tree in the corner behind the door, absolutely covered with flickering lights and tinsel, and presents wrapped up in shiny paper that reflects the room. One of the biggest and best trees I've ever seen. Mind, they ought to put it in the window in my opinion, not hide it away behind the door. Make the place more inviting from outside. I might mention that to the woman, if it doesn't seem rude.

"Look," says the man, trying to stand in front of me, trying to bar my way as I start moving along the hall towards the back of the house. "Now look here, I don't know who you are, but unless you have some reason for being here I must insist you leave immediately." And he points towards the front door, which is letting in quite a draught.

It's the kitchen I want now, so I duck under the man's arm—he's shorter than me, but I'm quicker than him—and as I head down the long hall, I hear him behind me saying: "It's all right, Sarah, you just stay there."

Before you get to the actual kitchen at Sarah and Tony's, you have to pass through the dining room. This is also beautifully laid out, with a pretty red tablecloth over a big round table—it'd seat six, easily—and there's decorations round the room and on the table itself, and Christmas crackers by each table-mat.

But I'm concentrating on the kitchen for the moment, so I walk straight through. The man's been following me, sort of snapping round my heels from room to room, and I haven't been paying much attention. Suddenly, now, I find his arm is around my neck and he's trying to steer me out of the back door, the door from the kitchen into the garden.

Too bloody cold for that, thank you, so I push him down on to a stool—it's a big kitchen, you hardly need a dining room with a kitchen this size—and he falls off the stool and bumps his bum on the floor. His wife, standing in the archway that leads back into the dining room, gasps, and cries out: "Oh my God, what do you want from us? It's Christmas, for God's sake!"

Funny thing is, I thought they didn't have Christmas, this lot. I don't know, maybe that's the Muslims, or whatever. So I look at them now, the man getting up off the floor, slowly, trying to get the stool between him and me, and the woman standing in the archway, arms crossed tight, shaking a bit. I look at them. Or, let *them* have a look at me, really. I've already seen them, corner-of-the-eyes stuff, now they can see me.

Now I'll listen to them. It's not that I haven't been hearing them before, all their questions, it's just that I've been busy. Had to have a good look around, see if this is the sort of home I thought it was. Like, have they done the place up nice? Got all the right grub in? Put up decent decorations, etc., like my gran would. I mean, not everybody bothers these days, I don't want to stay if they're not going to do it properly.

So I look at the man, look back at the woman, and now she's got a little boy with her. Behind her; don't know if she's seen him yet, I never heard him come in. About ten years old, just standing there, wondering what's going on. Pyjamas, dressing-gown, Fred Flintstone slippers.

"Hello, son," I say.

They both swing round, look at the boy. The man says, "Oh God," and the woman grabs the boy, holds him close.

We walk back into the dining room. Well, I walk in, they follow me. I'll tell you what, people say they're mean, don't they? Jews and that. But not this lot—I can tell that by the Christmas crackers. I've never seen crackers like them! Much bigger than the ones you normally see, much fatter, and the paper looks really classy, dead expensive. Still, people come out with a lot of prejudices, and they're not always accurate in my experience.

I put the parcel the barman gave me, and the bag of booze, on a small table by the window. I unwrap the parcel, using my penknife to cut through the string. I don't bother saving the paper, because it's not that sort of paper. Just ordinary brown paper: I screw it up and chuck it in a little waste-paper basket under the table. I take the gun out of the parcel, and put it on the table next to the carrier bag.

So then I turn round, look at them, give them a big smile.

"Hello," I say. "Happy Christmas."

"What do you want?" says the man. "Just tell us what you want."

"I've come to stay," I tell him. "I've come to stay for Christmas. Look," I say, "I've brought this." And I pull the bottles out of the bag. A big bottle of Scotch—malt whisky, for Christmas—and one of ginger wine. Seasonal fare. I hold them out to the woman, and after a moment she comes over and takes them.

"Thank you," she says, very soft, staring at me as she backs away.

"That's right, love," I says. "Just put them with the rest, eh?"

The boy's sitting on one of the chairs at the dining table. He'd better not mess up the place settings, they've been done beautifully. The man watches his wife take the booze, my festive gifts, over to a handsome sideboard behind the table, where there's bottles of every kind of booze you can imagine lined up in rows, glinting in the jolly light.

"Oh my God," says the man, so quiet I can hardly hear him. "Oh my God, he's mad."

Now the funny thing about that is the only reason they call me Madness down the pub is because I used to really like that pop group—the one that was called Madness. That's what's so funny about that.

The man looks at the gun, the pistol, sitting on the table. "Just tell us what you want," he says again. "We don't even know who you are, I swear we don't!"

So I pick up the gun and point it at the boy a bit. My finger's nowhere near the trigger, there's no danger. It's not mine, the gun, I haven't used one of these since I was a kid. It belongs to a big noise called Jim, only he's made a date with some pal on the robbery squad to raid his house on Boxing Day, so could I look after it for a couple of days (which obviously I can, no one's going to raid my bedsit, are they?), and he'll owe me a good drink, mate. *After* Christmas, naturally, when things have quietened down.

I smile at the man, smile at the woman. The boy looks a bit scared. In fact, I'm a bit worried about the boy. I mean, I haven't got anything for him—the booze is OK for his mum and dad, but I never thought to bring anything for a kid. It was all a bit spur of the moment, if you know what I mean. Never mind—I've had a good idea. Yeah, he'll love that, that'll do nicely.

Meanwhile: manners, Madness, please! Introductions first.

"I'm your cousin," I tell them. "I'm your cousin Madness, and I've come to stay for Christmas, I've come to surprise you for a lovely family Christmas. Happy Christmas," I say.

No response from the husband, but the wife—she's looking at the gun pointing at the boy—she walks over towards me, so she's standing between the gun and the kid, clever girl, and she says: "Happy Christmas." She swallows, there's a little tear there I think, then she says it again, louder: "Happy Christmas. I'm Sarah, and my son's name is Daniel."

"Happy Christmas, Daniel," I says, giving him a grin.

He doesn't look at his mum or his dad, he looks straight at me and says, "Happy Christmas, Cousin Madness."

I say Happy Christmas again, and laugh. We'll all have a laugh about that, later on, the way he says it with that straight face, like he thinks maybe I really *am* his cousin, only nobody's ever thought to mention me before! Good manners, that's what that is. Good decent family upbringing. "Good boy," I say.

Sarah looks over at her husband, sort of nudges him with her eyes, and says, "And this is my husband, Tony."

"Happy Christmas, Tony," I say.

He looks at his wife, looks at me, takes off his glasses and wipes his face with his shirt cuff. "Happy Christmas," he says.

He's got his hands underneath his armpits now, squeezing them, so I don't go to shake hands with him. Wouldn't be right, I don't want to embarrass him.

I put the gun in my belt. There: that's the formal part over with.

• • •

WE'RE in the living room, the room with the beautiful tree in it, having a nice Christmas Eve drink. Wine, in fact; they've opened a bottle specially, which is only what you'd expect from this sort of person. People of this quality, they're never thrown by unexpected guests. Nice drop of wine, as it goes, not my usual tipple, but it's going down very pleasantly.

I feel good. Sitting here, enjoying the lights from the tree, curtains drawn, fire up, all cosy. Christmassy. Wondering about the presents under the tree although, obviously, I know none of them can be for me. They weren't expecting me, that'd be asking too much, but even so, it's fun to wonder. That parcel there—is that a book? A record? That great big one, what's that: a bike for the lad? A DIY bench for Dad?

Which reminds me: presents. "I hope you like the Scotch, Tony? I see you're a wine drinker, if I'd known, obviously . . ."

"No, no, that's . . . that's fine," says Tony. "Isn't it, dear? That's, yes, that's lovely."

"Lovely," says Sarah. "Very thoughtful."

"It's a good one," I say, not boasting, but, you know, it is a good one.

"Yes," says Tony. "No that's, really, that's fine. My favourite."

"I am glad," I say. "We'll have a drop later, eh?"

Daniel's in bed. As he should be, of course, nearly one o'clock Christmas morning. Dreaming about his presents.

"Thing is," I say, a bit embarrassed, even though it's hardly my fault, "the boy—I just didn't think."

"Doesn't matter!" they both say at once. I've still got the gun in my belt, but to be honest, what I always think is, after the first few minutes—whatever situation you're in—a weapon doesn't really make much difference. Things are either calm or they're not, and if they're not, a weapon's just going to make things worse, right? Tonight, I rather wish I'd left it in the bag. Didn't really need it, not really, and there's always a risk it'll cause an atmosphere.

"No, well," I say, "maybe, but I've had an idea anyway." I reach into my pocket, bring out the knife, and chuck it over to Tony. He flinches: butter-fingers.

"It's not new, obviously," I say. "But it's in good nick, I've kept it nice. And it's a good knife, cost me a few bob. I was thinking, you know, perhaps Sarah could just wrap it up, bung it under the tree with the rest. I mean, I know it's second-hand, but I think he'll like it. Every boy likes a knife, right?" And then I look at Tony seriously, because it's his house, after all, his son. "Unless, you know, if you don't think it's suitable. I mean, if you think he's too young or whatever."

But no problem there, they're fine about it, thank me for the knife, Sarah says she'll wrap it, she's sure Daniel'll be delighted. So that's good. Anyway, it's getting late now, I'm feeling a bit knackered. Been mixing my drinks today, that's the truth, which is always a bad move!

"Well, all good things must come to an end," I say, and I stand up, stretch my arms over my head.

Sarah and Tony leap up like they've been bit by a dog. "Wait!" says Tony.

"Bedtime," I tell him.

They look at each other. "Oh my God . . ." says Tony, sinking back into the chair.

"Right," says the wife. "Fine. Well—Madness. Why don't you help yourself? Any room, they're all aired. And there's towels in the bathroom cupboard." She looks down at her husband, then back at me. "I think—Tony and I, we'll probably stay up for a bit, see if there's a film on or something."

I give her a smile. "I think we should all turn in, don't you? Late nights make cross mornings, that's what my old gran always said."

So we all turn in. Just as well: don't want to be grouchy Christmas morning.

• • •

ABOUT an hour and a half later, Sarah falls right over me, bang! Straight on the deck.

Not her fault—I'm lying on the carpet right outside their room, jacket for a pillow, gun in my hand.

She's got her dressing-gown on, and shoes. Outdoor shoes. And a torch. I help her to her feet, nothing broken, and we look at each other for a while. Slightly awkward moment all round.

She looks at the gun, can't help herself, then looks at me. "Are you angry with me?"

As if! I mean, come on, it's her family, isn't it? She's got to have a go, right, got to keep trying, else how would she live with herself if anything happened? Fair enough, hell, I understand all that. But then that's her, see: thinking of me, has she upset me, not thinking of herself. Smashing lady, Sarah.

"I hope your Tony knows what a lucky bloke he is," I say, but she pulls her dressing-gown round her more tightly and I think maybe she's got the wrong idea. So I take a step away from her, lean against the banister, light a ciggie, very casual.

"I usually go to my gran's," I tell her.

She nods. I offer her a cigarette—better late than never, Mr. Manners!—and she takes it, lets me light it, though it's obvious she's not a smoker. "Did your gran die?" she asks.

See what I mean? Thinks of others, notices things, works it out. Sympathetic.

But this is Christmas, and I've imposed enough already. I wouldn't actually mind crying on her shoulder, I'm not ashamed to say it, but it's not actually mine to cry on, is it? So I sniff, pretend a yawn, and say: "Well, better get some sleep, yeah? Big day tomorrow!"

I wake in the morning, rested and relaxed. Kipping on floors doesn't bother me, slept on more floors than beds, me. Anyway: it's Christmas morning! And there's that special feeling, I don't care how old you are, it never goes away, does it? The time ever comes when you don't feel that special excitement of Christmas morning—I don't care if you're nine or ninety-nine—then, son, you are ready for the grave!

Well let me tell you, no danger of Christmas morning not being special here, in this beautiful house, with these fine, kind people. It's like a dream! I wish my gran could've been here, she'd have loved it.

Great big breakfast, all the family together. Lovely grub. Nothing heavy, got to leave room for later, but very satisfactory. They both get the meal, Sarah and Tony, which is nice. Lady like that, she deserves a considerate husband, and I'm pleased to see she's got one. Because it can be a chore for the women, Christmas Day, if the men don't help out. So I volunteer for the washing-up, least I can do.

While I'm doing that, I take the gun out of my belt, slip it in my inside jacket pocket and hang the jacket behind the kitchen door. I feel better for that: guns and Christmas, you know, doesn't seem right, does it? Daniel sees me doing it—impatient to open his presents, he's come into the kitchen to find out what's keeping me—so I tell him he's not to touch my jacket, OK? And of course he says OK, good lad.

Opening the presents makes me a bit sad just for a while. Nothing for me, naturally, and that makes me think of Christmas at my gran's. She always got me a nice jumper, a record, whatever. Still, I cheer up when Daniel's so pleased with my knife. I don't think he's just being polite, I think he's really pleased. Well, it is a good knife, even if it is second-hand.

Before you know it, it's almost lunch time. We pull lots of crackers, especially me and Daniel—two daft kids!—and bloody good crackers they are, just as I thought. Really good gifts, things you can actually use, not plastic crap, and a big bang, and classy hats. But the jokes are still crap. "What do you call an octopus with seven legs? A seven-legged octopus." I don't think that's funny. I mean I *get* it, I just don't think it's funny. You pay this sort of money you should get a decent joke. Still, never mind. Minor point.

Daniel's allowed to put the telly on now, sits there in front of it playing with all his new stuff, as us grown-ups enjoy a little sherry while the meal finishes cooking in the oven.

Sarah coughs, clears her throat and says, "Well, a Merry Christmas to you, Madness, and a Happy New Year." She's looking more relaxed now, glad to have all the preparations over, I suppose.

"Actually, it's been a jolly bad year for me," I say. Well, why not? I'm amongst friends, don't have to be shy. Say what I'm feeling. "A jolly bad year all round. I'll be glad to see the back of it. Or at least, I would be if I didn't know that the next one will be just as bad, or worse."

"I'm sorry to hear that," she says. "Why has it been such a bad year, if you don't mind me asking?"

"Not at all," I say. "Kind of you to ask." But I don't really know what to say now. Don't want to tell them about the hospital, all that, don't want to put the mockers on. Ruin their Christmas with someone else's bad luck. So I say: "Oh, just this and that, you know." I put a finger in my mouth, waggle a tooth about. "Bad teeth, for one thing. Feels like they're all about to fall out. Keeps me awake, sometimes." Funny thing is, that's not a lie, I have had a lot of trouble with my teeth just lately.

"Have you," says Tony, "I mean, have you seen a dentist? I suppose you must have."

"No, I don't like dentists."

"My wife's brother's a dentist," he says.

Whoops. "No, no offence, I'm not prejudiced or anything," I tell her. "I'm sure your brother's a very good dentist, they can't all be crooks, can they? Anyway, I'm sure it wasn't your brother I saw last time."

"No," she says.

"Unless—he's not an Australian bloke, is he? Finchley Road?"

"No," she says.

"Red hair, big ears?"

"No, that's not him."

"Well," says Tony, "no, not Finchley Road. He's bald. He has got big ears, though." His wife gives him a look, and he shuts up.

It's nice in here. Warm, cheerful, few friends having a drink, rattling their jaws, chatting about their little troubles. A thought strikes me.

"What you two doing for New Year's, then?"

She gurgles, just for a second, very quietly. He opens his mouth preparatory for a quick stutter, but she puts her hand on his arm, says: "Well, you know, Madness, we, sort of, we don't in fact celebrate the same New Year. We're Jewish, remember."

Embarrassing! "Oh right," I say. "Sorry, no offence."

"None taken," she says, very gracious. "I hope you'll have a very happy one, anyway."

"Oh, sure," I say. "Well, never mind, New Year's different, eh? Pubs are open, last train on the tube's free. Go anywhere, New Year. Many options, several choices. Yeah, don't worry, won't be on my own New Year."

"You don't like to be on your own, Madness?" she says.

Very perceptive, that seems to me. A very unselfish lady, very open to thoughts about others. "Well," I say, playing it down, like it's no big thing. "It's just that, you know, I mean, you don't come into this world alone, do you? Your mum's there, and the nurse and that, and you don't go out of it alone, do you?"

"You don't?" says Tony.

"Actually, no," I say. "This bloke comes in the pub, he used to work in a crematorium, and he says they shove you through twelve at a time, saves on the fuel."

Bloody nice thing to talk about on Christmas Day! *Idiot.* I try to think of some way to make a joke of it, without making it worse, when there's a knock on the door and my hosts freeze, staring at each other.

Christ, now that is embarrassing. They were expecting company! And I never thought to ask, and they were too polite to mention it. But now I think, yeah, six places set in the dining room. Hell's bells.

The really embarrassing thing, of course, is that there's nothing I can do about it, not given the circumstances. We're just going to have to hope the visitors go away, and then we'll really have to get our heads together trying to come up with some excuse for later, for why Sarah and Tony didn't answer the door. And that's not going to be easy.

They do go away, but not quickly and not for very long. The phone rings all through lunch (great lunch, even if we are all a little distracted), and then just as we're settling down in front of the box again, the visitors return. Well they would, wouldn't they, when you think about it? I mean, they certainly know they haven't got the wrong day! And if we don't answer this time, chances are they'll get worried, call the cops.

"Right," I say, positioning myself in the living-room doorway. "Look, I'm sorry about this, but this is what we're going to have to do. Daniel?" He looks up from the telly. "Lend me your new knife a moment, will you? And come and stand over here with me." Because I don't fancy nipping to the kitchen to fetch the gun; the people outside might see me through the hall window. "Sarah, you stay there behind me. Tony, you go to the door, tell them they can't come in, you've got a contagious disease."

"Contagious disease?" says Tony, almost laughing at the idea. He wants to take things more seriously that bloke, no criticism intended, but he does. I know it's not a great plan, but it might send them away for a few minutes at least, long enough for me to fetch my jacket, dash off out the back. No time for good manners now, unfortunately.

"Go on, love," says Sarah. "Tell them measles, we've all got measles, and could they come back later when we might be feeling better." Good girl!

"And Tony?" I say. "Don't mumble, please." Daniel's standing right in front of me, I've got one hand on his shoulder, and the knife in my other hand. Obviously, I don't want to scare the boy, but Tony gets the message.

I keep out of sight, but I can hear him. "Measles . . . blah blah . . . not to worry . . . blah blah . . . give us a ring later, Jeremy . . . blah blah . . ."

It's worked. Won't work for long, I'll have to get out sharpish, and carefully too, but at least there's been no need for any of the sort of unpleasantness, which could have ruined Christmas for everyone.

The door shuts, I look round at the family—like, *phew!* Like, relax folks, panic over, back to the festivities. Only, I look at Sarah, and she's got that damn gun of Jim's—wish I'd never seen the damn thing, I really do—pointing right at me. Steady as you like, two-handed grip like the cops on telly, pointing right at the bridge of my nose. Well, fair enough, I didn't tell

Daniel "Don't mention it to anyone," I just told him "Don't touch it." It's not like he's disobeyed me.

I look at Sarah's eyes. Red flush from chest to cheeks, very angry. The funny thing is, I don't think she's going to shoot me. I'm not an expert on people or anything, but I've looked at a lot of faces in my time, and I don't think she'll shoot me. What I think she'll do is, I think she'll lock the gun up in a cupboard upstairs, not showing me where it is, then I think she'll go outside and throw the key down a drain, and then she'll say, like, "Right, let's all go back in and finish our cheese and nuts, and then I think you owe everybody an apology, Madness, don't you?" Maybe she'll even laugh and say, "Get my brother round to look at your teeth, shall we?"

I don't know for sure, obviously, I'm not a mind-reader, but I *think* that's what she'll do. That's what my gran would have done, anyway.

CAROLYN WHEAT

"Cousin Cora" centers on farm life and women's friendships in the early twentieth century. I awoke one morning after a vivid dream involving a teenage boy and a mysterious spinster, a dream that developed into this anti-detective story. Both stories are sad, filled with regrets and wishes that one had done things differently. As to the resolution the boy makes at the end of "Cousin Cora"—well, I have always wondered whether or not he kept that promise to himself. His name, it might be recalled, is Sam.

• • •

It took me all of ten seconds to choose "A Jury of Her Peers" as my favorite mystery short story of all time. It has haunted me from the day, at least thirty-five years ago, when I first came across it in To the Queen's Taste, a 1946 Frederick Dannay anthology. Susan Glaspell, Pulitzer prize–winning playwright, adapted the story from her one-act play, Trifles. First published as a short story in 1917, this tale of feminist detection and women's justice is firmly of its period yet as relevant as the latest Sara Paretsky.

COUSIN CORA

Carolyn Wheat

"Now the left hand," I ordered in my official Scotland Yard voice. The most dangerous criminal in London (portrayed by my six-year-old brother Lionel) placed his pudgy little paw in mine. I rolled the fingers one by one onto the satisfying squish of inkpad, then pressed them onto a sheet of Mama's best cream note paper. The result: a perfect fingerprint record, as guaranteed by the Hawkshaw Junior Detective Kit Company of Racine, Wisconsin.

I gave Lionel back his hand. "Mind you don't wipe them on your knickerbockers," I warned, "or we'll both catch Hail Columbia." Lionel nodded, his round blue eyes lending the scene all the solemnity any detective could have wished.

We were in the barn, temporarily renamed 221b Baker Street. I was the great Sherlock; Lionel had taken the parts, as required, of Dr. Watson, Mycroft Holmes, several Baker Street Irregulars, Mrs. Hudson, and Toby the dog. At the moment, he was basking in the notoriety of Professor Moriarty, the effect only slightly spoiled by a smudge of fingerprinting ink on his button nose.

It was the summer the very trees seemed to sway to the Merry Widow Waltz. It was the summer my feet (which were growing at a rate that alarmed even me) began to leave the barefoot path of boyhood. It was the summer

I sucked dry the bitter fruit of the knowledge of good and evil. It was the summer of Cousin Cora.

"Sa-am," a voice called in the distance. Lionel and I locked eyes, one thought in both our minds. What was the most dangerous criminal in London compared to our big sister Lucy, the most dangerous tattletale in Springfield Township?

"Sa-am, where aaare you?" Her voice was getting closer. She'd be in the barn any minute, and then she'd see Lionel's inky fingers, and then she'd spy the Hawkshaw Junior Detective Kit, and then—

It was a well-known fact that women were incapable of appreciating the Art and Science of Detection.

"Quick," I told Lionel, "scoot out the back and put your hands under the pump." He scooted. Even at six, my brother had a sound grasp of life's essentials.

I gathered up the fingerprint record of Professor Lionel Moriarty, closed the inkpad tin, and put both into the cardboard box containing the Detective Kit. Then I shoved the whole shebang into the corncrib, making sure a layer of cobs lay on top, so Lucy wouldn't see the scowling face of Hawkshaw the Detective on the cover.

I whipped my mouth organ out of my pocket and commenced to play—probably the Merry Widow, which I'd been trying to learn all summer just to get Lucy's goat. It was her favorite tune, but I didn't think she really cared for it on the harmonica.

"Sam, what on earth are you doing in this musty old barn on such a beautiful day?" My sister stood in the doorway in the stance favored by women throughout history for criticizing men: feet planted solidly apart, hands on hips, arms akimbo. Looking for all the world like an indignant milk jug.

I muttered something in which the term *beeswax* figured largely.

"What do you mean it's none of my—Why, Mama sent me to fetch you, so there."

"What for?"

"Mama's Cousin Coramae's come for a visit and Mama wants you to wash up and wear your Sunday collar to supper."

"Cousin Coramae?" My detective instincts leapt to the fore. True, Mama was Southern and therefore considered persons of the remotest connection her cousins, but why had I never heard tell of a Coramae? "And why didn't Mama say anything at breakfast?"

It was scarcely my intention to ask the question aloud, particularly of Lucy. Ever since turning seventeen and putting her hair up, she'd been impossible to live with. Putting on airs and looking down her nose at a fellow just because he was three years younger and didn't pomade his hair like the boys who went to Webley's Corners High School.

"I suppose you think Mama ought to consult you before asking her own kin for a visit," Lucy said, with a superior toss of her head. For a moment I thought her honey-blonde pompadour would shake loose from its moorings and tumble down her back, but no such luck. "And besides, how could she tell us when she didn't know herself? Cousin Coramae just turned up on the doorstep not twenty minutes ago. All alone." Lucy's eyes grew as round as Lionel's; her voice dropped into a conspiratorial tone. For a moment it was as if the bossy older sister had vanished, replaced by the pigtailed equal of former days.

"She didn't come in the hack." This momentous pronouncement was followed by another, equally startling. "And she brought no more luggage than a motheaten carpetbag and a hatbox."

This was news indeed. Mama's relations sent letters to announce their coming, telegrams to say they were en route, and invariably arrived in the depot hack with an army of bandboxes, steamer trunks, cowhide valises, and lesser impedimenta.

Cousin Coramae was a Mystery.

I hastened to the parlor, spitting into my hand and slicking down my hair as I raced past the kitchen garden toward the back door.

The house was dark and cool, sunlight kept at bay by heavy damask curtains pulled tight so the Turkish carpet wouldn't fade. I stood a moment outside the parlor door, conducting surveillance. Mama's voice was high and fluting, the way it sounded when she was making small talk with someone she didn't know well. The voice that answered was dryly precise, with a hard Yankee edge that surprised me. Mama's kin had Southern drawls, putting a lazy, questioning emphasis on the wrong words. Not like Papa's midwestern yawp, which came down as hard on consonants as a Baptist preacher on sin. Cousin Coramae's accent was different, as though she was related to no one but herself.

I was on the verge of stepping into the parlor to pay my respects when my mother's words fixed me in place like a chloroformed moth.

"—my husband. What shall I tell him?" Mama's voice sounded like a high end of the piano. "I'd rather die than have him learn the truth."

"Tell him nothing," the Yankee voice replied. "I have come for a brief visit. That is all anyone need know."

"Brief?" Mama seized upon the word as though it meant sure salvation. "How brief, Tommy?"

I no sooner had time to absorb the unexpected nickname than the visitor replied, "Until I get the money."

Silence followed, thick as barn dust. I crept forward, hidden by the half-closed door.

The mysterious cousin was a tiny woman. Frail, too, with bird bones and parchment skin stretched too tight over a pinched schoolmarm face. You'd have said she looked worn out, though she was about my mother's age, but there was an inner something that told me she was tough as twine.

Her hair was mud-colored and looked in need of a wash. Her skirt was travel-stained, and her high-button shoes were worn at the heels. At her throat she wore a lace jabot that looked the way my school collars did on Saturday night. My father would have said she'd been rode hard and put away wet.

She sat in the second-best chair.

The first-best chair—the green velvet plush with mahogany arms—was reserved for Grandfather Parsloe and other household gods. The third-best chairs (which had no arms) were reserved for whichever children were privileged to enter the parlor, and for Uncle Samuel, whose frequent indulgence in strong spirits no longer entitled him to chairs with mahogany arms. How did Cousin Coramae, with her pauper's luggage and her bedraggled appearance, rate the second-best chair?

I leaned in closer. Mama perched on the edge of the rose-colored chair as though afraid to lean back into its plush depths. A stranger would have thought Cousin Coramae the self-assured hostess and Mama the nervous guest.

"The money." My mother's tone was flat as an iron, hollow as an owl tree. "And just where do you think I can put my hands on such a sum?"

"Come, Lia, you married women always have little stores put by, amounts your husbands don't know about. Am I right?"

Lia. A name I'd never heard in my life. Mama was Lillian, Lily to her sisters, Lil to Papa in a joshing mood. Never Lia.

Mama's answering sigh was a surrender. "There's the butter-and-egg money, I suppose. But I had hoped to buy Lucy a dress for graduation."

"I *need* the money, Lia."

"You don't understand, Tommy. It *isn't* money, not really." Mama's words tumbled over one another like shelled peas rolling into a bowl. "Mr. Benbow at the General Store keeps an account of what he owes me, and then gives me credit when I need something special, like the silk for Lucy's dress."

"Couldn't you ask him for cash instead?"

"He'd be mighty suspicious if I did—and he'd tell Harry for sure. Men stick together."

"I see." Cousin Coramae sat still as a barn owl, her predator's eyes fixed on Mama. "Then we must concoct a story your husband will accept. An unpaid debt? Or perhaps I stand in need of a life-saving operation."

I stood behind the door, knowing how wrong it was to eavesdrop, but unable to move. If Cousin Coramae was an owl, it was I, not Mama, who was the mouse. Sweat poured down my back; I wiped my forehead with a hand still gray with fingerprinting ink. I had plenty of chores to do before supper, including scrubbing all evidence of ink off my fingers with Papa's lye soap. Yet nothing could have moved me from my vantage point.

"Why me, Tommy?" Mama asked. "Why not one of the others?"

The mysterious visitor shrugged. "You were the closest to the College. The train station was watched, I'm sure of it, so I didn't dare travel by rail."

This was better than the dime novel I had hidden under my mattress. A mysterious woman, arriving unexpectedly, unable to travel by train. The College, I was sure, meant Springfield State Teachers' College, where Mama went before she married.

"Are you so certain they suspect—"

"They suspect a great deal more than they can prove. But the family is both influential and persistent, and I decided discretion was the better part of valor. Still, Lia, I am sorry it had to be you."

"I know, Tommy," Mama said, her voice like the soothing syrup she gave me when I was sick. "I know. And I'll get the money on Saturday, I promise. That's when Harry takes me to Mr. Benbow's store to shop for the week."

The parlor looked as it always did: Great-grandmother Hartley's silver tea service resting on the mahogany butler's table alongside the bone china cups and saucers. I'd watched Mama pour tea into those cups countless times.

Today was different. Today blackmail hung in the air, heavy as honeysuckle.

• • •

THERE was plenty to occupy my mind as I sat on the back porch, shucking corn for supper. I pulled each ear free of its husk with a tearing sound that satisfied my soul and watched mounds of cornsilk billow to my feet. It looked as though every doll in the house had been scalped.

My first real case. No more playing Sherlock in the barn—I had a true-life female Professor Moriarty staying under my own roof. Deep secrets lay between these two strangers, one called "Tommy" and the other "Lia." Secrets my father wasn't to know.

What could I do? Tell Papa? I stripped the last ear of corn, running my hand along the pearly golden kernels, then setting it on the pile with the others.

No—telling Papa was betraying Mama, and that I would not do under any circumstances.

Confront Cousin Coramae—if she was even Mama's cousin, which I doubted—and tell her I knew everything, like a hero in a melodrama? She had only to threaten to tell Papa the terrible secret, and I'd be back where I started.

As I carried my load of corn into the kitchen for Maisie the hired girl to put on to boil, I reflected that there was nothing in the Hawkshaw Junior Detective Kit to cover this situation. I was on my own.

• • •

IT was one of Papa's town days. Although we lived on the farm his father and grandfather worked before him, Papa's real business was the Feed and Grain. He spent three or four days a week in Webley's Corners. Which meant that he was dressed for company when he walked through the front door.

We were all at the dining room table, empty soup plates resting on two layers of china before each place. My Sunday collar chafed my neck; Lionel squirmed like a tadpole. Lucy, in her new sprigged waist, sat next to me, still as a tree stump, showing how grown-up she was by her refusal to fidget.

Mama, at the foot of the table, seemed taut as a barbed-wire fence. Every time there was a noise at the door, she started. She lifted her glass of ice-water to her lips every few minutes, but seemed not to drink it, for the level remained the same. Her slender fingers played with the heavy silverware.

She looked everywhere except at Cousin Coramae.

As soon as Papa's tread was heard on the porch, she jumped from her seat, jiggling the table and spilling some of her water. "Harry," she called, in the high, fluting voice I associated with nerves, "you'll never guess who's come for a visit."

They talked in the vestibule, among the umbrellas and canes. I could only hear a few words: ". . . my second cousin twice-removed . . . I haven't seen her in so many years . . . it seems the letter she sent was lost in the mail, isn't that something?"

Papa's baritone was easier to hear, though he was trying his best to mute it. ". . . can't say I do remember, Lil, but then you have so many cousins. . . . Certainly she's welcome, letter or no letter. Now, let's have supper. I'm hungry as a bear."

Papa entered the room like a bear, his big masculine presence filling space out of proportion to the actual size of his body. He wasn't a tall man, but broad-shouldered, with thick brown hair and a mustache I envied with all my heart. Would I, someday, outgrow my weedy slenderness and thin, sandy hair, becoming a real man like my father?

"Harry, I'd like you to meet my cousin Miss Coramae Jones." Jones was not a name I'd ever heard in my mother's family. And since Mama had said "Miss," it wasn't her married name. Whoever our visitor was, I was willing to bet every marble I owned, plus my slingshot, that her last name wasn't Jones.

Supper began as soon as Papa took his place at the head of the table. Maisie brought out the soup, ladling it into the shallow bowls one by one. It was cherry soup, which I loved because it was cold and sweet and nobody else I knew had it for supper in their house.

"Cherry soup," Cousin Coramae said, her green-apple voice ripening just a bit. "This does take me back, Lillian."

Not Lia. Just as Mama said, "Remember, Coramae? We both learned to make it from that Swedish girl, what was her name?"

"Inga. Inga Gustavsen. A brain like a feather pillow, but cooked like an angel."

"I didn't know angels could cook," Lionel said. "What do they make, angel food cake?"

Papa's laugh boomed out. Mama and Lucy smiled. But Cousin Coramae exploded with laughter, as though something bottled up was being released. She pulled a dingy lace handkerchief from her sleeve and held it to pursed lips, but still the laughter came. Her eyes teared, as though the very act of laughing touched her in some deep way. Her laughter hurt, as though she'd all but forgotten there were things in the world to laugh about.

She dabbed at her eyes with her handkerchief, the tip of her nose red. She gave herself a good shake and said, "There now. I shall subside. I must apologize . . . difficult railroad journey." All at the table nodded, the notorious strain of travel upon the female sex too obvious to warrant remark. Only I knew that however Cousin Coramae had reached our farm, it hadn't been by train.

The thing about cherry soup was: Maisie had never learned to pit the cherries first. Each spoonful was a potential social disaster. Mama and Lucy ate with delicacy, gently removing each pit into their spoons and sliding it discreetly under the bowl.

I tried to do the same. Honestly, I did. But one pit got past me and slid down my throat, causing a coughing fit that sprayed red juice over my portion of the damask tablecloth. Lucy shot me a withering glance and said,

MASTER'S CHOICE VOLUME II   325

"Cousin Coramae, I must apologize for my brother. He isn't really house-broken."

My face burned as though stung with nettles. I wished Lucy at the bottom of Hale Pond, which everyone knew was bottomless.

Coramae Jones fixed Lucy with a stare only an owl could have duplicated. "In my day," she began, her tone as tart as a pippin, "it was considered the height of bad manners to call attention to someone else's *faux pas.*"

Lucy hung her head. Now her face looked as though it had had the nettle treatment.

Another piece of the puzzle fell into place: this woman had been a Teacher.

• • •

STARS fat as bumblebees hung low in the summer sky. I was outside, walking with Cousin Coramae. I was both afraid and curious, walking in the dark with a suspected blackmailer. There was excitement, too, in knowing that I was conducting my very first interrogation as a detective.

"Will you look at that moon!" The visitor pointed at a low point of sky, her finger twig-thin. We had passed the hitching-block and were well on our way toward the dirt road into town.

I looked; the moon was a crescent, but it lay on its side, points curving upward. "It looks like a boat," I said.

"Exactly," my companion agreed. "Like the gondolas I saw in Venice." In the pale moonlight, her weathered face took on a look of rapture.

"Have you really been to Italy?"

"Didn't your mother tell you?"

"My mother?"

"She was there too. We were a party of young ladies," she explained. "We toured Rome, Florence, and Venice. It was a very special trip for all of us."

Lia. An Italian pet-name from an Italian trip. A trip no one in the family had ever heard about.

I tried to keep my voice casual. "Did you ever visit Mama at the Teachers' College?"

"Why, yes, I suppose I must have. Once or twice." There was dismissal in the flat tone. We walked in silence for a minute or two, our shoes scuffling the summer dust. I could hear birds in the woods on the other side of the road; our side was rich-smelling alfalfa, and a little spring wheat.

My companion broke the silence. "The Hunter stalks tonight," she said.

"What?" It was not a polite reply, but I was too startled to remember manners.

"Up in the sky." The twig-finger pointed again. "There's Orion, the Hunter. See—the one that looks like an H with a crooked bar."

I found Orion without much difficulty. He was big, dominating his part of the sky the way my father dominated our dining room.

"Artemis, whom the Romans called Diana, killed him, and placed him among the stars. She was a huntress, the Virgin Goddess."

"You sound like a teacher." It was part calculated, part blurted-out, but I had to know.

"You are a very observant young man." She stated a fact, without judgment. "You notice things. You have eyes that catalogue, like an accountant. Or, perhaps," she went on, the tart-apple taste coming back into her voice, "like a spy."

It was as though the fugitive could see right into the barn, through the corncrib, under the dry cobs, to where the Hawkshaw Junior Detective Kit lay.

We passed the hollow tree where I'd seen a hoot owl the week before. The creek I fished in burbled in the distance. Up ahead was the water tower, looming over the horizon the way the Methodist Church steeple overshadowed the town.

I had to smile as I looked at the tower. There were some initials at the top I had reason to be mighty proud of.

"It takes considerable nerve to climb a tower that high," my companion remarked.

"What—what makes you think I climbed it, Cousin Coramae?"

"Please, call me Cora. I have always loathed my full given name, a fact I have some difficulty impressing upon your mother."

"Well, then, Cousin Cora,"—I had been brought up never to use an adult's name without some sort of title in front of it, so Cousin Cora she became—"the truth is that one night Red Beaudine, Spider Crowley, and I climbed clear to the top of that tower and painted our initials on the back. In red paint."

"Bully for you," Cousin Cora said. "That's one peck of wild oats sown."

Even Papa, who always wanted me to be manly, wouldn't have said that. My heart warmed toward the strange visitor, and I told her things that night I'd never told another soul. How I hated farm life. How I wanted more than anything in the world to set off for the city, maybe even California.

I didn't say a word about Hawkshaw Junior Detective Kits, or the conversation I'd overheard in the parlor. I kept a few secrets. But as to the rest, Cousin Cora made no criticism. Everything I said seemed reasonable to her. Every dream I expressed she agreed could be reality if I wanted it badly enough.

As we walked toward home, our way lit by a ghostly crescent moon, I decided I'd been reading too many dime novels. This skinny spinster lady who smelled of violet water was no blackmailer.

•   •   •

THE next morning, I was out with Papa mending fences by the dirt road. We were stringing new barbed wire and pounding the fence posts in tighter, so they'd withstand the summer rains. It was hot, dry work and we'd been at it since sunup. My arms hurt and my shirt was soaked with sweat; Papa looked the worse for wear, but I knew he could go till sunset without a pause or a meal if he had to.

When he lifted the heavy hammer over his head, his huge arm muscles knotted and tensed as the hammer rose high into blue sky, then struck the fence post with a force that shook the very ground. Bit by bit, blow by blow, the wood drove deeper into the caked soil.

I held the fence posts, my hardest job being not to flinch as the hammer swung down, all of Papa's strength behind it. I wondered if the day would ever come when I could swing the hammer while Lionel held the post. Right now, it was all I could do to lift the hammer, let alone hoist it with Papa's ease.

Hoofbeats caught my attention. Sheriff Caleb Anson trotted by on Midnight, his black mare. "What say, Cal?" Papa called out. He put down the hammer and gave the sheriff a straight-armed wave.

Sheriff Cal pulled his horse up short. "Say, Harry," he said. "Didn't your wife go to the Teacher's College in Springfield?"

"You know she did, Cal."

"Well, I'd surely hate to upset Lillian, but there's been a little trouble up that way." Sheriff Cal gentled his mare, patting her coal-black neck. Still the animal fretted and stamped, eager to trot. "I'd appreciate your letting me have a word with Lillian. Seems the woman who's involved was one of her classmates. She stayed on to teach at the College after they graduated."

At the word "teach," my ears pricked like a jackrabbit's. Hadn't I already deduced that Cousin Cora had taught school? I stood beside the fence, hoping to be taken for a fence post and ignored.

"Involved in what, Cal?" Papa asked. He pushed back his hat, wiping his forehead with his hand.

"Not before the boy," the sheriff said. Papa edged toward Midnight; the sheriff leaned down to speak as privately as possible.

I could only overhear snatches: ". . . family very upset . . . girl died of laudanum poisoning . . ."

Papa's voice was easier to hear. "Over a lover, I suppose. That's what all these young girls get up to." I was reminded how angry he got when Eddie Ruckleshaus came to take Lucy to the church social. You'd have thought Eddie was about to start my sister on the road to ruin instead of treating her to peach ice cream at Christian Endeavor.

". . . know how it is, Harry. All-female seminary . . . women cooped up together. These things happen."

"Disgusting!" Papa gave up any effort to keep his voice low. "If you dare bring filthy talk like that into my house, Caleb Anson, I'll—"

"Could be murder, Harry." Sheriff Anson's calm tone cut through Papa's anger like a wire cutter. "Leastwise, the Pargeters, the family of the dead girl, think so. And they've got a fair amount of influence in Springfield, so—"

"Springfield is Springfield," Papa interrupted, "and Webley's Corners is Webley's Corners."

I knew Papa in this mood: now the sheriff would be lucky to get directions to his own house from him. All I could think of were the words I'd overheard in the parlor yesterday, Cousin Cora talking about an influential family, and some reason she couldn't travel by train. Was it possible the woman I'd walked with under the stars the night before was a murderess? I should have felt excited. Instead, I felt sick.

"All the same, Harry, Lillian could—"

"Hellfire, Cal!" Papa shouted. He tore the hat from his head and slapped his thigh with it, raising a cloud of dust. The horse shied back; the sheriff pulled tight on her reins. "It's been nigh onto twenty years since Lil graduated that school. I won't have you upsetting her over something she can't possibly know anything about."

"Harry, I already told you." The sheriff's tone was patient but insistent. "This teacher, Miss Tomlin, was a student with Lillian twenty years ago. Your wife might just remember her, know where her family lives."

Miss Tomlin. Tommy. My ears buzzed, and for a moment, I could say nothing. Then I cleared my throat and said, "I never heard Mama mention anyone by that name."

"There now," Papa said. "If Sam here never heard of the woman, then Lily doesn't know her, and that's a fact. She's forever going on about that school. She'd have been bound to mention this Miss Tomlin if she'd known her. Right, Sam?"

"Right, Papa." I felt dizzy, as though the sun were frying my brain. Of course Mama knew Miss Tomlin. She called her Tommy, and was being blackmailed into helping her escape.

"So there's nothing more to say, is there, Cal? You won't be coming around to bother Lily, and that's that."

The sheriff raised his palm and eased Midnight away from the fence. "Can't say as I blame you, Harry. I guess I'd do the same if it was my wife." He dug his heels into the mare's flanks and Midnight gratefully accepted the hint. Man and horse disappeared in a cloud of dust.

Papa and I finished the fence posts in silence. I wanted him to tell me what the sheriff had said, wanted him to trust me man to man, but all he did was swing his hammer and pound wood deeper into hard-packed ground.

As soon as Papa and I finished, I made my way to the sewing room. On the wall, proudly framed in gilt, was Mama's diploma from Springfield State Teachers' College. In one corner, next to the workbasket, sat a two-shelf bookstand. The top shelf contained what I wanted: the yearbook of Mama's graduating class. I opened it, starting where I always did, with Mama's photograph.

She was Lillian Wanderley then. The face that looked at me was at once familiar as my own hand and as remote as the moon. She was my mother, but she didn't know me. Didn't know I would ever exist. Didn't know she would marry Papa and live in Webley's Corners.

She was President of the Poetry Society. Under her name was the quote: "Shall I compare thee to a summer's day?" Every time I read those words I thought how true they were. It wasn't just my mother's sun-bright hair and sky-blue eyes that made her seem summery, it was her laughter and lightness.

I turned the pages backwards, stopping at a picture of a dark-haired girl with huge black eyes in a thin face. Under the photograph was the name Letitia Coramae Tomlin. Secretary of the Poetry Society.

Papa had told Sheriff Cal the truth. Mama did go on about Springfield College, telling Lucy and me all about her friends, her teachers, the fun she'd had. I'd heard stories of every picnic, every midnight revel after curfew, every funny incident in class.

Why had I never heard of Cora Tomlin—or the trip to Italy?

• • •

THE next day, I rose at five, did my usual milking and swept out the barn. As I worked, I thought about Cousin Cora, and what I ought to do. It was wrong to let Cousin Cora take my Mama's money, wrong to let her go without telling the sheriff where she was, wrong to let her escape.

On the other hand, there was the terrible secret—whatever it was Mama was so desperate to hide. I remembered what Sheriff Anson and Papa had talked about. What if Cousin Cora really had killed the Pargeter girl? Could I let her go, knowing what I knew?

I needed more evidence. As I passed the corncrib, I took out the Hawkshaw Junior Detective Kit and hid it under the bib of my overalls.

It was just as well I did. On the way out of the barn, I met Lucy, dressed in a gingham skirt with a matching ribbon in her hair. "Going to town with us, Sam?" she asked, tossing her head. Practicing for the Webley's Corners beaux.

"Don't know," I replied. It was Saturday, the day Papa took Mama to Benbow's General Store. The day Cousin Cora would get her butter-and-egg money.

"Your sweetheart will be leaving today," she teased. "Mama says Cousin Coramae's taking the four-fifty to Chicago this afternoon. Don't you want to be there to say good-bye?"

"Not specially." I stuck my hands in my pockets and began to whistle, hoping to discourage conversation.

Nothing discouraged Lucy when she was bent on talking. "I don't know what you find so fascinating about Cousin Coramae," she said. "She's just a dried-up old stick, if you ask me." When my continued whistling convinced her she'd get nothing more out of me, Lucy flounced toward the kitchen door.

I thought Lucy wasn't wrong: Cousin Cora was like one of those stick-insects that looked like a twig and then scared the bejesus out of you when it started to move.

• • •

THE guest room looked as though no one had slept there for years. The bed, with its rose satin coverlet, was neatly made, the bolsters propped against the cherry headboard. The dresser, with its hand-embroidered scarf, was empty of Cousin Cora's personal belongings. The only evidence that she had ever occupied the room was the hatbox and carpetbag sitting beside the door.

Mama's Singer whirred in the sewing room next door. I was glad; no one would hear me with that noise going on. I pulled the Hawkshaw Junior Detective Kit out from under my overalls and opened it. Inside I had fingerprint powder, an insufflator, and special tape to lift latent prints.

There were plenty of surfaces in the room that ought to have given me prints: the top of the dresser, the night table, the washstand. None did. Every time I puffed away the excess powder with my insufflator, there was nothing there. The room had been wiped clean. Either Maisie had suddenly become the perfect housemaid, or Cousin Cora had erased all traces of herself.

I was so busy working I didn't notice at first that the sewing machine had stopped. I froze. Was Mama about to come into the guest room? What would I tell her if she did?

Then I heard the sobs.

I crept down the hallway toward the sewing room. The door was open, but I didn't go in. Mama sat in the rocking chair, her head in her hands, her shoulders heaving. On her lap was the yearbook.

"Mama?" My heart thudded inside me like Papa's hammer striking the fence posts. I could count on the fingers of one hand the number of times I'd seen my mother cry.

"Sam." Mama raised her tear-streaked face and gave me a watery smile. "I was just looking through my book, and so many memories came back. So many memories." She wiped her cheeks like a child, without benefit of handkerchief.

"Are—are you all right, Mama?"

"Yes, Sam. Please just let me be." She attempted a smile. "I was just reminiscing, that's all. You'll understand when you're older."

"Mama, I know the truth," I began.

"And what truth is that, Sam?"

I stepped over to where she sat and knelt beside the rocker. "I know about the dead girl at the College and about Cousin Cora's not being our cousin but being Miss Tomlin instead. And," I finished boldly, "I know you mean to give her money and let her get away."

Mama turned her gaze toward the window, where the last lilacs drooped on the bush. They were brown-edged now, but still filled the sewing room with a fragrance that reminded me of Mama.

"If you know that much, then you know I have to, Sam. I have no choice."

"But, Mama, couldn't we—"

"*No*, Sam." Her voice sharp as sewing scissors, she cut off my words. "Please, for my sake, don't ask any more questions. Just let it be."

I left her turning the pages of her yearbook. When she thought I was out of the room, she bent her head. A tear fell onto the page, and then another. I crept away quietly, as though from a sickroom.

What would Sherlock Holmes do? Find the truth at all costs. What would Papa do? Protect Mama at all costs. What was I to do?

I went back to the guest room. I didn't know what I wanted, the truth or comfortable lies or if I wanted to turn back the clock so that Cousin Cora had never entered our lives. I only knew that whatever I wanted, the truth was what I had to have.

I opened the carpetbag. Inside, among the neatly folded clothes smelling faintly of violet, was a small packet of letters tied with a black velvet ribbon. I drew them out, and recognized my mother's elegant penmanship.

Love letters, to someone not my father. Some were four and five pages of thick vellum, others were just notes. On the back of one of Mama's engraved calling cards: "I so loved our picnic by the river, Dear One." On monogrammed pink notepaper: "How do I love thee? Let me count the ways." On a torn-out sheet of school tablet paper: "I dare not ask a kiss, I dare not beg a smile."

I felt like a fence post on the receiving end of Papa's hammer. I was face-to-face with the terrible secret, the hold Cousin Cora had over my mother. Mama had had a lover when she was at the Teacher's College, a lover who received letters with poetry in them. Letters signed "Lia."

Someone besides Cora Tomlin had known my mother by that name. Someone she had met in Italy? And how had Cousin Cora come to have the letters?

The last note said only: "Since there's no help, come let us kiss and part."

It was when I put the letters back that I found the vial of laudanum.

I drew it out, turning it in my fingers. Cousin Cora, blackmailer, using Mama's letters to her lost lover as a weapon to extort money. Cousin Cora, murderess, using laudanum to poison a girl at the College. Had Cousin Cora blackmailed the dead girl, too, then killed her to prevent her telling anyone?

There was only one thing I could do. It felt like betrayal, and yet with murder at stake I had no other choice. Besides, Papa would understand. He often joked with Mama about the beaux she could have had back in her Virginia hometown. I took the letters out of the bag and put them in the pocket of my overalls.

Papa was in the bedroom, standing before his shaving glass, straight razor in his hand. His face was lathered, except for the precious mustache. Ordinarily, I loved watching Papa shave, taking mental notes so that I could handle the razor with ease when I had enough whiskers to worry about.

I came straight to the point. "Papa, there's something I have to tell you."

• • •

IT was as though an anarchist's bomb went off in our little farmhouse. Papa exploded out of the room, lather still on his face. He made straight for the guest room, picked up Cousin Cora's bags and tossed them out the front door. He ordered Maisie to tell Cousin Cora, who was out strolling in the woods, to hightail it off his property at once.

Then he marched to the sewing room. I hid behind the stairwell, feeling as though I was weathering a tornado. Papa's angry shouts filled the air, followed by Mama's tearful replies.

". . . phony cousin. Wanted by the police, of all things."

". . . don't understand, Harry. . . . not murder. The poor child took her own . . . wasn't Tommy's fault."

"Tommy! Is that what you call the creature?"

Lucy came down from upstairs, her face anxious. When she saw me behind the stairwell, she whispered, "What's wrong?"

"Not sure," I lied. But I couldn't look at her. Whatever was happening behind that closed door was my doing.

I felt even worse when Lionel came out of the kitchen, one half of a gingerbread boy still in his hand. He looked as scared as he had the day he nearly fell into the well.

"How could you, Lily?" Papa asked. It was a plea, a prayer.

"I was so lonely," Mama answered. "Away from home for the first time. . . . Tommy was good to me. I didn't understand at first, and then—I was in love."

"Love! You call that love?" Papa's voice sounded wrenched from him. "It's a sin, Lily, a sin against nature." His words ended with a sob.

The air felt heavy, the way it had when the baby died. Mama had been betrayed, but not by Cousin Cora. I'd wanted to protect her, but it was me she'd needed protection from.

The last I saw of Cousin Cora she was walking up the dirt road, back straight, carrying her carpetbag and hatbox in either hand.

Nothing was ever the same again. We never had cherry soup. Mama's sunshine nature faded like the lilacs. Papa worked later and later in town, sometimes staying over at Mrs. Hepwhite's boardinghouse. He never again called Mama Lil.

As for me, my detecting days were done. I swapped my magnifying glass to Red Beaudine for a pea-shooter and three immies I didn't really want. The rest of the Hawkshaw Junior Detective Kit I burned behind the woodshed. As the flames curled around the scowling face of Hawkshaw the Detective on the cardboard cover of the box, I decided hell was the right place for anyone who caused that much pain.

A JURY OF HER PEERS

Susan Glaspell

WHEN MARTHA HALE opened the storm-door and got a cut of the
north wind, she ran back for her big woolen scarf. As she hurriedly wound
that round her head her eye made a scandalized sweep of her kitchen. It
was no ordinary thing that called her away—it was probably further from
ordinary than anything that had ever happened in Dickson County. But
what her eye took in was that her kitchen was in no shape for leaving: her
bread all ready for mixing, half the flour sifted and half unsifted.

She hated to see things half done; but she had been at that when the
team from town stopped to get Mr. Hale, and then the sheriff came running
in to say his wife wished Mrs. Hale would come too—adding, with a grin,
that he guessed she was getting scarey and wanted another woman along.
So she had dropped everything right where it was.

"Martha!" now came her husband's impatient voice. "Don't keep folks
waiting out here in the cold."

She again opened the storm-door, and this time joined the three men
and the one woman waiting for her in the big two-seated buggy.

After she had the robes tucked around her she took another look at the
woman who sat beside her on the back seat. She had met Mrs. Peters the
year before at the county fair, and the thing she remembered about her
was that she didn't seem like a sheriff's wife. She was small and thin and

didn't have a strong voice. Mrs. Gorman, sheriff's wife before Gorman went out and Peters came in, had a voice that somehow seemed to be backing up the law with every word. But if Mrs. Peters didn't look like a sheriff's wife, Peters made it up in looking like a sheriff. He was to a dot the kind of man who could get himself elected sheriff—a heavy man with a big voice, who was particularly genial with the law-abiding, as if to make it plain that he knew the difference between criminals and non-criminals. And right there it came into Mrs. Hale's mind, with a stab, that this man who was so pleasant and lively with all of them was going to the Wrights' now as a sheriff.

"The country's not very pleasant this time of year," Mrs. Peters at last ventured, as if she felt they ought to be talking as well as the men.

Mrs. Hale scarcely finished her reply, for they had gone up a little hill and could see the Wright place now, and seeing it did not make her feel like talking. It looked very lonesome this cold March morning. It had always been a lonesome-looking place. It was down in a hollow, and the poplar trees around it were lonesome-looking trees. The men were looking at it and talking about what had happened. The county attorney was bending to one side of the buggy, and kept looking steadily at the place as they drew up to it.

"I'm glad you came with me," Mrs. Peters said nervously, as the two women were about to follow the men in through the kitchen door.

Even after she had her foot on the door-step, her hand on the knob, Martha Hale had a moment of feeling she could not cross the threshold. And the reason it seemed she couldn't cross it now was simply because she hadn't crossed it before. Time and time again it had been in her mind, "I ought to go over and see Minnie Foster"—she still thought of her as Minnie Foster, though for twenty years she had been Mrs. Wright. And then there was always something to do and Minnie Foster would go from her mind. But *now* she could come.

The men went over to the stove. The women stood close together by the door. Young Henderson, the county attorney, turned around and said, "Come up to the fire, ladies."

Mrs. Peters took a step forward, then stopped. "I'm not—cold," she said.

And so the two women stood by the door, at first not even so much as looking around the kitchen.

The men talked for a minute about what a good thing it was the sheriff had sent his deputy out that morning to make a fire for them, and then Sheriff Peters stepped back from the stove, unbuttoned his outer coat, and leaned his hands on the kitchen table in a way that seemed to mark the beginning of official business. "Now, Mr. Hale," he said in a sort of semi-official voice, "before we move things about, you tell Mr. Henderson just what it was you saw when you came here yesterday morning."

The county attorney was looking around the kitchen.

"By the way," he said, "has anything been moved?" He turned to the sheriff. "Are things just as you left them yesterday?"

Peters looked from cupboard to sink; from that to a small worn rocker a little to one side of the kitchen table.

"It's just the same."

"Somebody should have been left here yesterday," said the county attorney.

"Oh—yesterday," returned the sheriff, with a little gesture as of yesterday having been more than he could bear to think of. "When I had to send Frank to Morris Center for that man who went crazy—let me tell you, I had my hands full *yesterday*. I knew you could get back from Omaha by to-day, George, and as long as I went over everything here myself—"

"Well, Mr. Hale," said the county attorney, in a way of letting what was past and gone go, "tell just what happened when you came here yesterday morning."

Mrs. Hale, still leaning against the door, had that sinking feeling of the mother whose child is about to speak a piece. Lewis often wandered along and got things mixed up in a story. She hoped he would tell this straight and plain, and not say unnecessary things that would just make things harder for Minnie Foster. He didn't begin at once, and she noticed that he looked queer—as if standing in that kitchen and having to tell what he had seen there yesterday morning made him almost sick.

"Yes, Mr. Hale?" the county attorney reminded.

"Harry and I had started to town with a load of potatoes," Mrs. Hale's husband began.

Harry was Mrs. Hale's oldest boy. He wasn't with them now, for the very good reason that those potatoes never got to town yesterday and he was taking them this morning, so he hadn't been home when the sheriff stopped to say he wanted Mr. Hale to come over to the Wright place and tell the county attorney his story there, where he could point it all out. With all Mrs. Hale's other emotions came the fear that maybe Harry wasn't dressed warm enough—they hadn't any of them realized how that north wind did bite.

"We come along this road," Hale was going on, with a motion of his hand to the road over which they had just come, "and as we got in sight of the house I says to Harry, 'I'm goin' to see if I can't get John Wright to take a telephone.' You see," he explained to Henderson, "unless I can get somebody to go in with me they won't come out this branch road except for a price *I* can't pay. I'd spoke to Wright about it once before; but he put me off, saying folks talked too much anyway, and all he asked was peace and quiet—guess you know about how much he talked himself. But I thought maybe if I went to the house and talked about it before his wife, and said all the women-folks liked the telephones, and that in this lonesome stretch of road it would be a good thing—well, I said to Harry that that was what I was going to say—though I said at the same time that I didn't know as what his wife wanted made much difference to John—"

Now, there he was!—saying things he didn't need to say. Mrs. Hale tried to catch her husband's eye, but fortunately the county attorney interrupted with:

"Let's talk about that a little later, Mr. Hale. I do want to talk about that, but I'm anxious now to get along to just what happened when you got here."

When he began this time, it was very deliberately and carefully:

"I didn't see or hear anything. I knocked at the door. And still it was all quiet inside. I knew they must be up—it was past eight o'clock. So I knocked again, louder, and I thought I heard somebody say 'Come in.' I wasn't sure—I'm not sure yet. But I opened the door—this door," jerking a hand toward the door by which the two women stood, "and there, in that rocker"—pointing to it—"sat Mrs. Wright."

Every one in the kitchen looked at the rocker. It came into Mrs. Hale's mind that that rocker didn't look in the least like Minnie Foster—the Minnie Foster of twenty years before. It was a dingy red, with wooden rungs up the back, and the middle rung was gone, and the chair sagged to one side.

"How did she—look?" the county attorney was inquiring.

"Well," said Hale, "she looked—queer."

"How do you mean—queer?"

As he asked it he took out a note-book and pencil. Mrs. Hale did not like the sight of that pencil. She kept her eye fixed on her husband, as if to keep him from saying unnecessary things that would go into that note-book and make trouble.

Hale did speak guardedly, as if the pencil had affected him too.

"Well, as if she didn't know what she was going to do next. And kind of—done up."

"How did she seem to feel about your coming?"

"Why, I don't think she minded—one way or other. She didn't pay much attention. I said, 'Ho' do, Mrs. Wright? It's cold, ain't it?' And she said, 'Is it?'—and went on pleatin' at her apron.

"Well, I was surprised. She didn't ask me to come up to the stove, or to sit down, but just set there, not even lookin' at me. And so I said: 'I want to see John.'

"And then she—laughed. I guess you would call it a laugh.

"I thought of Harry and the team outside, so I said, a little sharp, 'Can I see John?' 'No,' says she—kind of dull like. 'Ain't he home?' says I. Then she looked at me. 'Yes,' says she, 'he's home.' 'Then why can't I see him?' I asked her, out of patience with her now. ' 'Cause he's dead,' says she, just as quiet and dull—and fell to pleatin' her apron. 'Dead?' says I, like you do when you can't take in what you've heard.

"She just nodded her head, not getting a bit excited, but rockin' back and forth.

" 'Why—where is he?' says I, not knowing *what* to say.

"She just pointed upstairs—like this"—pointing to the room above.

"I got up, with the idea of going up there myself. By this time I—didn't know what to do. I walked from there to here; then I says: 'Why, what did he die of?'

" 'He died of a rope around his neck,' says she; and just went on pleatin' at her apron."

Hale stopped speaking, and stood staring at the rocker, as if he were still seeing the woman who had sat there the morning before. Nobody spoke; it was as if every one were seeing the woman who had sat there the morning before.

"And what did you do then?" the county attorney at last broke the silence.

"I went out and called Harry. I thought I might—need help. I got Harry in, and we went upstairs." His voice fell almost to a whisper. "There he was— lying over the—"

"I think I'd rather have you go into that upstairs," the county attorney interrupted, "where you can point it all out. Just go on now with the rest of the story."

"Well, my first thought was to get that rope off. It looked—" He stopped, his face twitching.

"But Harry, he went up to him, and he said, 'No, he's dead all right, and we'd better not touch anything.' So we went downstairs.

"She was still sitting that same way. 'Has anybody been notified?' I asked. 'No,' says she, unconcerned.

" 'Who did this, Mrs. Wright?' said Harry. He said it businesslike, and she stopped pleatin' at her apron. 'I don't know,' she says. 'You don't *know?*' says Harry. 'Weren't you sleepin' in the bed with him?' 'Yes,' says she, 'but I was on the inside.' 'Somebody slipped a rope round his neck and strangled him, and you didn't wake up?' says Harry. 'I didn't wake up,' she said after him.

"We may have looked as if we didn't see how that could be, for after a minute she said, 'I sleep sound.'"

"Harry was going to ask her more questions, but I said maybe that weren't our business; maybe we ought to let her tell her story first to the coroner or the sheriff. So Harry went fast as he could over to High Road—the Rivers' place, where there's a telephone."

"And what did she do when she knew you had gone for the coroner?" The attorney got his pencil in his hand all ready for writing.

"She moved from that chair to this one over here"—Hale pointed to a small chair in the corner—"and just sat there with her hands held together and looking down. I got a feeling that I ought to make some conversation, so I said I had come in to see if John wanted to put in a telephone; and at that she started to laugh, and then she stopped and looked at me—scared."

At the sound of a moving pencil the man who was telling the story looked up.

"I dunno—maybe it wasn't scared," he hastened; "I wouldn't like to say it was. Soon Harry got back, and then Dr. Lloyd came, and you, Mr. Peters, and so I guess that's all I know that you don't."

· · ·

HE said that last with relief, and moved a little, as if relaxing. Every one moved a little. The county attorney walked toward the stair door.

"I guess we'll go upstairs first—then out to the barn and around there."

He paused and looked around the kitchen.

"You're convinced there was nothing important here?" he asked the sheriff. "Nothing that would—point to any motive?"

The sheriff too looked all around, as if to re-convince himself.

"Nothing here but kitchen things," he said, with a little laugh for the insignificance of kitchen things.

The county attorney was looking at the cupboard—a peculiar, ungainly structure, half closet and half cupboard, the upper part of it being built in the wall, and the lower part just the old-fashioned kitchen cupboard. As if its queerness attracted him, he got a chair and opened the upper part and looked in. After a moment he drew his hand away sticky.

"Here's a nice mess," he said resentfully.

The two women had drawn nearer, and now the sheriff's wife spoke.

"Oh—her fruit," she said, looking to Mrs. Hale for sympathetic understanding. She turned back to the county attorney and explained: "She worried about that when it turned so cold last night. She said the fire would go out and her jars might burst."

Mrs. Peters's husband broke into a laugh.

"Well, can you beat the woman! Held for murder, and worrying about her preserves!"

The young attorney set his lips.

"I guess before we're through with her she may have something more serious than preserves to worry about."

"Oh, well," said Mrs. Hale's husband, with good-natured superiority, "women are used to worrying over trifles."

The two women moved a little closer together. Neither of them spoke. The county attorney seemed suddenly to remember his manners—and think of his future.

"And yet," said he, with the gallantry of a young politician, "for all their worries, what would we do without the ladies?"

The women did not speak, did not unbend. He went to the sink and began washing his hands. He turned to wipe them on the roller towel—whirled it for a cleaner place.

"Dirty towels! Not much of a housekeeper, would you say, ladies?"

He kicked his foot against some dirty pans under the sink.

"There's a great deal of work to be done on a farm," said Mrs. Hale stiffly.

"To be sure. And yet"—with a little bow to her—"I know there are some Dickson County farm-houses that do not have such roller towels." He gave it a pull to expose its full length again.

"Those towels get dirty awful quick. Men's hands aren't always as clean as they might be."

"Ah, loyal to your sex, I see," he laughed. He stopped and gave her a keen look. "But you and Mrs. Wright were neighbors. I suppose you were friends, too."

Martha Hale shook her head.

"I've seen little enough of her of late years. I've not been in this house—it's more than a year."

"And why was that? You didn't like her?"

"I liked her well enough," she replied with spirit. "Farmers' wives have their hands full, Mr. Henderson. And then"—She looked around the kitchen.

"Yes?" he encouraged.

"It never seemed a very cheerful place," said she, more to herself than to him.

"No," he agreed; "I don't think any one could call it cheerful. I shouldn't say she had the home-making instinct."

"Well, I don't know as Wright had, either," she muttered.

"You mean they didn't get on very well?" he was quick to ask.

"No; I don't mean anything," she answered, with decision. As she turned a little away from him, she added: "But I don't think a place would be any the cheerfuler for John Wright's bein' in it."

"I'd like to talk to you about that a little later, Mrs. Hale," he said. "I'm anxious to get the lay of things upstairs now."

He moved toward the stair door, followed by the two men.

"I suppose anything Mrs. Peters does'll be all right?" the sheriff inquired. "She was to take in some clothes for her, you know—and a few little things. We left in such a hurry yesterday."

The county attorney looked at the two women whom they were leaving alone there among the kitchen things.

"Yes—Mrs. Peters," he said, his glance resting on the woman who was not Mrs. Peters, the big farmer woman who stood behind the sheriff's wife. "Of course Mrs. Peters is one of us," he said, in a manner of entrusting responsibility. "And keep your eye out, Mrs. Peters, for anything that might be of use. No telling; you women might come upon a clue to the motive—and that's the thing we need."

Mr. Hale rubbed his face after the fashion of a show man getting ready for a pleasantry.

"But would the women know a clue if they did come upon it?" he said; and, having delivered himself of this, he followed the others through the stair door.

The women stood motionless and silent, listening to the footsteps, first upon the stairs, then in the room above them.

Then, as if releasing herself from something strange, Mrs. Hale began to arrange the dirty pans under the sink, which the county attorney's disdainful push of the foot had deranged.

"I'd hate to have men comin' into my kitchen," she said testily—"snoopin' around and criticizin'."

"Of course it's no more than their duty," said the sheriff's wife, in her manner of timid acquiescence.

"Duty's all right," replied Mrs. Hale bluffly; "but I guess that deputy sheriff that come out to make the fire might have got a little of this on." She gave the roller towel a pull. "Wish I'd thought of that sooner! Seems mean to talk about her for not having things slicked up when she had to come away in such a hurry."

She looked around the kitchen. Certainly it was not "slicked up." Her eye was held by a bucket of sugar on a low shelf. The cover was off the wooden bucket, and beside it was a paper bag—half full.

Mrs. Hale moved toward it.

"She was putting this in here," she said to herself—slowly.

She thought of the flour in her kitchen at home—half sifted, half not sifted. She had been interrupted, and had left things half done. What had interrupted Minnie Foster? Why had that work been left half done? She made a move as if to finish it—unfinished things always bothered her—and then she glanced around and saw that Mrs. Peters was watching her—and she didn't want Mrs. Peters to get that feeling she had got of work begun and then—for some reason—not finished.

"It's a shame about her fruit," she said, and walked toward the cupboard that the county attorney had opened, and got on the chair, murmuring: "I wonder if it's all gone."

It was a sorry enough looking sight, but "Here's one that's all right," she said at last. She held it toward the light. "This is cherries, too." She looked again. "I declare I believe that's the only one."

With a sigh, she got down from the chair, went to the sink, and wiped off the bottle.

"She'll feel awful bad, after all her hard work in the hot weather. I remember the afternoon I put up my cherries last summer."

She set the bottle on the table, and, with another sigh, started to sit down in the rocker. But she did not sit down. Something kept her from sitting down in that chair. She straightened—stepped back, and, half turned away, stood looking at it, seeing the woman who sat there "pleatin' at her apron."

The thin voice of the sheriff's wife broke in upon her: "I must be getting those things from the front room closet." She opened the door into the other room, started in, stepped back. "You coming with me, Mrs. Hale?" she asked nervously. "You—you could help me get them."

They were soon back—the stark coldness of that shut-up room was not a thing to linger in.

"My!" said Mrs. Peters, dropping the things on the table and hurrying to the stove.

Mrs. Hale stood examining the clothes the woman who was being detained in town had said she wanted.

"Wright was close!" she exclaimed, holding up a shabby black skirt that bore the marks of much making over. "I think maybe that's why she kept so much to herself. I s'pose she felt she couldn't do her part; and then, you don't enjoy things when you feel shabby. She used to wear pretty clothes and be lively—when she was Minnie Foster, one of the town girls, singing in the choir. But that—oh, that was twenty years ago."

With a carefulness in which there was something tender, she folded the shabby clothes and piled them at one corner of the table. She looked at

Mrs. Peters, and there was something in the other woman's look that irritated her.

"She don't care," she said to herself. "Much difference it makes to her whether Minnie Foster had pretty clothes when she was a girl."

Then she looked again, and she wasn't so sure; in fact, she hadn't at any time been perfectly sure about Mrs. Peters. She had that shrinking manner, and yet her eyes looked as if they could see a long way into things.

"This all you was to take in?" asked Mrs. Hale.

"No," said the sheriff's wife; "she said she wanted an apron. Funny thing to want," she ventured in her nervous little way, "for there's not much to get you dirty in jail, goodness knows. But I suppose just to make her feel more natural. If you're used to wearing an apron—. She said they were in the bottom drawer of this cupboard. Yes—here they are. And then her little shawl that always hung on the stair door."

She took the small gray shawl from behind the door leading upstairs, and stood a minute looking at it.

Suddenly Mrs. Hale took a quick step toward the other woman.

"Mrs. Peters!"

"Yes, Mrs. Hale?"

"Do you think she—did it?"

A frightened look blurred the other things in Mrs. Peters's eyes.

"Oh, I don't know," she said, in a voice that seemed to shrink away from the subject.

"Well, I don't think she did," affirmed Mrs. Hale stoutly. "Asking for an apron, and her little shawl. Worryin' about her fruit."

"Mr. Peters says—" Footsteps were heard in the room above; she stopped, looked up, then went on in a lowered voice: "Mr. Peters says—it looks bad for her. Mr. Henderson is awful sarcastic in a speech, and he's going to make fun of her saying she didn't—wake up."

For a moment Mrs. Hale had no answer. Then, "Well, I guess John Wright didn't wake up—when they was slippin' that rope under his neck," she muttered.

"No, it's *strange*," breathed Mrs. Peters. "They think it was such a—funny way to kill a man."

She began to laugh; at the sound of the laugh, abruptly stopped.

"That's just what Mr. Hale said," said Mrs. Hale, in a resolutely natural voice. "There was a gun in the house. He says that's what he can't understand."

"Mr. Henderson said, coming out, that what was needed for the case was a motive. Something to show anger—or sudden feeling."

"Well, I don't see any signs of anger around here," said Mrs. Hale. "I don't—"

She stopped. It was as if her mind tripped on something. Her eye was caught by a dish-towel in the middle of the kitchen table. Slowly she moved toward the table. One half of it was wiped clean, the other half messy. Her eyes made a slow, almost unwilling turn to the bucket of sugar and the half empty bag beside it. Things begun—and not finished.

After a moment she stepped back, and said, in that manner of releasing herself:

"Wonder how they're finding things upstairs? I hope she had it a little more red up up there. You know,"—she paused, and feeling gathered—"it seems kind of *sneaking*; locking her up in town and coming out here to get her own house to turn against her!"

"But, Mrs. Hale," said the sheriff's wife, "the law is the law."

"I s'pose 'tis," answered Mrs. Hale shortly.

She turned to the stove, saying something about that fire not being much to brag of. She worked with it a minute, and when she straightened up she said aggressively:

"The law is the law—and a bad stove is a bad stove. How'd you like to cook on this?"—pointing with the poker to the broken lining. She opened the oven door and started to express her opinion of the oven; but she was swept into her own thoughts, thinking of what it would mean, year after year, to have that stove to wrestle with. The thought of Minnie Foster trying to bake in that oven—and the thought of her never going over to see Minnie Foster—

She was startled by hearing Mrs. Peters say: "A person gets discouraged—and loses heart."

The sheriff's wife had looked from the stove to the sink—to the pail of water which had been carried in from outside. The two women stood there silent, above them the footsteps of the men who were looking for evidence against the woman who had worked in that kitchen. That look of seeing into things, of seeing through a thing to something else, was in the eyes of the sheriff's wife now. When Mrs. Hale next spoke to her, it was gently:

"Better loosen up your things, Mrs. Peters. We'll not feel them when we go out."

Mrs. Peters went to the back of the room to hang up the fur tippet she was wearing. A moment later she exclaimed, "Why, she was piecing a quilt," and held up a large sewing basket piled high with quilt pieces.

Mrs. Hale spread some of the blocks on the table.

"It's log-cabin pattern," she said, putting several of them together. "Pretty, isn't it?"

They were so engaged with the quilt that they did not hear the footsteps on the stairs. Just as the stair door opened Mrs. Hale was saying:

"Do you suppose she was going to quilt it or just knot it?"

The sheriff threw up his hands.

"They wonder whether she was going to quilt it or just knot it!"

There was a laugh for the ways of women, a warming of hands over the stove, and then the county attorney said briskly:

"Well, let's go right out to the barn and get that cleared up."

"I don't see as there's anything so strange," Mrs. Hale said resentfully, after the outside door had closed on the three men—"our taking up our time with little things while we're waiting for them to get the evidence. I don't see as it's anything to laugh about."

"Of course they've got awful important things on their minds," said the sheriff's wife apologetically.

They returned to an inspection of the blocks for the quilt. Mrs. Hale was looking at the fine, even sewing, and preoccupied with thoughts of the woman who had done that sewing, when she heard the sheriff's wife say, in a queer tone:

"Why, look at this one."

She turned to take the block held out to her.

"The sewing," said Mrs. Peters, in a troubled way. "All the rest of them have been so nice and even—but—this one. Why, it looks as if she didn't know what she was about!"

Their eyes met—something flashed to life, passed between them; then, as if with an effort, they seemed to pull away from each other. A moment Mrs. Hale sat there, her hands folded over that sewing which was so unlike all the rest of the sewing. Then she had pulled a knot and drawn the threads.

"Oh, what are you doing, Mrs. Hale?" asked the sheriff's wife, startled.

"Just pulling out a stitch or two that's not sewed very good," said Mrs. Hale mildly.

"I don't think we ought to touch things," Mrs. Peters said, a little helplessly.

"I'll just finish up this end," answered Mrs. Hale, still in that mild, matter-of-fact fashion.

She threaded a needle and started to replace bad sewing with good. For a little while she sewed in silence. Then, in that thin, timid voice, she heard:

"Mrs. Hale!"

"Yes, Mrs. Peters?"

"What do you suppose she was so—nervous about?"

"Oh, *I* don't know," said Mrs. Hale, as if dismissing a thing not important enough to spend much time on. "I don't know as she was—nervous. I sew awful queer sometimes when I'm just tired."

She cut a thread, and out of the corner of her eye looked up at Mrs. Peters. The small, lean face of the sheriff's wife seemed to have tightened up. Her eyes had that look of peering into something. But the next moment she moved, and said in her thin, indecisive way:

"Well, I must get those clothes wrapped. They may be through sooner than we think. I wonder where I could find a piece of paper—and string."

"In that cupboard, maybe," suggested Mrs. Hale, after a glance around.

• • •

ONE piece of the crazy sewing remained unripped. Mrs. Peters's back turned, Martha Hale now scrutinized that piece, compared it with the dainty, accurate sewing of the other blocks. The difference was startling. Holding this block made her feel queer, as if the distracted thoughts of the woman who had perhaps turned to it to try and quiet herself were communicating themselves to her.

Mrs. Peters's voice roused her.

"Here's a bird-cage," she said. "Did she have a bird, Mrs. Hale?"

"Why, I don't know whether she did or not." She turned to look at the cage Mrs. Peters was holding up. "I've not been here in so long." She sighed. "There was a man round last year selling canaries cheap—but I don't know as she took one. Maybe she did. She used to sing real pretty herself."

Mrs. Peters looked around the kitchen.

"Seems kind of funny to think of a bird here." She half laughed—an attempt to put up a barrier. "But she must have had one—or why would she have a cage? I wonder what happened to it."

"I suppose maybe the cat got it," suggested Mrs. Hale, resuming her sewing.

"No, she didn't have a cat. She's got that feeling some people have about cats—being afraid of them. When they brought her to our house yesterday, my cat got in the room, and she was real upset and asked me to take it out."

"My sister Bessie was like that," laughed Mrs. Hale.

The sheriff's wife did not reply. The silence made Mrs. Hale turn around. Mrs. Peters was examining the bird-cage.

"Look at this door," she said slowly "It's broke. One hinge has been pulled apart."

Mrs. Hale came nearer.

"Looks as if some one must have been—rough with it."

Again their eyes met—startled, questioning, apprehensive. For a moment neither spoke nor stirred. Then Mrs. Hale, turning away, said brusquely:

"If they're going to find any evidence, I wish they'd be about it. I don't like this place."

"But I'm awful glad you came with me, Mrs. Hale." Mrs. Peters put the bird-cage on the table and sat down. "It would be lonesome for me—sitting here alone."

"Yes, it would, wouldn't it?" agreed Mrs. Hale, a certain determined naturalness in her voice. She picked up the sewing, but now it dropped in her lap, and she murmured in a different voice: "But I tell you what I *do* wish, Mrs. Peters. I wish I had come over sometimes when she was here. I wish—I had."

"But of course you were awful busy, Mrs. Hale. Your house—and your children."

"I could've come," retorted Mrs. Hale shortly. "I stayed away because it weren't cheerful—and that's why I ought to have come. I"—she looked around—"I've never liked this place. Maybe because it's down in a hollow and you don't see the road. I don't know what it is, but it's a lonesome place, and always was. I wish I had come over to see Minnie Foster sometimes. I can see now—" She did not put it into words.

"Well, you mustn't reproach yourself," counseled Mrs. Peters. "Somehow, we just don't see how it is with other folks till—something comes up."

"Not having children makes less work," mused Mrs. Hale, after a silence, "but it makes a quiet house—and Wright out to work all day—and no company when he did come in. Did you know John Wright, Mrs. Peters?"

"Not to know him. I've seen him in town. They say he was a good man."

"Yes—good," conceded John Wright's neighbor grimly. "He didn't drink, and kept his word as well as most, I guess, and paid his debts. But he was a hard man, Mrs. Peters. Just to pass the time of day with him—" She stopped, shivered a little. "Like a raw wind that gets to the bone." Her eye fell upon the cage on the table before her, and she added, almost bitterly: "I should think she would've wanted a bird!"

Suddenly she leaned forward, looking intently at the cage. "But what do you s'pose went wrong with it?"

"I don't know," returned Mrs. Peters; "unless it got sick and died."

But after she said it she reached over and swung the broken door. Both women watched it as if somehow held by it.

"You didn't know—her?" Mrs. Hale asked, a gentler note in her voice.

"Not till they brought her yesterday," said the sheriff's wife.

"She—come to think of it, she was kind of like a bird herself. Real sweet and pretty, but kind of timid and—fluttery. How—she—did—change."

That held her for a long time. Finally, as if struck with a happy thought and relieved to get back to everyday things, she exclaimed:

"Tell you what, Mrs. Peters, why don't you take the quilt in with you? It might take up her mind."

"Why, I think that's a real nice idea, Mrs. Hale," agreed the sheriff's wife, as if she too were glad to come into the atmosphere of a simple kindness. "There couldn't possibly be any objection to that, could there? Now, just what will I take? I wonder if her patches are in here—and her things."

They turned to the sewing basket.

"Here's some red," said Mrs. Hale, bringing out a roll of cloth. Underneath that was a box. "Here, maybe her scissors are in here—and her things." She held it up. "What a pretty box! I'll warrant that was something she had a long time ago—when she was a girl."

She held it in her hand a moment; then, with a little sigh, opened it.

Instantly her hand went to her nose.

"Why—!"

Mrs. Peters drew nearer—then turned away.

"There's something wrapped up in this piece of silk," faltered Mrs. Hale.

"This isn't her scissors," said Mrs. Peters in a shrinking voice.

Her hand not steady, Mrs. Hale raised the piece of silk. "Oh, Mrs. Peters!"she cried. "It's—"

Mrs. Peters bent closer.

"It's the bird," she whispered.

"But, Mrs. Peters!" cried Mrs. Hale. "*Look* at it! Its neck—look at its neck! It's all—other side *to.*"

She held the box away from her.

The sheriff's wife again bent closer.

"Somebody wrung its neck," said she, in a voice that was slow and deep.

And then again the eyes of the two women met—this time clung together in a look of dawning comprehension, of growing horror. Mrs. Peters looked from the dead bird to the broken door of the cage. Again their eyes met. And just then there was a sound at the outside door.

Mrs. Hale slipped the box under the quilt pieces in the basket, and sank into the chair before it. Mrs. Peters stood holding to the table. The county attorney and the sheriff came in from outside.

"Well, ladies," said the county attorney, as one turning from serious things to little pleasantries, "have you decided whether she was going to quilt it or knot it?"

"We think," began the sheriff's wife in a flurried voice, "that she was going to—knot it."

He was too preoccupied to notice the change that came in her voice on that last.

"Well, that's very interesting, I'm sure," he said tolerantly. He caught sight of the bird-cage. "Has the bird flown?"

"We think the cat got it," said Mrs. Hale in a voice curiously even.

He was walking up and down, as if thinking something out.

"Is there a cat?" he asked absently.

Mrs. Hale shot a look up at the sheriff's wife.

"Well, not *now*," said Mrs. Peters. "They're superstitious, you know; they leave."

She sank into her chair.

The county attorney did not heed her. "No sign at all of any one having come in from the outside," he said to Peters, in the manner of continuing an interrupted conversation. "Their own rope. Now let's go upstairs again and go over it, piece by piece. It would have to have been some one who knew just the—"

The stair door closed behind them and their voices were lost.

The two women sat motionless, not looking at each other, but as if peering into something and at the same time holding back. When they spoke now it was as if they were afraid of what they were saying, but as if they could not help saying it.

"She liked the bird," said Martha Hale, low and slowly. "She was going to bury it in that pretty box."

"When I was a girl," said Mrs. Peters, under her breath, "my kitten—there was a boy took a hatchet, and before my eyes—before I could get there—" She covered her face an instant. "If they hadn't held me back I would have"—she caught herself, looked upstairs where footsteps were heard, and finished weakly—"hurt him."

Then they sat without speaking or moving.

"I wonder how it would seem," Mrs. Hale at last began, as if feeling her way over strange ground—"never to have had any children around?" Her eyes made a slow sweep of the kitchen, as if seeing what that kitchen had meant through all the years. "No, Wright wouldn't like the bird," she said after that—"a thing that sang. She used to sing. He killed that too." Her voice tightened.

Mrs. Peters moved uneasily.

"Of course we don't know who killed the bird."

"I knew John Wright," was Mrs. Hale's answer.

"It was an awful thing was done in this house that night, Mrs. Hale," said the sheriff's wife. "Killing a man while he slept—slipping a thing round his neck that choked the life out of him."

Mrs. Hale's hand went out to the bird-cage.

"His neck. Choked the life out of him."

"We don't *know* who killed him," whispered Mrs. Peters wildly. "We don't *know*."

Mrs. Hale had not moved. "If there had been years and years of—nothing, then a bird to sing to you, it would be awful—still—after the bird was still."

It was as if something within her not herself had spoken, and it found in Mrs. Peters something she did not know as herself.

"I know what stillness is," she said, in a queer, monotonous voice. "When we homesteaded in Dakota, and my first baby died—after he was two years old—and me with no other then—"

Mrs. Hale stirred.

"How soon do you suppose they'll be through looking for evidence?"

"I know what stillness is," repeated Mrs. Peters, in just that same way. Then she too pulled back. "The law has got to punish crime, Mrs. Hale," she said in her tight little way.

"I wish you'd seen Minnie Foster," was the answer, "when she wore a white dress with blue ribbons, and stood up there in the choir and sang."

The picture of that girl, the fact that she had lived neighbor to that girl for twenty years, and had let her die for lack of life, was suddenly more than she could bear.

"Oh, I *wish* I'd come over here once in a while!" she cried. "That was a crime! That was a crime! Who's going to punish that?"

"We mustn't take on," said Mrs. Peters, with a frightened look toward the stairs.

"I might 'a' *known* she needed help! I tell you, it's *queer*, Mrs. Peters. We live close together, and we live far apart. We all go through the same things—it's all just a different kind of the same thing! If it weren't—why do you and I *understand*? Why do we *know*—what we know this minute?"

She dashed her hand across her eyes. Then, seeing the jar of fruit on the table, she reached for it and choked out:

"If I was you I wouldn't *tell* her her fruit was gone! Tell her it *ain't*. Tell her it's all right—all of it. Here—take this in to prove it to her! She—she may never know whether it was broke or not."

She turned away.

Mrs. Peters reached out for the bottle of fruit as if she were glad to take it—as if touching a familiar thing, having something to do, could keep her from something else. She got up, looked about for something to wrap the fruit in, took a petticoat from the pile of clothes she had brought from the front room, and nervously started winding that round the bottle.

"My!" she began, in a high, false voice, "it's a good thing the men couldn't hear us! Getting all stirred up over a little thing like a—dead canary." She hurried over that. "As if that could have anything to do with—with—My, wouldn't they *laugh?*"

Footsteps were heard on the stairs.

"Maybe they would," muttered Mrs. Hale—"maybe they wouldn't."

"No, Peters," said the county attorney incisively; "it's all perfectly clear, except the reason for doing it. But you know juries when it comes to women. If there was some definite thing—something to show. Something to make a story about. A thing that would connect up with this clumsy way of doing it."

In a covert way Mrs. Hale looked at Mrs. Peters. Mrs. Peters was looking at her. Quickly they looked away from each other. The outer door opened and Mr. Hale came in.

"I've got the team round now," he said. "Pretty cold out there."

"I'm going to stay here awhile by myself," the county attorney suddenly announced. "You can send Frank out for me, can't you?" he asked the sheriff. "I want to go over everything. I'm not satisfied we can't do better."

Again, for one brief moment, the two women's eyes found one another.

The sheriff came up to the table.

"Did you want to see what Mrs. Peters was going to take in?"

The county attorney picked up the apron. He laughed.

"Oh, I guess they're not very dangerous things the ladies have picked out."

Mrs. Hale's hand was on the sewing basket in which the box was concealed. She felt that she ought to take her hand off the basket. She did not seem able to. He picked up one of the quilt blocks which she had piled on to cover the box. Her eyes felt like fire. She had a feeling that if he took up the basket she would snatch it from him.

But he did not take it up. With another little laugh, he turned away, saying:

"No; Mrs. Peters doesn't need supervising. For that matter, a sheriff's wife is married to the law. Ever think of it that way, Mrs. Peters?"

Mrs. Peters was standing beside the table. Mrs. Hale shot a look up at her; but she could not see her face. Mrs. Peters had turned away. When she spoke, her voice was muffled.

"Not—just that way," she said.

"Married to the law!" chuckled Mrs. Peters's husband. He moved toward the door into the front room, and said to the county attorney:

"I just want you to come in here a minute, George. We ought to take a look at these windows."

"Oh—windows," said the county attorney scoffingly.

"We'll be right out, Mr. Hale," said the sheriff to the farmer, who was still waiting by the door.

Hale went to look after the horses. The sheriff followed the county attorney into the other room. Again—for one moment—the two women were alone in that kitchen.

Martha Hale sprang up, her hands tight together, looking at that other woman, with whom it rested. At first she could not see her eyes, for the sheriff's wife had not turned back since she turned away at that suggestion of being married to the law. But now Mrs. Hale made her turn back. Her eyes made her turn back. Slowly, unwillingly, Mrs. Peters turned her head until her eyes met the eyes of the other woman. There was a moment when they held each other in a steady, burning look in which there was no evasion nor flinching. Then Martha Hale's eyes pointed the way to the basket in which was hidden the thing that would make certain the conviction of the other woman—that woman who was not there and yet who had been there with them all through the hour.

For a moment Mrs. Peters did not move. And then she did it. With a rush forward, she threw back the quilt pieces, got the box, tried to put it in her handbag. It was too big. Desperately she opened it, started to take the bird out. But there she broke—she could not touch the bird. She stood helpless, foolish.

There was a sound of a knob turning in the inner door. Martha Hale snatched the box from the sheriff's wife, and got it in the pocket of her big coat just as the sheriff and the county attorney came back into the kitchen.

"Well, Henry," said the county attorney facetiously, "at least we found out that she was not going to quilt it. She was going to—what is it you call it, ladies?"

Mrs. Hale's hand was against the pocket of her coat.

"We call it—knot it, Mr. Henderson."

LAWRENCE BLOCK

Fredric Brown was a purely wonderful writer, producing a substantial body of distinguished work in two genres, crime and science fiction. Reading his work, I've always been struck not only by the deceptive ease of his writing style and the startling originality of his ideas, but by the sense of the human being behind the work. It is one of my regrets that I never got to meet him.

When I began writing crime stories in the late fifties, Brown was one of the writers I devoured. I read everything I could get my hands on and found something to like in everything I read. One time, at the end of a long week, I sat down with one of his novels and a bottle of Jim Beam. Whenever Brown's narrator took a drink, I joined him. Warning: Don't try this at home.

"Cry Silence" is one of the stories I read back then, over forty years ago. I never read it again, but I damn well remembered it, and managed to hunt it down in a friend's library the other day. There aren't many stories I recall so vividly after such a lengthy passage of time, but there are a few, and several of them had Fredric Brown's name on them.

• • •

"Sometimes They Bite" was written in 1975, during a month I spent at Rodanthe, on North Carolina's Outer Banks. There was a long pier there, and you could go out on it with a pole and fish, and that's what I did. I lived pretty much exclusively on what I hauled out of the ocean, and one day I wrote this story. Henry Morrison, my agent at the time, called a friend of mine and said he was worried about me. "I got this story from Larry," he said. "I've got a feeling he's been alone too long."

I don't know that the story owes anything to "Cry Silence," or to Fredric Brown, but I like to think it's one he might have enjoyed.

SOMETIMES THEY BITE

Lawrence Block

MOWBRAY HAD BEEN fishing the lake for better than two hours before he encountered the heavy-set man. The lake was supposed to be full of largemouth bass and that was what he was after. He was using spinning gear, working a variety of plugs and spoons and jigs and plastic worms in all of the spots where a lunker largemouth was likely to be biding his time. He was a good fisherman, adept at dropping his lure right where he wanted it, just alongside a weedbed or at the edge of subsurface structure. And the lures he was using were ideal for late fall bass. He had everything going for him, he thought, but a fish on the end of his line.

He would fish a particular spot for a while, then move off to his right a little ways, as much for something to do as because he expected the bass to be more cooperative in another location. He was gradually working his way around the western rim of the lake when he stepped from behind some brush into a clearing and saw the other man no more than a dozen yards away.

The man was tall, several inches taller than Mowbray, very broad in the shoulders and trim in the hips and at the waist. He wore a fairly new pair of blue jeans and a poplin windbreaker over a navy flannel shirt. His boots looked identical to Mowbray's, and Mowbray guessed they'd been purchased from the same mail-order outfit in Maine. His gear was a baitcasting outfit, and Mowbray followed his line out with his eyes and saw a red bobber sitting on the water's surface some thirty yards out.

The man's chestnut hair was just barely touched with gray. He had a neatly trimmed moustache and the shadowy beard of someone who had arisen early in the morning. The skin on his hands and face suggested he spent much of his time out of doors. He was certainly around Mowbray's age, which was forty-four, but he was in much better shape than Mowbray was, in better shape, truth to tell, than Mowbray had ever been. Mowbray at once admired and envied him.

The man had nodded at Mowbray's approach, and Mowbray nodded in return, not speaking first because he was the invader. Then the man said, "Afternoon. Having any luck?"

"Not a nibble."

"Been fishing long?"

"A couple of hours," Mowbray said. "Must have worked my way halfway around the lake, as much to keep moving as anything else. If there's a largemouth in the whole lake you couldn't prove it by me."

The man chuckled. "Oh, there's bass here, all right. It's a fine lake for bass, and a whole lot of other fish as well."

"Maybe I'm using the wrong lures."

The big man shook his head. "Doubtful. They'll bite anything when their dander is up. I think a largemouth would hit a shoelace if he was in the mood, and when he's sulky he wouldn't take your bait if you threw it in the water with no hook or line attached to it. That's just the way they are. Sometimes they bite and sometimes they don't."

"That's the truth." He nodded in the direction of the floating red bobber. "I don't suppose you're after bass yourself?"

"Not rigged up like this. No, I've been trying to get myself a couple of crappies." He pointed over his shoulder with his thumb, indicating where a campfire was laid. "I've got the skillet and the oil, I've got the meal to roll 'em in and I've got the fire all laid just waiting for the match. Now all I need is the fish."

"No luck?"

"No more than you're having."

"Which isn't a whole lot," Mowbray said. "You from around here?"

"No. Been through here a good many times, however. I've fished this lake now and again and had good luck more often than not."

"Well," Mowbray said. The man's company was invigorating, but there was a strict code of etiquette governing meetings of this nature. "I think I'll head on around the next bend. It's probably pointless but I'd like to get a plug in the water."

"You never can tell if it's pointless, can you? Any minute the wind can change or the temperature can drop a few degrees and the fish can change their behavior completely. That's what keeps us coming out here year after year, I'd say. The wonderful unpredictability of the whole affair. Say, don't go and take a hike on my account."

"Are you sure?"

The big man nodded, hitched at his trousers. "You can wet a line here as good as further down the bank. Your casting for bass won't make a lot of difference as to whether or not a crappie or a sunnie takes a shine to the shiner on my hook. And, to tell you the truth, I'd be just as glad for the company."

"So would I," Mowbray said, gratefully. "If you're sure you don't mind."

"I wouldn't have said boo if I did."

Mowbray set his aluminum tackle box on the ground, knelt beside it and rigged his line. He tied on a spoon plug, then got to his feet and dug out a pack of cigarettes from the breast pocket of his corduroy shirt. He said, "Smoke?"

"Gave 'em up a while back. But thanks all the same."

Mowbray smoked his cigarette about halfway down, then dropped the butt and ground it underfoot. He stepped to the water's edge, took a minute or so to read the surface of the lake then cast his plug a good distance out. For the next fifteen minutes or so the two men fished in companionable silence. Mowbray had no strikes but expected none and was resigned to it. He was enjoying himself just the same.

"Nibble," the big man announced. A minute or two went by and he began reeling in. "And a nibble's the extent of it," he said. "I'd better check and see if he left me anything."

The minnow had been bitten neatly in two. The big man had hooked him through the lips and now his tail was missing. His fingers very deft, the man slipped the shiner off the hook and substituted a live one from his bait pail. Seconds later the new minnow was in the water and the red bobber floated on the surface.

"I wonder what did that," Mowbray said.

"Hard to say. Crawdad, most likely. Something ornery."

"I was thinking that a nibble was a good sign, might mean the fish were going to start playing along with us. But if it's just a crawdad I don't suppose it means very much."

"I wouldn't think so."

"I was wondering," Mowbray said. "You'd think if there's bass in this lake you'd be after them instead of crappies."

"I suppose most people figure that way."

"None of my business, of course."

"Oh, that's all right. Hardly a sensitive subject. Happens I like the taste of little panfish better than the larger fish. I'm not a sport fisherman at heart, I'm afraid. I get a kick out of catching 'em, but my main interest is how they're going to taste when I've fried 'em up in the pan. A meat fisherman is what they call my kind, and the sporting fraternity mostly says the phrase with a certain amount of contempt." He exposed large white teeth in a sudden grin. "If they fished as often as I do, they'd probably lose some of their taste for the sporting aspect of it. I fish more days than I don't, you see. I retired ten years ago, had a retail business and sold it not too long after my wife died. We were never able to have any children so there was just myself and I wound up with enough capital to keep me without working if I didn't mind living simply. And I not only don't mind it, I prefer it."

"You're young to be retired."

"I'm fifty-five. I was forty-five when I retired, which may be on the young side, but I was ready for it."

"You look at least ten years younger than you are."

"If that's a fact, I guess retirement agrees with me. Anyway, all I really do is travel around and fish for my supper. And I'd rather catch small fish. I did the other kind of fishing and tired of it in no time at all. The way I see it, I never want to catch more fish than I intend to eat. If I kill something, it goes in that copper skillet over there. Or else I shouldn't have killed it in the first place."

Mowbray was silent for a moment, unsure what to say. Finally he said, "Well, I guess I just haven't evolved to that stage yet. I have to admit I still get a kick out of fishing, whether I eat what I catch or not. I usually eat them but that's not the most important part of it to me. But then I don't go out every other day like yourself. A couple times a year is as much as I can manage."

"Look at us talking," the man said, "and here you're not catching bass while I'm busy not catching crappie. We might as well announce that we're fishing for whales for all the difference it makes."

A little while later Mowbray retrieved his line and changed lures again, then lit another cigarette. The sun was almost gone. It had vanished behind the tree line and was probably close to the horizon by now. The air was definitely growing cooler. Another hour or so would be the extent of his fishing for the day. Then it would be time to head back to the motel and some cocktails and a steak and baked potato at the restaurant down the road. And then an evening of bourbon and water in front of the motel room's television set, lying on the bed with his feet up and the glass at his elbow and a cigarette burning in the ashtray.

The whole picture was so attractive that he was almost willing to skip the last hour's fishing. But the pleasure of the first sip of the first martini would lose nothing for being deferred an hour, and the pleasure of the big man's company was worth another hour of his time.

And then, a little while later, the big man said, "I have an unusual question to ask you."

"Ask away."

"Have you ever killed a man?"

It *was* an unusual question, and Mowbray took a few extra seconds to think it over. "Well," he said at length, "I guess I have. The odds are pretty good that I have."

"You killed someone without knowing it?"

"That must have sounded odd. You see, I was in the artillery in Korea. Heavy weapons. We never saw what we were shooting at and never knew just what our shells were doing. I was in action for better than a year, stuffing shells down the throat of one big mother of a gun, and I'd hate to think that in all that time we never hit what we aimed at. So I must have killed men, but I don't suppose that's what you're driving at."

"I mean up close. And not in the service, that's a different proposition entirely."

"Never."

"I was in the service myself. An earlier war than yours, and I was on a supply ship and never heard a shot fired in anger. But about four years ago I killed a man." His hand dropped briefly to the sheath knife at his belt. "With this."

Mowbray didn't know what to say. He busied himself taking up the slack in his line and waited for the man to continue.

"I was fishing," the big man said. "All by myself, which is my usual custom. Saltwater though, not fresh like this. I was over in North Carolina on the Outer Banks. Know the place?" Mowbray shook his head. "A chain of barrier islands a good distance out from the mainland. Very remote. Damn fine fishing and not much else. A lot of people fish off the piers or go out on boats, but I was surfcasting. You can do about as well that way as often as not, and that way I figured to build a fire right there on the beach and cook my catch and eat it on the spot. I'd gathered up the driftwood and laid the fire before I wet a line, same as I did today. That's my usual custom. I had done the same thing the day before and I caught myself half a dozen Norfolk spot in no time at all, almost before I could properly say I'd been out fishing. But this particular day I didn't have any luck at all in three hours, which shows that saltwater fish are as unpredictable as the freshwater kind. You done much saltwater fishing?"

"Hardly any."

"I enjoy it about as much as freshwater, and I enjoyed that day on the Banks even without getting a nibble. The sun was warm and there was a light breeze blowing off the ocean and you couldn't have asked for a better day. The next best thing to fishing and catching fish is fishing and not catching 'em, which is a thought we can both console ourselves with after today's run of luck."

"I'll have to remember that one."

"Well, I was having a good enough time even if it looked as though I'd wind up buying my dinner, and then I sensed a fellow coming up behind me. He must have come over the dunes because he was never in my field of vision. I knew he was there—just an instinct, I suppose—and I sent my eyes as far around as they'd go without moving my head, and he wasn't in sight." The big man paused, sighed. "You know," he said, "if the offer still holds, I believe I'll have one of those cigarettes of yours after all."

"You're welcome to one," Mowbray said, "but I hate to start you off on the habit again. Are you sure you want one?"

The wide grin came again. "I quit smoking about the same time I quit work. I may have had a dozen cigarettes since then, spaced over the ten-year span. Not enough to call a habit."

"Then I can't feel guilty about it." Mowbray shook the pack until a ciga-rette popped up, then extended it to his companion. After the man helped himself Mowbray took one as well, and lit them both with his lighter.

"Nothing like an interval of a year or so between cigarettes to improve their taste," the big man said. He inhaled a lungful of smoke, pursed his lips to expel it in a stream. "I'll tell you," he said, "I really want to tell you this story if you don't mind hearing it. It's one I don't tell often, but I feel a need to get it out from time to time. It may not leave you thinking very highly of me but we're strangers, never saw each other before and as likely will never see each other again. Do you mind listening?"

Mowbray was frankly fascinated and admitted as much.

"Well, there I was knowing I had someone standing behind me. And certain he was up to no good, because no one comes up behind you quiet like that and stands there out of sight with the intention of doing you a favor. I was holding onto my rod, and before I turned around I propped it in the sand butt end down, the way people will do when they're fishing on a beach. Then I waited a minute, and then I turned around as if not ex-pecting to find anyone there, and there he was, of course.

"He was a young fellow, probably no more than twenty-five. But he wasn't a hippie. No beard, and his hair was no longer than yours or mine. It did look greasy, though, and he didn't look too clean in general. Wore a light blue T-shirt and a pair of white duck pants. Funny how I remember what he wore but I can see him clear as day in my mind. Thin lips, sort of a wedge-shaped head, eyes that didn't line up quite right with each other, as though they had minds of their own. Some active pimples and the scars of old ones. He wasn't a prize.

"He had a gun in his hand. What you'd call a belly gun, a little .32-calibre Smith & Wesson with a two-inch barrel. Not good for a single damned thing but killing men at close range, which I'd say is all he ever wanted it for. Of course I didn't know the maker or calibre at the time. I'm not much for guns myself.

"He must have been standing less than two yards away from me. I wouldn't say it took too much instinct to have known he was there, not as close as he was."

The man drew deeply on the cigarette. His eyes narrowed in recollection, and Mowbray saw a short vertical line appear, running from the middle of his forehead almost to the bridge of his nose. Then he blew out smoke and his face relaxed and the line was gone.

"Well, we were all alone on that beach," the man continued. "No one within sight in either direction, no boats in close offshore, no one around to lend a helping hand. Just this young fellow with a gun in his hand and me with my hands empty. I began to regret sticking the rod in the sand. I'd done it to have both hands free, but I thought it might be useful to swing at him and try whipping the gun out of his hand.

"He said, 'All right, old man. Take your wallet out of your pocket nice and easy.' He was a Northerner, going by his accent, but the younger people don't have too much of an accent wherever they're from. Television, I suppose, is the cause of it. Makes the whole world smaller.

"Now I looked at those eyes, and at the way he was holding that gun, and I knew he wasn't going to take the wallet and wave bye-bye at me. He was going to kill me. In fact, if I hadn't turned around when I did he might well have shot me in the back. Unless he was the sort who liked to watch a person's face when he did it. There are people like that, I understand."

Mowbray felt a chill. The man's voice was so matter-of-fact, while his words were the stuff nightmares are made of.

"Well, I went into my pocket with my left hand. There was no wallet there. It was in the glove compartment of my car, parked off the road in back of the sand dunes. But I reached in my pocket to keep his eyes on my left hand, and then I brought the hand out empty and went for the gun with it, and at the same time I was bringing my knife out of the sheath with my right hand. I dropped my shoulder and came in low, and either I must have moved quick or all the drugs he'd taken over the years had slowed him some, but I swung that gun hand of his up and sent the gun sailing, and at the same time I got my knife into him and laid him wide open."

He drew the knife from its sheath. It was a filleting knife, with a natural wood handle and a thin, slightly curved blade about seven inches long. "This was the knife," he said. "It's a Rapala, made in Finland, and you can't beat it for being stainless steel and yet taking and holding an edge. I use it for filleting and everything else connected with fishing. But you've probably got one just like it yourself."

Mowbray shook his head. "I use a folding knife," he said.

"You ought to get one of these. Can't beat 'em. And they're handy when company comes calling, believe me. I'll tell you, I opened this youngster up the way you open a fish to clean him. Came in low in the abdomen and swept up clear to the bottom of the rib cage, and you'd have thought you were cutting butter as easy as it was." He slid the knife easily back into its sheath.

Mowbray felt a chill. The other man had finished his cigarette, and Mowbray put out his own and immediately selected a fresh one from his pack. He started to return the pack to his pocket, then thought to offer it to the other man.

"Not just now. Try me in nine or ten months, though."

"I'll do that."

The man grinned his wide grin. Then his face went quickly serious. "Well, that young fellow fell down," he said. "Fell right on his back and lay there all opened up. He was moaning and bleeding and I don't know what else. I don't recall his words, his speech was disjointed, but what he wanted was for me to get him to a doctor.

"Now the nearest doctor was in Manteo. I happened to know this, and I was near Rodanthe which is a good twenty miles from Manteo if not more. I saw how he was cut and I couldn't imagine his living through a half-hour ride in a car. In fact if there'd been a doctor six feet away from us I seriously doubt he could have done the boy any good. I'm no doctor myself, but I have to say it was pretty clear to me that boy was dying.

"And if I tried to get him to a doctor, I'd be ruining the interior of my car for all practical purposes, and making a lot of trouble for myself in the bargain. I didn't expect anybody would seriously try to pin a murder charge on me. It stood to reason that fellow had a criminal record that would reach clear to the mainland and back, and I've never had worse than a traffic ticket and few enough of those. And the gun had his prints on it and none of my own. But I'd have to answer a few million questions and hang around for at least a week and doubtless longer for a coroner's inquest, and it all amounted to a lot of aggravation for no purpose, since he was dying anyway.

"And I'll tell you something else. It wouldn't have been worth the trouble even to save him, because what in the world was he but a robbing, murdering snake? Why, if they stitched him up he'd be on the street again as soon as he was healthy and he'd kill someone else in no appreciable time at all. No, I didn't mind the idea of him dying." His eyes engaged Mowbray's. "What would you have done?"

Mowbray thought about it. "I don't know," he said. "I honestly can't say. Same as you, probably."

"He was in horrible pain. I saw him lying there, and I looked around again to assure myself we were alone, and we were. I thought that I could grab my pole and frying pan and my few other bits of gear and be in my car in two or three minutes, not leaving a thing behind that could be traced to me. I'd camped out the night before in a tent and sleeping bag and wasn't registered in any motel or campground. In other words I could be away from the Outer Banks entirely in half an hour, with nothing to connect me to the area, much less to the man on the sand. I hadn't even bought gas with a credit card. I was free and clear if I just got up and left. All I had to do was leave this young fellow to a horribly slow and painful death." His eyes locked with Mowbray's again, with an intensity that was difficult to bear. "Or," he said, his voice lower and softer, "or I could make things easier for him."

"Oh."

"Yes. And that's just what I did. I took and slipped the knife right into his heart. He went instantly. The life slipped right out of his eyes and the tension out of his face and he was gone. And that made it murder."

"Yes, of course."

"Of course," the man echoed. "It might have been an act of mercy, but legally it transformed an act of self-defense into an unquestionable act of criminal homicide." He breathed deeply. "Think I was wrong to do it?"

"No," Mowbray said.

"Do the same thing yourself?"

"I honestly don't know. I hope I would, if the alternative was leaving him to suffer."

"Well, it's what I did. So I've not only killed a man, I've literally murdered a man. I left him under about a foot of sand at the edge of the dunes. I don't know when the body was discovered. I'm sure it didn't take too long. Those sands shift back and forth all the time. There was no identification on him, but the police could have labeled him from his prints, because an upstanding young man like him would have had his prints on file. Nothing on his person at all except for about fifty dollars in cash, which destroys the theory that he was robbing me in order to provide himself with that night's dinner." His face relaxed in a half-smile. "I took the money," he said. "Didn't see as he had any need for it, and I doubted he had much of a real claim to it, as far as that goes."

"So you not only killed a man but made a profit on it."

"I did at that. Well, I left the Banks that evening. Drove on inland a good distance, put up for the night in a motel just outside of Fayetteville. I never did look back, never did find out if and when they found him. It'd be on the books as an unsolved homicide if they did. Oh, and I took his gun and flung it halfway to Bermuda. And he didn't have a car for me to worry about. I suppose he thumbed a ride or came on foot, or else he parked too far away to matter." Another smile. "Now you know my secret," he said.

"Maybe you ought to leave out place names," Mowbray said.

"Why do that?"

"You don't want to give that much information to a stranger."

"You may be right, but I can only tell a story in my own way. I know what's going through your mind right now."

"You do?"

"Want me to tell you? You're wondering if what I told you is true or not. You figure if it happened I probably wouldn't tell you, and yet it sounds pretty believable in itself. And you halfway hope it's the truth and halfway hope it isn't. Am I close?"

"Very close," Mowbray admitted.

"Well, I'll tell you something that'll tip the balance. You'll really want to believe it's all a pack of lies." He lowered his eyes. "The fact of the matter is you'll lose any respect you may have had for me when you hear the next."

"Then why tell me?"

"Because I feel the need."

"I don't know if I want to hear this," Mowbray said.

"I want you to. No fish and it's getting dark and you're probably anxious to get back to wherever you're staying and have a drink and a meal. Well, this won't take long." He had been reeling in his line. Now the operation was concluded, and he set the rod deliberately on the grass at his feet. Straightening up, he said, "I told you before about my attitude toward fish. Not killing what I'm not going to eat. And there this young man was, all laid open, internal organs exposed—"

"Stop."

"I don't know what you'd call it, curiosity or compulsion or some primitive streak. I couldn't say. But what I did, I cut off a small piece of his liver before I buried him. Then after he was under the sand I lit my cookfire and—well, no need to go into detail."

Thank God for that, Mowbray thought. For small favors. He looked at his hands. The left one was trembling. The right, the one gripping his spinning rod, was white at the knuckles, and the tips of his fingers ached from gripping the butt of the rod so tightly.

"Murder, cannibalism and robbing the dead. That's quite a string for a man who never got worse than a traffic ticket. And all three in considerably less than an hour."

"Please," Mowbray said. His voice was thin and high-pitched. "Please don't tell me any more."

"Nothing more to tell."

Mowbray took a deep breath, held it. This man was either lying or telling the truth, Mowbray thought, and in either case he was quite obviously an extremely unusual person. At the very least.

"You shouldn't tell that story to strangers," he said after a moment. "True or false, you shouldn't tell it."

"I now and then feel the need."

"Of course, it's all to the good that I *am* a stranger. After all, I don't know anything about you, not even your name."

"It's Tolliver."

"Or where you live, or—"

"Wallace P. Tolliver. I was in the retail hardware business in Oak Falls, Missouri. That's not far from Joplin."

"Don't tell me anything more," Mowbray said desperately. "I wish you hadn't told me what you did."

"I had to," the big man said. The smile flashed again. "I've told that story three times before today. You're the fourth man ever to hear it."

Mowbray said nothing.

"Three times. Always to strangers who happen to turn up while I'm fishing. Always on long lazy afternoons, those afternoons when the fish just don't bite no matter what you do."

Mowbray began to do several things. He began to step backward, and he began to release his tight hold on his fishing rod, and he began to extend his left arm protectively in front of him.

But the filleting knife had already cleared its sheath.

CRY SILENCE

Fredric Brown

IT WAS THAT old silly argument about sound. If a tree falls deep in the forest where there is no ear to hear, is its fall silent? Is there sound where there is no ear to hear it? I've heard it argued by college professors and by street sweepers.

This time it was being argued by the agent at the little railroad station and a beefy man in coveralls. It was a warm summer evening at dusk, and the station agent's window opening onto the back platform of the station was open; his elbows rested on the ledge of it. The beefy man leaned against the red brick of the building. The argument between them droned in circles like a bumblebee.

I sat on a wooden bench on the platform about ten feet away. I was a stranger in town, waiting for a train that was late. There was one other man present; he sat on the bench beside me, between me and the window. He was a tall, heavy man with an uncompromising kind of face, and huge, rough hands. He looked like a farmer in his town clothes.

I wasn't interested in either the argument or the man beside me. I was wondering only how late that damned train would be.

I didn't have my watch; it was being repaired in the city. And from where I sat I couldn't see the clock inside the station. The tall man beside me was wearing a wristwatch and I asked him what time it was.

He didn't answer.

You've got the picture haven't you? Four of us; three on the platform and the agent leaning out of the window. The argument between the agent and the beefy man. On the bench, the silent man and I.

I got up off the bench and looked into the open door of the station. It was seven-forty; the train was twelve minutes overdue. I sighed, and lighted a cigarette. I decided to stick my nose into the argument. It wasn't any of my business, but I knew the answer and they didn't.

"Pardon me for butting in," I said, "but you're not arguing about sound at all; you're arguing semantics."

I expected one of them to ask me what semantics was, but the station agent fooled me. He said, "That's the study of words, isn't it? In a way, you're right, I guess."

"All the way," I insisted. "If you look up 'sound' in the dictionary, you'll find two meanings listed. One of them is 'the vibration of a medium, usually air, within a certain range,' and the other is 'the effect of such vibrations on the ear.' That isn't the exact wording, but the general idea. Now by one of those definitions, the sound—the vibration—exists whether there's an ear around to hear it or not. By the other, the vibrations aren't sound unless there is an ear to hear them. So you're both right; it's just a matter of which meaning you use for the word 'sound'."

The beefy man said, "Maybe you got something there." He looked back at the agent. "Let's call it a draw then, Joe. I got to get home. So long."

He stepped down off the platform and went around the station.

I asked the agent, "Any report on the train?"

"Nope," he said. He leaned a little farther out the window and looked to his right and I saw a clock in a steeple about a block away that I hadn't noticed before. "Ought to be along soon though."

He grinned at me. "Expert on sound, huh?"

"Well," I said, "I wouldn't say that. But I did happen to look it up in the dictionary. I know what the word means."

"Uh-huh. Well, let's take that second definition and say sound is sound only if there's an ear to hear it. A tree crashes in the forest and there's only a deaf man there. Is there any sound?"

"I guess not," I said. "Not if you consider sound as subjective. Not if it's got to be heard."

I happened to glance to my right, at the tall man who hadn't answered my question about the time. He was still staring straight ahead. Lowering my voice a bit, I asked the station agent, "Is he deaf?"

"Him? Bill Meyers?" He chuckled; there was something odd in the sound of that chuckle. "Mister, nobody knows. That's what I was going to ask you next. If that tree falls down and there's a man near, but nobody knows if he's deaf or not, is there any sound?"

His voice had gone up in volume. I stared at him, puzzled, wondering if he was a little crazy, or if he was just trying to keep up the argument by thinking up screwy loopholes.

I said, "Then if nobody knows if he's deaf, nobody knows if there was any sound."

He said, "You're wrong, mister. That man would know whether he heard it or not. Maybe the tree would know, wouldn't it? And maybe other people would know, too."

"I don't get your point," I told him. "What are you trying to prove?"

"*Murder*, mister. You just got up from sitting next to a murderer."

I stared at him again, but he didn't look crazy. Far off, a train whistled, faintly. I said, "I don't understand you."

"The guy sitting on the bench," he said. "Bill Meyers. He murdered his wife. Her and his hired man."

His voice was quite loud. I felt uncomfortable; I wished that far train was a lot nearer. I didn't know what went on here, but I knew I'd rather be on the train. Out of the corner of my eye I looked at the tall man with the granite face and the big hands. He was still staring out across the tracks. Not a muscle in his face had moved.

The station agent said, "I'll tell you about it, mister. I *like* to tell people about it. His wife was a cousin of mine, a fine woman. Mandy Eppert, her name was, before she married that skunk. He was mean to her, dirt mean. Know how mean a man can be to a woman who's helpless?

"She was seventeen when she was fool enough to marry him seven years ago. She was twenty-four when she died last spring. She'd done more work than most women do in a lifetime, out on that farm of his. He worked her like a horse and treated her like a slave. And her religion wouldn't let her divorce him or even leave him. See what I mean, mister?"

I cleared my throat, but there didn't seem to be anything to say. He didn't need prodding or comment. He went on.

"So how can you blame her, mister, for loving a decent guy, a clean, young fellow her own age when he fell in love with her? Just *loving* him that's all. I'd bet my life on that because I knew Mandy. Oh they talked, and they looked at each other—I wouldn't gamble too much there wasn't a stolen kiss now and then. But nothing to kill them for, mister."

I felt uneasy; I wished the train would come and get me out of this. I had to say something, though; the agent was waiting. I said, "Even if there had been, the unwritten law is out of date."

"Right, mister." I'd said the right thing. "But you know what that bastard sitting over there did? He went deaf."

"Huh?" I said.

"He went deaf. He came in town to see the doc and said he'd been having earaches and couldn't hear anymore. Was afraid he was going deaf. Doc gave him some stuff to try, and you know where he went from the doc's office?"

I didn't try to guess.

"Sheriff's office," he said. "Told the sheriff he wanted to report his wife and his hired man were missing, see? Smart of him. Wasn't it? Swore out a complaint and said he'd prosecute if they were found. But he had an awful lot of trouble getting any of the questions the sheriff asked. Sheriff got tired of yelling and wrote 'em down on paper. Smart. See what I mean?"

"Not exactly," I said. "Hadn't his wife run away?"

"He'd murdered her. And him. Or rather, he was *murdering* them. Must have taken a couple of weeks, about. Found 'em a month later."

He glowered, his face black with anger.

"In the smokehouse," he said. "A new smokehouse made out of concrete and not used yet. With a padlock on the outside of the door. He'd walked through the farmyard one day about a month before—he said after their bodies were found—and noticed the padlock wasn't locked, just hanging in the hook and not even through the hasp.

"See? Just to keep the padlock from being lost or swiped, he slips it through the hasp and snaps it."

"My God," I said. "And they were in there? They starved to death?"

"Thirst kills you quicker, if you haven't either water or food. Oh, they'd tried hard to get out, all right. Scraped halfway through the door with a piece of concrete he'd worked loose. It was a thick door. I figure they hammered on that door plenty. Was there sound, mister, with only a *deaf* man living near that door, passing it twenty times a day?"

Again he chuckled humorlessly. He said: "Your train'll be along soon. That was it you heard whistle. It stops up by the water tower. It'll be here in ten minutes." And without changing his tone of voice, except that it got louder again, he said: "It was a bad way to die. Even if he was right in killing them, only a black-hearted son of a bitch would have done it that way. Don't you think so?"

I said: "But are you sure he is—"

"Deaf? Sure, he's deaf. Can't you picture him standing there in front of that padlocked door, listening with his deaf ears to the hammering inside? And the yelling?

"Sure, he's deaf. That's why I can say all this to him, yell it in his ear. If

I'm wrong, he can't hear me. But he can hear me. He comes here to hear me."

I had to ask it. "Why? Why would he—if you're right."

"I'm helping him, that's why. I'm helping him to make up his black mind to hang a rope from the grating in the top of that smokehouse, and dangle from it. He hasn't got the guts to, yet. So every time he's in town, he sits on the platform a while to rest. And I tell him what a murdering son of a bitch he is."

He spat toward the tracks. He said, "There are a few of us know the score. Not the sheriff; he wouldn't believe us, said it would be hard to prove."

The scrape of feet behind me made me turn. The tall man with the huge hands and the granite face was standing up now. He didn't look toward us. He started for the steps.

The agent said, "He'll hang himself, pretty soon now. He wouldn't come here and sit like that for any other reason, would he, mister?"

"Unless," I said, "he *is* deaf."

"Sure. He could be. See what I meant? If a tree falls and the only man there to hear it is maybe deaf and maybe not, is it silent or isn't it? Well, I got to get the mail pouch ready."

I turned and looked at the tall figure walking away from the station. He walked slowly and his shoulders, big as they were, seemed a little stooped.

The clock in the steeple a block away began to strike for seven o'clock.

The tall man lifted his wrist to look at the watch on it.

I shuddered a little. It could have been coincidence, sure, and yet a little chill went down my spine.

The train pulled in, and I got aboard.